VIEW
PARK

VIEW
PARK

ANGELA
WINTERS

KENSINGTON PUBLISHING CORP.
http://www.kensingtonbooks.com

DAFINA BOOKS are published by

Kensington Publishing Corp.
850 Third Avenue
New York, NY 10022

All Kensington Titles, Imprints, and Distributed Lines are available at special quantity discounts for bulk purchases for sales promotions, premiums, fund-raising, and educational or institutional use. Special book excerpts or customized printings can also be created to fit specific needs. For details, write or phone the office of the Kensington special sales manager: Kensington Publishing Corp., 850 Third Avenue, New York, NY 10022, attn: Special Sales Department, Phone: 1-800-221-2647.

Da███ and ███████████ ███████████████ Off.

ISBN-13: 978-0-75██-1260-█
ISBN-10: 0-7582-1260-7

First trade paperback printing: July 2006
First mass market printing: May 2009

10 9 8 7 6 5 4 3 2

Printed in the United States of America

*This book is dedicated to my agent, Peter Miller,
who stuck with me through this process and never
gave up.*

PROLOGUE

Meet the Chase Family

Steven Chase (the conqueror) Founder and CEO of Chase Beauty Corporation.

Born poor, Steven put himself through college and began a marketing career in cosmetics. He founded Chase Beauty, now a Fortune 500 company, for women of color. He is tough as nails in business and can be even tougher with his own sons.

Janet Chase (the socialite) Head of The Chase Foundation.

Raised in New York wealth, Janet is the perfection of balance in her role as a wife, mother, society maven and philanthropist. Her life has been building up her husband and preparing her children for success as their birthright.

Carter Chase (the reluctant gentleman) Head of Chase Law, LLC.

Deciding to go off on his own, the strife between Carter and Steven has been there forever and seems to have no end in sight. One of L.A.'s top lawyers and most eligible bachelors, he rules with a quiet, calm dominance that defies the drive inside of him.

Michael Chase (the favorite) EVP, Finance, at Chase Beauty.

Embracing his privilege, Michael is fiercely competitive and doesn't fight fair. He does the dirty work with pleasure and always comes out clean. He is obsessed with taking over Chase Beauty, with his only soft spot being his wife, Kimberly, and their twin sons.

Leigh Chase (the angel) Pediatrician.

The bleeding heart, Leigh has always devoted her life to helping others. Trusting and a bit naive at times, she goes out of her way to avoid the label of debutante but can't resist the urge to please her mother.

Haley Chase (the taker) Debutante.

Haley lives for herself, spending Daddy's money and using everyone for her own amusement. She leaves disaster in her wake, watching her mother clean up her messes while her father pushes her away.

Kimberly Chase (the outsider) Wife and Mother.

Kimberly left her troubled childhood behind for a modeling career in New York City, but an unplanned pregnancy marked the beginning of life as Mrs. Michael Chase. Everything she has, though, is threatened by Janet, who reminds her every day that she doesn't belong.

CHAPTER 1

That Chase mansion was something else. Nestled in View Park, the affluent mostly African-American suburb of Los Angeles, it is by far the largest house in the entire community. Glorious, elegant and intimidating begin to touch on it. Most people just call it big, not only because of its size, but because of its residents. A family couldn't be any bigger than Steven Chase and his clan, and no one was willing to admit how much they ached to know what went on behind the red brick and white columns.

The house, being only fifteen-thousand square feet was not as big as it could be considering the money the family had. All of the homes they owned around the world focused more on elegance and class than size. Still, it was impressive with seven bedrooms and nine baths, not to mention the exercise room, game room, media room, and library plus more, the home had taken eighteen months to build. Steven had purchased it when it was 8,000 square feet, but as his millions grew, the house next door was purchased, torn down and his wife, Janet, had taken it from there. The stature that blended a sturdy East Coast feel with a flirt of southern gentility rejected any hint of West Coast flash. It resembled something more likely to be in Bel Air or Hollywood Hills with its tall

gate, wide driveway filled with Mercedes, Jaguars and
Lexus SUVs, large pool with cabanas, basketball court
and a Caribbean colonial designed 2,000 square foot
guest house. Contemporary frames, marble flooring,
cathedral ceilings, granite countertops, five fireplaces and
a double staircase that caused mouths to drop while making *Town & Country*, *California Homes*, and *L.A. Magazine* salivate delivered a lasting statement to those far
beyond View Park.

The statement was class, sophistication and most importantly, power. It had to be. After all, the Chase family
was one of the richest and most powerful African-American
families in the country, the richest on the West Coast. No
one could put a label to them, white or black; no matter
how hard they tried, using every other rich family exist-
ing now and before them. The Chases never accepted any
of those labels, seeing themselves as originals in every
way. They were born leaders, attractive, well educated, phil-
anthropic and seemingly unfazed by anything. They stayed
away from the undesirable black wealth acquired by ath-
letes, actors or entertainers. Only lawyers, doctors, business-
men, educators and politicians made up the world the Chase
family ruled.

When it came to the various scandals, like any good
rich family worth their salt, they had plenty. The general
consensus among those who talk, and they all talked, was
that the Chase family was special. Special in a way that
any mistakes they made weren't as bad as their charitable
acts were good. None of their misdeeds seem to trump
their place as black royalty. It was a payoff that others
were willing to accept. More like . . . willing to embrace.

No matter how intense the scandal was, there was
never a feeling that the Chase family was out of control.
Steven Chase, *the conqueror*, raised his children similar
to the way he had built his business. The foundations
were strong and well supported, not only meant to last

long after he was gone, but to prosper and dominate far after that. He was the ultimate symbol of that power and his confidence left everyone in awe; especially his own children.

Only today, that confidence wasn't as visible as usual. In his home office, elaborately decorated in cherrywood and rich, dark leather, Steven, looking much younger than his fifty-three years, sat uncomfortably behind his desk. He was a distinguished man heavy on control and light on affection for anyone except his wife. Running his hands over his salt and pepper hair, he shook his head in disappointment, his chocolate skin darkened from spending the day before on the golf course; a rare retreat for him.

His eldest son, Carter, *the reluctant gentleman*, was thirty and better-looking than any man had a right to be. His conservative style and calm quiet demeanor drove his intense father crazy. Everything about Carter drove him crazy. The boy seemed determined to defy him since the day he was born. He seemed to take delight in doing anything other than what Steven wanted him to and making a success of his defiance.

Steven didn't expect today to be any different as he looked at Carter sitting in the chair across the desk from him. Those incredible light eyes he'd inherited from his mother stared back saying he refused to let his father's anguish affect him.

"So," Steven said as he sighed, trying to focus on something other than why his firstborn son wanted to be his enemy. "When exactly am I ready to say we should panic?"

"You don't panic, Dad." Carter was unwilling to accept the blame this time. Whenever things didn't work out at Chase Beauty like they should, he somehow shared the responsibility even though he didn't work there.

"There's a first time for everything," Steven scoffed. "And I think this might be that time."

He looked back at Michael, *the favorite son*, who was standing behind him, leaning casually against the bookshelf. It wasn't Steven's choice to make Michael his favorite and he would never admit to anyone, not even his own wife, that he was. He'd wanted Carter, but it became clear early on that that wasn't ever going to happen. It was better this way. Michael was more like Steven: aggressive, hungry and willing to do whatever it took.

Twenty-nine-year-old Michael was tall and dark, looking like a young Sidney Poitier. Unlike the carefully concealed fire inside Carter, Michael's flame could be seen miles away. It drove him. It gave him immediate respect from men twice his age. It made him dangerous. It made him the mirror of his father.

Michael leaned forward with a confident smirk on his face. He was used to this game. His father made it seem like the world was falling apart to light a candle underneath him when he thought Michael was slacking, which he never was.

"We have seventeen of the twenty," Michael offered. "It's just taking a little longer than we expected."

Steven stared him down. "I'm disappointed in you, Michael. I thought I raised my sons to never make excuses."

Michael blinked, but never lost his composure. There was something about this man that ripped at him. His approval could make him feel like he was king of the world, and his disappointment made him feel like a five-year-old boy. This business deal was the chance he'd been waiting for. He would be the one to take the leading cosmetics company for women of color to the next level . . . a chain of high-end hair salons and that board of directors seat was his.

"You're still on the timeline," Carter said. "You wanted to take over twenty of the top black salons in L.A. by the first of the year. It's only September."

Steven turned to him, a sarcastic grin on his face. "I love how you use these phrases 'you' and 'your'."

Carter rolled his eyes, knowing what was coming next. The almost daily reaming of accusations that Carter didn't love his father, his family and the family business because he'd decided to be his own man. It was a broken record and he didn't have the patience for it.

Steven leaned across his desk, staring pointedly at his son. "You may not work for me, a rejection I have learned to deal with, but you are still a Chase."

Carter felt his teeth grinding. Keep your cool, he told himself. He loves it when you let him get to you. "I know, Dad. I just meant . . ."

"So," Steven continued as if Carter hadn't spoken, "when referring to the success of Chase Beauty, 'we' is more appropriate."

Carter pressed his lips together noticing the sly grin on Michael's face. His little brother got a lot of entertainment out of these scenes, and even though Carter loved him more than anyone on the planet, he wanted to sock him right now.

"Hate to say it," Michael admitted, "but Carter's right. And I wasn't making an excuse."

Steven wasn't getting through to them. They were young, but they were Chases and that meant they had to act more than their ages. "Do you boys understand the point here? My vision was clear. We would buy these carefully selected salons and launch our own chain. The end of the year was the deadline to launch. Not buy the salons."

"Dad, we've offered them the world," Michael said. "Performance Salon and Essentials won't sell. It's time to get dirty."

"Like you haven't already?" Carter asked. "I've heard what you've been doing."

Michael smiled innocently. He kept very few secrets from Carter. Only sometimes, Carter's sensitivity to obeying the law made it necessary. "You haven't heard anything."

"How about Matt Leonard and those pictures you threatened to send to his wife?"

Michael laughed. "You thought that was dirty? I'm surprised at you, man. You ought to know dirty better than anyone. You're a lawyer."

"Michael is right," Steven said. "We have to—"

Carter raised his hand to stop his father. "Dad, I don't want to hear this."

"You're my lawyer," Steven stressed. "So it doesn't matter what you want to hear. Besides, I need your help with Essentials."

"I don't do your legwork." Carter watched as his father's eyes turned to slits.

"I'm your father," he answered back. "You'll do whatever I tell you to." Steven's gaze lingered a little longer on Carter to make his point before turning to Michael. "Michael, your hunger can go too far sometimes. Simple blackmail will . . ."

"I'm out of here." Carter stood up.

"Sit down, boy." Steven spoke in that tone that always got the desired result. No matter how big they got, he was bigger. He would never let them forget that, and as Carter sat back down in his chair, Steven knew they wouldn't.

"Blackmail won't do it Dad," Michael advised. "We're gonna have to take it to a new level with them."

Steven didn't like it when things got this way, but this was business. He'd learned that the hard way when he started Chase Beauty twenty years ago. He looked at Michael, his expression nothing less than deadly serious. "This needs to happen. So, do what you have to do. Carter will handle Essentials."

Michael's competitive spirit bit at him. He couldn't figure out why his father seemed to go out of his way to pull Carter in when he could handle this on his own.

Carter smiled, nodding. "Sure, why not? I've been looking for ways to lose my law license."

"I'm asking you," Steven said, "because we have to take the legal route with Essentials."

Michael smirked. "You get the easy stuff, Carter, since you're so soft."

Carter got up, starting for Michael, who quickly stepped around the desk, ready for him. With no patience for this, Steven stood up, the mere gesture having incredible power over his sons and they both immediately stopped, turning to look at him.

"Carter," Steven said. "Essentials has a shop in View Park and one in Baldwin Hills. They're both owned by Avery Jackson."

Carter shrugged. "Should that name mean something to me?"

Michael rolled his eyes. "She's the daughter of our chief of police, idiot."

"And she's not selling," Steven said.

"She's a bitch," Michael spat. "I've offered her twice what her piece of shit shops are worth."

"If they were a piece of shit, we wouldn't be going after them, idiot." Carter grinned while Michael gave him the finger.

Steven sat back down, focusing on the thick manila folder on his desk. "Revenue-wise, she's probably the weakest of the whole bunch. Location-wise, I've got to have those stores. I need a way to make her sell, but because of who she is, we can't use—"

"Me," Michael proudly offered.

Steven placed his hand on the folder and slid it toward Carter. Carter looked at it, but didn't pick it up, which he knew his father wanted him to do. "What exactly do you expect me to do?"

"You're the Harvard lawyer. You figure it out." Steven shared a stern look with both of his sons. "You need to understand the pressure we're under. Chase Beauty *is* our family's legacy."

Carter and Michael both sighed, having heard this speech too many times to count. Steven had built the business from scratch, ignoring the naysayers warning that an entire corporation focused only on black women could never rival the big players. Steven had showed them all, and he never let his sons forget it. He also never let them forget that a lot of people didn't like their success and were waiting in bushes like hungry lions for any chance to bring them down, and it was essential that they not get that chance.

"Nothing comes back to Chase Beauty," Steven ordered. "Do you both understand?"

"We understand," Carter and Michael answered in unison, as they had always to anything their father told them.

Janet Chase, *the socialite*, opened the office door without knocking, which was a sure sign she was angry. She didn't need to wonder if she had everyone's attention, because Janet always got everyone's attention. She was an exceptionally beautiful, elegant and classy woman who looked at least a decade younger than she was. That she was born into money was obvious to anyone with eyes and it took only a second's worth of time in her presence to see the best etiquette classes New York had to offer advertised in her every move and word. Including every look, like the dangerous one currently on her face as she eyed her husband and two sons.

"I knew you were in here." She placed delicately adorned hands on her trim, but curvy hips. She would not lose her temper. It wasn't her style, but she would be obeyed. "What are you doing?"

"Business, Janet." It amazed Steven that after over thirty years of marriage he still thought she was too good for him.

"Business is over." She had been Steven's mistress to his wife, Chase Beauty, for so long, but she wanted all the things its success gave her so she accepted it; only not today. "This is Leigh's day. She'll be here soon, and your guests are noticing your absence." She pointed her finger at her men, all of whom she loved with every inch of her. "I want you all out there in five minutes, and don't mess with me."

You just didn't mess with Janet Chase.

As Janet made her way down the long hallway toward her guests, she stopped at the edge of the expansive foyer, watching the crowd of the elite and other acceptables converse over fine wine and catered hors d'oeuvres. The finest black Los Angeles had to offer were all here for her daughter. No one declined an invitation from Janet Chase because she was the head of L.A. society; and everyone loved Leigh.

Now Haley was another story. Haley was a cross to bear that Janet gladly accepted, but she took it too far too often. Janet scanned the room as she had been for the last hour. She had already scoured upstairs and the girl wasn't there. She made her way to Maya, the woman who had helped her run this home and all of its inhabitants for the last ten years. Janet respected the woman's strive for perfection—not accepting any less in anyone who worked for her.

"Maya." Janet took her by the arm, pulling her aside. "Where is Haley?"

Maya looked at her as if she were demented to even ask. "I've checked everywhere, Mrs. Chase. She's not in this house. With your daughter, there's no telling where she is. Her cell phone is turned off."

"Keep trying."

Maya pulled her arm away. "You try. I've got a party to manage."

Janet's baby girl was her biggest challenge. She spoiled the young beauty too much, but there would be no spoiling tonight. If Haley messed up Leigh's homecoming, there would be hell to pay.

Congressman Jack Flay's boat was smaller than Steven Chase's boat, but Haley Chase, *the taker*, expected that. Everything her father had was bigger than most. Besides, the size of Jack's boat wasn't what she was interested in. The night they had met, at a fund-raiser for what Haley didn't care enough to remember, she was amused by his attention. With his wicked Irish charm, Yale education and perfect blonde wife at his side, his flirtations with her told Haley he was a man who liked to live dangerously. Not a good thing for a congressman, but a good thing for her. Haley loved danger.

The twenty-two-year-old debutante knew she was breathtaking and irresistible, and as she laid on top of him in the master bedroom of his boat, the desire in his eyes only confirmed that fact. Her large brown eyes, glowing caramel skin and that curvaceous body made a fool of any man who tried to tame her.

Haley loved it. Twice her age, Jack seemed positive he had her number, but he was all wrong. No man would ever get her number. She had theirs from the first moment she gave them the gift of her physical affection and she used them until she found someone else she'd rather use. She had to give it to him, Jack was great in bed. He had a wild side to him that she assumed his proper New England wife never saw and Haley was entertained by her ability to bring it out.

Lifting up, she smiled victoriously at him. She lowered her head a bit, allowing her long, wavy auburn hair to fall over his sweaty face. He was such an idiot, thinking he could outlast her. Haley screamed and laughed at the same time as he grabbed her by the waist and flipped her over. On top of her now, he leaned down to kiss her and she felt a little tingling in the pit of her stomach. It wasn't as strong as two months ago when they'd first had sex. The congressman's time was almost up and he didn't even know it.

His mouth trailed her neck and Haley grinned. She dug her nails into his back, letting him know she didn't have time to waste for foreplay this roll around. Jack got the message and went quickly to work. They were both too caught up to hear the boat that was probably half a mile away. When she wanted to, Haley made more noise than the average boat engine anyway.

Usually L.A. traffic was enough to make twenty-six-year-old Leigh Chase, *the angel*, put a gun to her head. Not today. She was fine with traffic going as slow as it wanted to. Thinking the last year of her life in South Africa working with women and children with HIV and AIDS was bad, she had forgotten how much harder it was to stand up to Steven and Janet Chase.

Riding in the backseat of the limo that had been waiting for her at LAX, Leigh couldn't deny she was happy to be home. The people she loved most in the world would be there waiting for her, but so was the life that she left behind a year ago and vowed she would never, ever return to again. A life so comfortable in all its protection and ignorance.

Leigh's innocence was genuine. She was the angelic, unassuming type of beauty with a gentle tone and demeanor that made men want to save her. With smooth dark chocolate skin and soft tender features, she looked like a princess and had lived like one most of her life. Going to Duke Medical School after Smith was an eye opener to the real world, but Leigh had had no idea what was in store for her when she'd signed up for Africa. Her parents had taught her that giving was an obligation of people like themselves, but they were the ones who protested vehemently when she told them her choice. Always one to please, it broke her heart to see her parents so upset, but Africa was something she had to do no matter what, much like what she had to do now.

Earl, the family driver for five years, glanced in his rearview mirror at Leigh, with an uncertain smile. "Your parents are very excited at seeing you. Your mother went on for months, thinking up schemes to get you back here."

"I don't doubt it." Leigh felt her stomach contract as the WELCOME TO VIEW PARK sign came into full view. It would only be a few minutes now. She was about to flip the switch on Mr. and Mrs. Chase and that never, ever went well.

Michael stood at the edge of the great room, sizing up his wife as she snatched a glass of wine from a passing waiter. Kimberly Chase, *the outsider*, was the hottest woman in the room. She was always the hottest woman in the room. She still looked like a model at twenty-five, even after twins, with café au lait skin, smoldering green eyes and full lips, she was a strikingly beautiful woman by anyone's standards and Michael's standards were the highest.

Kimberly didn't come from anything close to money, a fact his mother never let him forget, but she wore it well. Very well, and Michael loved the hell out of her. (He'd been obsessed with her since the moment he laid eyes on her at that club in New York almost six years ago, when he was in his first year at Columbia Business School.) As he approached her now, he slowly wrapped his arm around her waist, taking a second to squeeze her butt.

"You're enjoying yourself," he whispered into her ear before biting it. "That's what, number three already?"

Kimberly's mouth curved into an unconscious smile, feeling that familiar lightning jolt run through her body from her husband's touch. "This is how I survive Chase family weekends. I'm your wife and I live in this house, so I have to be here. Allow me what little enjoyment I can have."

"What has Mom done to you now?" Michael felt that the animosity between his wife and mother had lessened over the five years of their marriage, but Kimberly was never satisfied.

"Nothing today, but I'm waiting and I don't like your tone."

"What tone?"

"That tone suggesting your mother hasn't hated me from the first day she met me. She lives for making my life miserable."

Michael laughed, but quickly shut up when Kimberly glared at him. He knew her agreeing to live in his parents' home was a sacrifice she was making out of love for him. He tried to make it better for her by giving her everything else she wanted. "Honestly, Kimberly, I think my mother has more on her mind than hating you. Besides, Leigh is coming home. Mother has her favorite punching bag back."

Kimberly hadn't thought of much else. Now that Leigh was home, her inevitable clashes with Janet would give Kimberly some breathing room. Kimberly would never forget the saccharine smile on Janet's face when she first met her. The second Michael left the room Janet threatened to destroy her if she was lying about Michael being the father of her children.

Destroy? Kimberly had never heard someone use that word before but that was what Janet did. She destroyed anyone she didn't like and she hated Kimberly. She hated that Michael had to marry Kimberly because in the Chase family, there were no out of wedlock children. "Bastards" was the word Janet used, but Kimberly knew Janet had no problem with children of divorce and the woman was just waiting for the day Michael would cut Kimberly loose. That day was never going to come because Kimberly knew Michael loved her and she would never, ever let him go.

"Still," Kimberly argued. "It's another woman who thinks she has more claim to this sacred land than I do."

Michael gently touched her cheek with the back of his hand. Kimberly looked at him with love in her eyes and he knew he could convince her of anything. "Remember what I told you. We have the only grandchildren, and you're their mother. That gives you power, so use it." Michael planted a tender kiss on her cheek, loving the silky smooth feel of her flawless skin. "You're a great mother. Of all she tries to throw at you, she can't say anything about that. Use your strength."

Kimberly knew she had found a god among men when she met Michael Chase. Every word that came out of his mouth made her want to win, succeed and get what was hers. He encouraged her in a way that she'd had no faith men ever could. He made her feel that everything could be hers; should be hers. Her absent father, abusive brother, her pimp and every other man in her life had made her believe men like Michael didn't exist. But he did and he was hers. Just like everything else would be as soon as . . . The center of attention came into her sight. Janet Chase entertaining a circle of L.A.'s best; perfect in every way.

Standing at the doorway of her house, Leigh almost believed that it seemed bigger than when she left it just a year ago. From where she stood, you couldn't imagine it was anything but perfect on the other side. Leigh took another deep breath.

"Do you want me to . . ." Earl was carrying some of her suitcases, placing them at the door. He looked at her, puzzled.

"What did Mom say again? Just a quiet dinner, right?"

"That's what she said. They wanted you to have time to calm down. That's why they didn't meet you at the airport."

"All right," Leigh said, stepping aside as Earl opened the door.

Her eyes widened and she almost fell back as she was greeted with a room full of people yelling, "Welcome back!"

She stood stunned as Janet rushed to her with a warm smile and wide-open arms. Emotion took over at the sight of her mother and she hugged her so tight, neither of them could breathe.

"My baby." Janet looked her over, loving her perfection and overwhelmed by the only assurance of her daughter's safety she would accept: seeing her with her own eyes.

"What . . ." Leigh couldn't find words when Steven approached. God, how she missed her daddy. He was almost like an apparition.

"My angel." Steven spoke with a strained voice.

"I've missed you so much, Daddy."

Janet couldn't hold back the tears. All the nights worrying and wondering were finally over. It had almost been too much to bear. "You can't say you didn't know?" she asked, seeing Leigh's amazed face. "You had to be suspicious about us not picking you up."

"I thought . . . I thought you meant what you'd said. You wanted to give me rest."

"There's plenty of time to rest." Janet's instinct led her hands to Leigh's short hair, smoothing it out as she hugged her brothers. Her family was back together again. Well, almost. She pulled Leigh away from her brothers. "You have to say hello to your guests."

Leigh grabbed Carter by the shirt, pulling him close. "What's the radar?"

Carter leaned forward, whispering. "Mom and Dad have the most prestigious medical practices here to woo you. I think a couple of rich bachelors were added to the pot."

Rolling her eyes, Leigh mouthed a thank-you as she allowed her mother to drag her toward the waiting crowd. "Mom, where's Haley?"

Haley cringed as she heard Jack singing in the bathroom. She would have to talk to him about that one day. On the other hand, it didn't matter. She didn't plan on keeping him around much longer.

Rolling over on the bed to retrieve her watch, she noticed his wedding ring placed right next to it. She thought of his wife and their kids and wondered for a second if it was weird that she felt no guilt. Haley never felt guilt, but she would fake it sometimes to get sympathy, something she wanted or just to keep everyone from thinking she wasn't human. Leigh had always told her there was something wrong with her because she felt no remorse, but Leigh was weak and . . .

"Jesus!" Hopping out of bed, Haley yelled to Jack while she jumped into her clothes wondering how she'd managed to let the time get away with her again and again. Jack wasn't that good.

Jack rushed in with nothing but a towel around his waist. "What is it?"

"I was supposed to be home hours ago! My sister is . . . Mom is gonna kill me." Standing there, he suddenly looked like a fool to her. "Will you hurry up? Let's go."

"Don't worry. We'll be back on land in twenty minutes."

"Well, do it!" After he was gone, Haley stopped a moment to calm down and think of what lie she could come up with to get out of this one. It wasn't going to be easy. Leigh was the angel and upsetting her brought on Daddy's wrath. She would have to use her mother against him. But what was the excuse going to be?

Stepping out onto the deck, Haley tried to think of an excuse that could make her forget an event she promised to be at. Chase family events were priority number one. It pissed her off, the whole family thing. It was so fake, but her mother held on to it like it meant everything. Jack wasn't worth this, she told herself. She saw a challenge, an adventure, and went for it, no care for the consequences. She heard Leigh's "I told you so" ringing in her ears and part of her didn't want to show up at all. That would be something, wouldn't it? She loved her sister and missed her, but she loved stealing the spotlight even more.

She calmed down, taking a seat and a deep breath. Off in the distance, she noticed a boat that seemed to be still. Reaching under the seat to grab the binoculars, Haley watched with interest as she saw the two men arguing. Then, without warning, one man pulled out a gun and shot the other, just as he seemed to be reaching for his own gun. Haley screamed something incoherently, blinking several times as if she thought she was imagining things. She wasn't. The man who was shot was now lying on the deck and the other man poured more bullets into him.

Just as the boat roared to life, Haley watched in terror as the loud engine caught the attention of the killer. It felt almost like slow motion to her as she watched him point to the boat and yell something to someone she couldn't see. Then another man emerged from inside with a gun almost as large as he was. When Haley saw him point the gun toward Jack's boat, she threw the binoculars in his direction as if it would do anything.

She jumped out of the seat, hitting the floor as the boat's movement jerked her around. They were moving, that was all that mattered, and she didn't have the nerve to turn around and see if anyone was coming after them.

"Where do you think you're going?"

Her mother's cultured tone sent dread through Leigh who slowly turned around. She had thought she could escape just for a second alone, but there was no escaping this woman.

"Leigh, this party is for you."

"Mom, I've been flying for almost twenty-four hours straight."

"You're twenty-six. Stop acting like an old lady."

"I wish you had consulted with me before planning this big party."

Janet wasn't sure how to handle this side of her daughter. She seemed unappreciative, more like Haley. "You don't consult with someone when you're doing them a favor."

Leigh knew she was defeated. After the flight, she didn't have the strength to fight her mother this soon in the game. With her mother's hand firmly leading her, Leigh's expression pleaded with Carter for help as they passed, but all Carter offered was a sympathetic shrug. He was much more interested in the sexy young woman who was showering him with attention. Leigh knew it would be a long night.

As the woman's mouth moved, Carter didn't hear a word she said. He was trying desperately to remember what her name was. She was hot and new to Los Angeles.

She'd come as someone else's date, but Carter had an idea she was going to leave with him.

Michael was a charmer, but only selectively. If he didn't think you mattered, he was ruder than anyone Carter had ever known, which was why he didn't take too well when Michael joined him and all but ordered the woman with no name to go away. Carter didn't push it. He and Michael agreed they would never let a woman come between them. He certainly wasn't going to sweat one whose name he couldn't even remember.

"What do you want, Michael?"

Michael leaned in. "To know what you're gonna do about Avery Jackson."

Carter pushed him away with his shoulder. "I just found out about this. I haven't come up with anything yet."

"I have." Michael's face creased into a sudden smile. He loved these moments when he had the upper hand. Whenever their father was involved, he had the upper hand. Carter was the big brother, always making the right choice, so unassumingly confident. But he lacked the tenacious edge that Michael had and Michael relished the moments when that came in handy. When Carter's honest character put him a step behind. "What are you gonna tell Dad?"

"Dad doesn't expect me to—"

"Carter."

Carter turned to his father who seemed to come out of nowhere. He had a way of doing that and always with a face that let you know he'd been thinking about you and not in a good way. The man was overbearing, seeming twenty feet tall, and it killed Carter that he always felt like he was on a hot plate in his presence.

"What have you decided about Avery Jackson?" Steven asked.

Carter glared at Michael who didn't bother to hold

back an icy grin. "I'll figure out something. I haven't even read the file."

"It's gonna be harder than you think." Michael knew he was wicked, but he wanted Carter to succeed for two reasons. He loved his brother and he had come to hate Avery Jackson. "There's something seriously wrong with that woman."

"What are you planning for Performance, Michael?" Carter asked, hoping to deflect the attention from himself.

"You don't want to know." Michael turned to his father. "But I do have something planned, unlike Carter here."

Steven wondered if they were taking him seriously. He couldn't tell sometimes when they got in their stupid competitive mode. It annoyed him, but he knew that nothing would build their character more than competing with each other. No one else was at their level. He leaned into Carter. "Don't let me down."

"I won't." Carter blinked, cursing himself inside for doing that.

Chief of Police, Charlie Jackson, *the do-right man*, was an attractive, well-built man in his forties, whose dignity and poise was evident in the way he carried himself. He had his island parents' light complexion, but no hint of the accent since he left at the age of five. He had been poor most of his life, but a stellar career in the police force carried him and his family out of the ghetto and into View Park, where they lived an honest middle-class life. Still, Charlie couldn't get used to the other side of View Park. Ten million miles above middle class; the side the Chase family represented. When their maid opened the expansive doors to the home for him, he had to smile. He had never had any desire to live this well, but he loved the fact that black folks were.

"Can I help you, Chief Jackson?" Maya asked.

Charlie looked around the immense home. So many

homes in this town were extravagant, but there was something different about the Chase home. He felt it every time he came here, and every time he came here it was because of Haley Chase.

"I need to speak with Mr. and Mrs. Chase."

Expecting to see Haley, Janet rushed to the door. When she saw Chief Jackson, her chest tightened. She was a mother first and foremost. The expression on his face sent a chill through her. Something was wrong. She turned back, looking for her rock.

"Steven!"

Haley wanted to explode. She was cold and wet, wrapped in a thin blanket and sitting on a wooden seat that was harder than rock. The room was gray and morbid and nothing like the room she was in the last time she was at the police station, but that was another story. Her entire life was crashing down on her and facing her parents was still to come.

The detective in the room with her wasn't helping the situation any. He had introduced himself as if she gave a damn what his name was. She was shocked they sent her someone who looked like a college kid and pissed that he was staring down at her with judgment written all over his face.

"What are you looking at?" she asked.

Sean Jackson, *the Boy Scout*, rolled his eyes and turned away as the door opened. Grady McCann, a middle-aged uniformed officer entered and dropped a file folder on the table.

"She's got a little rap sheet of her own," McCann boasted. "Property damage, shoplifting and disorderly conduct. Surprisingly no convictions. Money goes a long way."

Haley wasn't insulted. Her last name made her better than him and certainly better than the junior detective.

"Thanks." Sean didn't need to look at it. He knew all about Haley Chase. Who didn't?

"You think you can handle her?" McCann asked. "If not, I can stay and help you."

"Go on home, McCann." Sean looked at Haley. "I can handle Ms. Chase."

"That's what you think," she mumbled under her breath just loud enough to be sure he heard her.

"You two should have a lot in common." McCann folded his arms across his very large stomach. "Both kids of big shots."

Did this guy think he could rile him up? Sean had heard every little jab about his father being chief of police since he'd joined the force five years ago. They all admired Charlie Jackson, but the son had to be getting a ride. The fact that he wouldn't look the other way when the blue did something wrong didn't make him their favorite person either, but Sean didn't care. He was a detective—a good detective—and the law was the law.

He just gave McCann a lazy, bored smile, refusing to give away anything, and McCann simply walked away.

"It's freezing in here," Haley snapped, but Sean didn't respond. He just looked at her and her frustration was building. Something about his look, she couldn't describe. It made her feel like she was on trial. "Are you hard of hearing? I said it's freezing, and it's too dark. This blanket isn't dry anymore. Get me a new one." Haley tossed the blanket at him, but he didn't even blink.

"Who do you think you are, looking at me like that?" She wanted to slap him. At least that would get a reaction out of him. She hated his calm demeanor. It reminded her of Carter, who annoyed her because he never indulged her. "I'm the victim here."

Sean smiled with an air of pleasure, knowing it would only anger her more. "You are some piece of work."

Satisfied with a response, she leaned back in the chair. "You don't know the half of it."

She was a deceptive one. Every time he had seen Haley Chase, whether dressed up like a spoiled princess or the mess she was now, she was incredible to look at and the raspy tone of her voice turned him on. If he hadn't known who she was, and how this all got started, he might think of her as a victim. "I know more than you think. I'm a good enough cop to see people like you coming a mile away."

"Your job is to protect and serve, not pass judgment. You can't get past my last name or who I was with on that boat, but that's none of your damn business."

"Whatever."

When he turned away from her, Haley wanted to throw something at him.

The door opened and Sean watched Steven enter. His family followed behind, but Sean was focused on the man of presence who stood before him. The great Steven Chase.

"Who are you?"

"Mr. Chase, I'm Detective—"

"Mr. Chase." Charlie entered the room, holding his hand up to stop his son. "This is my son, Sean. He's been keeping Ms. Chase company while she waits."

Sean's eyes widened. Had he just heard him right? Keeping her company? He had graduated at the top of his class at the academy, had the highest solve rate in the department and his father had turned him into a babysitter with one sentence.

"Detective Jackson," Sean added, unable to let that one slide.

Steven wasn't listening to him. He had turned his attention to his daughter, as had everyone else. Sean watched as they showered her with attention, kisses and hugs, and found it amazing how injured she suddenly appeared.

"You aren't hurt at all?" Janet asked.

"I'm fine." Haley leaned away. She looked at Leigh, envying her angelic features. "You've gained weight, Leigh."

Leigh had hoped some time would pass before she had to remember how nasty her little sister's jokes could be, but it didn't matter. "This isn't the time to be funny."

"You're the only person in the world who can go to Africa and actually gain weight." Haley chuckled until her mother pinched her arm.

"Chief Jackson," Steven said. "I want more information than you've given me. It's not enough."

Charlie knew how to deal with men like Steven Chase. "Sometimes drug deals get made at sea, innocent people stumble upon them and get caught in the crossfire. Your daughter and the congressman were lucky. For some reason they didn't go after them."

Michael slapped the wooden table, laughing as he spoke. "Hittin' it with a married congressman. I got to hand it to you, Haley."

"Shut up, Michael," Janet sniped. "Chief, that part won't get out will it?"

Here it goes, Charlie thought. "Mrs. Chase, we can't—"

"Chief." Steven approached him, already in a posture of negotiation. "We need to talk about how we can keep the situation with the congressman under wraps."

Leigh couldn't believe this. "Haley was shot at by drug dealers and you're talking about keeping secrets?"

"You've been gone too long," Haley said. "You forgot what's most important to Mom and Dad."

"They called the police on the way back to the dock," Charlie continued. "Our guys were waiting for them. When the Coast Guard went out there to look around, we couldn't find anything. Your daughter was too upset to help us identify any boats. She didn't want to go back out there."

"So they got away?" Steven asked.

"How did she get wet?" Carter asked.

"Jack was taking too long," Haley said with a shiver. "When he realized what was happening, he started freaking out. He couldn't even remember where he was supposed to dock. I jumped off the boat and swam to shore."

Janet smiled. She'd taught her daughters to save themselves instead of waiting for a man to do it for them. "Let's just get her home."

"We haven't interviewed her yet," Sean retorted.

Steven turned to the detective who looked no older than Haley herself, but held himself well. He had an eye for a man of character and he saw that in the man in front of him. "You won't tonight. She's been through enough."

Leigh flipped open the file on the table. "What is this? She's not the criminal here."

"According to junior, I am." Haley smirked at Sean's reaction to her choice of words.

Sean grabbed the folder from Leigh. "We needed to know who we were dealing with. When she got here, she was raising hell. She practically tore the place apart."

Haley innocently responded to everyone's stares. "I was upset. They were interrogating me."

"Is that right?" Janet laid an accusatory look on Sean.

Sean didn't bother to answer. The woman obviously didn't want to believe anyone but her daughter.

"What my son means," Charlie added, "is that we were trying to get information out of her so we could find the boat. Time was essential. We need Haley to—"

"Steven." Janet shook her head.

"Chief, we'll talk to you tomorrow," Steven said. "Haley is coming home now."

"What about protection?" Leigh asked.

"They didn't come after us," Haley explained. "It doesn't matter anymore."

Sean couldn't believe she was acting as if this were over. "If the man you saw get shot was at the helm, it's possible they just didn't know how to navigate the boat quick enough to get you."

"Nothing to say they won't try again," Steven said.

"I don't think they saw me," she returned. "I mean . . . my face."

"We can't take that chance," Steven said, already flipping open his cell phone. "We have a security company we work with. I'll have them come over tomorrow."

"We'll have two cops stay outside overnight," Charlie pointed out.

Sean watched as if in synchronized movement, the family stood up and walked out.

"And Chief," Steven called back. "No press!"

"He gets to walk all over us?" Sean asked as soon as they were out of earshot.

"It wasn't that bad, son."

Sean felt irritation riding up on him. "You're not supposed to call me that at the station. This delay could hinder our case."

"Don't worry. That man has power, but we're the law." Charlie hoped that sounded convincing.

CHAPTER 2

It was nine in the morning and Sean was already on his last nerve thanks to Haley. He was willing to forgive the fact that Steven somehow got his father to delay this interview for three days, even though he knew it was going to hurt his case. He was willing to forgive that he had to come to the Chase mansion to do the interview instead of her coming down to the station like everyone else. What he wouldn't forgive was Haley's attitude and the fact that her mother encouraged her self-pity by wrapping her arms around her like she was a helpless baby. Only Steven seemed to put forth any attempt at cooperation.

"I can't remember!" Haley slammed her cup of coffee on the table. What did these people want from her?

"I'm not asking you to remember exactly," Sean said. "Just estimate how far away the boat was or what you could see of their faces through the binoculars."

"I couldn't see their faces at all." She smirked. "See there, I helped you."

"I'll be the judge of that." Sean met Janet's angry glare with one of his own. He didn't care if he made her angry. Neither Janet nor the princess understood what was really going on here.

"She's doing the best she can," Janet argued.

"She's gonna have to do better," Steven said.

Haley glared up at her father, certain this man hated her. Maybe it was Leigh's return that had turned him so cold to her these past few days. He seemed impatient and unresponsive, but she wasn't going to let him get to her. She turned back to Sean. "I've told you all I know. Why aren't you asking Jack? He was there, too."

Sean wanted to strangle her. "You had to have seen something, like a design on the boat or outstanding physical characteristics of the shooter."

Haley felt her mother squeeze her hand and it urged her to try to play along. "I think they were white, but they could've been Latino. It was hard to tell. That's it. I don't remember anything about the boat."

"We're going to bring you a book and we'll need you to see if you recognize any of the boats."

Haley leaned forward with fire in her eyes. "Aren't you listening to me? I didn't pay attention to the damn boat."

Sean refused to even blink. He had dealt with murderers, rapists and thieves. He wasn't going to let a spoiled brat make him lose control.

"Haley, calm down." Steven leaned forward, placing a firm hand on her shoulder, which she promptly shrugged away.

"I'm through here." Haley got up and began walking away. Let the detective deal with that.

"Haley," Steven called after her. "Get back here right now!"

Haley turned around. "Don't yell at me!"

Steven didn't hold back. "He's only trying to help you!"

"They're trying to scare me!" Haley pointed at Jason, one of the goons her father had following her around everywhere standing in the corner. "I don't need him or the police stalking me. And I certainly don't need your fake attention, Daddy."

"Haley." Janet's tone was harsh for the first time that morning.

"No, Mom. He doesn't need to bother with me. His favorite daughter is home now."

As she stormed out of the room, Sean threw his hands in the air. It was like watching a freaking soap opera. "Mr. Chase, we can't help protect her if she's going to be—"

"A spoiled brat?" Janet asked, standing. "That's what you were going to say, wasn't it?"

Sean chose not to respond. He was more interested in the large man who had been standing in the corner and was now leaving to follow Haley. He was at least two hundred fifty pounds with a neck the size of a normal man's thigh. Sean had a sense about him. It was how he had gotten so far in his career, faster than anyone in the history of the Los Angeles county police. When something wasn't right, it just wasn't.

"Hold on, Jason." Steven waved the man back and introduced him to Sean as one of the two bodyguards he hired for Haley from the Attaché security agency.

Sean gave the man an icy greeting who returned it likewise. He waited until he was out of the room before questioning Steven on the choice.

"We've used the Attaché company for myself a few times." Steven appreciated the young detective's concern, but he shouldn't assume a man like himself hadn't done all the necessary research. "They've been here since Sunday and they're doing a good job."

"How many people know about them?" Sean asked.

"My husband knows what he's doing." Janet was on edge and needed a Valium. "Are you finished here?"

"Things have changed a little." Knowing this moment would come eventually didn't make it any easier for Sean.

"The department did everything it could to keep this a secret, but—"

Janet gasped. "Oh, dear God."

She had allowed the few days passing to give her hope, but she was asking for too much. As Sean showed her the rolled up issue of *South L.A.* magazine she squinted as if it was the glaring sun. It was worse. It was a picture of a wet Haley getting out of the back of a squad car in front of the police station with Congressman Flay clearly visible right behind her. Big bold letters atop read: "Another Chase Scandal!"

In seconds, Steven was in Sean's face, bearing down on him. "I thought I discussed this with your father."

Sean stood strong against the formidable man even though his stomach was tightening. "Sir, the chief of police made sure information on the incident was sealed. The article just speculates based on the photo."

"So what does this mean?" Janet asked.

"It means," Sean began, pulling himself together after Steven finally backed down, "that whoever went after Haley and Jack last Saturday, is probably checking around to see who is saying what. This might give them some ideas."

Janet and Steven looked at each other, able to speak without words after so many years together. Steven reached for her, wrapping his arm around her and squeezing tight. She had to know he would never, ever let anything happen to their baby.

Sean suddenly felt as if he didn't belong in this scene anymore. "Can I check Haley's room?"

"Take a left at the top of the stairs," Steven answered. "It's at the end of the hallway."

Leigh nodded to the detective as he left the room. She stayed at the edge, staring at her parents as they held each other. With so much to doubt in the world, the strength of her parents' marriage and love for each other had never been one of them and it was the foundation for everything

Leigh believed in. Strong black love. It was what kept her strong when she had been immersed in so much suffering the last year.

She didn't want to interrupt them, but she needed to reach out to them. She had been doing everything she could to lay the groundwork these past few days, trying to build up her confidence. Looking after Haley had distracted her a bit, but she was clearly on course for her goal. This was the next inevitable step and from the looks of things, it couldn't have come at a worse time.

She cleared her throat, entering the living room. "What's going on?"

"We have everything under control," Steven said. "It's going to be all right."

"I've been meaning to talk to you about what I plan to do now that I'm back."

Janet was grateful for some good news. "You don't have to pick the practice you want to join yet. We know you'll make the right choice."

Leigh produced a weak smile. "I hope you mean that."

Janet's smile faded. She knew her children too well. Caught up with Haley, she hadn't ignored Leigh's virtual absence at the house the past few days. She said she was visiting friends, but Leigh was a horrible liar.

"Because," Leigh went on, "I made up my mind about what I wanted to do a few months ago. I want to open up a free clinic in South Central for children with HIV and AIDS."

"A free clinic?" Janet's voice caught in her throat. "For poor people?"

"Yes, Mom." So it begins. "You say it like there's something wrong with that."

Steven took a heavy breath. "We donate to several clinics like that, but it's not the right job for you. You're a Chase, Leigh. If you want to show compassion, make a donation or find a safe clinic to volunteer at every now and then, but you're going to be a doctor of reputation and success and that only comes from having powerful patients and major hospital connections."

"That's your dream, not mine." Leigh begged herself to keep it together. She'd known this would be hard and she hated being such a coward. "What I experienced in Africa has—"

"Warped your mind," Janet pointed out. "You're just on a goodwill high. You'll come down."

Leigh shook her head. Her mother spent her life on philanthropy. What had it all been for? "You're wrong. HIV and AIDS among African Americans is an epidemic. Lack of education and access to care is what is killing our people, not the disease."

"Leigh." Steven loved the heart of this child. "Maybe there is some way you can continue to volunteer with these types of people, but not for a living."

Leigh didn't try to conceal her hurt. "Look, the truth is I need the Chase Family Foundation to help fund the clinic."

"No," Janet dictated. "I won't support this."

"Daddy."

"Leigh, I'm sorry. You know I love you and want you to be happy. We agreed to this stint in Africa, but . . ."

Agreed? Leigh specifically remembered threats were made. They fought her tooth and nail, but she did it anyway because it was her calling. So was this clinic.

Janet began anxiously fluffing the pillows on the sofa, unwilling to add this to her list of worries. "I can't deal with this right now."

"Think about it," Steven said. "You've glamorized this stuff. It's not—"

"Glamorized? I just spent a year in Africa! Look, I'm going to do this."

"Not with the Chase Family Foundation, you aren't."

Steven hated hurting her, but that was what a father had to do for his child's own good.

"Fine." Leigh knew that wasn't fine at all, but there was nothing else she could say. "I know people who want this as much as I do."

She had to bite her lower lip to keep from crying until she left the room. She had no reason to cry because, unfortunately, that had gone exactly as she'd thought it would.

Steven kissed his wife on the forehead even though it couldn't cure the pain in her eyes. "Baby, I have to go to the office. You'll stay with Haley?"

She grabbed his hands, feeling such a burden with her desperate need for him. He was the world to her. "Not today, Steven."

"I need to go to the office for at least a few hours today. You'll be here and so will the bodyguards." He ignored the guilt that he always felt when he picked Chase Beauty over everything else. Janet understood more than most wives, but she couldn't be expected to understand all the time. She would be cold to him when he got back home. He was used to this.

In her heart, Janet tried to smother the disappointment that came with Steven's choices. It was a sacrifice for him as well. She had to remember that and handle this day herself. Reaching into her pocket, she took out a small prescription bottle of Valium and swallowed a pill. She was used to this.

After graduating from college with a business degree, Avery Jackson, *the girl next door*, knew opening a hair salon wasn't what her parents expected, but they had always taught their daughter to find what she loved and the money would come. That advice birthed Essentials in

View Park, and three years later, Essentials II in Baldwin Hills; a neighborhood beauty salon where there would be no two-hour wait, and everyone would be in and out on time; even on Saturday. Service was better than the highest-end salons, but at neighborhood salon prices.

And she was only twenty-six.

Avery knew she should be the happiest woman in the world. Sometimes she wished she was better at fooling herself, but like most women, she wasn't able to separate her private life from her business life. Everything melted together, and as she sat in the back office of Essentials going through numbers that didn't make sense, all she could think of was Alex, her apathetic fiancé, and wondering why she let the phone call she had just hung up on get so out of hand.

She had tried to hold on to her emotions, because Alex only became defensive when she yelled. What was she supposed to do? He had been canceling their plans week after week, and wouldn't settle on a wedding date. He preached about the pressures of a salesman, telling her the solution was for her to work less. What was happening to them? She was so easily irritated and he was constantly annoyed. All of those qualities, Avery told herself, weren't as important as their love three years ago, but were becoming more important now after almost a year of being engaged.

"You wanted to see me?"

Avery hadn't even noticed Craig come into the office, let alone stand at the desk staring down at her with an anxious expression on his face. Craig Moon was a throwback from the eighties. He was a dead ringer for Phillip Michael Thomas in his *Miami Vice* days. An expert accountant, after four years he was now a minority owner in the overall business. Avery respected Craig's talent, but his secretive behavior in the past few months was bothering her.

"Craig, I was just going over last month's numbers and I think something is—"

"Knowing you can't count past ten." He laughed, scanning the documents on her desk.

"I can count, Craig. I have a business degree."

"I told you I would do that. That's why you brought me on. I'll handle it."

"We'll handle it." Avery worked hard not to seem so possessive of Essentials, but it was her baby and she wasn't going to stand for anyone pushing her out. With all of her frustrations with Alex, she ignored Craig's increasing tendency to push her away from the numbers. She had to regain her focus. "If we don't increase our profits, we'll never be able to open Essentials III."

Craig grabbed his keys on the hook at the door. "It'll pick back up."

"Where are you going?"

"I have some errands. Then I'm off to II."

Avery let him walk away even though she was angry. She hated coming down hard on Craig—on anyone. That was her problem. She was so preoccupied with keeping peace and making people happy that she was losing control of her business and her relationship. When had she lost her backbone?

Avery knew she had a temper, a spicy side to her, but she had bottled it down recently because it only seemed to anger Alex, making him push away from her. She preferred to hang up on him than deal with him. The old Avery would have called him back and cussed him out, putting him in his place, before asking him what he would like for dinner later that night. This Avery didn't want to bother starting something. She couldn't blame that all on Alex.

She needed a distraction. She needed out of this office. Tuesday was one of the slowest days of the week for Essentials, but she welcomed whatever distractions were there. Seeing her business—her child—thriving always made her feel better.

"What's going on?" Avery sauntered to the front window of the salon where most of the customers were standing, looking out.

"Outside, girl." Alexa Duchese licked her lips. "It's Carter Chase."

As she watched Carter Chase step out of his silver Mercedes SL-Class convertible across the street, Avery felt like she had a brick in her stomach. At least it wasn't Michael. She wasn't sure she could take another second of that one. Carter was different. He had a smooth way about him, not as abrasive, so she was told. She had never met him, but everyone knew everything about the Chase boys. Carter was the smooth character; laid back. Even the way he walked across the street, ignoring traffic as if he was sure nothing could ever happen to him, seemed to be in slow motion.

"I can't believe he's still single." Verona Dellis's hand spread over her heart.

Calabra Velasquez huffed. "I heard he's single because he's a big player."

"I could make him stay home." Lisa Tyson snapped her fingers. "But I like the younger one. Michael."

"He's married to that model thing." Calabra rolled her eyes.

"She trapped him," Lisa said. "Got pregnant and made him marry her."

Avery had heard enough. The black community's obsession with the Chase family was nauseating. "Okay, ladies. He may look good, but he's not worth letting your process burn through your head."

They returned to their places, but never took their eyes off Carter when he entered the store. Avery had no love for any Chase at this point. Not after the last few months of Michael, and she wasn't about to give Carter a chance either.

Carter flashed a winning smile for the woman standing in front of him, but she didn't seem impressed. Impossible. She was incredibly attractive in that suburban girl type of way, but this was about business so that didn't matter either way. Over the last few days, he had let his father's brooding looks and biting words get to him and he wanted to close this deal even if it meant being an ass. He didn't like it, but he was just as good at it as anyone. Better. "Can I speak with—?"

"No." Avery, hands on hips, was ready for him. With her current mood, a good-looking man meant nothing.

"Excuse me, but I need to speak with Avery—"

"That's me and the answer is no. You can leave now, Mr. Chase."

As she turned and began walking away, Carter started after her. "I was warned about your stubbornness, but I wasn't aware you were also unprofessional."

Avery swung around. "Unprofessional? What you and your brother are doing is what's unprofessional. Trying to push everyone around." She reached her office, planning to slam the door for effect, but Carter caught the door just before it closed. "I didn't invite you in."

"I don't push people around. Look, Ms. Jackson. If you would take a second, I can tell you why you should reconsider."

Avery sat down at her desk, eyeing Carter. Something about him was definitely different than Michael. Even though Michael was meaner, something told her Carter would be harder to fight. "I'm not selling my shops. Your obsession with me is a waste of time."

"Obsession?" Carter laughed for a second before becoming completely serious. "Don't flatter yourself."

"Am I going to have to get a restraining order against your whole family?"

"My brother can be a little—"

"Your brother isn't a little anything."

Carter knew now why Michael had been unsuccessful with this woman. She was too smart and Michael tended to underestimate women. He wouldn't make the same mistake, and he didn't need to make excuses for Michael. "I'm not my brother, but I'm prepared to offer you twenty-five grand more than his last offer."

Avery looked him dead in the eye. "No sale."

"You didn't even think about it."

"I don't need to. Unlike you, money isn't the deciding factor in why I do what I do."

Carter helped himself to the chair across from her, never once taking his eyes off her. "You don't know me well enough to pass judgment, so I suggest you watch your mouth before you put your foot in it."

Avery paused, her lips forming into a beautifully wicked smile as she thought of where she would like to put her foot. "Your charm is just wooing me off my feet, Mr. Chase. Listen, why don't I make a deal with you?"

Carter knew he was walking into it, but he would indulge her. "Let's hear it."

Avery leaned forward. "I'll watch my mouth if you get the hell out of my office."

Carter allowed her to lean back with an accomplished look on her face. She didn't know who she was dealing with. "That's a stupid move."

"There is just no end to your flattery, Mr. Chase."

"Call me Carter."

"Mr. Chase, like I told your brother the last four times he tried to buy me out, Essentials is my baby and it's not for sale."

"Everything is for sale, Avery. Even you."

The intensity of his light eyes caught Avery for a second and she couldn't think of the best comeback. "I already use all of your products. I've made enough of a contribution to the Chase wealth machine."

"You use Chase products because they're the best out

there. Everything we do is the best. And when we take over Essentials—"

"Not gonna happen. Now I have two shops to run. I don't have time for back and forth with Steven Chase's little boys."

Carter gritted his teeth. That one got through, but he wouldn't let it show. Casually, calmly, he reached into his tailored coat jacket, pulled a contract out of the breast pocket and tossed it on her desk. "At least look at it. It's much better than anything you've been offered. It's more money than your shop made any of the five years you've been open."

"How do you know how much my shops make?"

Carter ran down her revenue for the past three years, smiling at the sight of her unintentional blink. She was a privately owned business with carefully protected financial information. It was a guilty pleasure, seeing the look on someone's face when they realized they were dealing with a Chase. Nothing was that protected when it came to his last name.

"I also know," he added, "that Chase Beauty is going to own this shop as well as that other little joint you run and we're gonna make it bigger and better than anything you could have dreamed of making it."

Avery was digging her nails into her palms under the desk. He was different than Michael, all right. He was better. "So now you claim to know my dreams?"

"It's not about what I know," he explained. "You know that you could never do for Essentials what we can. And if you learned anything from that state college education you have . . ."

Avery couldn't stop her mouth from opening wide. She had lost her footing with him and she needed an out before he got any farther.

"You'll know," he continued, "when it's time to cash in and move on."

Unsure of how to verbally respond with words, Avery snatched the papers he had given her and ripped them into several pieces before tossing them into the garbage next to her desk. Carter showed no emotion and that unhinged her even more.

"That was a mistake, Avery."

"Are you threatening me?"

Carter smiled innocently, showing a genetically inherited smugness. "The police chief's little girl? I would never."

"If you're suggesting I need to hide behind my father to fight you, you're mistaken. I can handle you by myself. Now get the hell out of my shop."

Carter stood up. That was enough for now. Winning the big ones took patience, something Michael didn't have. When he was finished with Avery, she would beg him to take Essentials just to get him out of her life.

"You have a nice day, Avery."

When he was finally gone, Avery's head fell flat on the desk and she let out a moan. Although she would never admit it to a soul, he had intimidated her in a way his little brother was never able to, and Avery knew she hadn't seen the last of him.

Standing outside of Essentials, Carter took a deep breath as he pulled out his cell phone. He had intended to be as polite as professionally possible, but when she referred to him as one of Steven Chase's little boys, she declared war. This was his fight now, and unlike Michael who went right at you, Carter took the less expected route. From what his private investigator told him, Craig Moon was that route.

Sean thought of his entire apartment and surmised that it was probably the size of Haley's bedroom. Sizing it up, the only thing that really bothered Sean was the balcony.

He noticed the white garden climbing trellis with thick flowery vines on the right side against the house. It was sturdy enough to hold a normal sized person and reached all the way to the ground. The backyard was well manicured, with bushes and statues that could hide a considerable figure. He wondered how much of this big-neck Jason had figured out.

The room was at the west end of the home, which was separated from the neighbors by tall eucalyptus trees. No gate on the sides, which wasn't good. He knew the family must have a top-notch security system outside as well as in, but sometimes the richest families were the most absent-minded when it came to security. He'd seen the results of their mistakes; especially when they didn't give a damn, which perfectly described Haley. He had to get his mind around that girl.

Returning from the balcony, Sean came face-to-face with a scowling Haley just as she closed the door behind her.

"What in the hell are you doing in my room?" she asked.

"Checking for safety. Your father gave permission."

"Well, it's not his room, is it?"

Sean found her sense of entitlement incredible. As if she didn't owe everything to her father. "You want to make the rules, why don't you get a place of your own? That way you can give all the permission you want."

Haley's lips formed a prissy smile. He was a slow learner. "So I can live like you? No, thanks. Keep your middle-class fantasy. I like my life just fine."

"Well, if you want to keep that life, I suggest you check that attitude and get with the program."

"I'm not with anyone's program but my own." She looked him over. "You'll find that out sooner or later. Now get out so I can take a shower."

What hit Sean wasn't what she said, but that her eyes

told him she really meant it. She wasn't just trying to be tough. This girl was a serious bitch. "I'm not leaving until I've finished my work here."

"I know what you're doing. You don't care about my safety. You're here to get a peek, aren't you?"

"You overestimate yourself."

"That's not possible."

"Either way, I'm not leaving yet."

"Fine." Haley's mouth curved into a put-your-seat-belt-on smile. "Then I'll just have to take the shower with you here."

Sean couldn't have turned away if he wanted to and as Haley let her robe drop, revealing her naked body in all its perfection, he knew he didn't want to.

She smiled victoriously because he couldn't take his eyes off her. No man could resist her, she knew that much. She had long legs and a curvy body that had brought better men than Detective Jackson to their knees. She walked past him into her bathroom wondering how long he would be frozen in awe. She hoped it was long enough to learn his lesson. No one said no to Haley Chase.

When he entered his downtown L.A. penthouse condo, Carter was too preoccupied with thoughts of Avery to notice something was wrong. He wondered if he could count on Craig to keep their conversations secret. He wanted to feel bad for what he was doing to Craig, but Avery's stinging words reverberated around him. It was his father in him. Michael embraced that willing-to-do-anything quality, but Carter tried to draw lines. He wasn't a lawyer because he wanted to be rich. He knew he would be rich no matter what he'd chosen to do. He was a lawyer because he believed in right and wrong, no matter how inconvenient that belief might be at times. Times like this, when he knew what he was doing was wrong, but the Chase blood in his veins urged him to look beyond it. Oh, yes, he was also a lawyer because he had a bloody thirst to win.

It was late, past nine. He was a workaholic, but his law firm was still growing and he wouldn't ask his lawyers to work till nine if he wasn't willing to. His father hated him for choosing to start his own law firm instead of working at Chase Beauty and that fueled his already ambitious heart to make Chase Law better than successful.

He heard a noise in the distance, stopping him cold. Usually pitch black when he came home, there were some dimmed lights coming from the dining room. Tossing his keys and briefcase on the console, he cautiously headed down the hallway. Michael always stopped by uninvited.

He stopped at the edge of the dining room, noticing the perfectly set table with catered food and candlelight. Definitely not Michael.

She stood at the entrance to the dining room with a seductive smile on her face. Tall and elegant with long black hair and eyes like coal, her dark skin favored perfectly with the silky peach dress that hugged her curves. Carter's lips slid into a smile. "Lisette McDaniel."

"In the flesh." Her English accent was decidedly upper class. She placed a hand on her hip with a slow tilt of her head. She was a master in the art of enchantment. It was what attracted Carter to her in the first place. He had jumped in too fast and learned his lesson the hard way. Lisette was too expensive for him. Three years after breaking up, every time she came back into his life she wanted one thing. Money.

"When did you get back from London?" he asked.

"Yesterday." She took a step toward him. Then another. "I had to sleep off a little jag. I miss the *Concord*. Travel is brutal without it."

"I don't remember ever giving you a key." Never give a woman the key to your home. She'll assume it's the same as an engagement ring.

"I don't need keys to get anywhere I want. You should know that by now."

Carter wrapped his arm around her waist, pulling her to him. She smelled . . . expensive.

"It's been a year," Lisette said. "I assumed you've missed me terribly."

"What if I had come through that door with my girl-friend?"

"Like that would matter to me."

Carter was always intrigued by her honesty. The woman wasn't any good and she was proud of it. "That's not a good girl."

"I don't have to be a good girl." She rubbed up against him. "Because I know you're a good boy. If there was a woman in your life, you wouldn't have laid a hand on me. So shut up rich boy and give me a kiss."

Carter kissed her, remembering immediately the fire they had together. Brief, but hot. Like so many of his rela-tionships. Something inside him was turned on by the confusion of getting everything he wanted from a woman and still being unsatisfied. Suddenly, an image of Avery came to him. Sitting at her desk, lips pressed together, every inch of her ready for a fight she knew she wouldn't win. Carter leaned back, wondering what was wrong with him thinking of that witch at a time like this.

"What is it?" Lisette asked.

"Nothing," he answered. "I . . . I've had a long day."

"I'm good for long days. You used to think so, at least."

Lisette was exactly what Carter needed tonight even though he knew he would pay for it tomorrow. He grabbed her tighter and kissed her harder this time.

* * *

Haley laid still as night under her bedsheets as she heard her bedroom door open. Jeff, the other goon sitting outside of her room, looked in every half hour, so she planned everything perfectly. When she heard the door close again, her covers went flying. She felt that familiar tingling sensation at the idea of doing something wrong and knowing she was going to get away with it. She almost wished she could see the look on their faces when the idiot went crying that she was missing.

She tiptoed to her vanity, checking herself in the mirror. Tight, red silk, BCBG top, black suede, low rise hip-hugging Missoni pants, her hair thrown aimlessly around and a dab of MAC mink satin lipstick. It was a crime to keep someone who looked this good inside. She grabbed her cell phone off the dresser and quietly made her way to her bathroom, closing the door so her phone call would not be heard.

Carly Longoni had a sore throat and she wasn't supposed to be going out either, but neither of them found any interest in doing what they're supposed to. The plan was for Carly to wait at the corner on Kelly Street until Haley, who was sneaking off her trellis, got there.

Exiting the bathroom, Haley tiptoed through her room. She stopped for a second certain she heard something fall or clank like glass or porcelain. Her eyes focused on the doorknob, but it didn't move. After what seemed like a full minute, she slowly reached for her favorite club purse, a tiny Burberry, dropped her cell phone inside and slid it up her arm. She heard a slight squeaking sound as she slid the balcony door open and wasn't about to risk it to slide it closed.

As soon as she reached the ground she had her path marked out. She had done this plenty of times. Her feet firmly on the ground, Haley didn't have a chance to scream before a strong hand grabbed her by the shoulder and forced her back. Another hand muffled her screams as she struggled to get free. She wasn't going out like this. She hadn't taken two self-defense classes in college for nothing.

Her leg went up and back, her hard-heeled Pradas connecting with his groin. She heard a loud groan as she was let go. Haley knew she should have just run, but being the curious cat she was, she turned around for one more kick while he was down so she could have a head start in getting away. Seeing Sean struggling to get up both surprised and amused her, but angered her more than anything.

"What in the hell are you doing here?"

"Trying to protect you!" Sean finally stood up, his body still vibrating with pain.

"Protect me? You're the one on the ground."

"What do you think you're doing?"

Haley wondered if he was even worth lying to. "I was just trying to get some air without that goon upstairs trying to follow me around."

"Dressed like that? Please. You're probably off to meet one of your other married boyfriends."

The amusement gone, Haley jabbed him in the chest with her elbow. "Get out of my way." When he grabbed her by the arm, she tried to break free, but his grip was too strong. "What just happened to you the last time you grabbed me?"

"You got lucky that time." He swung her around, his grip tightening. "You're getting back in that house."

Sean ignored her threats as he dragged her across the immense yard and around the house. He wanted to get some sleep at home, but the balcony kept nagging him and he was glad he'd come back if for nothing than just to spoil her plans.

"You need to get a life," Haley said, already thinking

of how she was going to make him pay for this. "I can do whatever I want."

He stopped suddenly, jolting her as he pulled her to him. He stared into her eyes, using her shock to his advantage. "When your life is in danger, you can't do whatever you want."

Haley pushed away from him. "You know I'm not in danger. This is just so you can feel important."

"Just shut up and come on."

Haley quickly changed her strategy. Her bellowing was only making him feel superior and when her mother greeted them at the door, she knew playing up his more brutal tendencies would work in her favor and it did. More than her anger at Haley's attempt to escape, Janet was incensed at Sean's aggressive grip on her daughter and spent most of the trip back to Haley's bedroom warning Sean of the repercussions if even the slightest bruise showed up on Haley's delicate skin. When Haley observed Sean's mounting frustration, she realized this was much more fun than sneaking out for the night. He was about to explode.

Janet's incessant nagging ceased to exist when Sean realized what was before them. Still in the chair outside Haley's bedroom, Jeff was hunched over and he wasn't moving. As Sean rushed to him, Haley attempted to follow him but Janet held her back.

Sean lifted the heavy man's upper body. He checked for a pulse and felt it faintly before noticing the cup of coffee half spilled on the floor. "Who gave him this?"

"It had to be Maya," Janet said.

"This man was drugged." Sean reached for his gun, pulling it out of his holster.

"Haley, don't." Janet reached for her daughter, but Haley escaped her grip. She followed her, adrenaline running through her veins. Whatever was happening, she wanted to get her child out of there.

"There's no one here." Sean came out of the bathroom. "We need to search the rest of the house."

Haley looked around her room, the hair on the back of her neck standing straight up. She felt the same fear as she had on Jack's boat. Who had been in here? What had they touched? How had they gotten in? What were they planning to do to her? It was too much. Her knees began to give out on her as she called out to her mother.

In the minutes after the intrusion, Sean ushered everyone into the kitchen while they waited for the police and ambulance to arrive. With her mother's arms around her, Haley watched feeling helpless as chaos ensued around her.

Sean interrogated an anxious Maya even though he didn't suspect she had anything to do with the drugging. She confessed to making the coffee to help keep Jeff awake, leaving it alone for less than five minutes to chase after Daniel, one of Michael and Kimberly's twins, who had escaped his bedroom and was traveling the house. Whoever it was had been roaming the house for some time. He had more questions for Jason, who responded with defensive anger toward him and a livid Steven whose yelling was upsetting everyone.

Michael seemed upset that his and Kimberly's bathroom sex romp was interrupted more than anything, and Janet's insistence that Kimberly's negligence was to blame started an argument that brought Haley to the edge. When she screamed for them all to shut up, the sheer volume caused immediate obedience. Everyone looked at her in a way that made her feel damaged, only angering her more.

Sean felt a certain sense of compassion for her, but was glad she finally got it.

Janet looked to her husband. "Steven, I want more police officers here."

"Make that possible, Detective." Steven approached Sean.

"Mr. Chase . . ." Sean wanted to head him off. With baseball playoffs for the Dodgers, and Athletics starting, the Kings' first home game and the Lakers playing the Spurs, there wasn't going to be a free cop for days.

Steven leaned in close, his hand firmly but not too aggressively grasping Sean's elbow. He knew what he was doing. "I know you'll get it done. What I'm concerned about is now. You saved my daughter's life."

Sean tried to ignore the sense of pride a compliment from a man like Steven Chase brought on. "I caught her sneaking out of the house."

"You're the only one I trust to protect her."

Grateful for the ringing of his cell phone, Sean turned away, hoping he hadn't gotten himself into something he would have to go through hell to get out of.

"Damn!" Only seconds later, Sean faced the curious crowd. He looked at Haley whose eyes were so wide they made her look like a child. "On the way to the hospital, Jeff had an allergic reaction to whatever was given to him. He went into cardiac arrest. He's dead."

CHAPTER 3

Avery checked her watch, looking out the window into the parking lot of Roscoe's Chicken and Waffles on Pico Boulevard. Alex was now ten minutes late. If he didn't show up in the next five minutes, his Friday wasn't going to go anything like he planned. A week ago, Avery would've considered ten minutes not much to worry about, but this past week things had changed. Ever since her encounter with Carter she had been on edge. She found herself both anticipating and dreading the next time she would see him. When she arrived at the shop Thursday to find a bouquet of lilies from him, she was a mess for the rest of the day. What game was Carter playing?

What game was Craig playing? He hadn't been in the shop for two days and wouldn't return any of her phone calls. Avery wasn't suspicious by nature but she believed in her own intuition and Craig was up to something at the worst possible time. Avery was under siege and she needed the people on her side *clearly* on her side. The message she left for him last night turned out to be more of a warning than she intended, but she had been nice too long.

"No," was all Avery could say as, instead of Alex, Carter slid into her booth. "It's too early in the morning for you."

"You like the flowers?" Carter asked.

"Why are you following me?"

"I don't follow people. I have them followed. Actually, I'm surprised to see you here." There was something about her appearance this morning that was softer and more vulnerable than the other day, but Carter was too far in the game to let that distract him.

"I sincerely doubt you're surprised by much of anything." The way he appeared so comfortable and absolutely blameless annoyed her.

"You're turning down an opportunity that you can't even see you need desperately."

"Desperately?" She laughed. "You know something I don't?"

"I know a lot of things you don't know, but that's for another discussion." He broke into a leisurely smile as her full lips pressed together. "I know that you want to take my offer, but you won't just to spite me."

"Reverse psychology." Avery stared at him. "How original. You know what amazes me?"

Carter leaned back. "Those tedious everyday things in your painfully average life?"

"That sounds like something out of your brother's book." She wrinkled her small nose. "A little beneath you."

Carter knew he had Craig in his pocket and whatever last chance he was going to give her just flew out the window.

"You never even asked me why I won't sell," she said.

"You're attached and that's understandable. Something like a hair salon would mean a lot to someone like you."

Avery's hands formed into fists under the table as she felt her stomach tightening. It wasn't what he said that got to her, rudeness wasn't impressive. It was the way he looked when he said it; so harmless as if the words hadn't come from him.

"Yes, I am attached to my shops, but I'm not stupid. I know a good opportunity when I see one. I walk away with a fat check, on to my next business venture, but what about everyone else?"

"Who else is there?"

"Not everyone has a Chase trust fund. There are a lot of regular people, just like me, who can't afford a hundred dollars for a wash and set."

"Is that what they're going for these days?" he asked, laughing.

"Don't mock me."

He straightened up. "Avery, everything with the Chase name on it is going to be high end. Women will pay whatever it costs to get their hair done if it's done right. Business is business, not charity."

"Finally, he's come," the waiter said as he reached them. "We've been waiting for you."

"No," Avery announced. "This is not the man I'm waiting for."

"Her fiancé is a smaller man," Carter said. "He doesn't look nearly as good, nor dress as well as I do."

Avery was fuming now. "You know nothing about my—"

"Alex Conner?" Her naiveté made her attractive, but it was also how he was going to demolish her.

Carter reached for a menu, but Avery snatched it from him, turning to the waiter. "We aren't ordering. He's leaving."

"Where is our fair-skinned sales boy?" Carter asked, knowing it was killing her that he knew the details of her personal life. "He likes to make you wait, doesn't he? It's how he wields his power over you."

Avery shifted in her seat, knowing she had already lost the second round. She was going to have to prepare better.

"Or even worse," Carter added. "He doesn't care whether you wait or not. If you were my woman . . ."

Avery was ready to light into Carter for going there, but realized she no longer had his attention. Her eyes followed him as he slid out of the booth and headed for the entrance to the restaurant; for a man who'd just entered. Avery was trying to put the man's familiar face to a name when Carter's fist connected hard with his right cheek, with enough force to throw him to the ground. Everyone in the restaurant sat stunned.

Carter looked down at Congressman Flay. "Because of you someone tried to kill my baby sister three days ago. If anything happens to her, I'll kill you."

Everyone's eyes followed Carter as he left the restaurant with strong, meaningful strides. Avery, still shocked by what she had seen, couldn't prevent the little smile that formed at the edges of her lips.

As Leigh climbed the walkway to the tattered one-story building she'd bought, she tried to look as optimistic as her friend, Alicia Spender, who was standing in front of it. "Sorry I'm late Alicia."

"Do you have the keys?" she asked. "I can't stand out here in this sun. I'm sure after Africa this is nothing for you, but to us pale Irish girls with freckles and red hair, it's torture."

Leigh waved the keys at her. She had just been to the lawyer's office and finalized the purchase of the building they were going to make their clinic. Alicia had been doing the legwork for the last month, and without her parents' help, Leigh had to accept the best their pooled resources could get. It was a one-story, two-thousand-square-foot former veterinary clinic that had been abandoned for two years.

"We're sure this place isn't condemned?" Leigh asked.

"It's not." Alicia grabbed the keys. "I went through

with two separate inspectors, whom we have to pay, by the way. It's actually very sturdy. It just needs some cosmetic work. We have the money for that."

"My yearly trust fund allowance isn't that big," Leigh said.

"Maybe if I talk to them," Alicia suggested. "This is my dream, too. I shouldn't make you do all the begging."

"They've never met you and my parents don't listen to people they don't know." Leigh looked around the neighborhood, knowing what this clinic could mean. "It's hard to explain to people like them, but I'll try again."

"Without your mother," Alicia said, "I don't see how we can do this."

"I wouldn't give you a dime if it were me."

Leigh looked over Alicia's shoulder as a rugged-looking, caramel-skinned man in jeans and a Chicago Cubs T-shirt came from the side of the building. This was not the neighborhood to be popping out from behind buildings. "Who are you?"

Alicia grabbed Richard by the arm, pulling him towards Leigh. "Meet Richard Powell. He's a doctor at L.A. General. He just moved here five months ago from Chicago. He wants in on the clinic."

Richard held his hand out to Leigh, who hesitated before accepting it. "I was listening in on your conversation."

"Obviously," Leigh said.

"I didn't mean to sound rude. I was just suggesting that . . . well you both sound defeated already."

Leigh's arms folded across her chest. "If you had been paying closer attention you would've heard that I'm not giving up."

He nodded. "Those were your words, but your tone says 'I give up.'"

"You don't know me," Leigh said. "I don't give up."

"After everything Alicia told me about you, I would assume you wouldn't. I have some suggestions if you're interested."

Alicia stepped between them. "Please."

"I don't have any money, but I know some guys in construction who can give us a discount and we can pay anyone in the neighborhood here to help clean up and paint. That will save us more money for equipment."

"Then there's marketing, advertising, insurance." Alicia sighed.

"There are a lot of places who will do that stuff pro bono for a clinic like this. We'll have to weed them out. You didn't expect Mommy and Daddy to do everything, did you?"

Leigh watched his unflinching smile, thinking that he better be a good doctor if he wanted to join this group, because he wouldn't get in on charm. "I was relying on them because our family's foundation does exactly this type of thing."

"Her mother is known for her fund-raising expertise," Alicia added.

"Alicia told me they refused to help you."

Leigh's tone gave away her embarrassment. "They want me to join a prestigious practice."

Alicia rubbed Leigh's arms. "Leigh's family is very—"

"He doesn't care what my family is like," Leigh interrupted. "Besides, he's living in L.A. now. He'll find out soon enough."

"I read about your sister in the paper earlier this week," he said. "Is she okay?"

Leigh was taken back. She expected judgment, gossip, ridicule, accusations, and pity like she'd gotten from everyone else, but not genuine concern. "Yes, she's okay. Thank you."

"If your parents know all of the right people," Richard said, "then don't you know them, too?"

Leigh shrugged. "I guess, but not as well as my mother."

"Then you don't really *need* her," he maintained. "You have the contacts. You have the last name. You be the fund-raiser."

"I don't know how to do that," Leigh said.

"You just came back from Africa. Your experiences must have been incredible."

"They were life changing."

Richard took a step closer, smiling. "I can't wait to hear about them."

Alicia cleared her throat, but it failed to distract Leigh and Richard from each other.

"You're right," Leigh said, getting her second wind. "I've got to go."

"What?" Alicia called after her. "I thought we were going to go over—"

"Not now," she yelled back. You can't put inspiration on hold.

Chase Beauty now took up four full floors at 777 Tower in downtown L.A. Steven's corner office was, in size, almost equal to his ego, and was undergoing its third redecoration by Janet. Its current style was Manhattan minimalist. He wasn't crazy about it, but he would rather suffer anything than disappoint his queen. Right now he was more focused on Carter who made it a practice to show up late to every scheduled meeting. He knew Carter treated his other clients better even though they didn't make him ten percent of what Chase Beauty made him.

He looked at Michael, leaning back on the leather sofa, the only soft piece of furniture Janet allowed him to keep. Michael, greatly lacking in the art of sensitivity, always reminded him of how undesirable his office was. All that mattered to Steven was that Michael wanted this office and would do anything to get it. A lesser man would be threatened, but Steven was proud. He had to be on guard against his own son and he liked that.

"Hey." Carter rushed into the office. "A client lunch got away from me."

"Does that client pay you as well as I do?" Steven asked.

"So," Michael said. "How's it hanging, Cassius?"

Carter sat across from his brother, a thin smile on his face. "Word travels fast in this town."

Steven got up, leaning against the edge of his desk. "One of the men with Flay was a WKLA reporter."

"I did what I felt I had to do."

"I only wish I could have done it," Steven murmured. "I've been trying to reach him, but he's been covered like he's the president."

Carter wasn't sure, but he thought his father had just given him a compliment. "Is this why you called me here?"

"I called you here for business," Steven said.

"I got Performance to agree to our terms today," Michael said. "They're signing the contract tomorrow."

"That was fast," Carter said. "Care to share with us how you did that?"

"I don't want to know," Steven said. "All I know is it's been a week since I gave you Avery Jackson, Carter."

"Well, since I can't lower myself to kidnapping family members, I think it might take me a little longer."

"It's just two stores," Michael teased. "Two little stores."

"I'm using her partner to get in." Carter socked Michael in the left arm. "She's clean, but he has a lot of skeletons in his closet."

"I already did a background on him," Michael said.

"I did a better one."

"Are you being careful?" Steven asked.

Carter didn't answer that and Steven knew he wouldn't. He could see the resentment in his son's face at his questioning. He should feel guilty about it, but he didn't. Besides, if Carter didn't want this tension between them, he knew what he could do to change things. Come work at Chase Beauty. "I'm giving you one more week."

"Or what?" Carter asked. He wasn't going to be threatened by anyone.

Michael wondered why in God's name Carter pushed their father like that. This was the one thing he envied about his brother. He watched as the two men stared each other down, knowing he could never have the nerve. Carter would blink first. He always did, but each time he lasted longer and Michael wondered if it were possible that one day, Steven would be the first to blink. He didn't think so.

Carter blinked.

"Get out," Steven said, satisfied. "I've got work to do."

Carter was fine with leaving, but Michael never let him just walk out.

"Why haven't you checked in on Haley?" he asked.

"Who are you now, Mom? Haley might not want to see me after she finds out what I did."

"You think she actually cared about that guy?" Michael asked, laughing.

"I lost my head for a second."

Outside of Michael's office, Carter stopped and grinned at his little brother. He had been ready to tell him everything he had going on with Craig, but not now. He would slap him with it a few days from now.

"Come in," Michael said.

Carter knew why Michael always invited him into his office when he stopped by Chase Beauty. He enjoyed the momentary affliction of envy Carter felt when he saw Michael's throne. Carter did love his father and he was proud of Chase Beauty. Here Michael was, basking in it all and he never let Carter forget it.

"You think you're going to get a promotion out of this, don't you?"

Michael's expression was very serious, no signs of his usual sarcasm. "This was my idea and it's gonna be gold. You're damn right I'm getting a promotion."

Carter checked his ringing cell phone. It was Lisette and he placed the phone back into his pocket, leaning against the wall. "So, how many laws did you break to get Performance on board?"

"Laws?" A wicked grin crossed Michael's face. "Never heard of the word."

"I hope I'm interrupting something." Kimberly sashayed into the room looking like a million dollars. Her hair flowing, her hips tempting; it was a sight Michael never tired of. She rubbed against him, flipping her head back as if on cue from a photographer.

"Unusual to see you here, Carter," she cooed. "Oh yeah, that's right. You're on retainer."

"Something you and I have in common," Carter noted jokingly. Michael certainly had his hands full with this woman. "I'm out of here."

"What was that about?" Kimberly asked after Carter left, closing the door behind him.

Michael tightened his grip around her. He knew he was too possessive, but something about Kimberly made him feel like he was always trying to keep her. "What is this about?"

"I'm having lunch with an old friend downtown." She leaned away when he tried to kiss her.

"Old?" He frowned. "From the modeling days?"

"She's in town doing a show."

"Jealous?"

"Well, she does have her own house."

Michael lifted her onto his desk, maneuvering himself between her legs. "When I get this next promotion, we'll move into a house built to your every desire. Right now, I need to stay close to Dad. He's making up his mind about me, and I need to be everywhere he is."

Kimberly felt his hand make its way up her thighs and she was already melting. "Promises, promises."

"It is a promise." He held her chin in his other hand, looking into her eyes. He wanted to see them when he touched her. "But until then, maybe this will hold you."

Kimberly let out a gasp as her body shivered all over. She grabbed his head, pulling it to her, and pressed her lips against his so hard it hurt. She loved it on his desk with the door unlocked.

Avery was venting her frustrations as she tossed the dinner she'd prepared into her kitchen garbage. Alex was supposed to be there at 7:00 and it was 7:30. She had let it go that he was fifteen minutes late for breakfast at Roscoe's yesterday, because the whole scene with Carter and Congressman Flay was entertaining enough, but he wouldn't be that lucky tonight. She hated feeling this way. Used, unappreciated and taken for granted. She wasn't high maintenance, only expected what any woman would want; some attention and a guy who was on time every now and then. Apparently three years into a relationship, that was just a little too much to ask.

She looked down at the two-carat ring on her finger, wondering if this symbol on her saying that someone loved her was what she really wanted and not marriage. That was what she thought of most now; the ring, the dress, and the wedding. Not Alex so much anymore. It made her want to cry thinking of what it could all mean. She didn't want to accept failure, three years coming to nothing and, God forbid, returning to the dating world where men like—

"It's been a while since the Chase family has given us so much to talk about. I think we've all missed them a bit."

Avery wondered if she was hearing things. She rushed

into the living room where the local FOX news station was on the television, her only company after a long Saturday at the salon. The female reporter conveyed the story as if just talking about the Chase family caused a stir within her. Avery couldn't get the effect these people had on everyone.

"Right on the heels of Haley's scandalous encounter with Congressman Jack Flay, the usually clean Carter Chase is making the news. Will he be charged with assault after his attack on the congressman yesterday, which according to witnesses left Mr. Flay in need of a trip to the dentist?"

Avery huffed. Assault, please. Well, actually it *was* an assault she thought after a second, but the man was protecting his sister's honor. What little of it Haley had.

"To discuss this latest news," the reporter continued, "we've assembled a panel of . . ."

Avery turned the television off. A panel? Was she mad or was it the rest of the world? Did people really want to hear this? She thought for a second how this would make Carter feel, but refused to feel sorry for him or anyone in that family. Maybe if they got in enough trouble of their own, they would stop making trouble for her.

When she heard Alex's key in the door, Avery tried to refocus.

Alex had that textbook charming smile on his face and an apologetic tone. "I know you hate me baby, but I couldn't help it. I was playing hoops with the guys, and the time got away from me."

Avery just stood there, hands on hips. A voice way back in her head told her he was lying, but she couldn't deal with that right now. They hadn't had sex in a couple of weeks, but she never believed Alex would actually cheat on her. That would be unforgivable.

"I know I forgot to call," he said. "I meant to, but when

I thought about it, I was already on my way over here, so . . ."

Avery's eyes narrowed. He was definitely lying.

"So." Alex seemed apparently satisfied with his own explanation. "What did you make for dinner?"

"Nothing," Avery said. "This kitchen is closed. Go home."

"Go home? Avery, I live on the other side of L.A. You're kidding, right?"

"You must be insane," she exclaimed. "Cancellations; showing up late. How much of this did you think I would put up with? The sight of you makes me sick, Alex. Go home and decide what you want to do. Either something changes or everything changes."

The textbook smile faded. "Is that a threat?"

Avery was surprised at the words herself. "Maybe it is. I don't know anymore. I can't tell what I mean or what I feel. I'm just so . . . unhappy with us."

He leaned back, his defensive posture beginning to form. "So, what are you saying?"

"I love you, Alex. I want to marry you, but either I come first for you, or not at all."

When she entered the house, Leigh came face-to-face with the last person she wanted to see: her mother. It wasn't just because she had a look on her face that warned you not to mess with her, but Leigh felt guilty going behind her back to fund the clinic which was why she slipped a quick greeting out and headed for the kitchen.

"Where have you been?" Janet asked. She hadn't spoken more than two words to her since knocking down her ridiculous idea to work in the middle of a war zone with prostitutes and drug addicts. "I went to sleep at eleven last night and you weren't home. And you left early this morning."

"I was in Malibu with some friends." Leigh never thought she'd say this, but right now she wished she could be more like Haley. Haley let a lie roll off her tongue as smooth as butter.

Janet didn't want to argue with this child even though she knew she was lying. She had just gone twelve rounds with a frustrated Haley who, only four days after an attempt on her life, wanted out of this house. "I didn't like the way we left things."

"I really want you and Daddy to understand. I want your support."

"We love you so much, Leigh. I hope you understand that."

"I do, but this is my life. I've got to make my own choices. I want this clinic. If you would listen to our case for—"

"I know the clinic is a good idea," Janet said. "You don't need to convince me of that. But it's not for you."

"You've made a career out of charity. Why can't I?"

"You can't possibly compare what I do with the Chase Foundation with what you were thinking of doing. Let's be serious." Janet could see the hurt in Leigh's eyes and it wasn't what she'd intended. Being a parent was painful and Leigh was so sensitive. "I want everything for you, Leigh."

With nothing to say, Leigh turned and walked away. Her mother would never understand that any of her children had a right to their own lives. She preached the importance of who they were and what they meant to the community. The choices they made couldn't be just theirs. That's why they had to pick the right friends, the best colleges, at least two degrees, careers of the highest regard, walk the right way, talk the right way and dress a certain way. Taking everything into consideration before any choice was made was the price for privilege.

Leigh could only hope that after she got the clinic up

and running, her mother would become a part of it. She wasn't sure she could do it any other way. Her mother's approval meant the world to her.

Janet felt emotion well in her throat. She had been so hopeful that things could be different between them after all of this time.

"I want you to be safe. I can't tell you how many nightmares I've had over the last year. All those nights not knowing, and hearing the horrible things going on there. Now with Haley, I just can't take it."

Leigh turned back, her mother's words reaching inside her. "Who would we be as black people in this country if we let fear stop us from helping our brothers and sisters?"

"Everything your father and I have done is so that you don't have to be a savior. No matter what you say, this is not the right choice for you."

"Either way, it's my choice."

Janet looked into her eyes, believing her sincerity. There was so much about who they were and what they stood for that Leigh never understood; never tried to. She couldn't let her do this. She wouldn't.

CHAPTER 4

As she finished ringing up her last customer for the night, Avery was so tempted to call Alex she felt like the phone next to the register was vibrating. She hadn't spoken to him since kicking him out Saturday night. It was Wednesday and she hadn't heard a word. They had fought before, too many times to mention, followed by a short time to calm down. A few days, one time a whole week. Only this time seemed different and Avery's heart was tearing apart at the idea that she may have made a serious mistake.

Her desk was a mess and that was a sure sign that Craig had been using it. He'd barely spoken to her when she'd come in earlier today and didn't want to talk about what was wrong with him. Avery had so much on her mind that she didn't push, and right now she had to think about what she was going to say to Alex. If she let her emotions get to her she would lose her point.

"Write it down," she said to herself.

She saw Craig's message pad and reached for it. Craig was adamant all calls for him be put on this pad. It was an accountant thing. It was already on the last page so she flipped back a few pages and ripped one out. She could write on the back of . . .

This was interesting.

Message To: Craig

From: WNS

WNS was code for Would Not Say, when someone didn't want to leave a name. Avery couldn't help but be curious because of the way Craig was acting. She went back to the pad and scanned the last few pages of messages going back to the beginning of last week. Three messages from WNS with the same phone number in the past week.

This was wrong. She hated nosy people and didn't want to be in anyone's business, but Avery had a feeling she couldn't ignore. She dialed the number, with her hand on the button to hang up as soon as she saw the Caller ID, but when the number came on the screen, the name above it froze her solid. Unable to accept it, she put the phone to her ear and listened to the message that came without rings.

"You've reached Carter Chase. I can't . . ."

She hung up, feeling a sense of panic rip through her. She flipped desperately through the message pad as the room seemed to spin around her. Craig's erratic behavior began the day after Carter's first visit to the salon. She thought of Carter's lack of pressure since their first encounter, and now these messages. They had been communicating! She had assumed Carter would try to get to Craig, but when she'd talked to Craig about it he'd promised to let her know any- and everything.

When the phone rang, Avery almost jumped out of her seat. It wasn't Carter. It wasn't Alex. It was someone named Lauren Palnak. "Essentials, can I help you?"

"Is Craig there?" The woman spoke with a high-pitched voice.

"Craig left a couple of hours ago."

"I thought . . . I wanted to catch him before he went to dinner because my plans have changed. I can meet him after he's done."

"Sorry, he's not here."

"Would anyone there know where he's at?"

"No, I don't." Avery was about to hang up.

"Well, ask somebody," she nagged with attitude. "I'm his girlfriend, Lauren. They know me there. His dinner was about the salon, so someone there ought to know."

Avery felt like she was kicked in the stomach. "What do you remember? Maybe I can help."

"It was Italian," she said. "I remember he's been wanting to go there for—"

"Angelo's." Avery was almost whispering, focusing more on her thoughts than her words.

"That's right! Oh, thank . . ."

Avery hung up, her hand gripping the phone so tight it hurt. Carter had been one step ahead of her since the moment he walked into her shop. She had been playing fair with someone who didn't know the meaning of the word, but no more. Some heads were coming off and she wasn't talking about the ones on top of the shoulders.

The phone rang again and Avery almost ignored it, but Alex's name and number came on the ID.

"Alex?"

"What's wrong?" he asked.

"Nothing. What do you want?" Avery was too angry to be conscious of her tone.

"I was hoping we could go to dinner tonight. You know, so we could talk about—"

"Fine," Avery said. "Let's go to Angelo's. Pick me up in ten minutes." She hung up the phone so mad she could barely breathe.

Carter knew he was wrong to make the comparison, but it was so obvious Craig was a much lesser man than he. He wondered how a man made it, always struggling to do what came so easily for him. It wasn't all about money. Carter had seen many men with more money than he had with no control over their own destiny; who couldn't stand up for themselves to save their own lives.

Craig was visibly shaken, this being their first face-to-face encounter. Carter didn't want to come off as threatening, but he knew there was probably no helping that. He had lost his patience. This had taken longer than it should have. Even now, sitting across from him for almost a half hour, Craig could barely make eye contact with him.

Craig had hung up on Carter the first time he called, but after a while he was singing a different tune. Craig was dead broke. He was being sued for child support by two women and had gambling debts that were being called in by some pretty dangerous folks. Most importantly, he had been stealing from Essentials for the last three months to keep his head just above water. He wanted to know how Carter knew so much about him, but Carter assured him all that mattered was that it was all the truth and he wanted the papers. He felt some pity for Craig, knowing the man was never really in the game.

"You made these choices, Craig," he admonished.

"Spare me the speech, man. You're no different from me. You're blackmailing me to get at that bitch, and . . ."

"Let's keep this civilized." Carter gestured for him to keep his voice down. "For the record, I am absolutely, positively nothing like you and Avery didn't make you do this."

"She thinks she's better than everybody else. Pretending to be perfect, just keeping everyone at enough distance to never forget they aren't worthy of her. I know who she really is. She's an insecure mess and that marriage ain't gonna happen."

"I don't give a damn," Carter said. "Don't think about Avery. Think about—"

"Don't think about her?" Craig laughed. "She's the reason this is all happening. I wanted to sell when your brother came around. I needed the money, and now I'm—"

"I'm offering you the money," Carter said.

"I can't do anything with my shares without Avery signing off."

"I'm a corporate lawyer, Craig. I told you I'll take care of that."

"Where's the money?"

Carter reached into his briefcase and placed the thick yellow envelope on the table. As he began sliding the down payment across it, a delicate hand reached in and picked it up not so delicately. Both men looked up to see a fuming Avery standing over them.

Craig's eyes were wider than his head. "What are you—"

Avery waved the envelope in front of their faces. "This wouldn't by any chance be cash for your share of Essentials?"

Carter eyed Craig, wondering at first if he was up to something, but the look on the man's face told him Craig had no idea how Avery had figured this out. He reached up, grabbing the envelope from her. "I'll take that back, thank you."

"I'll deal with you later." She felt her adrenaline running at mach speed. "How could you, Craig? I thought you were my—"

"Friend?" Craig laughed. "You've got to be kidding me."

Carter saw the emotion in Avery's eyes and ignored the fact that it sort of mattered to him.

Avery didn't know what to say. She was seeing hate in Craig's eyes and she couldn't begin to know how she had caused this.

"There are friendships," Craig said, "and there is money."

"And Avery doesn't have either to offer you," Carter

interjected, "so don't try to make it like you can help him."

Avery's hands formed into fists as she stared Carter down. "This is between me and Craig."

"No, it isn't." Craig slid out of the booth. "I've had enough reality for tonight."

"Craig!" Avery couldn't believe he was running away like a child.

"Let him go," Carter said.

"What did you tell him?"

"None of your damn business." Carter gritted his teeth. This woman. How was he going to recover this? Tell his father, what? He needed a drink.

"Did you threaten him?" Avery had to control the feeling of vulnerability she now had.

"Like I said, none of your business." He stood up, throwing a handful of bills on the table. "Thanks for ruining my evening."

"Ruining your—" Avery was astounded and livid. "I swear Carter, from this moment on you better stay away from anything related to Essentials or—"

His sudden closeness as he leaned in shocked her. His face was only inches from hers and his expression was beyond serious. That calm, cool demeanor was nowhere in sight.

"Or what?" he asked.

Avery swallowed, asking for the strength to speak. She knew she had to stand tall now or she might as well give him Essentials for free. "Or you're going to be sorry," she said in a voice not as strong as she had wished it would be.

A surge of energy swept through Carter as he grabbed Avery by the arms, pulling her closer. A mixture of anger and lust ripped through him, the second coming unexpectedly. "Don't threaten me. I don't think you want to see the side of me that gets cornered."

"Get your hands off me!" Avery was rattled through and through. When he let her go, she wasn't sure if she could stand on her own. "I know what you're up to, and it's not going to work."

Carter watched her as she backed away from him. "You have no idea what I'm up to, and it always works."

The anger inside him began to temper as he watched her walk away, only to get another rise as he saw who she was walking to; her somewhat confused fiancé, Alex. Why that bothered him, he didn't know and he didn't care. He had bigger problems on his hands.

Sean knocked on the door to Haley's bedroom for the second time. He knew she was in there. She was the one who'd called to tell him something about the case. He wasn't sure she was telling the truth, but it had been a week and a half since the break-in and every lead had grown cold. As the second knock came unanswered, he began to suspect her motives. When he opened the door, she was in the middle of getting dressed with an unbuttoned shirt and pants half pulled up.

"What are you doing?" Haley asked.

"There's supposed to be someone outside your door."

"Maybe he died, too. I'm getting dressed."

"I've seen the whole show, remember?" He certainly hadn't forgotten. "Where is the bodyguard, Haley?"

His patience was too short for Haley to enjoy teasing him. She preferred the buildup for her own entertainment, but she had to behave tonight. She needed his help if she was going to get out of there. "He went to the bathroom. Hopefully no one will try to kill me before he comes back."

Sean was disappointed. "Somebody wanted you dead."

"But I obviously don't know anything," she said. "I

couldn't recognize anything from those pictures you showed me. Maybe they realize that and they're giving up."

"What are you getting dressed for?"

"I didn't tell you? I'm going out."

"No, you're not."

"That's why I called you over." Haley ran behind him and closed the door. "The Yankees are in town for the playoffs. There's a big players' party tonight."

Sean felt like an idiot. "I'm leaving."

"Wait. I'm not playing games. I do take this seriously now. I'm very frightened." She could tell from the look on his face that he was close to buying it. Well, it wasn't actually a lie. "I know I need to be guarded, but I can't stay in this house anymore. It's been two weeks and I'm losing my mind."

"I can understand it's hard, but if he can get in your house—"

"The party I'm going to is for the players. It's extremely exclusive. The VIP list is highly scrutinized and all of the players' security will be there."

Sean had to admit, it was probably a safe environment. Several high profile players in one spot. Not to mention the stars who would show up with their security.

He shouldn't have done that, Haley thought to herself. His little sigh told her she was making some sense. He was hers now. "This place has metal detectors and cameras on the ceilings."

Sean was shaking his head, but his resolve was fading as she moved closer to him. "You'll still be exposed before you get inside and when you come out."

"Not if I have both of those bodyguards," she said. "And you."

"Me?" Sean knew he should have asked to be on that new case about that missing drug dealer. It was less dangerous than Haley.

Men were so easy; especially the younger ones. "You saved my life. My daddy trusts you. He likes you. He'll let me go if I'm with you." Still some hesitation. "You'll have fun. There will be beautiful girls there and I promise I'll behave."

His brows narrowed. That was a lie if ever he heard one.

"Derek Jeter," she teased.

Haley was already slipping into her shoes. "We need to pick up Carly and Olivia before we get there."

When they arrived at the party at ten, Sean was on edge. He was thinking of Steven's threats if anything happened to Haley and Jason's indignance at his instructions. Neither he nor Erik, the new bodyguard, appreciated his advice, but he didn't care. They would be able to see Haley from every angle and he would personally never let her get more than three feet away from him. When the players started showing up, Sean expected he would have a hard time concentrating on Haley, but it was nothing like that. He couldn't take his eyes off her.

She tried to escape him time after time, talked to her girlfriends with the mouth of a sailor, drank too much and went from pretending he wasn't there to teasing him continuously. Sean hadn't touched a drop of alcohol, but there was something intoxicating about her bad behavior. It was so genuine to her that she almost made it seem innocent. He was completely disgusted with her and drawn to her at the same time. She knew it, which only made him angrier, but didn't seem to make him want to stop. Not even when she pulled him onto the dance floor.

A little buzz began to flirt in Haley's ears as she danced around Sean. Out of his element, which he definitely was right now, he didn't have that holier-than-thou attitude. It made him more attractive; more interesting. He would hate himself in the morning for having so much fun with her and that amused her more than anything. He had a strong sense of morality and professionalism, but in a few hours she had become his weakness. As the music changed to a slow beat, Haley grabbed Sean by his shirt and pulled him to her. He was still a boy in so many ways, but he wasn't awkward. He was too turned on by her for that. She could see the hint of denial in his eyes, holding on to all he had to resist her, but she would break that soon. She would break him and it would be the most fun she'd had in a while.

Sean looked down at her, knowing that a woman this sexy could never be any good. She wrapped her arms around his neck, smiling up at him as if she held a secret he should be willing to give his life to know; and Sean believed he would.

If Leigh was in a better mood she could appreciate Richard's kind words praising the work she'd done. The work they had all done. He was a good guy, contrary to what she might have thought when they'd met over a week ago. Since then he had managed to come up with over ten thousand dollars in donations from L.A. General. Alicia hadn't been able to come up with anything, but she had already given her entire savings for the down payment on the clinic and Leigh couldn't ask for more.

While Richard walked Alicia to her car, Leigh sat on the floor of the clinic determined to make the numbers work. They had spent the last week cleaning the place up from floor to ceiling, inside and out, with help from people in the neighborhood.

Next were the repairs, which would cost a couple thousand dollars. Richard had come through again. He worked tirelessly, even though he was pulling heavy hours at the hospital and somehow finding time to raise funds. There was still the furniture and the equipment, which would cost tens of thousands.

Using her mother's connections, Leigh already had five grand in checks in hand and was promised another fifteen by the end of next week. With at least thirty more people to see, she really believed this was going to happen and that was enough to get her aching body up every day. Still, she hated lying to her parents, her mother especially, and knew it was just a matter of time before they found out what she was doing. She only hoped she would be far enough into this to give her the backbone to stick with it.

"You ready to go?"

Out of her daze, Leigh looked up at Richard unsure of how long he'd been standing there. She shrugged as he sat down on the floor across from her.

"Or do you want to talk?" he asked.

He had compassion in his eyes. They were tender and soft, contrasting with his rugged exterior. Leigh's heart had been broken too many times by men not living up to the standards she refused to let go of. She didn't think she had the heart or the time to try again so soon. Her life should be about the clinic, not a man. But those eyes.

"I want to talk," she answered.

Haley was leaning on Sean as they quietly made their way to her bedroom. He had to hand it to her. She was the best actress he had ever seen and that was saying a lot living in L.A. Even though it was three in the morning when they got home, Steven and Janet were up waiting for them. Haley acted completely sober and so grateful that Steven offered Sean the guest room for the night. Sean was certain he'd said no, but he heard "yes, thank you."

Everything Sean was made of told him to walk away, but he didn't. He sat her on the edge of her bed and stood there, wishing she would tell him to get out. When she patted the space next to her without looking up, Sean sat down without even thinking twice.

"It's dangerous."

"What?" Haley flipped off her shoes.

"Staying out all night. Having too much to drink."

"You didn't drink anything."

"Then why do I feel like I did?"

"You're just tired."

"Just as dangerous to be tired as drunk. Both are bad for the reflexes."

Haley rolled her head around, giving her neck a good stretch and Sean forced himself to look away. He attempted to stand up, but Haley grabbed him by the arm. She should have been satisfied with her accomplishments tonight, but she wanted more. She always wanted more.

"Why do you hate me so much?" she asked.

He looked at her, wondering if this was another one of her games. "I don't hate you."

He was burdened by his attraction to her and Haley felt a hint of pity for him, but it passed quickly. "You certainly don't like me."

"Well, you haven't exactly treated me with respect. I am a man, Haley."

"Every man has to have his damn respect."

"See," he said. "Look at you now. Mocking me. It's true."

"So does every woman, but you don't have any respect for me."

"That's not true." He didn't think so, at least.

"You think I'm a ho because of Jack."

It was what he thought when he first met her and hadn't seen anything to make him think differently now, but he did. "I just . . . I don't understand why you'd want to embarrass your family like that."

Haley laughed bitterly. "My family."

"Mocking again, but it's a very serious thing."

Haley didn't like the way this conversation was going. "You don't know my family. My parents are Republicans for God's sake." She noticed him swallow and look away and she couldn't hold back her laugh. "You're a Republican?"

"Don't try to change the subject."

"You wouldn't get it. Your family is probably perfect."

"My family has problems, too," Sean said. "Everyone's family does."

"Well, then maybe it's just you," she teased. "You're perfect."

"I'm not perfect," Sean said. "But I care about the people I love."

"I care." Haley hoped she sounded genuine. She didn't give a damn, but this was working.

The tortured tone of her voice as it caught in her throat made him look at her. Her eyes made him lean toward her. The sound she made as her lips parted made him kiss her.

"So this is your style of protection?"

Sean leaped from the bed in one swoop, facing Janet standing in the bedroom doorway.

"Weren't you going to sleep?" Haley asked.

"Shut up." Janet didn't even look at her daughter.

Sean couldn't find words for his humiliation. "Mrs. Chase . . . I . . . I . . ."

"I don't want to hear it," she said.

"It was nothing, Mother," Haley said. "It was just for fun."

Sean looked back at Haley, feeling a little stab by her nonchalant tone.

Janet's small lips curled into a tiny smile as she saw Sean's reaction. He didn't know who he was dealing with. Haley probably had him thinking this was his idea.

Sean headed for the door, making sure to keep his distance from Janet who made no attempt to step aside for him. "I should have been . . . I'm gonna get going."

"The only good idea I've heard you come up with yet," Janet replied. "I've made up your room for you."

Sean looked at her with wide eyes, wondering if she was serious or sarcastically telling him to get the hell out. The woman hated him and she was daring him.

"Thank you," was all he answered. Maybe because he was tired or because he liked living dangerously.

Closing the door behind him, Sean leaned against it, trying hard to remember the last time he had been such an idiot.

"No luck, huh?" Jason positioned himself in the chair with a satisfied look on his face.

"Mind your own business." Sean wondered if the background check he requested on this guy from the department was ready.

"Well, don't worry. I'll take it from here."

Her mother's insistent staring was about to drive Haley crazy. She was tired and wanted to go to bed, but she knew there was a lecture coming. "Just come out with it, Mom."

"I'm just making sure you get in bed safely."

"You're staring me down."

"Don't worry about what I'm doing," she said.

"Can you get over Jack Flay, please?"

Janet sat on the bed helping her pull her covers up. "No. I look at you loving you more than life and crying myself to sleep because I can't believe my own daughter has become the type of woman I fear."

"What?"

"I'm a married woman over forty, Haley. Women like you are all around and would love to drag my husband into their bed and away from me."

"Mom, I'm not—"

"You're not what?" she asked. "He was married and he had a family. I know he's responsible for what he did, but you didn't think twice before jumping into bed with him."

"That's not true." It was true, but damn this was brutal.

"These are not our values, Haley."

Haley pulled her sheets tighter. "I don't want to talk about it."

Janet pulled the sheets back. "I'm not concerned with what you want to talk about."

"I said I'm sorry."

"I raised you to be a person with dignity and pride." Janet stood up. "You're proving yourself to be anything but. You're going to apologize to this family for what you've done."

"Are you serious?"

Janet didn't respond. The look on her face said enough.

"I can't believe this!" Haley screamed. "I feel bad, okay! Isn't that enough? I didn't mean to hurt or embarrass anyone."

"You should have thought of that before you slept with another woman's husband."

"Is that it?" Haley asked. "Or would you like me to scrub the bathroom floor with a toothbrush now?"

Janet made her way to the door. She hated hurting her children, but she loved her daughter too much to toss aside this type of behavior. "There is something else."

"If it will make you get out, anything."

"Spend some time with your sister. I want to know what she's up to."

"Why are you always trying to get me to spy on her for you?"

"Because she never talks to me." She ignored Haley rolling her eyes. "And Haley, don't get any ideas about that detective. I don't like him."

"Whatever."

At first, Sean assumed the tossing and turning he was doing all night was guilt from kissing Haley or getting caught by Janet, but it clearly became something else as the night went on.

Jason.

Sean sat up, looking around the room to let his eyes adjust. Something wasn't right. It was in his gut and he had to heed it. He flipped the covers off and sat on the edge of the bed. It was five in the morning. Remembering the smug look on Jason's face as he said *I'll take it from here*, Sean grabbed his gun out of the holster hanging on the bedpost.

Jason pulled out his gun with one hand and a silencer with the other. Screwing the silencer in, he hovered over Haley's sleeping body. Haley didn't hear his feet on the soft, carpeted floor. She couldn't see his shadow draped over her. She smelled him. Cheap cologne was like poison because cheap cologne meant a cheap man.

She was disoriented as she opened her eyes. It was dark, but there was something looming over her. The second Haley opened her mouth to scream, Jason covered it with his hand, using the other to put the gun to her head. Haley was still unable to figure out what was going on or if it was really happening at all.

"You should have stayed asleep," he whispered. "It would have been better for you."

Just as his finger rounded the click, the bedroom door burst open and Sean rushed in; gun up and rearing to go with the light from the hallway illuminating him.

"Drop it, Jason!"

Haley tried to move away, but an increasingly anxious Jason grabbed her tight.

"Let me go!"

Jason's voice was more a growl than a tone. "Doesn't anybody ever sleep in this damn house?"

Sean's gun was aimed right at Jason's head. All or nothing. "Put the gun down, now!"

Jason pulled Haley closer to him. "I have a job to do."

"Who hired you?" Sean asked. "We can help you."

Voices heard down the hallway were enough of a temporary distraction for Jason to allow Haley to jerk away from him, flinging her body over the other side of her bed just out of Jason's reach. Sean leaped for him and both men tumbled to the ground. Sean realized he was dealing with a man almost twice his size, but he was trained for this. One blow to the gut, a kick to the groin and another blow to the head and Jason was down.

Haley was peeking over the bed. "Kill him, Sean!"

Sean ignored her as he kicked Jason's gun away.

Rushing into the room, Steven saw the scene before him and was consumed with a murderous rage. He was only able to get one kick to Jason's side before Sean grabbed him and pushed him back.

"Just call the police!" Sean yelled.

"Leave me alone with him, Sean."

"I can't do that." Sean stood between Steven and a moaning Jason.

Looking down at the man, Steven contemplated many things. He was a powerful man and this asshole had tried to kill his baby. His demons urged him, but thoughts of his family pulled him back and he reached for the phone.

Sean slammed his foot into Jason's back as he tried to

stand up. Flat on the ground, Jason protested and pleaded but Sean had no mercy.

"Unless you're telling me who made you do this, shut the fuck up."

"She's dead one way or another," he winced.

Sean looked up at Haley who was standing on the other side of the bed taking it all in. She fell down on her hands and knees and threw up.

CHAPTER 5

Carter's otherwise calm Saturday morning was shattered by his mother's phone call about Haley. Here he was, trying to avoid Lisette while obsessing over Avery and how to get back in the game. Avery wasn't supposed to matter anymore, but another call from Michael just as he was about to leave his condo let Carter know that Haley was just the beginning of a very, very bad day.

"You read the early edition Sunday *Times*?" Michael asked. "Front cover of the business section."

"Michael, I don't think this is the time to . . ."

"Just read it and get over here. Dad is gonna kill us both." As usual, Michael hung up without saying goodbye.

Opening his front door, Carter reached down, picked up his copy of the paper and discarded the front section. "Chase Beauty's Dirty Tactics To Take Over Local Businesses."

Carter groaned. "Avery!"

As soon as Carter entered his father's office at the mansion, Steven lit into him and he had no defense. Avery had gathered some of the salon owners and together they laid out a number of complaints regarding the tactics used to get them to sell. Avery had followed through on her threat. Still, Carter was more interested in Haley than getting ripped a new one by his father.

"He's saying that it was his idea," Steven said. "That he didn't like the way Haley treated him and he wanted to kill her."

"That's bull," Michael protested. "We'll get the truth out of him."

Steven recognized the look on Michael's face was the look he had when he saw Jason lying on the floor in Haley's room. "The last thing we need is for him to get away with this because he's been mistreated."

"No one has to know," Michael said.

"That's enough," Steven announced abruptly. "We're in enough trouble. Carter, how in the hell did you let this happen?"

"Dad, I didn't let this happen. I had no idea she was . . ."

"No idea?" Steven couldn't believe these words were coming out of one of his sons. "Please don't tell me that, Carter. I refuse to accept that you're that stupid."

"She's making us look like the mob." Michael understood the irony in his own statements.

Carter could have placed all the blame on Michael. After all, every accusation was probably true and definitely his doing. "I just . . . I just made a mistake. I underestimated Avery."

"What about your new angle?" Steven asked.

"She found out," Carter said.

"Your genius was supposed to keep that from happening," Steven said. "You know the difference between genius and stupidity is that genius has its limits."

"It's not just her," Michael jumped in, hoping to avoid the explosion that could come from his father's insults. "It's that reporter. He took liberty with her words. We need to sue, Dad."

"I'll take care of this," Carter said.

"Like you have so far?" Steven stood up from his desk and approached Carter. The boy didn't flinch as he got to within a few inches of him. "I wanted to keep this under the radar. Now, it's front page and it's a failure."

Carter tried to control his temper. "I said I'll fix it."

"You're not going to get the chance," Steven maintained. "No one touches Avery Jackson or her salons. We have to let it go."

Carter couldn't believe what he was hearing. "We're not giving up. I can—"

"What you're going to do," Steven said sternly, "is deal with the legal fallout from this article. If you think you can handle that without it blowing up in your face."

Carter eyed his father defiantly and for a second, a short moment, Steven saw himself in his son.

"No." Carter wasn't going to let this man hold this over his head forever like he did with everything else. "I'll get Essentials."

Steven let a blip of a smile curve his lips for only a second. "Today, we focus on Haley. Everything else . . ."

He watched as Carter stormed out of the office.

"What about the timeline?" Michael asked.

"I'm not worried," Steven answered. "Not anymore."

As she wiped the tears from her eyes, Avery felt her heart beating so hard she thought it might burst from her chest. She didn't know how long it would take her to recover from the scene she'd just had with Craig. She hadn't been able to reach him since breaking up his private meeting with Carter, but Saturday was payday and she knew he'd be there and she was ready.

He came with apologies and excuses, but Avery wasn't having it. There was no room for forgiveness or second chances if she was going to save Essentials. The way the contract was put together, she had the right to terminate the partnership and buy Craig out without notice and without his approval.

Avery kept calm, not letting him get to her. She had been the nice girl for too long. This was business, but Craig quickly made it personal with erratic switches from hurt to anger, then accusations and threats. He objected to everything and Avery was fine with his objections until she told him she was hiring an outside accountant to look at their books and calculate a fair settlement. She thought the impartiality of it would satisfy him, but it made him angry enough to throw a box across the room.

Avery's entire body was shaking when Craig left, slamming the back door of the office behind him. Everything was made worse when she called Alex for compassion he couldn't seem to muster for her.

"What do you want me to do, Avery? Call the police?"

"I want you to come over here."

"I have the guys over," he said. "It'll take me forever to get into—"

"Alex, are you hearing me? He threatened me and I'm frightened."

"We're talking about Craig, here. He doesn't have the balls to do anything. You cut his heart out. If you ask me, it's Carter you should be—"

Avery slammed the phone down as hard as she could. Her stomach was a mess and she could barely breathe. She had to get out of there.

Standing outside the shop, she felt too exposed. Rushing across the street to her car, Avery had a frightening sense of losing her grip. Her relationship with Alex was plummeting fast. She was under siege from rich ruthless men and she couldn't trust anyone. She was seeking refuge in revenge, knowing it would only diminish her character. Was this the reward for trying to be a good person?

Just as she reached the door to her car, Avery could hear footsteps behind her. She jerked around, expected to see Craig with a gun. Instead it was Carter, who looked even angrier than Craig had.

Carter's rising desire to bring this woman to her knees was immediately tempered at the sight of her. Her eyes were red from crying and she looked drained. He should be happy, but it made him pause.

"What are you, stalking me?"

"There you go again, flattering yourself." He waved the newspaper in his hand. "This was dirty, Avery."

"I took a page from the Chase guide to business."

"Attacking my father to get back at me?"

"How is that different than going through my partner to steal from me?"

"Your partner was a full and willing participant." Well, not exactly, but fuck her for trying to make the comparison.

"It was your idea to play this game, Carter. You shouldn't have started what you couldn't finish."

"You have no idea what you've done, do you?"

"I stood up for myself."

"Do you think this is still about your little shop?" He came closer, urged by the confusion on her face.

Avery felt a surge run through her. It was a mixture of excitement and fear that was completely unfamiliar to her.

"Do you know how many companies try to shove us out of the way every day? What they'll do to put a successful black-owned business out of circulation? They eat up stuff like this. They'll take it to our customers, our partners."

"I did what I had to do to save my business, but I didn't say anything that wasn't true; so if there is any backlash, it's all on Chase Beauty. I'm sorry if—"

"Bullshit," Carter spat. "You're not sorry for anything. You got what you wanted. You're happy, right?"

Avery couldn't remember the last time she was happy about anything. Carter tossed the newspaper at her feet and stormed away. She just stood there wondering how in the world she allowed him to make her feel guilty. Suddenly she was dealing a blow to black businesses everywhere.

In the interrogation room, Sean stared unrelenting at Jason Seitz. Jason's defenses were down and he was ripe for a confession. He'd been left in the room alone for several hours with no water or food. Sean delayed his request for a lawyer as long as legally possible. Full of justified fury Sean tried to get the picture of him holding a gun to Haley's head out of his mind, but he couldn't.

"I want a lawyer!" he screamed at the top of his lungs.

"Takes a while on Saturdays. You ready to deal?"

"You guys can't keep me in this hole forever and it don't take this long to get a damn lawyer."

Sean slammed his fist on the table. "If you want a deal, I can work with you, but when the lawyers come in, all deals are off. You decide."

"And how do I know you'll go through with it?"

"You don't," he offered. "Now talk."

"I want a smoke."

"Fuck that. Talk."

"I'll talk after I have a smoke." He turned away. "That's it."

Sean sneered at him, knowing he was going to get the man a cigarette. "I'll be back, and you better talk or I'm gonna burn that cigarette into your cheek."

As he headed for the desk area, Sean was thinking about Haley and wondered if she was okay. His attempts to get her statement were thwarted by Janet, and Steven was being uncooperative in more than a few ways. A dangerous calm came over that man that Sean had seen before. It usually meant a person had decided to take the law into their own hands and for a man as rich and powerful as Steven Chase, it would be easy to get done.

"Anybody got a smoke?" Sean asked the room of detectives.

Detective Madden held the phone up to him. "It's for you."

"I'm busy." Sean accepted a cigarette from another officer. "I need a match, too."

"He said it's about your guy," Madden added. "The guy you got back there. He say's he'll only talk to you."

Reporters. It was out that someone had tried to kill Haley. The flashing police cars for blocks took care of that, but Sean was pretty sure nothing about the suspect was revealed.

"Detective Jackson. Who is this?"

"Detective Sean Jackson?" The woman's voice scratched like that of a lifelong smoker.

"Yeah." Sean listened to complete silence, quickly losing patience. "Can I help you? Hello? Hello?" Hearing a dial tone, Sean cursed as he slammed the phone down. "Who did she say she was?"

Madden shrugged. "Just said she needed to speak to you about Jason Seitz."

Sean's alarm went up. "She said his name?"

"Yeah. That's his name, isn't it? Jason Seitz."

Sean barreled out of the desk area and down the hallway, pushing aside the officers, detectives and other people who had no business clogging up the area. Charging into the interrogation room, Sean fell to his knees at what he saw. Just a few seconds and the bullet had gone clean through Jason's heart.

Leigh was hot and tired, but she didn't want to stop. After five days, the repairs were done and today they were determined to paint the entire clinic before leaving. She felt a little overwhelmed after trying to be there for Haley, and keeping secrets from her parents was taking its toll on her. The only thing that saved her was the progress of the clinic and the funds that were continuing to come in. The power was on and the air-conditioning would be complete tomorrow.

"Hey, kid."

Richard's friendly smile was contagious. Leigh tried to focus on his face because his shirtless chest revealed a perfect six-pack that was like a magnet for a woman's hand. The more she got to know the man, the more she considered breaking her rule of not getting involved with people she worked with. He was flirting with her shamelessly and Leigh was finding it harder and harder to resist.

"You look tired. Why don't you take a break and get a drink?"

"I'm fine," she lied. "This is helping me, really."

"I'll snatch that brush out of your hand if you don't put it down."

Leigh stared him down, but he was serious and she did as she was told. "I appreciate your concern, but . . ."

"You think this is courtesy?"

The way he looked at her with those light eyes made Leigh feel like he could see right through her. She held on to the belief that men as fine as this weren't any good; especially the doctors and lawyers. A black man with good looks, education and money was a player and a heartbreaker.

"How's your sister?" He leaned in closer as she backed up against the only part of the wall that wasn't painted.

"I honestly can't tell you," she disclosed. "There's no way to read that girl."

"You don't have to be here," he offered. "This is gonna be done in the next hour, and no one would think badly of you, Leigh. You've put in the most work and you're the heart of this place."

"I can't believe that man was in our home, walking down our hallway. We didn't even get to know who he was working for before he was killed."

"Your father is a very important man," he said. "It shouldn't make a difference in getting justice, but it does. The police won't let this linger."

Leigh leaned back, studying him a bit. With a confused grin on her face, she asked. "When is the shoe going to drop?"

"Excuse me?" he asked.

"You're being too nice to me. There has to be some reason for it."

Richard broke into a wide-open smile. "All I can say is that you've made an impression on me."

"You're kind of a flirt." Leigh leaned closer.

"And you're a very smart girl."

"Woman."

"Forgive me; woman."

"Don't forget it."

He looked her up and down. "How could I?"

A good guy wasn't any good if he didn't have a little naughtiness in him. As if gorgeous, smart, kind, giving and courteous wasn't enough. Here goes nothing, Leigh thought.

"Why don't we go for drinks later this week? You know, after things have calmed down at home."

He leaned back with a spark in his eyes. "Sounds like a plan. Now quit your whining and get back to work."

Haley stood at the edge of the sun room, looking out over the verandah that led to the swimming pool. The guest house had been her own personal apartment for a short time, but a wild party and some fire damage had changed all of that. Carly and the other girls would come over and they would sit by the pool, drinking and playing music as loud as they could get away with before Janet made them turn it down. It seemed like just yesterday her life was great and now all she could do was look out a window. The house had become a fortress with security everywhere. It had to stop. She had to let go of this fear. Jason was dead and the small amount of pleasure she had from that was cut short by the fact that he was their only link to whoever really wanted her dead. She felt like she was going mad. This was her life!

Then there was Sean who hadn't called or come by. He only spoke to her father, who in turn told her mother everything. Haley was getting filtered information and it made her mad as hell. She wanted Sean to be her game, her challenge, but she was becoming . . . eager for him and it made her feel weak. She hated Sean for that and for not wanting to see her. It wasn't the game she was playing with him that made her think this way. It was that partic-ular moment in the horror of her room when Sean burst in. The way he had looked at her was a promise that she would not die.

Death was better than fear, wasn't it? Haley felt the rage fill up inside her. She couldn't take it anymore. Be-hind her, she heard the shuffling feet of her bodyguard. He sat in silence, staring at her ass, and she wanted to stab him with a spoon. She wanted her freedom back and she had been planning and scheming all week. The secu-rity shift was at six. With her balcony bolted down, she had scoured the house in search of an alternate route but had been too scared to try it. Not today. Today she was going to do what Sean couldn't. Where and how, she had no idea, but she had to get out of the house and do some-thing.

The security guard, reading a magazine, hadn't noticed Sean standing in the doorway of the kitchen staring at Haley, resolving himself to his attraction for her. When it came to his personal life, practical had Sean's face in the dictionary. To a sin, he never jumped into anything. He thought it out, weighed the pros and cons and ruled out the best path. Haley was the worst possible path in more ways than he could count, but looking at her now he imagined her being better than any fantasy he could create.

"Haley."

Haley swung around, unable to fight the smile on her face at the sight of him. The man had saved her life, but he had also ignored her for almost a week. "Where in the hell have you been?"

"Handling the investigation," he answered, "not that it's any of your business."

"It's my investigation, so I think it is."

"Can you be civil for five minutes? I came to check up on you." As she seemed to glide over to him, Sean remembered how she downplayed their kiss to her mother. The tone of her voice was cold and careless and he remembered it more than he wished he would. This girl didn't give a damn about him.

"What did you expect me to do?" she asked, only inches from him. "Get on my knees and thank you for some of your valuable time?"

"Sarcasm in the face of death. How brave."

"Fuck you."

"Watch your mouth." For a second, the look in her eyes warned Sean that she was about to slap him, but she didn't.

Haley gathered herself together. He was back and that was all that mattered. Game on. "I'm sorry. I can't help it. It's my mother. She's smothering me."

He looked into her eyes, knowing the girl couldn't tell the truth if it meant her life and it probably meant his life to remember that. "It has to be torture here. How big is that screen in your media room? Five feet wide? How do you survive?"

"She's making me fill out grad school applications even though I don't want to go."

"Then don't go."

"Don't be stupid." She rolled her eyes. "I don't have a choice in the matter. To my family, a bachelor's degree is like graduating from junior high."

Sean heard the flap of expensive heels on the kitchen floor and took a deep breath before facing the dragon. In the few times he'd come face-to-face with Janet this past week he could see she resented the fact that she had no excuse to be rude to him anymore. He had saved her daughter's life, and that gave him a free pass forever.

"Is there something you came to tell us, Detective?" she asked.

"He came to see me," Haley said.

Janet ignored Haley. She was being terrible, but she would allow the girl anything at this point. "My husband is still very upset about that . . . incident at the station."

"I'm glad he's dead," Haley said. "Sean doesn't need him."

"I was just on the phone with Mr. Chase," Sean exclaimed. "We've been bringing in everyone Jason knows. I'm on my way to check up on a lead right now."

"Who?" Haley felt her entire body tense and scream out to her that today was the day. "Where?"

"Excuse me, Mrs. Chase." The bodyguard stood up. "It's six. Time for a shift change."

"Fine." Janet kept her attention on Sean. "If you have a lead, what are you doing here?"

Haley watched the bodyguard leave. She would have less than five minutes.

Sean cleared his throat. "I wanted to make sure Haley was . . ."

"Excuse me." Haley was halfway out of the room already. "I forgot Maya wanted to see me about something."

As she skittered away, Sean shook his head. He would never be able to read that girl.

"Haley!" Janet called after her. She didn't want her going anywhere in this house without a guard. "As you can see, Detective, she was elated to see you. Now you can get back to finding the person who is trying to kill her."

So much for that free pass, Sean thought.

Alone in the kitchen, Janet opened the spice cabinet and reached far in the back. She took out the stash of Valium she kept there and took one pill before heading to the refrigerator for some water. One daughter on a drug dealer's hit list and another just as invisible as if she were still in Africa. What was it about her family that just attracted drama?

Hoping it was Steven, she picked up the ringing phone. "Hello?"

"Hello, Janet. It's Giovanna."

"Hello, Giovanna." Janet rolled her eyes, but her tone was as polite as an angel. "What can I help you with?"

"It's about Leigh; that precious daughter of yours."

Strip clubs were a sorry sight in the middle of the day. The few that were open always had five or six losers, most of them alcoholics, staring with their mouths open at the girls who were usually the worst-looking, dancing with zombielike expressions on their faces. Sean flashed his badge to the bouncer who looked at him like he had just killed his mother and cut her into pieces when he passed him. So much illegal activity went on at most of the clubs in Los Angeles, especially the strip clubs. Sean had been on club duty right out of the academy and was able to bring down an ecstasy ring that netted over seventeen million dollars and put thirty criminals in jail.

The back room of El Cubano resembled a corporate lobby more than a strip club, with the exception of the well-strapped enormous man in a wife-beater T-shirt that stretched the word *Humongo* to its limits.

"I hope you have a license for all those." Sean pointed to his various guns.

"Every one of them," he answered in a voice that sounded only half-human.

Sean flashed his badge. "I want Rudio."

"He ain't here."

"Then you'll do." Sean waved him over. "Let's go down to the station."

"Hey, wait." He looked behind him. "He's back there."

Sean entered Rudio Saldana's office without knocking. He knew in this type of environment busting into a room could get a brother shot, but it also wielded an advantage when someone was caught off-guard. It turned out to be a waste of time either way, as television monitors in the office, showing every inch of the club, gave him away the second he stepped inside.

Rudio was a short thin man with tattoos everywhere. Sean knew he thought it made him look tougher, when in actuality it only made him look like a walking STD.

Sean flashed his badge.

"I'm a busy man, Officer Jackson," Rudio said calmly.

"It's detective," Sean answered back not surprised the man already knew his name. "And I don't plan to take up much of your time. I just came by to congratulate you. You've got some balls, getting someone to commit murder in a police station."

Rudio's face turned as hard as stone. "I don't know what you're talking about."

"Yes, you do, but I'll get to that." Sean leaned back.

Since dealing with Haley, he wanted to be taken off babysitting duty and put on the case of the missing drug dealer, but after some investigation he realized they were highly likely one and the same.

Haley stepped into the club behind two burly bikers and hurried over to the corner where the pay phones led to the bathrooms. The place had bad lighting and was mostly dark, which worked in her favor. That, along with the wig, floor-length trenchcoat and oversize hat she'd stolen from Maya's room.

Sean lifted his feet onto the man's desk. "Rudio, because of you, two people are dead. Three, actually, if you count Jorge Nesco, whom you killed on the boat. You've been busy staking claim to his territory."

Rudio shrugged. "I don't know anything about murders. I'm a businessman. As for Nesco, I haven't heard of a body. No body, no crime. He's a grown-ass man. What can I tell you? He told me he was looking for an early retirement."

"And you gave it to him," Sean said. "We both know drug dealers don't retire. They die. You see, the problem with guys like you is that you never know how to temper your reach." Sean knew from Rudio's stare that the man didn't know what he meant and that made him angry. He was making a fool of him in his own territory.

Haley approached the bar wondering where Sean had gone. Escaping through Maya's room, Sean was already at the end of the street when Haley pulled out of the driveway, but she was a better driver than anyone gave her credit for.

"What you want, baby?"

She looked at the bartender. "Gin and tonic."

"Can I see some ID?"

"You got to be kidding me." She didn't have any ID and she didn't have any money. "Just forget the drink."

"It's a two drink minimum." He laid his hands flat on the table. "Buy something or get the hell out!"

Haley didn't know what made her look down, but when she did, the tattoo of a curling black and orange snake on the back of his left hand catapulted a lightning bolt of terror through her.

When Sean heard the scream, he searched the video monitors. He saw the coated figure backing up from the bar, screaming bloody murder, and was out of the office in a flash.

"Haley!"

She heard Sean scream her name, but when she swung around, Haley couldn't see anything but lights flashing. Her heart was beating out of control when she felt a hand grip her arm. It was Sean and she grabbed him back as tight as she could.

"It's them," she choked out.

When they reached his car, Sean looked back at the club and saw Rudio standing in the doorway with his crew surrounding him. The look on Rudio's face told Sean all he needed to know, but he wouldn't try anything right now. Not with Haley to deal with.

"What are you doing here, woman?"

"That was it," Haley said, shaking all over.

"What was it?"

"That man's tattoo was on the side of that boat!"

"Did you recognize him?"

"No, but that creepy snake was on that boat." She could see it clearly now.

"Okay, Haley." Sean rubbed her arm to calm her. "This is good. This helps a lot."

She looked back at the club entrance, but no one was there. They wouldn't dare come after her with Sean at her side . . . would they?

"Call the cops. Have them arrested before they can . . ."

Sean opened his passenger door, helping her in. His beeper was going crazy; no doubt Steven Chase. "It doesn't work like that. We need more evidence. You have no idea what you risked today, do you?"

"I had to do something," she retorted as soon as he got in the car. "I hated feeling helpless and scared. I just . . . I thought I could help."

"You can help by staying alive. I'm taking you back home."

As he backed out of the parking lot, Sean kept a steady eye on the club. He could hear Haley crying and was afraid of what the sound stirred in him. When he reached over and placed his hand on her shaky thigh, he was afraid of a lot more.

Leigh stood at the edge of her parents' bedroom, enjoying the anonymous view of her mother as she quietly brushed her long wavy hair sitting in front of the antique vanity. Her mother was the most beautiful woman she had ever seen. Not in the way Kimberly was just drop dead gorgeous, but pretty with demure gentility that made her simply incredible. Leigh worshipped her mother in many ways; a woman as strong as an ox, but with the beauty of a swan.

Only right now, something seemed wrong about her posture and it bothered Leigh. "You wanted to see me, Mom?"

Janet turned around with a smile that came a little too slow. "Come in, Leigh. Sit down."

"Is this about Haley?"

"I don't want to talk about her." There wasn't enough Valium to get her through this day. "She's fine. I received a call from Giovanna Bridges."

Leigh swallowed hard. Time to pay the piper. It was horrible to think, but compared to Haley escaping, her lies couldn't possibly matter now. "I'm not doing anything you haven't done."

"You call what you're doing fund-raising? Showing graphic pictures of dying children and telling stories that scare people to death."

"Sometimes reality is graphic and scary. I've gotten—"

"I know what you've gotten. I've been making some calls of my own."

Leigh fought the anger. The way her mother invaded everything she had and turned it around to seem as if she was letting her in on her own life drove her out of her mind. "Mom, if you're not going to help I wish you would just stay out of it."

"Just me, then?" Janet asked, feigning confusion. "I just spoke to your father and he told me you dropped your little proposal off at his office."

"It's a business case."

"You're not a little girl anymore, Leigh. You can't turn your father against me to get what you want like you used to."

Always her mother's perception, but never the truth. "I wasn't trying to do that. It's just that Dad has a good head for business and he . . ."

"Do you know what it looks like to have you pandering to our friends?"

"I'm doing what I have to do for my dream. I'm sorry if it embarrasses you. It doesn't have to be that way."

Janet wondered how someone so intelligent could be so dense. "You're doing this the wrong way, Leigh. It's going to blow up in your face."

Leigh stood up, her head held high. "Actually, it's going to be the most successful thing I've ever done with my life. It's going to be something people will remember about our family for generations."

Janet let her leave without a word, the Valium making her too tired to argue at the moment. How could she make the girl understand? She was so proud of her heart; it was wider than the ocean. She had always taught her children the value of giving—the obligation of giving—but none of that held a candle to the nightmares she was having. Nightmares of a needle breaking through a glove and seeing herself crying at her baby's funeral. Nightmares of gang members waiting for her daughter outside at night.

Carter waved the waiter away and seated himself across from Michael and Kimberly in the corner of the new "it" restaurant of the moment. Michael had intended to tease his big brother the second he saw him, but the look on his face told him this wasn't the time. Five days since "the story" broke, they had been putting out fires all over the place. It seemed like the more work they did, the more bad publicity they got. Michael was stuck between Carter and their father, who could do nothing but argue. A volcano was coming, especially now that Carter wouldn't even take Steven's calls anymore.

To the average person, Carter looked as cool and calm as usual, but Michael knew him well enough to see that the pressure was wearing on him. It was wearing on all of them.

"How you holding up? Michael asked.

"Fine, why?"

"I heard Dad leaving one of his messages for you. It wasn't pretty."

"Unlike you, I don't let his every word run my life."

He turned to Kimberly who was applying lipstick to her perfect face. "Hello, beautiful."

Kimberly winked at him. "You've caused a little stir, Carter. I like that about you."

Michael pulled at his tie as he took a sip of scotch. "Dad is psychotic, man. The reporters were literally on the steps of the building. No one could get anything done. The PR people are all ready to quit."

"That's not all we have to worry about," Carter said. "The Mabrys called the firm threatening to sue if we didn't give them their salon back."

Michael searched his memory bank. What had he done to get the Mabrys on board? Yes, that could be a problem. "It's not a problem."

"You don't think so?" Carter asked sarcastically.

"We'll work this out." Michael looked intently at his brother and Carter nodded. It was the two of them, struggling to keep their heads above water; all to please King Chase. As always.

Kimberly leaned in, whispering. "Your touched-in-the-head sister escaped and almost got herself killed."

"Is she all right?" Carter couldn't believe Haley sometimes.

"She's fine." Michael waved it away as a mischievous expression framed his face. "Forget Haley. I called you down here to show you the present I got for you. Check it out."

Following Michael's nod, Carter scanned the room. It didn't take long because she stood out. Avery was sitting in a booth at the other end of the restaurant with Alex. Carter cursed himself for noticing how sexy she looked in that fitted red dress. He watched silently as Avery's tender, unhappy face tried to fake a smile. As her fingers circled her wineglass, her engagement ring sparkled.

"I had to hold Michael back when we saw her come in," Kimberly said.

Carter wasn't listening. He couldn't take his eyes off Avery. She looked as if she was about to cry and Alex was sitting there talking on and on not noticing a thing. Carter knew the man was a fool.

Then finally she sighed, flipping her hair back. That was when she saw him. When her eyes locked on his, he reveled in the look of surprise on her face. Carter didn't frown or smile, just stared at her letting her wonder what he was thinking. He wanted her to know a little bit of the hell he was going through, to know even though she'd won the last two rounds, she should keep her gloves on because he was still fighting.

Michael didn't like this at all. He knew his brother better than anyone and the look on his face wasn't the hatred he expected. There wasn't the hatred that should be there. "What in the hell is wrong with you?"

Carter blinked, ripping his eyes from Avery. "Nothing. I just hate that woman."

"You sure?" Michael asked. "I mean, you should, but I've seen that look on your face before and it looks more like you want to go down on her instead of bring her down."

"Don't be stupid." Carter flipped open his menu, but he was too revved up to even concentrate.

"It's been five days," Michael said. "What are we going to do about her? We can't let her get away with it."

"I'm biding my time," Carter revealed. "Don't worry. Avery Jackson is all I'm thinking about now."

When he looked at her again, he could tell she was trying hard not to look at him and that gave him a certain sense of satisfaction. His eyes lowered to her neck, her skin was glowing and he wanted to touch her. He also wanted to strangle her. *Go down on her or take her down.* When she turned to him again, her eyes seared through him and her full lips parted just a bit. Carter knew he wanted to do both and he would. He could do anything.

* * *

Standing outside the restaurant, Avery felt a chill run through her as she thought of the way Carter had been looking at her all night. She was still afraid of Craig even though she had no clue where he was and was more consumed with waiting; waiting for Carter to get his revenge. Tonight, the way he was looking at her made her feel like she was naked prey and he was the hunter.

"You barely finished your dinner."

Avery felt all the hair on her arms dart up as Carter stepped beside her. She didn't look at him, keeping her eyes focused straight ahead. "I'm not hungry."

"What made you lose your appetite?"

She would never give him the satisfaction. "If you came for another one of your hit and runs, don't waste your time."

Carter took a deep breath. It was a nice early October night. A little dry, but a good breeze. "I don't run away from anything, unlike your cheap boyfriend."

Avery's eyes widened as she turned to him. "I beg your pardon?"

"Valet is only fourteen bucks, Avery. Yet he chooses to park and make you walk to the restaurant. He did make you walk, didn't he?"

This had to be part of his game. He wouldn't even mention the purple elephant in the room between them. Make her wait and become more anxious, if that was possible. "Go away, please."

Carter could feel her anxiety and he enjoyed being the cause of it. "You should be happy. You won."

An impulse made him reach for a strand of her hair that had fallen loose, but she moved her head to avoid him.

"Don't touch me."

That was okay. Carter was patient. Soon enough she

would be begging him not to stop touching her. "Essentials is safe from the grasp of the evil empire."

"It was always safe."

"You know better than that, but I don't hold a grudge. I never really wanted it."

Avery sensed the indignation in his voice. "Then what did you want?"

Carter leaned in close to her, his smooth lips curving slightly. Avery's eyes widened as she leaned back.

"I make you nervous," he said. "I don't know why. You're the victor."

"I'm not happy." Avery wondered how many glasses of wine she'd had to feel so light-headed right now. "I . . . I thought I would be, but . . ."

"But what?" he asked, enjoying her discomfort. She was attracted to him, he knew that much.

Avery turned away, ashamed. "That person who decided to play so dirty wasn't me. I'm not . . ."

"Like me," Carter finished. "That's what you were going to say, right?"

"I just felt cruel and dirty. It makes me sick to my stomach." She stared at him, unable to read any emotion in his face. She couldn't believe what she was doing, but she had to remind herself it wasn't for him. It was for her. "I'm sorry, Carter."

"I don't want your pity, Avery."

Avery wanted to slap him in the face. "It's not pity, you jerk. I was wrong. Not to want to hold on to Essentials, but in the way I went about it. I'm sorry whether you believe me or not."

When he leaned in closer, Avery knew where the light-headedness was coming from and it was joined by a pull in the pit of her stomach. Her lips parted, waiting.

"Leave her alone!"

Carter hadn't heard Alex's car pull up, but didn't care.

His mind was already made up and this man wasn't even worthy of the title of competitor.

"He's not bothering me." Avery stepped toward the car, feeling like her body was a couple hundred degrees.

"What does he want, then?" Alex asked.

"Nothing from you." Carter stared the man down. If he wanted to go, Carter was ready. He was in enough of a mood to beat the hell out of somebody today anyway.

"Then you can leave." Alex's voice caught just a bit.

"I can do whatever I want," Carter responded. *You'll learn that soon enough.*

Avery closed the passenger side door. "Let's just go."

Watching them drive away, Carter realized he had a lot to figure out. He was a man of many talents, but this wasn't going to be easy. How was he going to destroy a woman and steal her from her fiancé at the same time?

CHAPTER 6

Sean kept his distance watching Rudio emerge from his boat at the Carr Yacht Club docks. Rudio didn't have a boat registered anywhere under his name, so Sean had to hope following him 24/7 would lead him to the boat Haley had described.

There was one problem. The boat didn't have the insignia Haley described and that was going to make it hard to get a warrant and have the CSI team scour the place for blood. All he saw was the name *El Cubano*. A little redundant.

He gave the surveillance team the thumbs up and headed for the dock when his cell phone rang. He looked at the ID. Bad timing, but he couldn't say no.

"What's up, Haley?"

"When are you coming over here again?"

She flirted with him nonstop only to go dead cold on him in a second. He knew he was being played, but wasn't putting up much of a fight.

"You remember something?"

"I just wanted to know what was going on."

"Haley, I told you I can't tell you everything."

"It's my case! You can't keep things from me."

"I'm going to hang up now. I'm in the middle of something."

"What," she asked. "What is it?"

"I'll be at your house in a half hour." He hung up on her. That would keep her occupied for a while.

Staying on the dock at the edge of the boat, Sean waited for Rudio to come outside. He searched the boat and was hopeful his eyes were telling him the paint was fresh. That was enough for a warrant.

"Get a good look, Detective?" Rudio leaned over the edge of the boat.

"Nice boat. Looks like you've had a new paint job."

Rudio's hands were tucked firmly in the pockets of his white silk pants, smiling down at Sean wide enough to reveal all the gold teeth in his mouth. As Humongo came up behind him, practically blocking out the sun, Sean found the stereotypes boring.

"I hated to see you leave so soon last week, Detective. Who was that young lady, by the way?"

"You know damn well who that was."

"Maybe if you rub her the right way, she'll buy you one of these."

"It is a nice boat," Sean said. "You and your boyfriend there taking it out for a sail?"

Humongo made a growling noise, but Rudio put his hand up to silence him. "You don't amuse me anymore, cop."

"You two ladies have a good day." Sean turned to leave.

"You too, Junior."

Sean didn't turn around. He wasn't surprised Rudio knew who he was. He probably had a connection in the department. How else could someone have gotten away with killing Jason Seitz? He wasn't stupid, but he wasn't smart. Not smart enough to know that every boat had to register a photo with the dock and Sean was betting his life the picture on file for *El Cubano* hadn't been altered yet.

Avery didn't handle guilt well. She tried to excuse the feelings that made her want to kiss Carter, by claiming temporary insanity. With everything happening with Craig and her love life in a shambles, she didn't know what she was doing.

It was early Monday and Calabra had already banished her to the back of the shop because she *had enough attitude to fill a stadium and needed to get her act together*. She was trying desperately to figure out at what point her life had turned in this direction. She was engaged to a man who had taken to treating her only a step above a booty call. She'd put her trust in a partner willing to betray her the first time someone waved a few bucks in his face.

Then there was Carter and his underhanded attempts to take Essentials. Why didn't she hate that man? She had every right to, every reason to. Maybe she was taking the whole Christian principal of forgiveness too far. Especially considering he hadn't even apologized and she knew he never would.

It was all part of Carter's game, she was sure of it. He had done something to make her think she was attracted to him. He was smooth, but she had a defense against him that he would never understand. Values and morals were Greek to Carter, but Avery had lived her life by them and they were going to keep her strong.

She answered the phone wishing that it was Alex but it was Karen McNamara, the lawyer she hired to deal with Craig's settlement.

"Do you have Craig's check ready?" Avery asked after greetings.

"You know I haven't been able to reach him."

"So we mail it to him."

"That's really not the problem."

Avery had a feeling things were going to get much worse. "What's wrong, Karen?"

"I've gone over your records several times and . . . we need to talk."

"Just tell me now." Avery gripped the edge of her desk.

"Well." Another long pause. "It looks like Craig has been stealing from you."

Avery put the phone on her lap and stared into space. She took a deep breath before putting it back to her ear. "I'll be over in ten minutes."

Janet definitely approved. Sitting poolside over tea with Giovanna Bridges, she knew she made the right choice. She always made the right choice. Giovanna had class and pleasant grace, and even though she was a newcomer to L.A. society, Janet knew almost everything about her. Giovanna's father was a famous black general who married an Italian woman just a few steps removed from what used to be royalty. Giovanna made her way to the States via Harvard University, where she married a prominent Boston doctor and raised one son. Recently named head of Internal Medicine at Los Angeles County Hospital, her husband uprooted the family to L.A. only six months ago.

Janet felt for her. In high society circles, there were hierarchies and that made it difficult to move into a new group, especially one on the other end of the country. She was a smart woman, knowing the first person she needed to get to know was Janet, who hadn't been too quick to receive her. Only now that she remembered there was a thirty-year-old single son who was now in L.A., things would be different.

"Leigh will come around." Giovanna sipped her tea. "She'll see things your way."

"Don't get me wrong," Janet said. "That girl is the jewel of my heart, but I just worry about her so much."

"She is an exceptional young woman. All you need is to find something to direct her interests elsewhere. There has to be a cause or—"

"No cause will take her mind off of this." Janet appreciated the setup. "I was thinking more along the lines of a man."

Giovanna's smile showed the tiny lines on her sixty-year-old face. "They can be a distraction or a disaster if you don't pick the right one."

"None of these young men in our circles are the quality of their fathers. They've lowered themselves to acting like—"

"Any other man," Giovanna finished. "But they aren't any other man. They're our sons and they don't seem to want to hold that responsibility. Not like your sons, Janet."

"Or yours," Janet returned.

Janet assumed Giovanna's turning away to clear her throat was nerves, but found it an unusual reaction anyway.

"Leo is something," Giovanna said. "I was so happy when Goldman Sachs agreed to transfer him to L.A."

Janet had made calls to her contacts in New York, but hadn't been able to get much information on Leo except that he was very private. It was okay. Giovanna and her husband were aboveboard and Leo was only intended to be a distraction.

"Is he dating anyone?" she asked.

He had no appetite. His mind was all over the place. He was full of anxiety. Carter was beginning to feel sick at the sight and smell of the uneaten food on his desk. He couldn't think about anything but Avery and Essentials.

His father coming to his office had really thrown him off balance. Steven never came to anyone, especially his sons, and he hadn't been too impressed with Carter's plan to back away and pounce when Avery was off-guard. Carter didn't take the bait when his father gave him one of his Nazi pep talks. He had his own plan.

Craig was of no use to him anymore, so he refused to take any of the several calls he had made to him in the past few days. There had to be another way and he needed to find it quick. He wanted her; there was no denying that, but she was a hard one. He would need more than his usual skills to get her in bed, considering he was going to take away the thing that mattered most to her.

Spin the press and make her believe Essentials was no longer in play because he was more interested in her than her business. He would get her into his bed and then she would be his. She wouldn't deny him anything—including Essentials—after that.

He would have everything he wanted. Essentials for Chase Beauty, a taste of Avery Jackson for himself and his father off his back.

Carter knew he was crazy to think he could get away with it. He wasn't Michael and Avery wasn't going to be anywhere near that easy anyway. She knew who she was and what she stood for. She didn't care about his money or his name. She would fight him to the death no matter what it cost her. She was the only woman to keep his attention for more than a minute in a long time and that made him think his outlandish idea was worth a try.

"Carter." Patricia, his secretary, came over the intercom. "It's the queen of England."

Patricia had obviously not gotten over the way Lisette had treated her years ago. "Send her in."

Lisette rushed into the room with the urgency she always had about her and sat like a queen on her throne in the chair across from him. "You've got to do something about her."

"I'd be nothing without her," Carter admitted. "And if you can't take it, don't dish it out."

"How genuine." She rolled her eyes. "Carter, I've been calling you."

"I've been busy working on something for my father."

"I've been reading."

"What can I help you with?" He hadn't seen her since she was waiting for him at his apartment a few weeks ago. The sex was great and she was gone before he woke up the next morning, which he was grateful for.

"I need your help," she said.

Here it comes. "Your dictionary says that means money."

"You know me too well, Carter."

"Unfortunately." He leaned back in his soft leather chair.

"You have it and I need it."

"You have it, too. Last I remember your second husband left you plenty."

Lisette pressed her lips together to stifle her anger. "I don't want to talk about that. His damn kids have taken it all back. I've got nothing. Honestly, Carter, I'd rather be dead than poor."

"Wouldn't we all? How much are we talking about?"

She took a deep breath. "Somewhere in the area of one hundred grand would keep me going until I find . . ."

"A new sponsor," he said.

Lisette had a devilish smile. "Like I said, you understand me."

"And when could I expect to see this hundred grand back?"

Her brows rose. "You want it back?"

Carter didn't smile. "I'm really busy, Lisette."

"Carter."

"You have got to be kidding me," he uttered more emphatically.

"I'm not," she said. "I'm desperate, Carter. I would only tell you that and if you repeat it, I'll put a contract out on your life."

"With what?" he asked. "You don't have any money."

Lisette wasn't laughing now and Carter was inclined to believe her. He had given her money before and never expected to see it back, but one hundred grand was a lot.

"Carter, I've burned bridges and I don't have anywhere else to turn. I have some things in motion now. I'll be able to pay you back sometime."

"Things in motion?"

"There are a few gentlemen who I'm building a strategy on."

She couldn't have been divorced more than a year, but money was all that mattered to Lisette and this was the easiest way for women like her. "Would I be mistaken to assume these few gentlemen are on the wrong side of seventy-five?"

"Fuck you, Carter." Lisette was obviously tired of the damsel in distress act.

"I'll have to think about it," he said. "It's a lot of money to just give away."

"It doesn't have to be like that," she said. "I'm sure there's something I could do for you."

When Richard slid a shot of Scotch toward Leigh at the bar, she recoiled a bit. She was already regretting her promise.

"You can't back out now," he said, taking his own shot. "A promise is a promise."

Richard's promise had come the weekend before their first date, dinner in Studio City. The clinic would have all its necessary furniture by the end of the week. Leigh didn't doubt him, but she was feeling a little superstitious. Things were going too well. Since finishing the paint job, Alicia had secured an advertising firm pro bono and secured interviews with the top three urban radio stations to announce the opening. Leigh found a neighborhood company to cater the opening and Richard promised a full waiting room, examination rooms, offices and front desk and she was getting a little nervous.

Whoever loses buys drinks, real drinks straight up. Not that she needed an excuse to see him again. Richard was a brother on top of his game. He had a rugged guy's look about him, loved sports and listened to something other than rap. He was politically aware and could carry a conversation about the cover of *Newsweek* and *Black Enterprise*.

"Let's go." He brought the shot to his lips.

Leigh did the same, her eyes shutting tight as if that would spare her anything. She could smell it and she thought she was going to throw up.

"One . . . two . . . three."

Leigh felt like she was on fire, and from the look on Richard's very amused face, she must have looked the same. Richard ordered two more shots.

"Hey! I only said one."

"You said shots," he argued. "Notice the *s* on the end? I remember distinctly."

"How can you be so sure?"

His smile softened. "I remember everything from that night. Don't you?"

Leigh knew she was in trouble. This guy was hitting all the right notes with her and she wasn't in a place to defend herself against a seduction. The truth was, she was horny as hell. She hadn't been dating before leaving for Africa and barely had time to sleep let alone think about a man while she was there. Looking at Richard, sitting only a foot away with that earnest smile, she wanted to jump on top of him. The careless way he carried himself was so sexy and it made Leigh want to put her inhibitions aside.

"One more." She wrapped her fingers around the shot glass. "This time, I count."

"Go ahead."

"And I toast." Leigh thought for a moment. "To Hope Clinic!"

"To Hope Clinic!"

Leigh hit the shot, gripping the edge of the bar to take the fire that trailed her throat. When she looked at Richard the look in his eyes told her he was ready for whatever she wanted. It was all up to her. Everything was going her way.

Zipping through L.A. traffic, Carter was having another one of those moments. He called them family moments, pondering the state of his family and his position within it. He was thinking of his father and the rift that seemed to eternally exist between them. He wanted to blame Steven, but he knew he was just as much at fault. He loved the man, and in many ways he worshipped him. When other men had drug dealers, prisoners or deadbeats for fathers and some not even knowing who their father was, Carter knew he was lucky.

He had been brought up in a loving home with two married parents who loved each other and led their lives as an example for him. He went to sleep every night knowing his father was down the hallway and would be there when he woke up. He had always felt loved, needed, believed in and safe. He also always felt expected of, pressured and obligated. That was at the root of it. Steven wanted his firstborn to be just like him and Carter wanted to be like no one but himself. That wasn't understandable to a man like Steven, who, like any self-made man, worshipped his creator.

He was thinking of Michael and Kimberly, wondering why Michael had been the one to find real love. Although it was mostly cloaked in a sexual obsession they had for one another, Carter knew that they would do anything for each other. The boys only brought them closer in a marriage that everyone was certain was doomed from the start.

He was thinking of Leigh and how close they had once been, but he had practically ignored her since she returned. Not to mention Haley, whose life was in grave danger and he couldn't even remember to call her. He had to find a way to make it up to the little brat even though he didn't expect her to respond.

Then there was Avery and that image of her in the red dress with those sad eyes. It was sketched on his memory and it made him doubt if he had the balls to go through with this. He had been calling her every day since deciding to take the seduction route, something he would have never, ever done for any woman. She wouldn't take his calls and never returned his messages. If she thought that would do the trick, she had a lot to learn. Carter knew he was a selfish bastard, but come hell or high water he wanted everything, and he was going to get it. He wasn't so different from his father after all.

"Carter here," he said into his cell phone as he answered it.

"It's your best friend, brother!"

Whoever it was, they were drunk as a skunk. "I'm about to hang up."

"It's Craig Moon, Chase."

"The offer is off the table, Craig. That's what happens when you take too long to make up your mind."

"That bitch messed up everything for everyone, but you and I can make a new deal."

Carter turned off the expressway. "You're drunk. Otherwise you'd know you had nothing to offer."

"I'm doing you a favor." Craig's tone was clearly angry. "This is just as much for you as it is for me, brother."

"I'm hanging up now."

"You can get Essentials!" came out quickly.

"I'm listening," Carter said.

"You need the location, right?" he asked. "You can build a shop there."

Carter didn't respond. This didn't sound good.

"I can give you the location," Craig said. "After tonight, it'll be yours."

"Go on."

"After tonight, Avery is gonna regret ever crossing either of us."

Carter pulled alongside the curb. "What in the hell are you talking about?"

"And if you don't pay me what I want," Craig continued, "I'll make it look like you did it."

Carter tried to use the calmest voice he could find. "Okay, Craig. Tell me what you've done"

"Essentials is gonna blow tonight, and after that she won't have anything. Her loopholes are ghosts. She'll have to sell to you at whatever you offer her. I think I deserve something for that."

What an idiot. "Someone could get hurt!"

"The shop closed an hour ago. Now let's talk about . . ."

Carter tossed the phone in the passenger seat as he swerved back into traffic. He could only hope that Craig was a crazy drunk, but he had a distinct feeling that he wasn't; and if that was true, all hell was about to break loose.

As soon as he opened the double doors to the Chase mansion, a smiled crowned Sean's face at the sight of Haley coming toward him. When she reached him, he barely had time to duck before her closed fist came swinging at his head. Haley went falling forward and he caught her in his arms.

"What's the matter with you?"

She pushed him away so mad that her stomach hurt. "You're a liar."

"What did I do now?"

"You know what you did!"

Haley had been willing to give Sean the benefit of the doubt after he stood her up on Monday. No one stood her up, but when he told her what he'd been doing she forgave him. Only, he'd done it again today. He was supposed to be here in the morning, but it was almost nine. She was more frustrated that all of her hard work seemed to have no effect on him. He should be willing to do anything to see her, but he obviously wasn't.

"No, I don't, but I'm not inclined to care if you're gonna act like this. I came over here to give you good news."

Hands on her hips, Haley tilted her head. He was frustrating the hell out of her and she had to put a stop to it. It was her game, not his.

"I'm sorry I'm late, but we got a break in the case and I had to stick around." He knew his attraction to this damn high-maintenance woman was gonna be the death of him.

"That's no excuse." Haley turned to walk away. "I don't want to talk to you now."

When he reached for her, she pulled away but he reached again and pulled her to him. She moved her head to the side when he lowered his mouth to kiss her; she wasn't giving in that easy. He jerked her arm to let her know the games were over, but she only smiled, knowing that they were just beginning.

His lips came down hard on hers, partly in lust, partly in a bit of discipline. He wanted to teach her that she couldn't toy with him, but as she kissed him back, his body's reaction told him that this girl could pretty much do whatever she wanted with him.

Haley pushed him away, looking fiercely into his eyes. He thought he could tame her? She would give it to him; that kiss lit a fire, but he had another thing coming if he thought he was going to control this. He'd see who's about to learn a lesson.

"This is not what I came here for," he said.

"I don't give a damn what you came here for." Haley grabbed him, leading him toward the stairs.

"Wait a second." He pulled back. "Where are your parents?"

"Who cares?" she asked. "There's a lock on my bedroom door."

"Look, Haley." He broke free of her. "This is not the time to be messing around."

Haley stood, stunned. He couldn't possibly be rejecting her.

"Put a smile on your face," he said.

"That's what I was trying to do," she answered.

Sean smiled, thinking how nice it would be to take her right there on the stairs. No, there was work to be done. "Rudio didn't clean up as well as he thought he did. We found some blood on his boat and forensics matched it to Jorge Nesco. We have his DNA on file from a sex crimes case two years ago."

"That's good, right?"

He shrugged. "It could be if some other things come together. What's really good is that the picture of the boat on file with the yacht club matches your description."

Haley smiled in relief. "I'm gonna be free again. Is he in jail now?"

"Not yet, but it's moving forward. We're picking him up tonight at his club, in front of all his boys for effect. We're gonna try to keep him all night to see what we can get out of him. We need you to come by in the morning and pick him out of a lineup."

Haley felt her stomach tighten. She would actually be near him. "Do I have to?"

"We need you to try."

"I barely remember." Haley sat down on the bottom step, feeling queasy. "I don't think I can—"

"You can." Sean sat down next to her, putting his arm around her. "You remembered the snake after you saw it."

She leaned her head on his shoulder. Fear made her feel weak and she hated it. "What if I don't?"

"Then we'll find another way to bring him down." He cupped her chin, lifting her face to his. "Whatever happens, I promise you we will get him."

Haley took a deep breath. "I want my mother there."

Walking out of the bar, Richard wrapped his arm around Leigh's waist and she leaned into him. She was sending him every message possible and he'd better be getting it, because this was as bold as she had the nerve to get.

"So what's the plan?" he asked as soon as they were outside.

"I don't . . ." Leigh let him pull her aside as a group of women entered the bar. "I don't think driving would be appropriate."

"We can leave the cars here. I've done it before. I only live a few blocks away, but you . . ."

"I can take a cab," she said.

Richard smiled with a shrug, a casual invitation for her. It seemed like slow motion to Leigh as he leaned in and kissed her. Backing into the wall, she wrapped her arms around him and gave in to the feeling. Man, how she missed this. He was so deliberate as his hands caressed her hips and he pressed his body against hers. Leigh felt something surge inside of her. It had been so long and every second longer he kissed her, the more she knew Richard wouldn't only scratch her itch. He would scratch it good.

"Come home with me, Leigh," he whispered into her ear through heavy breathing.

Leigh tugged at his shirt as he kissed her neck. His lips were like fire on her skin. *You're a good girl*, she told herself, but Richard's lips told her she was a stupid girl if she didn't do this. "You're trying to seduce me."

"I was waiting for you to seduce me, but you were taking too long. So I decided to lay it on you."

"Lay it on me?" she asked, unable to control her laughter.

Richard's lips pressed together to keep from laughing. "That's what I call it. When I seduce a woman, I lay it on her."

"Very mature," she mocked. "That needs some work."

"Maybe that's why I can't get anyone into my apartment."

Leigh didn't believe for a second he had a problem getting women into his apartment or into his bed. "Aren't you glad I pointed it out to you?"

"Eternally grateful." He kissed her again, this time longer, harder. "I'll work on it, and maybe next time . . ."

"Next time?" she asked.

"Next time," he answered, "it might work."

Leigh pulled him to her, kissing him to clear up any confusion. "I said it needed some work. I didn't say it didn't work."

"Police? Yes, I need to report an emergency."

Carter rushed to the front door of the salon. It was closed with bars over the windows and pitch black inside.

He was thinking more of himself right now. If Craig meant even half of what he said, this was going to make things a mess for him.

"I think there might be a bomb at the Essentials Hair Salon on Eastern Avenue in View Park."

Stretching his neck, Carter looked as far back as he could. Just as he was about to assume no one was there, a slit of yellowish white light hit his eyes. It was coming from underneath the door to the back office.

"Just hurry! 7722 Eastern Avenue."

He hung up, rushing down the block toward the alley. The thought of Avery having to pay for his devious acts and that nut Craig made him forget the danger. She hadn't deserved any of this, but especially not this. In the alley, he leaped over a gate to reach the back of the store and when he did, all he could hear was music blaring.

Avery gulped the wine straight from the bottle and slammed it back on the desk. Wiping the tears from her eyes, she looked at the papers Karen had given her. It was right there in front of her face. Craig had been stealing from both of her stores and she'd let him do it with her eyes wide open. She might as well have given him permission!

She cranked the radio up a notch, thinking the wine and noise could make her drown out the insanity she was feeling. What a fool she had been about everything; Craig, Carter and even Alex who wasn't returning any of her messages from his hotel in Philadelphia.

She had let these men break her down. She pictured her father's arms around her mother as they watched television in peace and quiet and didn't have the strength to share this with them right now. They were so proud of her and she was too embarrassed to let them know they had placed their pride in an idiot.

She wanted to strangle Craig. She thought of calling the police, but couldn't even deal with it yet. The thought of having to act rational for whatever time it would take to explain wasn't something she could manage yet. What was worse was that she really meant it. If she saw him right now, Avery was sure there wasn't anything that could keep her from trying to kill him. She, the daughter of the chief of police, wishing she could kill someone. Look at what she had let him turn her into.

Her greater sense told her that this wasn't the end of the world, but she didn't think she had the strength to fight another day. Maybe she should just give up on it all. Essentials and Alex.

Carter banged harder on the door. "Avery, open up!"

"No!" Avery screamed out loud to all the demons she felt around her, letting them know she refused to give in to the thoughts they were putting in her head. She was strong and she would fight this. She hadn't been brought up to be a crying, helpless victim. She had worked too hard to let men like Craig Moon take her down.

As the CD wound down its last song, Avery heard the faint sound of banging on the door and it scared her to death. Craig!

"Avery, open the door!"

She reached for the phone, dialing 911. "I'm calling the police!"

"It's Carter, Avery! Open up."

She faintly heard the 911 operator pick up.

"Carter?" Phone still in hand, Avery slowly walked toward the door.

"Open the door! You're not supposed to be here!"

She opened the door and was shocked by the panic stricken look on Carter's face. "Carter, what are you—"

Before she could say another word, Carter grabbed her, pulling her toward him. She heard an explosion so loud, her teeth shattered and she felt a rush of heat behind her as the two of them were lifted from the ground and tossed into the air. Avery heard herself screaming, but couldn't feel herself doing it. Then, everything went black.

CHAPTER 7

Avery's mother had gone to the cafeteria to get something to eat, but Carter knew there was still a nurse in her hospital room so he waited, having already ditched his own parents claiming he had to use the bathroom. He couldn't get rid of them even though the doctor told them he was just fine.

He looked down at the bandages on his left hand. A few cuts from flying debris wasn't too bad. The painkillers they gave him the night before would hold him well for a while. He had been lucky, but he didn't really care about himself. He wanted to see Avery and make sure she was all right. The doctor's reassurances weren't enough.

Finally the nurse left the room and Carter cautiously looked around. He made sure his arm was prominent. With new clothes his mother had brought him, the arm was the only thing that told anybody he might have a right to be there.

Avery was halfway sitting up in the bed, drinking juice from a straw. With the exception of a couple of scrapes and bruises, she looked perfect. Relief wasn't what Carter was feeling and he wasn't interested in figuring out what it was. Right now he just wanted to watch her peacefully and just be happy she was okay.

When she saw Carter standing at her door, Avery didn't know what to feel. The events of last night were still a little fuzzy to her, but she knew that he had probably saved her life. She wanted to know so much more even though every thought made her head pound.

"Hey." Carter approached, standing at the side of her bed. She was looking at him like she didn't even know who he was. "How you feeling?"

"Still a little dizzy." She tried sitting up a bit more.

He placed his hand gently on her shoulder. "No, don't bother."

"You saved my life."

Carter looked into her tired and confused eyes feeling the need to comfort her even though he had no right to. He reached over, placing his hand on hers at the edge of the bed.

Avery couldn't tell, but she was feeling something sweep over her from his touch. His eyes were so tender, so caring, so unlike anything she had seen from him before. There was no way to know if it was genuine coming from someone like him, but right now she needed to believe it was, so she did.

"What happened?"

"I got a call from Craig. He was drunk."

"You're still dealing with him?"

"No, Avery, I . . ."

"I need to know where he is. I have to talk to him."

"He's been stealing from you, and . . ."

"You knew . . ." Her attempt to sit up rushed to her head and the pain was overwhelming. She bellowed, leaning over and Carter reached for her, but she slapped his hands away. "You knew and you didn't tell me?"

"I didn't tell you because I—"

"Because you were using it against me to take my shops." Avery felt tears well in her throat at the thought of

Essentials. She didn't even want to know what it looked like.

Carter didn't have a response for her because what she suspected was true. "I had no idea he was crazy."

"What are you talking about?"

"He called to tell me he was blowing up the shop."

"Where is he?"

"I don't know." Carter could see the disbelief on her face. "Really, I don't."

Avery looked away from him, not wanting that humble expression on his face to cloud her thoughts. She was having a hard enough time thinking as it was.

Carter had always known the right thing to say in whatever the occasion was, but he was at a loss right now.

"What in the hell are you doing here?" Alex stood in the doorway in a department store business suit, staring at Carter with hate in his eyes.

"What you should be," Carter said. "Where have you been?"

"Are you questioning me?" Alex's hands formed into fists.

"Thanks, Alex, I'm doing fine." Avery was disgusted. The first time seeing her since she was almost killed and all he could do was start a pissing match with Carter.

Alex looked at her with a guilty smile. "I'm sorry, honey. I didn't mean to— The nurse told me you were okay. I've been trying to reach you."

"My mother has been calling you since last night."

"I did the best I could." His tone was defensive. "There aren't many night flights from Philly to L.A."

"There had to be one that could get you here before now," Carter said.

Avery knew now wasn't the time to say, but her mother had told her earlier there were two flights before the one Alex took.

"You aren't even supposed to be here," Alex sneered. "You're a suspect in all of this." Alex beamed at the sight of Avery's eyes widening. "Didn't you know that, honey?"

"What—" Suddenly she remembered Carter's words from last night. *You're not supposed to be here.*

"I've already spoken to the police," Carter said, "and I told them it was Craig."

Alex casually took a seat on the other side of Avery's bed. "Craig doesn't have the balls to do something like this and that's what I'm gonna tell the police the first chance I get to speak with them."

Carter eyed Alex intently. "You wouldn't know the first thing about having the balls to do anything. If you did, you would've been here a long time ago."

Avery watched as the two men stared each other down. Alex swallowed hard and it hurt her heart to see him re-sign himself to being the weaker man. It hurt her even more that she had resigned herself to it before he had.

"Since you're such a man," Alex challenged, reaching for the phone, "then you'll have no problem sticking around while I call the police."

"Stop it," Avery said. "Carter was leaving anyway."

Carter looked at Avery, seeing the doubt in her face. He didn't want to leave, but he knew what staying would lead to. "I'll talk to you later, Avery."

"Why in God's name would you let him in here?" Alex asked after he was gone.

"I didn't," Avery said. "I don't want to talk about Carter. Alex, my mother said—"

"Have you talked to the police yet?"

Avery just stared at him as he looked down at her. She wanted him to touch her, to hug her or act like he gave a damn about her. She wanted him to reach out to her the way Carter had. "Briefly, but I was tired and the doctor sent them away."

"The place is gone, Avery." He began pacing the room. "I drove by on the way here. It's completely destroyed. He couldn't stand that you won, so he blew your place up."

"Carter is an asshole, but he wouldn't try to kill me."

"I don't think he knew you were there," Alex said. "Maybe he did."

"It could have been an accident," she said hopefully. She had almost kissed the man just a week ago.

"Don't be stupid, Avery."

"I'm not stupid!" Yelling made her entire body hurt.

Alex stopped pacing. "I . . . I didn't mean that. I'm sorry. I'm just upset and I thought you'd be."

"I have been," she answered. "Since last night, but you weren't here to see that."

"I did the best I could, Avery. Besides, I'm here now."

"I don't want to talk about Carter anymore. Besides, he says it's Craig, and—"

"That article did it," he said. "It pushed him over the edge. You touched someone who thought he was untouchable. He couldn't have Essentials, so no one could."

"I don't know."

"You can't say you don't think it's possible, can you?"

Avery reluctantly shook her head, remembering *you're not supposed to be here*. "It's possible."

"So why did you let him stand next to your hospital bed?"

"That wasn't my choice," Avery specified. "But I won't let it happen again."

In the very early hours of the morning, Leigh was sleeping soundly in Richard's arms when she was rudely awakened by her cell phone ringing nonstop. Seeing her home number she knew it was her mother wondering why she wasn't home. She would love to ignore it, but she knew Janet wouldn't leave her alone. When she found out what her mother was really calling for, she stumbled over herself trying to get dressed.

Richard rushed her to the hospital before heading off to L.A. General to pick up some donated equipment for the clinic.

Leigh waited in the cafeteria with her parents, her concern for her mother growing. Janet seemed ready to fall apart after taking a Valium even when Steven had asked her not to. She hadn't even asked Leigh where she had been and Leigh knew that meant she was heavily sedated. After seeing Carter was okay, Leigh wanted desperately to stay with her mother, but a call from Richard less than a hour after he left brought on a desperation of another kind. She had to go.

Leigh felt her heart drop into her stomach when she pulled up to the clinic. Three police cars were parked out front. She just kept hearing Richard's apology over and over on the phone, urging her to get over there, and when she ran up the walkway toward him, the anguish on his face made her knees go weak.

She reached for him. "Just please tell me no one was hurt."

"No matter what," he urged, "believe me when I tell you everything is gonna be okay."

Inside, Leigh was stopped in her tracks. A tornado had come through Hope Clinic. Windows were smashed, graffiti was everywhere, most of the furniture was either destroyed or missing, and the floor looked tarnished by fire or chemicals. Leigh was speechless as her hands went to her imploding chest.

Richard grabbed her tightly in his arms to keep her from falling. He spoke to her in whispers. "It's all cosmetic, Leigh. We have insurance, remember that?"

Leigh nodded, trying to remember what the insurance man had told them about the rates rising if they had substantial claims because of the neighborhood. "What does it look like in back?"

"It's the same."

Leigh was feeling dizzy. First Haley, then Carter and now this. "Who did this?"

"We don't know yet," he said. "They think it was a bunch of crack addicts or gang members. They broke in the back door. No one saw anything, but we've gotten to know these people pretty well. Someone will come around. You know how it is here. They don't trust the police."

"What difference does it make? They can't fix this."

"We'll fix it." Richard's brows centered in frustration. "I'm so damn sorry this happened to you—today of all days."

"I want to see what's back there." She headed for the back before an officer held his hand up to her.

"This is a crime scene, ma'am. We're gonna have to ask you all to leave here."

"My clinic," Leigh said, "is now a crime scene."

"Come on." Richard was leading Leigh out of the clinic. "I'll take care of this. I know you want to be at the hospital."

"What about Alicia?"

"I haven't been able to reach her yet, but I'll call her and she'll help me."

"We'll all do it," Leigh said.

"Not necessary. We need better locks, and bars around the windows. We'll just call the construction people back. They'll work fast like they did last time."

"They can't even go in there, Richard! It's a crime scene."

"I'll call the insurance man today and take care of this."

"They're gonna raise our rates," she complained. "They were already too high because of the area. We can't afford this."

Richard touched her cheek gently, wiping a tear away. "I won't deny that it's a setback, but that's all it is."

Leigh laughed bitterly. "Just a setback?"

"What else can I say? At least no one was here."

"You're right." Leigh knew he was doing everything he could to hide that he was just as angry and worried as she. He was trying to be strong for her and that made her want to love him.

"Go be with your parents," he said.

"My parents." She felt a wave of nausea sweep over her. "They're gonna love this."

"Please, Mom!" Carter waved Janet's fussing hands away as she tried to prop the pillows on his living room sofa around him.

Janet wished he was coming back to the mansion, but he refused. Now back at his place, he wouldn't even go to bed. "I know what I'm doing."

"There's nothing wrong with my head." He held up his hand to stop her from touching him.

"You're lucky as hell, you know that?" Steven stood at the edge of the room, watching them. He hated feeling scared and he had been scared to death when the police came to the house last night.

"Steven." Janet refused to let her husband turn this into an argument.

"You shouldn't have gone there," Steven said. "You should have just called the police."

Carter was amazed at how this man found a way to make everything he did wrong. "Thanks for the advice, Dad. I'll keep that in mind next time I try to—"

"Don't get smart with me!"

"Steven." Janet turned, her tone warning. "Carter is a hero. He saved that young woman's life."

Steven grumbled, crossing his arms over his chest.

"The press is going to be all over us for this. They'll blame it on us no matter what happens with that Craig person."

"Have I embarrassed you, Dad?" Carter's words were laced with sarcasm.

Steven ignored his wife's searing eyes. "The police are suspicious of you. You're smart enough to pick up on that, aren't you?"

Janet sat next to her son, her heart saying a prayer at the sight of his bandaged hand. It could have been so much worse. "We've talked to Chief Jackson. I'm sure it's going to be okay."

"I told them who did this," Carter snapped.

"Carter." Janet placed her hand on his chest, leaning toward him. "You are a hero, you know this, right?"

He smiled at his mother, always eager to make up for the disapproving father. "I think I was just really lucky."

"We'll have to invite her for dinner," she said. "She was worth you risking your life for, so I would like to meet her."

"Have you both gone crazy?" Steven asked, believing his ears were playing tricks on him. "This woman hasn't just put our chain stores in jeopardy. She can take down Chase Beauty now. Not to mention Carter's freedom."

"This isn't her fault," Carter claimed. "Her crazy partner did this."

"She does business with psychos," Steven said. "That is her fault. Dammit, Carter. You said you had this taken care of!"

"Enough," Janet announced. "Whatever has happened before, everything has changed. Steven, you will do whatever you have to in order to fix the salon venture and protect the company. Carter will do whatever it takes to make sure this woman doesn't suspect we're behind any of this."

"The police will figure out the truth," Carter said.

"I'm going to talk to Chief Jackson again," Steven offered.

"Don't push him," Carter said. "It'll look like—"

"Did I ask you for advice?" Steven asked. "You've done enough already."

"I'm sorry, Dad. I wish I could have died for you. That would have been better, wouldn't it?"

Steven glared down at his son, feeling guilty. He knew he was at fault in all of this. They held a stare, only broken by Janet's cell phone ringing.

"That's probably Haley," he muttered. "We have to go now. She's being taken to the station for a lineup."

"Don't let me stop you." Carter grabbed an issue of *Black Enterprise*, trying to calm himself down. He could feel his father's eyes on him.

"Carter," Steven said. "Look, I'm sorry. I—"

"It doesn't matter." Carter didn't look up. "Just go."

"What?" Janet, still on the phone, stood up in a panic as she looked at Steven. "Was she hurt? No, okay. Thanks, we'll be right over."

She hung up and took a deep breath wondering if her heart could take any more of this. "That was Maya. She said Leigh came home in tears. The clinic was robbed and vandalized overnight. She's devastated."

Steven looked at his watch as he let out a litany of curse words. "You go to the station with Haley and I'll go home to Leigh."

Janet leaned forward, kissing Carter's forehead. "I'll be back tonight with some dinner." She turned to Steven as she stood up. "I have to go to the bathroom first."

Steven watched her leave, knowing what she was going to do. He wondered how many she had already taken since last night. Right now, he had to deal with Leigh and somehow get back to the office without another one of his children bringing the sky down on them.

Carter waited for them to leave before dialing the hospital and asking for Avery's room. She picked up with voices in the background.

"Avery, It's Carter."

"Carter?"

Avery's stomach tightened at the sound of his voice. She looked at her family, circled around her, and Alex leaning against the wall. Silence spread across the room at the sound of his name. She looked at her mother, Nikki, who shook her head in the way she had when Avery was a five-year-old about to do something dangerous to herself.

"Avery, I wanted to finish what I was going to tell you last night."

Avery swallowed, finding this harder than she'd expected. "Carter, I don't want to talk to you. Don't call me again."

"Avery, wait—" He heard the click and then the dial tone. He thought of everything Alex might be telling her, fueled more out of jealousy than fact. He wasn't going to let this happen. He had to make Avery understand for more reasons than he was ready to admit to right now.

Haley sat in the interrogation room trying to fight back tears. She was exhausted from all the emotions she was feeling. It had all begun when another officer, instead of Sean, showed up to take her to the station in the morning. She didn't give a damn what had happened to Sean's sister. He had promised to be there for her and he wasn't.

Things only got worse when her mother showed up at the station, her eyes glazed over. Her father's decision to be with Leigh instead of her made Haley bitter and angry. She knew he loved Leigh more than her, but how could he choose her at this time of all times? A stupid break-in.

Who gave a damn about the break-in of an empty clinic in the ghetto? She was gonna make him pay for this. She had made a career out of knowing her father's hot buttons and she was going to push away.

Her mother's reaction to her anger was cold and scolding, accusing her of thinking only of herself, and she was right. Haley didn't care about anyone but herself because nobody else seemed to.

Then there was the lineup, but Haley shivered at the thought of it and refused to dredge it back up. Although the officers assured her he would be nowhere near her, she knew Rudio was going to kill her like he had Jason. She didn't trust anyone.

When Sean entered the room, she expected to deck him and was certain this time she wouldn't miss, but she didn't even try. She ran to him, hugging him tightly as he wrapped his arms around her.

"It was horrible."

"I'm sorry, Haley." Her sobs were reaching deep inside of him. "I wish I could have been here."

Haley leaned back, looking at him. "I ruined everything, didn't I?"

He shook his head trying to hide his concern. "It was a long shot from the beginning."

"Why did they have everyone in there look like him?"

He grinned. "That's the point. To increase the certainty."

"Or increase the confusion."

"It has to be undeniable in court."

"I tried, Sean. I did. I just wasn't sure and his lawyer was so mean. She kept nagging at the officer who was trying to help me."

Sean tried to get past the confusion of this moment. Here he was holding Haley in his arms, rushing as fast as he could to be there for her. At the same time, he was supposed to believe her brother tried to kill Avery. It was all a little incestuous for his taste, but he couldn't stay away.

They both turned to Janet when she entered the room. Sean saw the undeniable look of distaste on Janet's face at the sight of them together and it was undeniable to him that it didn't matter anymore.

"I would like to take my daughter home now," Janet said. "I've cleared it with the other officer."

"Sean, will you come with me?" Haley asked.

"No, he can't," Janet asserted. "He's got work to do."

Sean reluctantly let Haley go. "She's right. We've got to figure out what to do about Rudio now that we've got to let him go."

"No, you can't," she pleaded. "He's going to kill me. I know it."

"He will not," Janet said. "Detective, don't you have the blood evidence?"

"The ID of the boat only proves you saw that boat. He's got an alibi for now that we weren't able to crack. Jorge Nesco was on that boat all the time. There's no way to prove he was murdered, especially without a body."

"Then you find a body," Janet said. "Haley, let's go."

"I can't go out there." Haley could hardly breathe. "He's out there and he's going to kill me."

Sean gripped Haley's shoulders, looking straight into her eyes with an urgency felt around the room. "Haley, believe me when I tell you this. I will not let him hurt you, ever."

Haley smiled, leaning into him. She had to believe him, and she did.

Steven handed the cup of hot tea to Leigh at the kitchen table and sat next to her, grateful she was calming down. It hurt him to the core to see tears falling from the eyes of the daughter who would always be a baby girl in pink dresses and unruly curls no matter what age she was. He was her daddy and it was his job to make sure she never cried.

"I'm sorry you're hurting, but now you understand that we were right."

"Is that all you're concerned about?" she asked.

"All I've ever been concerned about was your safety. That place is dangerous. No one was there last night, but how can you guarantee that the next time? You're talking about servicing children whose parents are likely drug addicts. Those people are trying to survive not be educated."

Richard stood at the edge of the kitchen, and Steven, not trusting much of anyone these days, gave him a cautious look. "Who in the hell are you?"

"I can come back," he said awkwardly.

Leigh placed a hand tenderly over her father's. "Daddy, this is Richard Powell. He's one of the doctors I was telling you about. He's been dealing with the insurance people."

"Did they drop you?" Steven asked.

"Not exactly." Richard sat in the chair Leigh directed him to. "But it isn't good."

"Just give it to me straight," Leigh said.

"The good news is they will replace the furniture and pay for the repairs. That means a delay, because it will only happen after the police investigation confirms that none of us are to blame."

"Who are these people?" Steven asked. "I'll call them and take care of this."

"Wait, Daddy." Leigh found it somewhat ironic that he wanted to get involved now. "How long do you think this will take?"

Richard shrugged. "Not sure, but there's more."

Richard explained that because the policy was only

two weeks old, a full investigation by the company would accompany the police investigation. Even if the cause was cleared, they would only be reimbursed for the damages. The worst was that they were raising the rates on the clinic, effective next month, with a new down payment due in thirty days. If they wanted to stay insured, they would have to give proof that a professional security company had been hired to install a system and have it in place before the new equipment would arrive. The cost was going to be astronomical.

Leigh was letting it all sink in, ignoring whatever it was her father was advising her of and promising to get done before storming off.

"You want me to be honest?" Richard asked. "You want me to tell you whether or not we have the money for this? The answer is no."

"I can try to do more fund-raising and Alicia is still working on those grants. She's certain one of them will come through within the next six months."

"We won't last three more months unless we get more money."

Leigh's face fell into her hands. Her parents had warned her of this, but she was positive doing the right thing would have its own rewards.

Richard leaned in, putting his arms around her. "You're overwhelmed, baby, but you're stronger than this."

"We made a commitment to that community," she said.

"What we need now is the money to pay for the repairs, repainting and replacing the furniture. We have almost half of that. We need to raise enough to get the other half and we might be able to hold on until the insurance company reimburses us and the grants come in."

Leigh wasn't going to put off the reality of the situation. Richard's suggestion was a best case scenario and they both knew better. There was nothing else left.

"I'm going to fix this, Richard."

"There is no I, Leigh. We're in this together."

She reached up, gently touching his cheek. "I know what I can do for my part."

Richard frowned, seeming uncertain. "Talk to me, Leigh."

"I'll call you when it's done. Just let me do this, Richard. It'll make everything better for all of us. I promise." Leigh mustered her resolve. "Let me show you out."

Avery let out a groan as she labored to sit on the sofa. Even four days after the explosion, her body was still sore. Still, she was happy to be home after spending her recovery at her parents' house, being smothered by her mother. Nikki Jackson, *the peacemaker*, was a twenty-first-century hippie artist with brownish blonde corn-rows that traveled her back and endless holistic healings for every ailment. After three days of having her aura cleansed, Avery just wanted it all to end. Unfortunately, her mother had set camp at her own apartment and Avery couldn't get a second to relax.

"You want some juice?" Nikki stood over Avery trying to hide her concern. All things considered, her daughter had been taking this all too lightly.

"You gonna stay for dinner?" Avery asked.

"I'm staying until you get better," Nikki said. "I have Jorga watching the gallery for me. Don't worry."

A local artist whose paintings were famous in Los Angeles and Orange County, Nikki's successful art gallery was five years old. Avery found it an inspiration for a woman who married her high school sweetheart one month after graduating, was a stay-at-home mom raising three kids, to choose at the age of forty to start such a large venture. Even with an active gallery to run, Nikki had taken it upon herself to help all the girls who had worked at Essentials move to Essentials II or work at the art gallery.

"You got a call while you were sleeping," Nikki said. She could see from Avery's expression she thought it was Carter, who had been calling nonstop. "It was Taylor. She wanted to talk to you."

"I should call her."

Nikki shook her head. "She's in classes until three today. Then she has some Spellman-Morehouse meet-and-greet thing. Beginning semester stuff."

"I'll call her tomorrow. What about Alex?"

Nikki rolled her eyes. "You should know that I've asked him not to come over."

"Why did you do that?"

"You know how I feel about him."

"He's my fiancé, Mom."

"If he was any good you two would be married by now." Nikki could never put her finger on it, but Alex had always rubbed her the wrong way.

"That's not all his fault."

"You need to make some serious decisions about him," Nikki said. "Not today, but soon. After three years with someone, you either get married or you break up."

"Not now, Mom."

"He called, too," Nikki said after a short pause.

"Carter? Did you pick up?"

"You told me not to so I didn't, and no, he didn't leave a message. He's determined to get to you. That tells me he's guilty."

Avery shrugged, looking down at her hands on her lap because she didn't want her mother to read what she was really thinking. Just then, the phone rang and Avery looked at her mom who looked back at her.

"Let it ring, Mom. It's Carter."

Nikki couldn't comprehend the look on Avery's face

and that troubled her. She knew her children like the back of her hand, but Avery was holding something back from her and she had never done that before.

"Are you afraid of him?"

If she couldn't be honest with her own mother, who loved her more than anyone ever would, she couldn't be honest with anyone. "I don't know what I feel about him, Mom. I almost kissed him once."

Nikki's mouth fell open.

"I'd rather not get into it right now," Avery responded. "I already feel guilty."

They heard the door opening and keys jangling and knew it was Charlie. When he appeared in the dining room, he went straight to Avery.

"How you doing, lil' bit?" He bent down, kissing her forehead. Charlie took a deep breath, taking a seat at the table. "I came to give you some updates."

Avery was becoming obsessed with finding Craig. She had wanted to kill him, but after her own life coming so close to the wire, she wouldn't think as lightly of the word.

"We haven't found Craig yet, but we found his appointment book with an entry that said 'meet Carter, plan bombing' on it."

Avery thought Alex would love this, certain the two of them had plotted together against her. "That's a little too obvious."

"We also found Craig's cell phone," Charlie continued. "It shows several outgoing calls to Carter, including one to Carter's cell phone just minutes before the explosion."

"It doesn't make sense," Avery pointed out. "Why did he try to save me if he wanted me dead?"

Charlie wondered if Avery was being absentminded or deliberately forgetting one of her most vivid memories from the incident.

"Why haven't you arrested him?" Nikki asked.

"He's a Chase." Charlie stood up. "It's not that simple. We have to have better evidence. I've got to get back to work. I'll keep in touch."

After he left, Nikki stared her daughter down. She didn't want to attack Avery, but something was seriously wrong. "You have feelings for this man?"

"I . . . I . . . No. I used to hate him, but I don't anymore."

"I don't want you to hate him," she said, "but I want you to understand that he probably blew up your shop."

"He could have been set up," Avery said. "Besides, I just . . . It was the way he looked when he came into my room."

"He's trying to charm you." Nikki walked to the phone. "Looks like he left a message this time. I want to know what he wants."

Avery was determined not to make up her mind until they found Craig. He was at the center of all of this. That was the only thing in this world she was sure of.

"Avery." Nikki lowered the phone, with a concerned look on her face. "It wasn't Carter. It was the insurance company. They need to speak to you and it's urgent."

Sean parked his car behind the detectives watching Rudio's massive Beverly Hills home from a half block away. He glanced at his watch. It was another hour before he was supposed to replace them and he wanted to show his gratitude by letting them off a little early. Gibbs and Rodriguez had been helping him out the entire weekend because staking Rudio out was the only option for now.

Sunday, the soon to be ex-congressman Flay agreed to lead him to the place where he and Haley had been. Almost a month since this all began, he was still being very difficult with the police. He had shipped his family off to his wife's parents in New England and he himself was lawyering up and eluding the police with frequent trips to Washington, D.C. After what had happened to Haley, he was under tight security, but it didn't seem like Rudio cared much about him.

When Jack called, his tone held acquiescence to it as he explained he would announce Monday he was stepping down from his office and wanted to help more where he could. Sean wanted to feel sorry for the guy. His career, which he had spent twenty years building, was gone, and the local papers reported his wife had filed for divorce, but none of that seemed to matter. Out on the water with Jack, all he wanted to do was toss the man overboard.

It was all about Haley. While Jack walked him through the boat, Sean couldn't help but picture him and Haley on that bed going at it, and it filled him with jealousy. When they reached the spot and Sean directed the divers to check out the site, he knew they wouldn't find anything. If any sign of Jorge had been floating around it would be long gone by now, and if it had been sunk the floor of the ocean here was too deep for the divers.

While the divers were down, Sean watched Jack break down on the deck. The man was sobbing over how regretful he was and even though Sean was cursing him inside, all he could say was *I understand, I understand.* He didn't understand. It was Sunday and he wondered if Jack had ever actually listened in whatever church it was he went to. No one was perfect, but it didn't take perfection to keep your pants zipped. The man was just weak and that's what he admitted to, but the way he did it only disgusted Sean. As if it wasn't at all his fault. His weakness had done him in and he made no indication that there was anything he could do to keep his weakness from doing it again.

Sean didn't even expect him to try. Still, he kept it together until Jack started talking about Haley and how the touch of her made him forget anything else in the world existed. Sean had to excuse himself at that moment and when he was alone, he was filled with rage. Not for Jack or for Haley, but for himself for wishing that he could touch Haley and feel that way.

"How's it going?" Sean asked as he leaned into the driver's side window.

"Nothing." Rodriguez said a few words in Spanish to signify his boredom. "Five hours and nothing. How long we gonna do this, man?"

"Until we catch him doing something. He's a drug dealer. He'll do something soon."

"We're going to get him for drugs?"

"We'll get him for anything we can," Sean said. "Until we can get him for murdering Jorge or anyone else we're sure he's murdered."

"Hey! Hey!" Gibbs was talking through a mouthful of sub sandwich as he hit Rodriguez in the shoulder.

"Give me the binoculars!" Sean reached down and grabbed them from Rodriguez.

The oxblood red Mercedes backed out of the underground garage and turned toward them. Sean looked closely. It wasn't Rudio, but he had an idea that it was still important. A man like Rudio doesn't do his own dirty work. He had men like Humongo, aka Armand, do it for him.

"You guys stay here." He tossed the binoculars back in the car. "I'm gonna follow this guy."

"Hey! What about relieving us?"

"You still have an hour." He pointed at his watch. "I'll be back."

As Rodriguez and Gibbs leaned down in the seats, Sean rushed to his car. He followed Armand a few cars behind, his mind going over what had made this case more personal to him than most. He cared about every case he had. He had even been attracted to some of his witnesses, but never let it show. Haley had changed all of that.

He didn't blame himself for being attracted to her. Even with her personality flaws, too many to mention, most men would want to go, but Sean had always thought himself stronger than most men. His life as a police officer and now as a detective meant a lot to him. The values his parents had instilled in him taught him there was virtue in denying yourself something you knew wasn't good for you; especially when that something could hurt others.

As he followed Armand into a strip mall parking lot Sean thought of Jack, almost on his knees sobbing like a little girl over Haley, thinking he would rather shoot himself in the head than be brought to that by any woman. He could tell himself just to stay away from her, but he knew he wasn't going to do that. He wanted her and he wasn't going to rest until he had her.

Sean parked two aisles behind Armand, leaning back in his seat as he watched Armand swagger into the Carlson Travel Agency office. Was Rudio planning on going somewhere? He had family in Florida and Cuba, based on Sean's records, but a man with drug money could go anywhere he wanted.

While he waited, Sean thought of the old stakeout days with his old partner, Luke Klane, who had left the force two months ago to join his father-in-law's security business in San Diego. The salary was twice what he was paid as a detective. Sean missed him and wasn't looking forward to a new partner coming soon.

After about twenty minutes, Armand left the travel agency and returned to his car. Sean decided to keep following him. His hour was running out and he knew he could check up on the travel agency after his shift was over.

Janet waved Leigh over to her table in the country club dining room. She ignored any nerves she felt at asking so much of her daughter.

The first thing she noticed as Leigh sat down was the dark circles beneath her eyes. "Are you hungry? You look like you haven't eaten."

"I'll just have the usual." Leigh accepted the menu Janet handed her. "You don't look happy, Mom. What's wrong?"

"Is that a serious question?" Janet almost laughed. "Things have been tough on all of us and I wish you were around more."

"You know how busy I've been with the clinic," Leigh said. "Which is why I wanted to talk to—"

"I'm going to spare you, Leigh." Janet reached across the table, placing her hand over her daughter's. She felt its trembling and it touched her heart. "Your father told me everything. I know why you're here."

"I'm sorry, Mom. I know how going to Daddy first makes you feel. It's just that—"

"You were encouraged by his interest after your problems with the insurance company, I know. Your father loves a challenge. Apparently, so do you."

Leigh was a little confused at the veiled compliment. "I'm a Chase, right?"

"You certainly are." Janet leaned back, adjusting the napkin on her lap. "I am truly, truly sorry about the clinic. You're my baby and anything that hurts my baby, hurts me. You may not believe me, but—"

"I believe you, but I don't want pity."

"You're definitely a Chase." Janet was proud of her; pity was for the weak. "Trust me, I wasn't even considering pitying you. I want to give you an apology."

Leigh was completely confused now. Which way was this conversation going?

"An apology," Janet continued, "for making you work harder than you should have to get this started. As much as I hate the idea of you down there—"

"We're going to get a security system and hire a security guard."

"Your father told me. He also told you that he would use his contacts to lean on the insurance company. You went along with that?"

Leigh's head lowered. "I don't think it's right, but . . ."

"That's where you go wrong, Leigh. Having power isn't just good for helping others. It's also good for getting what you want for those that you love. I don't always agree with your father's tactics, but it is what it is."

"Insurance companies are powerful."

"So is your father," Janet said. "He'll do what he can, but the Chase Foundation is mine."

"That's what he told me and that's why I'm here."

Janet could see that Leigh was close to tears and she had cried enough herself over the past weeks. "I'm going to help you, Leigh."

Leigh's eyes widened, wondering if she'd just heard what she wanted to hear. "You're . . . What?"

"The Foundation will help the Hope Clinic. I'll set up a quick fund-raising dinner for start-up and secure operations funding for the next six months."

"Are you kidding me?" Leigh was crying and laughing at the same time.

"I may be crazy," Janet said, "but I'm not kidding. I can only give you six months because that's what we always promise start-up charities."

Leigh was no fool and as Janet dismissed the waiter who came for their orders, she leaned in and studied her mother's demure smile. "What's going on? You can't tell me you suddenly believe in what I'm doing."

"I've always believed in everything you've ever done, Leigh." Janet watched as Leigh's face softened and her lips turned up in a proud smile. "You're the most incredible person in this family and that's why I've chosen to do this for you. I know you'll understand what I'm asking."

Leigh swallowed, her shoulders lowering a bit. It didn't matter, really. She was going to do anything and she couldn't wait to tell Richard and Alicia. "What?"

"I need you to make more of a commitment to this family. Leigh, you're like a ghost and you were that way well before you left for Africa. It's as if you're embarrassed by your name. There are societal responsibilities attached to it."

Leigh always felt the entire system was set up to make a few feel better by excluding most. No one was ever good enough. What put the Chase family on top was Janet's bloodline and Steven's power and money. No one could match both. Not in L.A. Some had the family names but only middle- or upper-class economic status. Those who had all the money but no name might as well be homeless ex-cons.

When Janet spoke of societal responsibilities she meant events, mostly masquerading as charity. They were all about trivializing their privileges, degrading those who didn't have them and figuring out the best way to separate themselves from everyone. Most people, black or white, didn't meet their standards and for a person like Leigh, who wanted to bring people together, it was nothing short of sickening.

"You should be proud of who you are."

"I am," Leigh said honestly.

"You aren't. You don't see it, but you wear shame on your face for being blessed. You're embarrassed that you've been given so much only because everyone else hasn't. You don't realize what it means to be a Chase and how embracing that could do more for your people than you'd ever believe."

Leigh didn't really want to hear this. "I know how important our family is to the community, Mom. What do you want me to do?"

"I've always asked all of you the same thing," Janet said. "Educate yourselves as much as possible, reach for the highest goals, and never compromise your principles and your civility. Understanding how simply the way you live your life is the greatest contribution you can give to society."

"I've tried to do that."

"And you've done it the best, Leigh. That's why I need you to help me represent our family right now. Carter has his own problems and I can't count on your father and Michael right now with the mess Chase Beauty is in. That doesn't change our obligations and I need your help. The press can't possibly write anything bad about you."

"So you're pimping me for good press for the family." Leigh regretted it as soon as it came out.

"Your little sister's vocabulary has been rubbing off on you."

"I'm sorry, Mom." Leigh had to remember this wasn't about her. "I understand and I can do whatever is needed."

"You understand this will take you away from your time at the clinic?" Janet asked. Leigh nodded, making her feel like a bully. She knew she was doing this for the right reasons. She glanced down at her watch, realizing she didn't have any more time left. "What are your plans today?"

"I have to stop by County Hospital at two. They're donating some supplies. I need to store them at home, if that's okay?"

"Fine. I'll be working at the foundation offices today, so come by and we'll work everything out."

"Mother, I can't begin to thank you for all you're doing. It just means so much to so many people."

"I only care what it means to you," Janet said, "but spending more time on this family is not all I'm asking."

Inside, Leigh screamed at herself not to protest. Even if it was unbearable, she had to do this. It meant too much. "What else?"

"I'm setting you up on a blind date and you must—"

"Mother!" Leigh held her hand up. She hadn't told her about Richard yet, but only because spreading news about her love life hadn't seemed appropriate with everything that was going on. "I never like the guys you set me up with. They're always snobs."

"This one is an exception." Janet halted her protest. "Listen to me. I'm just asking that you spend some time with him. A few dates maybe with some of your friends along. I know you'll like him. I've met him and he's not like any of the other men I've set you up with."

Leigh was still shaking her head.

"It's all I'm asking," Janet said, "but . . . well, I'm asking it all. I'm already going to get flack for contributing to my child's venture when there is a line of charities waiting. This is how it will happen. I mean, it's not like you're seeing anyone."

Looking at her mother's indignant stare, Leigh knew now wasn't the time to tell her about Richard. She had to be smart and give her mother what she wanted. To have the clinic up and running and fully operational to serve its much-needed patients was worth a few dates with a society brat. After a while, she could tell her mother about Richard and let her know this young man, whoever he was, just didn't do it for her.

Leigh noticed her mother look toward the door to the dining room and wave someone over. She looked behind her noticing an attractive elderly woman walking toward them, her hand in that of an even more attractive young man.

"It would be boring for me to give you a bio," Janet said, "so I invited him to lunch."

CHAPTER 8

In the back room of Essentials II, Avery was trying to pull herself together even though she was shaking all over. Essentials II was all she had left and she didn't believe she would have it much longer. She heard the words the insurance agent said over and over again but was having a hard time believing them. Craig had made it so that she lost everything no matter what happened to him.

She had to be strong even though it felt like the devil and all his demons were conspiring to bring her down to hell with them. She would lose everything now, but she was young and had the will to start again. With the grace of God, five years from now she would be even more successful than she had been before all this mess started. That's how it worked, wasn't it? Place all your faith in God and He will provide. He would show her the way.

She repeated the scripture that came to mind every time she thought she couldn't take it. II Corinthians 12:9: My grace is sufficient. Grace: Underserved Kindness. It would be enough to get her through all of this, and as long as she didn't lose faith, she would be rewarded. Honestly, all she really wanted was to get through this without slitting her wrists.

"Avery!" Calabra rushed in, struggling to close the door behind her. "I told him you don't want to see him."

She was pushed aside as Carter entered with an intimidating frown on his face. Avery watched him struggling against the petite woman and if she had been feeling better, she thought she might have enjoyed this.

"I'm calling the police!" Calabra yelled after Carter won the door fight.

"It's okay," Avery said. "Go on back to work."

"Your first day back?" he asked, waiting for a response that didn't come. "If you don't want to talk to me, why did you let me in?"

"What you're doing could be considered stalking, Carter."

"I just want to talk to you." He'd done more pride-swallowing in his pursuit of her than ever in his life. "I know Alex has been filling your head with . . ."

"I make my own decisions."

"I don't want to argue with you, Avery. I just want to talk." He leaned against the side of the desk, looking down at her. "I just want to apologize."

"There's nothing you can apologize for." She was trying to look into his compelling eyes with some dignity.

"I'm to blame for some of this," he said.

"You're to blame for all of it." She didn't take any pleasure in the hurt look on his face even though she wanted to.

"I accept that, but you have to understand I would have never done this if I knew Craig was sick. He never gave me—"

"Save it," she interrupted. "I know everything you told the police about how you blackmailed Craig."

Carter scratched at his chin, wanting to say she was making it sound worse than it really was, but that was a waste. He had let his animosity toward her erase his conscience.

"I had nothing to do with that bombing. I told Craig our business was over. That's when he tried to blackmail me."

"I would be happy to hear you got a taste of your own medicine, but the only problem with that is that I ended up paying for it." Avery was only holding herself together because of a need to make him understand. "When you tempted him with the answer to all of his problems, there was no turning back. He thought he was saved and when that was ripped from him it made him all the more desperate. You set this in motion with the first call you made to him."

Carter wanted to say *If only I had known*, but that was the point. That was why you didn't do these things, because you don't know. "What else have the police told you?"

"The only reason they haven't arrested you is your last name. Your father."

Carter nodded, unable to protest. He knew it was the truth, but it wouldn't last long. He resisted his father's advice to hire a criminal lawyer because more than what that might do for him, he thought of what that would look like to Avery.

"Carter, I've spoken to you like you wanted. So please go."

"Not before I tell you something. I know you don't want to hear this, but I won't really believe it until I hear myself say it to you." He stepped only inches from where she was sitting.

"Then this is for you," she said. "Not me. Everything is for you."

"Avery, shut up."

She looked up at him ready to cuss him out, but a sense ran over her and it scared her half to death.

"I care about you," he said. "I thought at first it was pity and guilt that I felt because of what I've caused, but it's not. It's . . ."

Avery backed out of her chair and jumped away from the desk like he was a roach coming out of the dark. She backed into the wall to get as far away from his confused stare as possible.

"How could you do this to me?"

"What? I—"

"How could you lay this on me right now?" She didn't believe this man was even capable of really caring about anyone other than himself. "With everything you've already done to me, you want me to believe you care about me? What are you trying to do, seduce me into not suing you and your father?"

"I don't expect you to believe it now." He backed away. "I just wanted to say it before I do what it takes to make you believe it. I'm doing everything I can to find Craig. I'll find him and you'll know the truth."

"The truth is you still tried to steal my company and now you want me to—"

Unable to hold on any longer, Avery fell to her knees crying. She hadn't thought she could feel worse, but this fake admission of affection from Carter pulled at something inside of her; it was really the last straw. She pulled away when Carter rushed to her.

"Get away from me!" she yelled. "You've got everything now. Every shred of dignity I've ever had. I'm gonna lose everything and I don't care about how you feel or what happens to Craig."

"You'll rebuild," he said. "I'll help you. Until then, this store is—"

"There's not going to be any rebuilding and this store isn't gonna be doing anything for much longer. I don't have any insurance. Craig cancelled the policy three months ago. He forged my signature to cancel it and was pocketing the payments."

Carter blinked at the unexpected turn, but he didn't let it cloud him for more than a moment. Kneeling down on the floor, he came face-to-face with Avery's tortured inner child. "He'll pay for this, Avery. I'll make sure of it."

"I don't want anything from you," she stressed. "And don't act like this isn't what you wanted; me losing everything for turning you down."

"All I want is to find Craig and make him pay for what he did. Whatever that costs me, I'm willing to accept."

The desperate anger on his face and the strain in his voice made Avery want to believe he was telling her the truth, but she hated him as much as anyone right now.

"You're strong enough to handle this," he said.

She shrugged, too far beyond embarrassed. "God never gives you more than you can bear."

"Unless you die of something." He found a small victory in the smile that briefly flirted on her face. "You can count on me, Avery."

Maybe I can," she said, "but I can't return these feelings you say you have for me. I love Alex."

Not for long. Carter wasn't accepting defeat here, but getting her away from Alex wasn't more important than finding Craig and getting Avery back on track. He wanted to hold her, his ego convincing him he could make any woman feel better with his charm and comfort. Avery was much more than any woman and he wasn't going to let any feelings she had for Alex get in his way.

"Wait out here," Haley ordered her bodyguard as she and Sean headed into the library. "I want to be alone with him."

Sean could see from the look on the bodyguard's face that he was happy to get rid of Haley. Sean didn't like the way she talked to him—or anyone for that matter—but he hadn't seen her in three days and nothing else mattered. She was all over him the second the door closed behind them. Sean tried to reach the leather sofa a few feet away, but Haley dragged him to the floor. She was kissing on his neck, unbuttoning his shirt. He told her to slow down, only because he knew she wouldn't listen. Any nervous tension he felt from being in Steven's home evaporated the second he got his hands on her. Frantically, he slid them under her thin silk tank and up her stomach. She had large, firm breasts and her skin was as soft as satin.

"Shouldn't we be in your—" He stopped as she slapped her hand over his mouth. It kind of hurt, but anything she did right now was okay.

"My bedroom?" Haley was disappointed. He wasn't learning what she wanted quickly enough. He should be desperate enough to have her by now to know better. She bit his earlobe before whispering into his ear. "My parents have sex in their bedroom, Sean. This is much more exciting."

He leaned back looking around the massive room filled with oversized, leather-bound books and antique furniture. Every piece in the room cost more than his yearly salary. "Haley, we can't do this here."

Haley leaned on her knees looking down at him. This was starting to get on her nerves. Any other man would be ready to sell his mother after waiting this long. "You were telling me on the phone how much you wanted to see me, so do you want to do this or not?"

"You have no idea," he answered, "but not in your parents' house."

"This is my house, too." She pushed him to the ground and straddled him. "And no one rejects me."

"I'm not rejecting you." He didn't resist when she started unbuttoning his jeans. "I thought our first time would be in a more—"

"What are we, virgins?" She was starting to cool down a bit. "I need to work off my nervous energy, Sean. Is it going to be you or someone else?"

Sean's hands fell away from her hips as he felt himself go limp.

Haley rolled her eyes. He looked like a normal, red-blooded American male and when he touched her he made her feel great, but she couldn't get it. How could he resist her?

"I'm not interested in being your stress relief." He would accept being anything for her. Still, a man had to stand on his principles. "And I'm sure as hell not interested in being one of your *either/ors*."

"Why are you so damn sensitive? You're a man, aren't you?"

"You're really blowing me away here." He laid his hands on her thighs and squeezed. "Your mother is here, isn't she? And she knows I'm here, so we won't get very far without getting caught."

Haley eyes lit up. "Isn't that the whole point?"

"You're not taking this seriously," he said. "We're not just a man and woman having sex. I'm the lead detective on a case where you're the victim and only witness. We can't get caught doing anything."

"You're really serious, aren't you?" Haley was at least glad there was a reason. She liked Sean more than she was willing to admit to herself, but she didn't wait for anyone.

"I'm trying to maintain some professionalism here." Sean was already breaking too many rules to sleep through the night. "When things calm down, we can go—"

"Things aren't ever going to calm down. That asshole is free and he's gonna keep me locked up in this prison till I die!"

"I've already told you that's not true."

"All you do is tell me things. Why don't you deliver on any of it? Like now for instance."

Sean knew Haley wouldn't understand. Like her father, she was used to getting whatever she wanted when she wanted it. They were both driving him crazy.

"It's hard when you do it right. It takes longer."

"Then do it wrong," she ordered. "My father knows—"

"Please don't tell me that." Sean was worried because Steven had already insinuated he was going to handle things from his end if Sean didn't get on it quick.

Balancing on her hands, she lowered down on him. "I'm serious. I know exactly what he looks like now. Give me another chance to ID him."

"That's not legal," he said.

"You'd rather he kill me?" she asked.

"Stop it, Haley."

"Carly was over today," she said. "Remember her from the club? She said that since they let him go, he knows I can't identify him. So maybe he doesn't care about me anymore."

"Would you stake your life on Carly?" he asked. "Besides, I told you not to talk to people about this case. The less people know, the better."

"I can't go anywhere. I can't talk to anybody. You have to understand how much anxiety this is causing me. If you did, you'd know how much I need you right now."

She was undoing the top buttons to her shorts when the door to the library flung open.

Janet's mouth hit the floor at what she saw. "What are you doing?"

When Sean got that Haley had no intention of moving, he took it upon himself to lift her off of him. "Mrs. Chase . . ." Looking at Haley, he could see this was exactly what she had wanted. She was bored and entertained herself by using, shocking, and offending. "I'm sorry. This is—"

"Don't apologize," Haley said. "She's seen this before."

Sean looked at her, feeling the sting of her words. Why in God's name did he want this woman?

"You might want to zip your pants up before you leave." Janet had too much to deal with today to let Haley's exploits with this boy get to her. Haley would be done with him soon enough.

"He's not leaving," Haley said. "He's staying for lunch."

"I haven't set the table for him," Janet stated.

"It's okay." Sean really wanted to leave.

"Leigh's guest is here, so please pull yourself together and join us." She never took her eyes off him as he zipped back up, tucking his shirt in. He was completely humiliated and that would satisfy her for now.

Standing in the doorway, Leigh felt awful. Leo had been a great lunch guest, but all she wanted was for him to leave. It was a shame, he was an attractive brother. Dark and handsome with jet black eyes and strong features, not to mention all the charm a well-bred boy should have. He was a stockbroker, and Leigh had no love for that, but it didn't matter. She was falling in love with Richard and every time she looked at Leo, Richard was all she thought of.

She laughed at Leo's jokes and agreed to go with him to a party at the Beverly Hills Hotel on Saturday. He was extremely flattering and complimenting, but it was all for nothing. She was lying to him by making him think she was interested, lying to her mother for making her think she was giving this a try, and lying to Richard by not telling him what she was doing. She reminded herself time and time again that this was for the clinic, but she never bought into the idea that the end justifies the means.

"Leigh?"

She blinked, realizing she'd been lost in her thoughts while he was talking to her. "I'm so sorry, Leo."

He smiled, showing perfect white teeth. "I was just saying that you and your mother are so much alike."

"How do you mean?"

"I don't know," he said. "Perfect, I guess."

"Nobody's perfect, but thanks anyway. We really enjoyed having you."

"I'm really looking forward to Saturday night." He leaned against the entryway. "I think we've really hit it . . ."

Leigh was distracted by the phone ringing. She wondered if it was Richard and if her mother would answer.

"Thanks again for coming by." She started closing the door very slowly. "I guess I'll see you Saturday?"

He nodded, looking as if he wanted to stay longer but stepped away anyway.

Just as Leigh rushed to the phone, it stopped ringing. Picking it up, she listened quietly for the sound of her mother's voice, but only heard Maya.

"Is that you, Leigh?" she asked.

"Yes, I thought . . ."

"Hi." It was Richard.

"Thank you, Maya." She leaned against the sofa waiting for Maya to hang up. "Hey, sexy, you on a break?"

"I'm off rounds, actually. Neo, the guy I subbed for last week, is making it up to me. How you doing?"

"Okay." For a liar, she was doing just fine.

"The construction guys are coming to the clinic for repairs tomorrow," he said. "Your mother really came through for us."

"Yes, she did. It took a lot, but she has come around."

"I want to come over and thank her myself. I don't think flowers were enough."

Especially since Leigh intercepted the flowers before they got to her. "She's not here right now."

"Then tomorrow, because I . . . we all really owe her."

"Want to meet me somewhere?" she asked, trying to change the subject.

There was a short pause before he said, "How about Trinity? A drink and then maybe a movie?"

"Sounds perfect." Leigh stood up when Janet walked into the room.

Janet sighed impatiently as she held up her watch, but Leigh lowered the phone a bit and shooed her mother away.

"We have to go," Janet said loudly. "We have an engagement."

Leigh placed her hand over the phone, hoping Richard hadn't heard. "Just a second, okay?"

"We have to go to the museum to plan the fund-raiser. It's for your clinic, remember?"

Leigh remembered. She remembered her promise and how this was all for the clinic. A few weeks and they would be back where they were before this all went downhill. Back on track. Back on track. Waiting for her mother to leave, she took a deep breath before returning to the phone.

"Who was that?" he asked.

"Maya." She cringed at her own lie. "Richard, about that movie; can we push it back a little?"

To Steven, seeing Janet lying on the sofa against the window in their bedroom was like looking at a painting. She was the picture of perfection calmly lifting her head from her book and sending him a smile that warmed him throughout. He loved this woman to no end and, although he should be home more often, coming home to that smile was a blessing.

"It's late." She kissed him on the lips, wrapping her arms around him. She felt the tense muscles in his back and shoulders. "You're working too much these days."

"You always say that." He loved the feel of her soft familiar body and she still had a way of making him feel like he was the king of the world because she had forsaken all others for him.

She removed his tie, tossing it on the bed before she led him to the edge of it. "Lie down. Let me loosen you up."

"That's what I'm talking about." He leaned back onto the massive bed, reaching out for her. With a wife like Janet, a man didn't need Viagra.

Janet slapped his hands away playfully. "Turn around and take your shirt off."

"However you want it."

"Stop being dirty and lie on your stomach. I'm going to give you a massage. You're tense all over."

Steven let out a moan as Janet kneaded the muscles in his back. He hadn't realized how much he needed this until she grabbed his shoulders and began turning. She began with the polite "how was work" conversation, which always led to something more serious and this time it was Carter's predicament.

"My legal staff is having a problem," he said. "Carter is being too hard on them; barking orders left and right."

"Sounds like you."

"He's a natural leader, but they work for me, not him."

Janet rested her weight on him. "Did I just hear you give Carter a compliment?"

"Stop it, Janet. You know I love that boy."

"He's not a boy, he's a man, and I know you love him. He just needs to hear it every now and then."

"He is a boy," Steven said. "He's only thirty and he has yet to comprehend the magnitude of this—"

"What about what I just said?" Janet usually tried to avoid the role of mediator in their relationship because Steven begged her to stay out of it. "I called him today and he said he hasn't spoken to you since last week."

"We're both busy trying to clean up the mess he made."

"The mess you gave him." She squeezed a little harder this time until he groaned.

"I can't talk to that boy. It's like he resents everything I've done for him. I've made him the man he is today. I taught him strength, responsibility and the keys to success."

"You sound like you gave him a gift. You're his father, Steven. You're supposed to do all of those things, and more."

"It was my job, I know." Steven sighed. "I don't want a thank you. I'd just prefer not to get a fuck you."

"That's not fair. Carter loves you."

"I know he loves me, Janet. I want him to respect me."

She leaned down, speaking harsh words tenderly. "He respects you, Steven, but that's not what you want. You want him to worship you and Carter is too much of his own man to worship another one. He got that from you, too."

Steven grinned at the thought of it, but it bothered him that he couldn't think of a way to fix what was going on between him and his son. "Can I go this evening without a lecture on Carter?"

Janet wasn't going to push anymore. She knew when to pick her battles, but she was concerned about this feud between the two of them. If they didn't work this out, their relationship could be irreparable. That, she couldn't bear.

"What is Maya making?" he asked.

"Some Caribbean dish. I don't know."

Steven's stomach grumbled. He hadn't eaten all day. "I thought I smelled curry."

"It stinks up the entire downstairs," Janet said. "I tell her time and time again not to cook that, but she says you like it."

"I do."

"She works for me, not you."

"We all work for you." He reached back, squeezing her thigh. "I tried to call him yesterday."

Janet stopped for a moment, sensing the strain in her husband's voice. "And?"

"I left a message for him to call me. To come over to the house, but he never called me back."

Janet sighed. Carter was just as stubborn as his father. "It's just one day. He'll be here Saturday at least."

"What's Saturday?"

"I've invited Avery over to the house for dinner." She leaned back as Steven quickly sat up, looking at her like she was psychotic. She expected as much.

"You invited that woman to our house?" Both Carter and Janet's infatuation with Avery was beyond ridiculous. "That woman could destroy us."

"Stop being so dramatic." Janet slid off the bed and went to her vanity. "If that innocent woman could destroy Chase Beauty, then Chase Beauty was never meant to be."

"Innocent?"

"She's incredibly pleasant. I only spoke to her on the phone, but she was polite and well spoken."

"That's nice, considering she thinks our son tried to kill her."

"Your son has been working some magic with her. I don't know what he's done, but she didn't seem to hold any animosity toward Carter when she spoke of him."

"That's because from the phone you couldn't see the voodoo dolls in the back of her shop." Steven wasn't giving up even though his wife had that look on her face that told him protest would be a waste of time. "I don't want her here. She's the enemy."

"She isn't the enemy, Steven, and she's coming."

"This isn't going to go well." He sat at the edge of the bed, facing her. "You got lucky with Leigh, so you're hedging your bets."

"Steven, in all the years you've known me, have I ever

done anything that wasn't in the best interest of this family?"

He didn't need to answer that. It was an unequivocal *no*.

"Then Saturday it is," he said. "Now I'm gonna go tear up some curry."

"You can't be serious!" Alex leaned across Avery's desk in the back office of Essentials II. "You can't tell me you're going over there?"

"I've already made up my mind," Avery said.

"What exactly did she say to you? That woman has a master's in charm. She can charm a million dollars out of anyone for her foundation. You must have been easy for her."

"I'm going to ignore that." Avery had been easily induced by Janet Chase's invitation. She'd made it impossible for her to refuse. By the time the woman ended, she had Avery feeling like she owed the family.

In the two days since the invitation, Avery must have picked up the phone ten times to cancel, but a call from Carter sealed the deal. He was trying so hard to spend time with her and it was driving her out of her mind because she was beginning to get used to him.

He wasn't too happy when she made him agree to stop if she came to the house for dinner, but he agreed nonetheless. Avery didn't believe it for a second, but at least she knew if he kept trying to see her after that, she didn't have to be nice to him anymore.

"It was an incredible gesture."

Alex sat in the chair near the door, looking around. "This place is a mess, Avery. Why can't you get one of those girls to clean it up?"

"We've all been a little busy lately." Avery was beginning to become numb to his ambivalence about her professional life.

"If you think it was such an incredible gesture," he said, "then why did you wait till today to tell me?"

"Alex, I'm just asking you to come with me."

He threw his hands in the air. "There is no way I'm setting foot in that house and neither are you!"

"I beg your pardon?"

"I'm putting my foot down, Avery. If you don't care about what these people have done to you, then I'll care for you."

"You're not gonna do anything for me," she said, "and you can put your foot up your ass."

Alex looked stunned for a minute, but snapped out of it. "This is about Carter, isn't it? I know he's trying to get with you, Avery. I've been reading the log on your caller ID. I know he's—"

Avery shot up from her chair. "How dare you? All I've asked you for is your support in what is undeniably the worst time in my life and you refuse to give it to me. All you give me are orders and insults and you have the nerve to accuse me?"

Alex just stared at her. Avery could see he was shutting off. It was what he always did when he was about to lose an argument. He would shut off and give her the cold shoulder in his passive-aggressive way of punishing her for being right. Avery didn't really care right now. She had too much to deal with to be concerned with Alex's hurt feelings.

"I'm doing the best I can," he answered after a while. His face held no expression at all. "You don't make it easy. You're just feeling sorry for yourself."

She couldn't deny that completely. "I'm sorry, but I'm stressed out. I can't do this on my own and you're not helping me. I'm going to have to take out a second mortgage on this place to pay off what I owe for Essentials."

"You can't afford that."

"Is that the advice you have for me?" she asked sarcastically. "Well, it's very helpful."

"Stop your whining," he said. "Get rid of this place."

Avery was too stunned to respond and too familiar with Alex to think she heard him wrong.

"You sell this place to pay them both off and sue the Chase family to make up the rest. When we get married, you won't need to work anyway."

"Alex, Essentials is my life."

He rolled his eyes. "It's a hair salon, Avery. It's so . . . working class. You'll be able to go to business school with what you get from the Chase lawsuit. Unless, of course, you go over there and play into their game. I'll catch you later."

Avery stood in the middle of the back office for several minutes just staring at the door. She was beginning to realize that the Chase family's game wasn't the only one she had played into.

Leigh laughed as Richard grabbed at her under her shirt. She pushed his hands away even though she loved it. "There are other people here."

The other people at the clinic were Alicia and the man installing the new security system.

"They aren't paying attention to us." Richard leaned in, kissing her. "I want to be alone with you."

Leigh was really falling in love with Richard. When they finally got together on Wednesday, they skipped the movie and dinner and went right to his place for nonstop sex and pizza delivery. She couldn't get enough of him and the way he made her feel. He made her forget the clinic was being delayed and she had become her mother's indentured servant. He hadn't been able to make her forget she was lying to him, and the more she fell for him, the more afraid she became that she could lose him over this.

"Can't you guys get enough?" Alicia asked. She was carrying an encyclopedia-size book on how to operate the security system. "Isn't that why you guys were late getting over here?"

"Actually, it was." Richard reached for the book. "Let me take that. I don't want to stress your brain."

Alicia snatched it away from him. "Listen, Doctor, I bet I scored higher than you on the MCATs, so watch it. I'll be teaching you how to work this thing in a couple of minutes."

"We'll get together tonight and do it," he explained. "We'll learn it together."

Leigh nervously shook her head. "I can't do tonight. Avery Jackson is coming over and Mom demands that we all be there for the event."

"Good luck with that." Alicia rolled her eyes before turning and heading for the security technician.

"I'm so sorry," Leigh said. "I forgot to tell her."

Richard rubbed her back comfortingly. "My fault. You told me and I forgot. Your mother has you running through hoops, doesn't she?"

"I don't mind. I just hate being away from the clinic so much." She wrapped her arms around him. "I hate being away from you."

"Maybe I can come over," he said. "I still need to thank your mother."

Leigh backed away, feeling her nerves charge into high gear. "No, you don't want to come over. When my mother hosts these family dinner things, it's overwhelming for me and I've been doing them all my life. It's not the time to introduce anyone."

Richard hesitated with a frown. "Okay. Well, look, whenever you think it's right, but I am eager to meet your parents."

"I want you to. They'll love you."

"So what about tomorrow night? Let's do that movie thing that didn't work out on Wednesday."

"I . . . No, I can't. My parents are going to some banquet and I promised to keep Haley company."

Richard's hesitation was a little longer this time. "Well, um, I guess I can do some babysitting. It can't be that hard considering she's twenty—"

"Maybe we should do something in the daytime. My parents don't want anyone coming over while they aren't there. Security and everything."

Richard sighed. "What is it, Leigh? What's going on? You've been acting weird all week."

"I'm just nervous, Richard. I'm sorry for being so inaccessible, but I just want to make sure my mother is happy with what's going on. Trust me, you don't know her. She could pull out of this and I can't let that happen."

"I'm sorry. I know this has been hard on you."

He reached for her, but Leigh's shame caused her to back away. She hadn't thought before she did it, but the second she did she regretted it. The look on Richard's face was undeniably hurt.

"Leigh, what have I done?" He backed away, seeming resigned to not connecting with her. "You're obviously upset with me, but I can't think . . ."

"You haven't done anything." Leigh didn't know how much longer she could lie to him. "You've been better to me than I could have expected. I'm just stressed out. I have to go." She heard him call her name again, but didn't turn around, and when this was all over, she wasn't sure if she would lose Richard—but she knew she deserved to.

CHAPTER 9

When Avery drove up to the Chase mansion, Carter was standing at the door with a boyish look on his face. It made her smile even though she warned herself to be on guard this evening and not give too much. When she stepped out of the car, she promised to leave her emotions there.

"You look nice." Carter had been doubtful until the end whether she would come.

"I get door service?"

"I'm here to warn you," he said. "My mother put a lot into this evening. My entire family is here and they can be—"

"I can handle myself, Carter."

Carter wondered if her cold edge was her selected mood for the evening or just geared toward him.

"I know you can handle yourself," he said. "I think you've proved that ten times over. You're healing well." His finger gently touched the tiny scratch on her forehead from the blast. Covered by bangs, it was barely visible.

Avery recoiled at his touch. She didn't like this caring side of him. It was too convincing. She had to forgive what little attraction she felt for Carter already because it was only human. He was fine; the devil always is.

When Carter opened the door, his parents were already heading for them. Only Janet had a smile for her and even though Carter had gone out of his way to avoid his father this past week, if he intended to give Avery a hard time, Carter intended to give him one in return.

Avery was taken back by Janet's response to her outstretched hand. She ignored it, grabbing her in a warm hug in comparison to Steven who only offered a cold nod. She could see in his eyes that he blamed her for everything, including his own choices.

"Maya hasn't finished setting up yet," Janet said. "Carter can entertain you until then. The bar is set up near the pool."

How nice, Avery thought. The bar is set up near the pool. Just like at her house.

"Come on." Carter gently placed his hand to her back, grateful she didn't pull away, as he led her toward the back of the house.

Steven leaned into his wife, whispering as Carter and Avery walked away. "You see that?"

Janet grabbed his hand, squeezing it tight. "You behave tonight."

"This isn't about him helping Chase Beauty," he said. "He wants that woman and you know it."

Janet turned to him, guiding his face to hers. "It still works in your favor, doesn't it, dear?"

Steven smirked. "It's just another way he can do something I wouldn't want him to."

Michael tugged at Kimberly as she said a few last words to Avery by the pool. He had done what his mother wanted and greeted her even though he couldn't stand the woman. It was bad enough she barely mouthed a greeting in return, but now Kimberly was acting like she had just met her new best friend.

"Take it easy." Kimberly pulled her arm out of his grip.

"What's the matter with you?"

"I'm being polite like Janet ordered us to."

As soon as they were inside, he held her against the wall. He leaned in, kissing her hard as his hand slid up the inside of her thighs. She tried to stop him, but he laughed, slapping her hand away.

Kimberly didn't want him to stop, but Janet could walk in any moment and all she needed was another lecture on decorum and proper behavior. She tried to slide away, but he kept her where she was, tilting his head a little to the side to catch a glimpse of Carter and Avery.

"Look at them," he said. "They're sharing a reclining chair like high school kids."

"He's trying to make her feel comfortable. It can't be easy for her being here. I should know."

"Why are you being so nice to her?"

"I like her." He frowned and she grabbed his chin, squeezing his face. "Stop being such a baby. I'll hate her if you want me to, but I don't want to. She seems like a normal person and that's a rarity in this house."

"Avery's not going to have anything to do with this house after tonight, so don't get excited. And yes, I want you to hate her like I do. She's made a mess of everything."

"Damn her," she mocked. "Who does she think she is standing up for herself and trying to keep her business? Doesn't she know who deserves it more?"

Michael didn't care for her biting wit right now. Kimberly had a way of digging into him that only made him angrier. It turned her on when he lost it because she knew there were places only she could take him. She used it to remind him that she owned him and he resented that even though he gave in to it every time.

"Don't start with me, woman. I told you that night at the restaurant he's after that woman, and the closer he brings her inside, the more dangerous she is."

"You overestimate her interest in you." Kimberly saw the real issue here.

Whenever Carter got serious about a woman, Michael got jealous. He liked being the most important person in Carter's life. Michael wanted everything all the time. They were brothers, enemies, and best friends. The way they fought just to turn around and be a rock for each other amazed her.

"You're not seeing the point here." She rubbed his chest to calm him down. "The more Carter knows her, the better he'll be able to protect the family from her. You don't think he'd pick a woman over family, do you?"

"I do," he said. "If she was the right woman, he might. But you wouldn't turn on the family, would you?"

"Of course not." Unless it meant getting rid of Janet, in which case she'd do it in a New York second. "No one comes before you, Daddy."

"Then you get close to her," he said. "You can pretend to be normal, can't you?"

She socked him in the chest. "I'm the only normal person in this house."

"Then she'll like you. You get close to her and find out what she really wants."

This wasn't the first time he'd used her to get information and Kimberly didn't like it one bit. If only she could say no to this man, but she couldn't, so she agreed to become Avery's new best friend, and she let Michael's hand reach up her thigh again as his mouth took hers. Damn Janet. The world could walk in on her for all she cared. She was under this man's spell.

Avery and Carter were both preoccupied with Michael and Kimberly going at it just inside the house near the verandah. Avery at first wondered if they knew they could be seen, but from the way they touched each other, she realized they didn't care.

"They seem pretty fond of each other," she said.

"That's one way to put it," Carter said. "They act like a couple of horny teenagers all the time. I'm surprised they only have two kids."

"Where are Daniel and Evan?"

"How do you know . . ." He caught himself, remembering who he was. Everyone knew everything about his family and he didn't like it one bit. "They're inside. Maya is giving them their dinner in the kitchen. Trust me, the night will be wild enough without them."

Avery couldn't turn her eyes away from Michael and Kimberly and had to admit it was affecting her. Not sexually really, but emotionally. She saw their passion for each other and it was raw and untamed. It was something she had never experienced.

"I'm sorry about that." Carter wished Michael and Kimberly would take it upstairs. "They forget people are around."

"I don't mind." She took a sip of her wine. "It's nice to see married people express passion for each other."

"So you would have done something like that in public if you had married Alex?" he asked.

Avery turned to him, speaking before thinking better not to play his game. "I *am* marrying Alex."

Carter leaned against the back of the chair. "I don't know. I just don't see it happening."

"Stop it, Carter."

"And I'm sure if it did, you two would be nothing like Michael and Kimberly there."

He didn't have time to react before she dumped the rest of her wine on him, splashing his face and soaking his white linen shirt.

He sat up straight, laughing out loud. "I was just kidding, Avery."

"So was I," she said. "Isn't it more fun when we both do it?"

"Fine." He wiped himself down. "Game over. What do you want to talk about?"

Avery smiled, grateful for any little victory she got in life these days. "What about this house. Where is your room?"

"I don't live here."

"I know you don't live here, but you had a room here, didn't you?"

He looked up at the back of the massive home, pointing to the right. "I think it's somewhere up there toward the front."

"You don't know where your room is? Didn't you grow up here?"

He was thinking of changing his shirt. The night was too damp to dry it, but he didn't want to leave her right now. "No, I didn't as a matter of fact. I grew up in a little middle-class home in your neck of the woods."

"Baldwin Hills?"

"I was a junior in high school when we moved into this house. I didn't live here because I was in New York at prep school."

"Your parents sent you all the way to the East Coast?" Avery couldn't imagine being that young so far away from her family. "It must have been lonely."

He shrugged. "It was fine. My parents didn't think any of the West Coast schools compared to New York and D.C."

"So you were only here for the summer?"

"Not really. My parents have a house on the Vineyard. We used to spend the whole summer there. My mother's family owns the house, actually, but we don't really go anymore. Too inconvenient and my father would never stay because of the company. My mom hates to be away from him for long. I was home for the holidays, though."

Avery felt for him. His voice was reticent and held regret. She took all her childhood summers and comfy nights at home with her family for granted. She wouldn't have traded it for the best education in the world.

"So you don't really know this house, do you?"

"I went to college and then law school in Boston. I went traveling across Europe with friends during those summers. In law school, there was this girl . . ."

Avery laughed at his tentative tone. "All good stories start with that phrase."

"I thought I was in love."

"You weren't?"

Carter looked at her, thinking back. "No, I was in love. We got an apartment and I stayed in Boston. After that, I worked in New York and we lived together for a few years."

"What happened to her?" Avery was more interested in the answer to that than she had a right to be.

"That we don't need to go into," he said. "When I came back to L.A., I got my own place."

"You must have missed your family so much."

"Can you keep a secret?" he asked, leaning forward. "I stayed away because my father and I fight all the time. When I came home, it was because I missed my brother. We were all each other had in prep school. He went to college in New York while I was in Boston, so we're close."

"What about the rest of your family?"

"I missed Leigh, and my mother, too, but I never really got close to Leigh until I was back for good. I love her to death now, though."

"What about your dad—"

"I don't want to talk about my father."

Avery was struck by the serious expression he held and it made her want to know everything about his relationship with Steven. "What about Haley?"

"I don't really know her." He noted the look of shock she quickly tried to conceal. Someone like Avery couldn't imagine family members being anything but deathly close. "I love her. She's my baby sister, but she was a baby when I left and I never really got to know her that well. She's a little hard to get close to, but that's my fault. I'm her big brother and we should be close."

The regretful look on his face reached deep inside of Avery. She wanted to tell him it wasn't too late, but she couldn't do that. It was too intimate and none of her business.

Carter felt like a fool. He'd intended to be this suave charismatic bachelor that she couldn't resist, but that was all gone now. He had given himself up and she probably pitied him. Good luck getting her in bed now.

He stood up, looking down at her. "Will you be okay for a second? I need to go change my shirt."

"I'm uh . . . I'm sorry about that." She suddenly regretted every bad thing she had said or done to him.

"I deserved it. I'll be back."

Avery made her way to the bar to pour another glass of wine. It was probably dangerous, but she needed something after that. She was in trouble with a man she thought was the devil himself.

"Hello, Avery."

Dressed in raggedy jean shorts and a pink tank top, Haley stood in front of Avery looking at her like she wanted to kick her in the face. Avery held her hand out to her, but Haley didn't budge so she let it fall to her side.

"So what is Sean doing tonight?" Haley had already completed her survey of the woman. It only took a few seconds. She was softball and despite the glass of wine she threw on Carter, Haley figured the woman probably had no backbone.

"I'm not sure," she stated. "I haven't seen him today. He's really busy on your case."

"I sincerely doubt that," Haley said. "Considering he's

spending all his time taking care of you. You don't seem like the injured little bird he seems to think you are. Maybe you could tell him you don't need him to baby you and he might remember other people exist."

Avery was speechless. This woman couldn't be a day over twenty-one and she was fierce. She held a boat load of anger and Avery wasn't interested in going up against it even though she was curious to know why she seemed so interested in Sean's time.

Nothing to say, Haley thought. That was easy. Moving on. "You've certainly got my brother wrapped around your little finger."

"You're mistaken. I—"

"I'm never mistaken," Haley spat back. "I was watching the two of you."

Never mistaken? So sleeping with a married congressman was the right choice? That's what Avery wanted to say, but unlike Haley, she had manners. "There is nothing going on between me and Carter."

"You can say that now all you want, but if he wants you, he'll get you. No woman has ever turned him down and you certainly don't have the guts to do it. You're the emotional type and you'll fall for him, but you won't last six months before my family breaks you down. Then he'll toss you aside."

Haley paused to take in the bewildered look on Avery's face. This woman had played the victim enough. It was time everyone returned their attention to the real story, her and the hell her life was becoming. Especially Sean. There was no way she was going to get him to worship her the way he should if his big sister played the emotional edge.

"So glad you could come." She pasted on a saccharine smile before turning and walking away.

*   *   *

Avery wasn't as quick as she would like to be during dinner. Janet was loading her with questions that were all flattering and light, but she was distracted by the daggers Haley and Michael were sending her way. Leigh didn't seem to be aware that she or anyone else existed and Steven ignored her completely.

Then there was Kimberly, who was the only person at the table with a genuine smile. Avery tried not to stare at her, but it was hard. Kimberly was probably one of the most beautiful women she had ever seen.

"Where is your friend this evening?" Janet was running out of conversation topics. She was a master at hosting; making everyone feel comfortable was her gift. It wasn't working well tonight.

"My friend?" Avery asked.

"She means Alex." Carter wished his mother hadn't brought the man up.

"Oh, yes." Friend? What did that mean? "He had to work tonight. He's very busy."

"Doing what?" Michael ignored the pinch Kimberly gave his thigh as well as Carter's indignant stare.

"He's a salesman, right?" Janet asked.

"I know what he does." Michael resented this woman being treated like a visiting queen while he was getting railed daily by his father because of her. "I was just wondering because a couple of years ago, he won best salesman, didn't he?"

"That's right," Avery answered cautiously. Be ready for this one. "He actually won it twice, but you know that because you know everything about me after all your snooping."

"It's called business research," Michael said. "I was just curious, because he used to be so good. From what I hear now, he couldn't sell whiskey to an Indian."

There were several gasps around the table and some forks scraping the plates.

"Quit it." Carter's lips pressed together as his brows narrowed in, matching his brother's stare.

"Haley." Steven frowned at his daughter who hadn't stopped laughing. "That's enough."

Haley glared at him before returning to her food. "I thought it was funny."

"It's not funny," Leigh said. "It's racist."

"It's just a saying," Michael said.

"I don't care what it is," Janet lectured. "I don't want to hear it at my dinner table. I'm sorry, Avery."

Avery nodded, pretending as if her food was more interesting than Michael.

Carter leaned in and apologized, still staring at Michael who stared back.

"What's the matter?" Michael asked, finally turning away from Carter. "Am I not being appropriate? Mom, I sincerely doubt you can call me on that when you're practically pimping your daughter."

"What?" Janet gasped.

Kimberly had to put her napkin over her mouth to hide her laughing. Nothing amused her more than Janet being called out.

"I know what you're doing with Leigh," he said. "Pimping her off to Leo Bridges so she'll hang out with you more."

Steven slammed his fist on the table, making everyone jolt a bit. "Don't you ever talk to your mother like that."

Janet was doing what was best; she had to keep telling herself that. "It's okay, Steven."

"It's disrespectful and Leigh would never allow herself to be treated that way anyway." He looked at Haley. "If you don't stop laughing, Haley, I swear—"

"You swear what?" She tossed her napkin across the table and it landed right on Avery's plate. "If Leigh laughed, you wouldn't mind, would you?"

"Leigh wouldn't laugh at something like that," he replied.

"Of course she wouldn't." Haley pushed away from the table, standing up.

She knew this was all about her affair with Jack. Ever since that had come out the man barely spoke to her, even though her life had been threatened and she was crying out for his attention. He was ashamed of her and she wasn't going to let it go by anymore.

"Leigh is so perfect!" She shouted loud enough to make one of the bodyguards enter. "She would never let herself be treated like that. Not like your other daughter, the ho. The ho who's been stuck in this damn house forever and no one seems to give a shit!"

"Haley!" Steven had had enough.

Janet swallowed hard, looking at Avery whose eyes were as wide as her open mouth. She had intended for Avery to see a civilized, refined family that would never do anything to hurt anyone. Instead this was turning into an episode of the *Jerry Springer Show*.

"Sit down," Steven asserted as calmly as he could. "Right now."

"The hell with that." Haley kicked her chair out of the way before storming out of the dining room. She had successfully ruined the evening for everyone and that would hold her until she thought of something else.

Avery looked at Carter who simply smiled an I-warned-you smile.

"Avery." Janet could barely speak she was so embarrassed. "I am so sorry."

Avery smiled nervously, trying to take everything in without showing it on her face. She remembered the hell there was to pay for even saying shut up at the dinner table. "It's okay . . . It's not . . ."

"Isn't anybody going to go after her?" Leigh asked, pushing away from the table.

"There's been a lot of stress," Janet continued. "I'm sorry for Haley and Michael."

"Don't apologize for me," Michael said. "I meant everything I said."

"Shut up," Carter warned. It would be his last warning.

"It's okay, Carter." Avery knew if she let someone else stick up for her, she didn't have a chance. "Nothing Michael says bothers me. It never has." She leaned in, seeing the anger rise in his eyes. "Because honestly, his skills pale in comparison to yours."

Carter leaned back in his chair, smiling. She had told him she could handle herself. She didn't need him at all.

"Just back off," Michael told Carter as the two of them entered the great room. Carter could warn him all he wanted to. He was on a roll now. "I know what I'm doing."

"Keep it up and I'm gonna beat the crap out of you."

"You wish."

When they reached the women, Kimberly was talking Avery into lunch at the country club and Carter didn't know what to think of that. He loved Kimberly because she was his sister-in-law, but she was on Michael's side with everything. It was curious she would be so nice to her after Avery had embarrassed her husband.

Avery watched as Michael sat on the sofa behind Kimberly, pulling her onto his lap like she was a little child. He kissed her passionately, completely ignoring Avery's presence. Honestly, she wanted to get out of there, but Kimberly was making it difficult.

"So you survived." Carter leaned over the sofa. She still looked a little shell shocked, but was managing a smile. "I'm sure you want to leave now."

Thank you, Avery screamed inside. "That would be okay, I guess."

"She's having fun with me." Kimberly nudged Michael

away as he bit at her shoulder. "You're over all of that mess at dinner, aren't you?"

"I'm sure it was just the stress that everyone has been under," Avery said.

"No," Kimberly said. "It's pretty much like that all the time."

"You mean Haley does that regularly?" she asked.

"What business is that of yours?" Michael asked.

Avery shrugged. "She just seemed very upset."

"Really?" Michael asked, laughing. "Wow, that's very intuitive of you. You must have graduated top of your class."

Carter stood up, crossing his arms over his chest. "Michael."

"I know what you meant," Kimberly replied. "You meant beyond what was obvious. She just really wants more attention, but there's a lot going on."

"Thank you," Avery answered. "That is what I meant."

Steven was standing in the archway to the great room, watching the interaction. If things got bad and Avery decided to take legal action, Steven wondered if he could count on Carter to be on the right side.

"Boys." He stepped into the room. "I need to talk to you for a few minutes. It's business. Get into my office." He turned away, but quickly turned back. His eyes set on Avery. "Good night, Ms. Jackson." He didn't wait around for her to respond.

"They'll be in there forever," Kimberly said after they were gone.

"Then I should probably be leaving." Avery stood up. All she needed was to say thank you to Janet and get out of there. Maybe a letter would do.

"Not yet." Kimberly stood up, grabbing her hand. She knew what Michael told her to do, but she actually liked the woman. "I want you to meet my boys. They're upstairs."

* * *

Avery was admiring Kimberly's unreal closet when she thought she heard yelling. Daniel was pulling at her leg, deciding that she was his girlfriend after having met her only ten minutes ago while Kimberly was struggling with a tantrum-throwing Evan who didn't want to get ready for bed. Avery didn't consider herself a materialistic woman, but as she looked at the Dolce & Gabbana, Versace, St. John, Burberry, and Armani that flooded the closet, she wanted to burn her own Target collection.

"Did you hear something?" Kimberly asked.

This got Daniel's attention and the second his screaming stopped, the yelling became much clearer. It was Steven.

Kimberly stood up. "Boys, stay here and I mean it."

Avery followed Kimberly down the hallway, knowing she probably didn't want to find out what the yelling was about. She had an eerie feeling it was about her, and when they reached the top of the stairs, that feeling sank into her stomach.

"You can't do this," Janet yelled as Chief Jackson placed the cuffs on Carter.

"He's under arrest, ma'am." Charlie knew this was going to be hard, which was why he chose to come instead of sending an officer or detective like usual. "I have to take him in."

"You're gonna be sorry for this!" Steven was pacing in front of them. Michael tried to still him, but he pushed away. The sight of his son being arrested for attempted murder wasn't anything he ever expected to see and not anything he would let pass.

Janet ran to Carter. "We're coming with you. We'll get you out of there tonight."

Drawing in a slow steady smile, Carter tried to calm her. She seemed like she was ready to break down. "It's okay, Mom. It's nothing. Don't worry."

"This is personal!" Steven yelled. "This is about your daughter and you don't care about the evidence. Charlie, when I'm done with you, you won't even be able to get a job as a mall security guard."

Avery held onto the banister, not sure her legs could hold her.

Carter intended to turn to his father to tell him to shut up, but his eyes caught halfway at the figure on the top of the stairs. Avery was looking down at him with her mouth opened wide. He couldn't look away from her even though he was humiliated.

Everyone followed Carter's eyes and soon all were staring up at Avery.

Charlie's grip on Carter loosened as he blinked, thinking he was seeing things. "Avery?"

Avery slowly made her way down the stairs, looking from her father to Carter. She glanced briefly at Steven and Michael and for a second she wasn't sure she would get out of this house alive. She tried to smile, but her lips made a line then fell.

"Daddy, what are you doing here?"

"What am I doing here?" He was amazed at the sight of her.

Explaining would make no difference.

"Can we get this over with?" Carter asked.

"You're going to regret this, Chief," Steven said, calmer now.

"What's going on?" Haley asked, rushing down the stairs. "Carter's getting arrested?"

Avery felt ashamed by the way her father was looking at her. He turned away, reclaiming his grip on Carter. She hadn't told her parents about this, because she knew they wouldn't approve. Now she felt like a liar.

Steven turned to Michael. "Call Josh Haffley. Have him meet us at the station."

"I have my own lawyer, Dad." Carter just wanted to get out of there.

Janet threw her hands in the air. She needed her Valium. "I can't believe this. You can't possibly have enough evidence to . . ."

"We found explosive materials in the garbage dump outside the building where Carter works. The garbage has been tossed, but traces are still there. It's solid evidence."

Steven didn't even blink. "It's bullshit."

Carter looked at Avery. "It's Craig."

She nodded because she believed him. Carter might be many things, but he wasn't stupid. It had Craig written all over it.

"Let's go." As Charlie led Carter out, he didn't want to look at Avery. He didn't know what to say to her, but there would be a conversation. It was unacceptable for her to be here.

"We have to go," Janet said. "First I have to get my—"

"Don't, Janet." Steven couldn't have her down at this moment. "I mean it. I need you here. Let me find Michael and we'll go."

Avery felt a chill run through her at the look Steven gave her as he walked past.

"Well, Avery." Haley waited for her to turn around and look at her. "You just seem to be the gift that keeps on giving."

"I . . . I"

"Ignore her." Janet wiped her own tears before taking Avery by the shoulders. "This isn't your fault, dear. Everyone is just upset. You should go home now. We have to go with Carter."

As she closed the door behind Avery, Janet rushed into the kitchen to grab her stash of Valium. No matter what Steven said, she wouldn't make it another hour without those pills. Maybe this was her fault. She kept saying things couldn't get worse and they just kept getting worse.

Avery drove as far as a block away before she pulled over. She sat in her car for almost an hour in a daze. What in the world had just happened?

CHAPTER 10

Carter indulged his mother as long as he could, but enough hugging was enough. "I'm fine, Mom. I was in jail overnight, not ten years."

Janet touched his cheek, squeezed his arms. He could hide it all he wanted to, but she knew her children. He was rattled.

"Stop it, please." He pushed away from her.

Carter emptied the envelope of his belongings. His wallet with a couple hundred in cash, titanium credit cards and a twenty thousand dollar watch. "It's View Park, Mom. Not L.A. I've been in jail before."

"Overnight in a campus jail for being drunk in public doesn't compare to an attempted murder charge."

"There aren't any charges yet," he reminded her. "Thanks for bailing me out."

She held on to his arm as they headed out. "Your father called everyone he could think of, even the district attorney. He's out of control."

"Where is Dad?" Carter was strangely comforted by the news.

"He's outside." Janet stopped. "First, I want to tell you something."

"Can we get out of here first?"

"I know what Steven puts you through," she said, "but you know he loves you."

He nodded, but he wasn't so sure. "I know he's upset with me. He blames me for all of this."

"He blames himself. You should have heard him last night, Carter. He's so upset about this. He regrets ever asking you to do this. He regrets all the things he makes you and Michael do to please him. He's afraid his need to push you is going to end up costing you everything."

Carter didn't have a response. It would be too much to ask for his hard-ass father to say anything like this to him.

"I'm telling you he's in pain over this. He was the most emotional I've seen him in years last night." She wanted to add that the only time she ever saw Steven cry was when Carter was born, but she had to save that truth for the edge of war. "He gives you a hard time because you're the only man on this earth who can stand up to him and get your way. You challenge him more than anyone and you've been doing it for thirty years."

Carter was feeling her love, believing her words and feeling ashamed, but he couldn't let it show. His father wouldn't respect that. "Have you heard from Avery?"

"No, but I'm going to call her to apologize again and I'll put in a good word for you."

"It's going to take more than that, Mom." He held the door open for her.

"From the way she looked when Chief Jackson took you away," she said, "I don't think so."

Carter was stopped in his tracks by what he saw outside the station. A gaggle of reporters were listening intently to his father who was speaking with Josh Haffley at his side. Carter believed that somewhere deep down inside, his father loved him, but he knew that his father loved Chase Beauty more and that was what he was saving now. That was why Carter held so much resentment for it.

"Are you ready?" Janet asked.

"Of course I am." Carter held his head up and headed with powerful strides to his father. The reporters darted for him, swarming him with questions and microphones. This was what being a Chase was all about. Your business was everybody's business. It was okay. He could handle it.

Sean drove into the strip mall in front of the Carlson Travel Agency. He had been there later the day he followed Armand, but the store was closed. When he followed up later, he was told the only person who had been in the office that day wouldn't be back until Saturday. He did a background check on Marrissa Donnelly before returning and was eager to meet her because, based on what he knew, there was very little reason for a Scottish immigrant grandmother in her fifties with not even a parking ticket, to know Armand.

Standing at the door to the agency, he saw her sitting at her desk on the phone. He hated having to tell himself to focus, but he did. He was thinking of Haley and what was going on in her mind after Carter's arrest for the attempted murder of his sister. He wanted to take a club to the brother of the woman he wanted to take to bed. The sick thing was that he assumed she didn't give a damn either way and he was counting on that.

He had never before had to remind himself the case was his first priority. The pressure Steven was putting on the department was taking its toll on everyone and that all came down on him. Not to mention Steven who had gone against all warnings to use his unlimited resources to get all of Rudio's businesses, including the club, closed down. The media was combing over Rudio with a fine-tooth comb and at least four private investigators on Steven's payroll were wearing Rudio's nerves down. It was only going to lead to disaster and Sean had a bad feeling Haley was going to pay the price.

"Marissa Donnelly?" Sean flashed his badge. She said something he couldn't understand, but followed it with a welcoming smile.

"Can I help you?"

"Do you know a man by the name of Armand Castaneta?"

"No, I don't. Is he a customer?"

He observed her reaction to Armand's picture. She didn't even blink. She had no idea who this guy was. "Can you check the walk-in customers you had on Monday? You might remember him then."

"This past Monday?" she asked.

He nodded, noticing her expression change. She was suddenly nervous. "So you do remember him?"

"I wasn't here Monday," she whispered.

"Yes, you were. Your manager said you were the only person in the office Monday until two in the afternoon."

"That's what she thinks." She looked around again before gesturing for him to come closer, but he didn't. "Okay, look. I was supposed to be here Monday, but I couldn't."

She stood up, coming around her desk to where she was only a few inches from Sean. "I had a date. You see, www.scottishsingles. com. Ever heard of it?"

Sean just looked at her.

"Of course not," she said. "Well, it's true. I wasn't here."

"Then who was?"

"I had one of the girls take my place, but we didn't tell 'cause I've been taking a lot of time recently."

Sean believed her; for now at least. "Can I have her name?"

The name she gave him almost knocked him over.

* * *

"I want to play solitaire," Haley stated as Carly laid the cards out on her bed.

"You can't play solitaire with two people," Carly snapped.

"You can watch me." Haley pushed her cards away and Carly cursed at her. "What's your problem?"

"You're acting like a baby." Carly didn't look up while gathering the cards. "You wanted to play cards. I wanted to watch videos."

"I didn't ask you to come over here, Carly."

Carly looked at her, her eyes red and tired. "You ask me to come over all the time, Haley."

"Not today I didn't. You called me, remember?"

"Fine, play your solitaire." Carly tossed the entire deck at her and reached for the remote.

Haley knew Carly could be a bitch sometimes, but she was confused. When she called earlier that day, she sounded like she was crying. Haley invited her over. She was dying inside that house and wanted anything to get her mind off Sean.

"You know what's going on with my brother, Carly. I'm stressed out, okay? I wish you'd be a little more understanding."

"Nothing is gonna happen to your brother." Carly's voice was edged with anger. "Nothing ever happens to anyone in your family."

"Still," Haley said.

"You don't know what it's like to suffer, Haley. You never have." Carly turned away, wiping tears from her eyes.

Haley's mouth dropped open as her arms opened wide. "Hello! Someone tried to kill me! I'm stuck in this prison for the rest of my life because nothing is ever gonna happen to him. I'm falling for a man who probably makes two hundred dollars a week and I've had to wash my own hair for the past month!"

Carly rolled her eyes. "You've never had your father walk out on you and your mother and leave you desolate."

"I wish he would get the hell out of here." Her father hadn't bothered to say anything except to warn her if she ever saw Sean Jackson again, he would send her to relatives in Paris.

"Yeah, only he would leave you with a million dollars."

"My mother would get way more than a million dollars," Haley said. "Don't blame me because your mother was too stupid to get a good lawyer. Besides, she married that mattress guy and got millions out of him."

"But what about my life in between?" Carly asked.

"What do you care now?" The more appropriate question was *what do I care at all?*

"Mom went manic when Dad left us." Carly was speaking in between choked tears now. "I had to take care of her and my little brother, Alex."

"My mom says that kind of stuff builds character. You should be grateful."

Carly's eyes squinted to slits as she looked at Haley. "You don't understand. I would do anything for Alex. Anything."

Haley was at a loss. "Calm down. Besides, Carter doesn't need me to help him with anything."

"If anything happened to Alex, I would . . ." Carly fell flat on her face on the bed, sobbing uncontrollably.

Haley stared at her for a few minutes, wishing to God she would stop. When it was clear she wasn't going to, she reached over and patted her back. "Look, Carly, I don't have any weed, but I have a nice bottle of gin in my drawer. I'll make you some."

"I can't do it." She pushed away and jumped up from the bed.

Carly was quickly turning into a train wreck and it was scaring Haley enough to ignore her ringing cell phone. If this woman had a nervous breakdown in her room, her parents wouldn't let anyone come over again.

"I can't!" Carly grabbed her purse, grasping it tight to her stomach. "I'm so sorry, Haley. I . . . I didn't want to."

Haley jumped ten feet high when her bedroom door burst open and two security guards rushed in, guns drawn. They were yelling for Carly to hit the ground and she did, tossing her purse away.

"What's the matter with you?" Haley screamed at them. "She's my friend. She's always over here. Stop it!"

One of the guards lifted a wire from under his collar to his mouth and yelled. "Subject under control."

"I'm sorry, Haley," Carly said, flat on the ground. "I didn't want to."

Haley was grabbed by the arm by another guard who rushed in the room. She fought the man as he attempted to drag her away. "Stop it! You're all crazy."

"She's not your friend," the guard argued. "She's connected to the man trying to kill you."

Time seemed to come to a halt as Haley called Carly's name over and over again before she finally looked up.

"He threatened to kill Alex," she exclaimed. "I'm sorry, Haley. It's . . . Alex is everything to me."

On pure adrenaline, Haley dragged the guard halfway across the room as she rushed Carly, hoping to beat the life out of her, but the guard regained control and pulled her back. As she was being dragged out of the room, Haley was threatening to kill Carly, her brother and anyone else she could get her hands on.

Alicia stood next to Leigh, surveying the finished paint job at Hope Clinic. "It looks even better than the last time."

It did look better, Leigh thought. There was something about this second time around that made it feel more victorious, more deserved. With everything that was going on in her life, every little bit of happiness meant so much more.

The doorbell rang and Alicia and Leigh looked at each other. The complicated new security system was stressing them out. IDs and security guards made it resemble a government facility more than a neighborhood clinic. They both rushed to the door and looked at the monitor. Richard was staring up at the camera, waving his hand.

Alicia punched in the code that opened the door.

"The sign is up," Richard said as he entered.

Eager to see it, Leigh started after Alicia, but Richard closed the door in front of her. She looked at him and the look on his face told her he wasn't interested in a few seconds alone to mess around.

"I want to see it," she said.

"You're not going anywhere until you talk to me."

"Richard, honestly. Let's not get into this today. You know what happened to my brother."

"Sorry, but I'm not waiting any longer. You're being so damn cold to me. You just want me to look the other way, but that's not how this is going to go."

"Since when did you start calling the shots?" she asked, feeling a little cornered.

"Since right now," he fumed. "You've been calling the shots from the beginning and now I'm out in the cold. I'm not taking it anymore. You're telling me why you're lying to me now."

"I'm not lying to you!"

"When I called you Wednesday you said your mother wasn't there, but I heard her voice in the background. You said it was Maya, but that voice didn't have her accent."

Leigh looked down and sighed, flattening her palms against her thighs. "God, Richard. I'm sorry. I'm so sorry."

"I know what this is about. You're ashamed of me."

Leigh gasped.

"I know everything about what you come from. I'm just a poor kid from Chicago trying to make it as a doctor and that's not like the men you're used to taking home."

Leigh reached out to him, but he backed away. She could see the hurt in his eyes and she hated herself at that moment.

He nodded tensely at her, stuffing his hands in his pockets. "I've become obsessed with finding out everything I can about your family and the types of men you dated, hoping that there was some way I could be more like what you wanted, but I can't do that. I am who I am and I'm not going to be ashamed of it."

She reached for his hands, lacing her fingers around his. She pulled him to her, placing one hand on her chest. "Richard, whatever it is you think I wanted, you're wrong. I have never, ever met a man like you and you're not just good enough, you're too good. The way you make me feel; strong, powerful, soft and feminine at the same time. I love you. I'm not ashamed of you. I'm ashamed of myself. That's what this is all about."

Leigh tried to confess everything to him, but she wasn't sure she could completely explain her reasons. She couldn't explain her mother's possessive behavior or her compelling need to please that woman even if it meant making herself unhappy.

"What have you done with this guy?" he asked.

"Nothing, I swear. It's just a few dates and I'll tell Mom it's not working out. She'll leave me alone then."

"Why don't you just tell her now? About him, about me."

"I've explained that to you. My mother wants her way and you'll be a glitch in that. That's not how I want to introduce you to her. She'll resent you for it."

"This guy is going to think you're . . ."

"It doesn't matter what he thinks." She placed her

hand on his cheek, but she could feel he wasn't warming to her. "I said I love you and that's all I care about."

He backed away, shaking his head. "It's too much for her to ask of you and for you to ask of me. I'm supposed to what, just stay home and watch the game while you go out with this guy?"

Leigh knew that men thought on different planes than women. He couldn't see past the idea of Leo and what that did to his ego. "This changes nothing between us, Richard."

"It's already changing everything between us. Lies, cover-up, hiding the truth. I never thought you would do something like that, Leigh. I thought you were better than that."

Leigh felt the tears welling in her throat. "I'm doing what I have to do for this clinic. For you, me, Alicia and all of those people depending on us. We need my mother!"

"I need you!"

"Richard, please."

"No," he stated. "I know what your intentions are, but it's wrong. It's wrong to us and it's wrong to this guy. I want you to stop seeing him and tell your mother the truth. I can deal with what she thinks of me. I can't deal with my pride being slapped around while you pretend like I don't exist."

"Richard!"

Alicia jumped aside just in time to avoid being knocked over by Richard on his way out. "What's wrong with you two?"

"It's all blowing up in my face," Leigh said, reaching for her ringing cell phone. "I'm going to lose him."

"Is it anything a good pint of rum raisin couldn't solve?" Alicia asked, smiling nervously.

"More like a rum straight up." Leigh answered her phone, assuming it was a reminder from her mother of their luncheon at the country club. "What's up, Mom?"

"It's Haley," Janet said. "Just come home."

* * *

The kitchen had always been a refuge for Avery. Growing up, she would sit at the table coloring while her mother prepared dinner. The family always gathered in the kitchen before dinner and the room held warmth and reflection for her. Without meaning to, it made her think of Carter and all the nights he came home to a dorm room with a cafeteria instead of a family kitchen and she felt for him.

Putting the dishes away after a silent, animosity-filled lunch with Alex, Avery tried to get back to her own, happier memories. All she could think of now was dinner at the Chase mansion. Janet's warmth and Steven's coldness; Leigh's distance and an obvious sadness that no one seemed to notice; Haley's jarring rudeness and Michael's insults. What stayed with her the most was Carter by the pool, talking about his detachment from his family. It made her reflect on all the things she thought about him before, all the names she'd called him, and she regretted it all. She'd tried to make it simple by labeling him cruel and rude, but Carter wasn't simple at all and neither were any of his motives or actions.

She couldn't excuse either his actions or her feelings for him, but she couldn't ignore them, either. It was all too dramatic for her, a woman used to a simple and mostly predictable life. Whatever man Carter really was, it was he and his family who'd brought this all on. Craig had no reason to blow her store up. He was getting what he wanted until Carter threatened to take it away. Still, she found herself fighting the urge to call him even though she had no idea what she would say.

"Avery!" Alex yelled from the living room in between laughs. "Come in here, you gotta see this."

What she saw was a picture of Carter standing outside the police station talking to reporters.

"I'm lovin' this," Alex said. "He's getting what he deserves and you know it's killing him."

The sight of Carter looking tired and haggard bore into Avery. She hadn't expected to hurt so much at the sight of his suffering. She only hoped the reason she didn't believe he blew up her shop was for more than just that she wanted to.

The screen switched to the reporter. "Those were the only words we've heard from the Chase camp, but there are still too many questions to count. No charges have been filed yet, which says the district attorney is still investigating, but it's safe to say a Chase wouldn't have been arrested without some evidence."

"That's for damn sure," Alex added.

"Carter Chase," the reporter continued, "whose very public assault on former congressman Jack Flay didn't even make a blip on the department's screen, has a lot at stake this time: his reputation as a leading lawyer; his firm; his license to practice; and of course, his freedom. When asked how this investigation will effect the investigation into the recent attempt on his sister Haley Chase's life, Chief Jackson had no comment."

Avery couldn't take it anymore. When she was in the kitchen again, she placed her hand on the phone, trying to reach inside her heart to know the right thing to do. When the phone actually rang, she jumped back a few feet. Picking it up, she accepted the sign that was given her. Whatever direction she was going, this call had to be a clue.

It was Aaron Hanson, the loan officer from the most recent bank she had applied to for a loan to keep her from drowning. From the tone of his voice, she got the feeling he was about to break what was left of her heart.

"I'm sorry, Ms. Jackson, but the financing isn't going to come through for your shop. Unfortunately, there's nothing we can do for you. I can give you the names of some other banks that might . . ."

". . . charge me twenty percent interest. I don't think so. Thanks, Mr. Hanson, but I'll take it from here."

Hanging up, Avery leaned against the counter, refusing to cry. This was it; her sign. For some reason God didn't want her to keep Essentials. As upset as that made her, she was willing to accept it. After all that had happened and all she had done, there was no way she could win this one and she had to believe she wasn't meant to. Whatever plan He had for her, it was to start after Essentials would end.

She picked up the phone, taking a deep breath before dialing. It was ironic in a way. She finally had a reason to call Carter.

"What are you talking about?" Sean asked the security guard standing outside the Chase mansion. "I'm the detective on the case!"

"I'm sorry, sir." He blocked the door as Sean tried to pass him. "We have specific orders not to let you in the house."

"You can't be serious," Sean said. "Now, step aside. I'm a police officer, man. I'm not asking you."

"You don't have a warrant," he answered back.

Sean took out his gun. "I have this. Is this good enough for you?"

"I have one of those, too," the guard smirked.

"Well, I'm ready to use mine," Sean added, watching the smirk slip away from his face. "So unless you are too, I suggest you step aside."

Inside the house, Sean found it eerily quiet. There weren't any guards in sight and barely a sound. It felt empty. He had a bad feeling that something had gone wrong. It had been some time since he'd called the security detail to detain Carly and met them at the police station to interrogate her. He'd wanted to see Haley first, but he had to do his job. Since the interrogation, he hadn't been able to reach her at all.

After rushing up the widening staircase, he turned straight for Haley's room. There was the chair, but no guard outside. Getting closer, Sean heard voices and with one hand on his gun in his holster, he opened the door. Steven and Janet turned slightly to see before completely turning to face him.

"Where is she?" he asked, too anxious for small talk.

"How did you get in here?" Janet asked. "I specifically told them not to let you in."

"Where is she?" Sean asked again.

"It doesn't matter to you," Janet said. "Not anymore."

Steven placed a hand on Janet's tightening shoulder. As much as he wanted to punish anyone related to Chief Jackson, Sean had saved Haley's life, so for Steven, this was regretful but necessary. "Detective, I want to thank you for what you've done for—"

Sean couldn't take this anymore. "Tell me where she is, please."

"I'm having you taken off this case."

"You can't do that."

"He has," Janet answered back. "It's a conflict of interest."

Sean knew Carter's arrest would bring problems, but he couldn't believe it would have to come to this. "This is my case. I'm working it and I'm making progress."

"You have," Steven affirmed. "I'm sorry, Sean. Our lawyer is already talking to the lieutenant and the DA. After this situation with Carter, it's just not right."

Sean knew it probably wasn't right, but that wasn't what mattered. "I'm a professional only focused on solving a crime that has nothing to do with Carter."

"She's his sister," Janet said. "I don't know how your family works, but when something happens to one of us, it's happening to all of us. There's no way you can be trusted to put your all into finding justice for the woman whose brother you think tried to kill your sister."

"You can't say it doesn't affect you," Steven said. "You're human."

Sean could only shake his head. "I'm so close."

"In more ways than one," Janet offered.

Steven observed the exchange of looks between Sean and his wife. "What's going on here?"

Sean didn't want it to come out this way, but that was exactly why Janet was going to make sure it did.

"He's been carrying on with Haley," she maintained. "I caught them having sex in the library just the other day."

Steven's lips pressed together, his brow pulled into an affronted frown. "Do you understand what kind of a delicate state she's in right now?"

Sean had to believe this man was talking about a different person than Haley. She was stronger than they were giving her credit for. "Sir, I care about your daughter very much, but we weren't having sex."

Janet huffed. "I have four children. I think I know what sex looks like."

"Stop it," Steven said. "This is something we'll deal with later. Including, Janet, how long you've known this without telling me."

All the time, she was left alone to deal with their children while he went off and made millions, but now he was going to question her?

"Just let me talk to her," Sean pleaded. "Then I'll leave."

"She's not here," Steven said. "I've sent her somewhere safer."

"I understand. Where?"

"You can't talk to her." Steven noticed the desperation in the young man's eyes. How had he missed this? "No one can see her. Not even Janet or I can see her and since you're not on the case anymore, neither can you."

Sean couldn't believe this and he wasn't going to accept it. He was trying to keep his wits about him, but the two of them together was like a fortress. "I think you're making a mistake, sir, asking me off this case. We're too close to change leadership now."

"Tell that to your father," Steven said.

After he got back in the car, Sean leaned back in his seat and gripped his steering wheel. He had to think of how to handle this with his father, the lieutenant and the D.A. He couldn't stand the thought of being taken off this case, but the situation with Carter made it seem impossible for him not to. Why had his father insisted on being the one to arrest Carter?

Either way, Sean didn't believe he stood much of a chance of staying on this case, but that wasn't going to stop him. He was going to get Rudio one way or another and he was going to find Haley. With all her stubborn pride, she had to need him right now. He certainly knew he needed her.

It was almost November in Los Angeles, and Avery felt a little nip at her nose as she sat on the park bench. It reminded her of the Christmas she spent in New York with her cousin. She was sweet sixteen and had never seen or touched snow in her entire life. She loved it. Then it kept falling, and falling and falling. Thirteen inches later, she was stuck in the small Harlem apartment, begging to go back to her beautiful California.

She knew Carter was somewhere near thirty, so being ten years earlier, he would have been in Boston at the time. She imagined him traveling to New York to visit Michael at college and passing her on the street. She imagined him being one of those guys she'd smiled at and wished she had the nerve to stop and talk to. She thought of all the choices people made every day and what course that placed their lives on.

One year ago, Alex's proposal had meant everything to her. She loved him and wanted making him happy to be all that mattered. What choices had she made in the past year to change that? Had it really changed, or was she just working through the next stage with him?

Hearing Carter's footsteps snapped Avery out of her trance. She studied the way he walked, wondering if it was a conscious decision to look so in control, so self-assured all the time.

"A smile for me?" he asked, joining her on the bench.

Avery hadn't even been aware she was smiling and it embarrassed her. "Just 'cause it's a great day."

"Any day under seventy degrees I can do without." Carter felt the tease of anticipation as he looked at her. She looked different. She looked happier than usual and it only made him think good things about why she wanted to see him today.

"Coming from church?" she asked, gesturing to his spotless Ralph Lauren outfit.

"No time for church. I'm a busy man."

Too busy for God. She slid away from him. "I don't want to be near when the lightning strikes."

"So you go to church every Sunday?"

"It's the highlight of my week. What about you?"

"You're the highlight of my week," he answered.

Avery watched a couple as they walked by, hand in hand, and was fully aware that Carter had gapped the distance she'd just placed between them. "I'm glad you came."

"I've been wanting to see you, Avery."

She looked at him, seeing the affection in his eyes and

admitting to herself it was what she wanted to see even though she knew it was wrong. "Carter, I asked to see you about Essentials II."

Carter leaned back. She was determined to make this hard on him. "If you want me to believe this is about business then I will."

"I'm with Alex," she said. "I thought you understood that."

"I heard what you said," he answered.

"But did you understand?"

He wasn't going to answer that. "What about Essentials II?"

"I'm selling it to you. If your father still wants the shops. I mean, he'll have to rebuild the first one, but it's all his."

"Avery, I told you I wasn't going to let you lose your shops. If I say something isn't going to happen, then it isn't going to happen."

"It is happening." She wasn't willing to rehash the situation. She was only looking forward. "I only ask that you give me some type of reasonable price. I have some loans to pay off."

"You're willing to walk away?" he asked.

"Carter, this is a business transaction. Don't ask me personal questions."

"You're getting pretty old, aren't you?" he asked. "Memory loss is the first thing to go with old ladies like you."

She tried to stifle a laugh. "You must be under the impression I won't slap you."

"You must be under the impression I wouldn't like that." He held her eyes for a while, feeling the tension build between them. If only she realized that she was his already this could be a lot easier for both of them. "I promised you, didn't I?"

"What are you saying, Carter?"

He reached into the back pocket of his jeans. "I was going to give this to you after you gave me some, but—"

"Will you stop it?" she asked, unable to hold back her laughter.

"A smile and a laugh in one day," he said. "It must be my birthday. I accept that I'm not getting any today, so I'll just give it to you now and go home and take a cold shower."

Avery took the business card. "Who is Reggie Sawyer?"

"Reggie is an old Harvard buddy of mine who just happens to manage the retail loan department at Redding Bank."

"Redding?" Avery was really laughing now. "Are you kidding me? That's a bank for people like . . . you. Millionaires bank there. What can he do for me?"

"He's going to approve a loan for whatever amount you need him to." Carter watched her expression change from disbelief to amazement. He didn't smile. He was serious and he wanted her to know it. He was pounding his chest a bit, but what good were connections if you couldn't use them?

"How can he do this?" Avery asked, feeling so overwhelmed by the opportunity that it didn't even seem real. "Doesn't he have rules to follow?"

"The rules at banks like Redding are different," Carter said. "He'll approve you. Trust me."

Avery bit her lower lip to keep from crying. What was this, a test? She had been praying nonstop and the answers had come to her. She had to stick with the direction they were sending her in.

"Thanks, Carter." She handed him back the card. "I'm sorry, but I can't take it."

"Avery—"

"I appreciate it," she explained. "I really do, but you

don't understand. I'm meant to let Essentials go. This has all happened for a reason. I'm going to do something else with my life. Essentials was a great accomplishment, but it's over."

"You love those shops," he said.

"I always will." She placed her hand over his hand holding the card and closed it. "I know what I'm doing."

Carter knew it would be a waste of time to try to push any further. She had this look about her that he recognized clearly. It was the same look he had a few years ago when he made the decision to start his own law firm instead of what everybody assumed he wanted: Chase Beauty.

"It's not going to be easy," he admonished.

"If it was easy," she said, "what would be the point of doing it?"

Damn, he liked this woman! He needed that strength and purpose in his life. He needed a woman who had the spirit and drive to explore and create like he did.

"I'll have a contract on your desk Monday morning."

"How much exactly?" she asked.

"You know my last offer."

Avery's mouth dropped open. "Carter, you can't. That was for two stores. Essentials is gone now."

"I know what I'm doing. Besides, I'm hoping I'll get a kiss out of it."

"You have to stop this." She fought the smile, but it was useless against his charm.

He looked down at his watch. "Come have lunch with me."

"No." Avery stood up. She was smiling as if it didn't matter much, but inside she knew she better get out of there because she really, really wanted to have lunch with him.

"What about coffee?" he called after her.

She waved her hand at him, not bothering to turn around. He enjoyed the view as she walked away. Carter wasn't a fool. She was falling for him and he knew it. Hard didn't mean impossible. Nothing was impossible.

Leigh relished the quiet of the house right now. The security guards, except for one outside, were all gone and the rest of her family was at church. She was able to spend a quiet Sunday morning in the sun room drinking coffee and thinking of Richard and the clinic. They seemed to be the only two good things in her life right now.

When she showed up at Richard's apartment yesterday, she didn't think he would let her in, but he did. She must have looked how she felt and at this point, Leigh was willing to accept pity. She poured her heart out to him about Haley's most recent close call and he held her, saying nothing. He was the best listener Leigh had ever known.

As much as a pain her sister was to her, she loved Haley and she could only imagine what she was going through now because Haley had been removed from the house and taken somewhere that no one would tell her. It was Richard who wiped the tears from her eyes and told her that he loved her and would be there for her. He made love to her in the most tender and caring way ever.

In his embrace, she promised to fix everything. He just wanted Leo out of the picture and agreed to give her plan a chance. He made no promises and Leigh didn't complain. She was counting her blessings; especially the one that held her in his arms.

As Janet, dressed in the most elegant Sunday best, and Maya came into the kitchen, Leigh accepted the peaceful solitude being over. She watched as her mother barked orders for the dinner menu that evening, acting as if she hadn't even seen her. Leigh had a weird feeling. Her mother was behaving more and more erratic every day. She couldn't be blamed considering everything that was going on, but she was being cold now and that wasn't her style at all. Janet didn't pull any punches, but she was never cold with her children. When Janet finally looked at her, Leigh waved with a smile, but Janet barely smiled back before asking Maya to leave.

She could tell from the look on Leigh's face that she knew something was coming. Janet couldn't find it in her heart to feel any guilt about what she was about to do. Not after everything that had happened in the last few months. She had given all she could and she was getting nothing in return but more heartache.

"Who is Richard?"

Leigh's mind was racing a mile a second as their eyes locked. She felt awful for thinking she had an advantage with her mother in such an obvious state of weakness. Usually Janet could catch a lie, but she wasn't herself today. She hadn't been for a few weeks now.

"He works at the clinic. I told you it's the three of us."

"The three of you work together." Janet had low tolerance for bullshit today. "So you let Alicia grab your butt while you make out with her on the street too?"

Leigh blinked and swallowed hard. When Janet got crass it meant she was at her wit's end. She lowered her head. "Richard is my boyfriend."

"Look at me when I'm talking to you."

"Don't talk to me like I'm a child." They eyed each other and Leigh looked away. She knew she had no guts when it came to this woman. She shouldn't even try.

"After all that happened yesterday, this is who you go to?"

"Are you having me followed, Mom?" Leigh knew no

one her mother associated with would be driving through
Richard's neighborhood.

"After that man got out of jail, your father and I both
felt we couldn't take chances with any of you."

"You could have told me."

"Is that really the point you want to make with me
right now?"

The look of disgust on her mother's face made Leigh
want to find a crawl space to hide in. She gave her mother
her history with Richard, but seeing no softening of her
expression, refrained from any expression of love.

"I'm your mother," Janet said. "Keeping something
from me is the same as lying to me."

"Not every aspect of my life is your business."

"How could you betray me like this?"

Janet began crying right in front of her and the scene
shattered Leigh. The anchor of her family who always remained strong in the midst of every storm was sobbing
now and Leigh couldn't contain herself. She rushed to
her mother, wrapping her in her arms.

"You made a commitment to me, Leigh. You knew that
you weren't going to give Leo a chance. You used my
hopes to get money for your clinic."

Janet shrugged out of Leigh's arms and Leigh felt it
like a dagger through her chest.

"You were all I had left, Leigh. After these past few
months, you were the only thing I could really be proud
of. I thought we were getting closer. I thought I could de-
pend on you."

"You can, Mom."

"Then why can't you give Leo a chance?" Janet didn't
even know herself why she was holding on to this. She
didn't care anything for Leo, but it meant her sanity to
have something she wanted work out. Nothing was left
but Leo.

"There's no chemistry," Leigh claimed.

"You never gave it a chance." Janet said.

"Mom, please stop crying." Leigh couldn't take it any-more. She was hurting everyone. "I can fix this. I promise. Just please stop crying."

CHAPTER 11

Sean pulled up to the curb across from Rudio's house. He didn't care if he was seen. He wanted to be seen, as a matter of fact. He was full of anger and didn't know what else to do with himself. He was off the case and there was nothing he could say to anyone to change their minds. He almost came to blows twice with Davis, the new detective on the case. The man wasn't interested in any advice suggesting that his ten years as a detective told him all he needed to know. Sean glanced down at his watch. It was time for Davis to show up for surveillance but he wasn't in the spot.

Not seeing Haley was killing him. More, it was killing him wondering if she was feeling anywhere near the same. He knew she didn't love him, wasn't sure if Haley was even capable of that, but he wanted her to need him just a little bit. He hadn't spoken to her since Carter's arrest and it was making him nuts wondering what she was thinking and what that mother of hers was feeding her mind.

He had saved her life! Didn't that matter to anyone? He was a good detective. He knew how to keep a secret and had a right to know where she was. Even Davis knew and that made Sean want to rip his head off. This case and that woman were driving him out of his mind. He was thinking of doing things to her, for her, and because of her, that he would never have thought he would do.

Sean gripped his steering wheel as Rudio's garage door opened. With Davis not there, Sean resigned himself to following the car, but it wasn't going anywhere. It backed into the street halfway and stopped. When Rudio got out of the passenger's seat, Sean got out of his car. He was ready for anything and he wanted something to happen.

Rudio stood a few feet from Sean with a wide grin on his face. He tucked his thumbs into his pants, holding his hands at his sides like a cowboy. Sean just stood there, staring at him. Out of the corner of his eye he kept notice of Armand who was still in the driver's seat of the car looking on.

"You look like a man with a lot of free time," Rudio said.

"You can't get rid of me that easy," Sean stated. "I've become too attached to you."

"I have that effect on people." Rudio looked around. "Where's the real cop at? I mean, you got other things your daddy wants you to do now, don't you?"

"Worried about my workload?" Sean smiled. "How considerate of you, but don't worry. I'm working on what I need to be working on."

"I'm on my way to the station to meet your replacement. I've graciously agreed to fill him in on who I believe had reason to kill Jorge Nesco even though I doubt the man is dead." Rudio looked Sean over. "I hope this new guy is at least worth my time. You sure as hell haven't been."

"Conspiracy to commit murder." Sean was shaking his head. "You know what that means?"

"I don't know what that little ho is talking about. I don't even know her. She was using me as a scapegoat. I'm sure as much of a bitch this Chase girl is, everyone she knows wants to do her."

Sean gritted his teeth. "Including you, right?"

"I got no reason to kill the trick." He shrugged. "As a matter of fact, if I wanted to kill her, which I don't, I wouldn't send someone to just shoot her. I'd have her brought to me first, so I can have some fun with her before putting a bullet in her—"

Sean's fist came like lightning across Rudio's face and he hit the ground like a sack of salt. Sean reached for his gun and aimed it straight at Armand who was already around the car headed for him.

"Don't you move!" Sean could hear his loud, heavy breathing. He was sweating all over even though it was cold outside.

"That's assault!" Rudio screamed as he unsteadily helped himself off the ground. He turned to Armand. "Call the cops. Now!"

Sean lowered his gun, trying to calm himself down. He was in so much damn trouble.

Janet stood in the middle of her dining room trying to figure out what she was going to change. She was grasping at straws at this point. She was finding it hard to live with herself after bullying Leigh into giving Leo a chance and dying over not being able to see Haley. She was trying to find something to fill her every moment with work to keep her mind distracted. Besides the Chase Foundation, redecorating was her therapy. Whenever she was depressed, changing one or more rooms in the house could make her feel better. She'd spent over two hundred thousand dollars on the kitchen and breakfast room after

Leigh left for Africa. After the humiliating dinner with Avery, the dining room was the hands down winner for change.

"Mom!"

Carter and Michael were both looking at her like she was crazy and she wondered how long she had zoned out.

"You okay?" Michael asked.

"Of course. I'm just thinking about redecorating this room. It needs a new look."

"Dad's gonna flip," Michael said.

"It's nice to see you." Standing on her toes, she kissed Carter's cheek, noticing that he didn't look very good.

"I came over to play some hoops out back." Carter had been fired by one of his best clients today in the fallout of the arrest and he was getting the feeling it wouldn't be the last. "I'm not in the mood to be stared at in the gym."

"You'll stay for dinner, then?"

And deal with Steven on top of everything else? "I have to get back to the office."

"Let's go." Michael was heading out the sliding doors when Carter took out his cell phone. "What are you doing, man?"

"I just want to check first." Carter couldn't pass on any of his messages. He was hoping Avery would call, but he refused to call her again if she hadn't yet.

"How about you?" Janet asked Michael.

"We're going to the country club with the boys." Michael was studying Carter and whatever he was hearing wasn't good. With everything going on, Carter wasn't talking to him at all lately and it was pissing him off.

"Dammit!" Carter slammed his fist on the table. Another client wanted to talk and his tone was nervous and uncomfortable, which only meant one thing. "I gotta go."

"Come on, man!" Michael threw his hands in the air.

"Michael!"

They all froze at the sound of Steven's bellowing tone. "He's not at the office?" Carter asked. "Michael."

Michael shrugged. "I didn't know. What do you care? He's not yelling your name."

Steven stood in the archway to the room, surprised to see Carter there. "Where in the hell have you been, Carter? I've been calling you all day."

"I got your messages." Carter wasn't ready to deal with this.

"Did you think you could get this past me?" Steven asked.

"Not now," Carter said. "I have to go."

Steven fumed, raising his voice. "You'll go when I tell you to go! Did you know about this, Michael?"

"What?"

"This offer to Avery Jackson!" He tossed a crumbled up piece of paper at Carter. It hit him in the chest but his son didn't flinch.

"You made an offer to Avery?" Michael asked, but Carter didn't even look at him. He hated when his brother acted like this.

"Isn't this good news?" Janet asked. "You wanted the shops, right?"

"That's right, Dad," Carter proclaimed. "You said you wanted the shops so I got them for you. Essentials is yours, so what in the hell are you so upset about?"

"Don't want to get smart with me, boy." Steven started for Carter, but Janet stood in front of him, placing her hand gently on his chest. She knew how to calm him and he stopped, taking a deep breath.

"At any cost," Carter said. "Those were your words, right?"

Steven sneered at his indifference. "You're pretty generous with money that isn't yours."

"How much did you give her?" Michael asked, beginning to feel like he wasn't even in the room.

"I'm a Chase, too." Carter was too angry to care that he was making it worse. "Isn't it 'our' money?"

Steven wanted to clock him right now, but he wouldn't. He knew Carter was going through a lot. Still, he wasn't going to let his pursuit of a piece of ass hurt Chase Beauty's bottom line any more than it already had.

"What did you pay her?" Michael grabbed Carter by the arm to turn him around, but Carter pushed his hand away.

"Tell him, Carter." Steven held a smirk on his face. "Michael's the one who has to answer for it. It's his budget. Tell him that you paid her more than his last offer."

Michael couldn't believe that. Carter wasn't that stupid. "No way. He wouldn't do that."

Seeing the satisfied look on Steven's face only angered Janet. "Steven, I don't know what you're doing, but stop it now."

"You better answer me," Michael said. "What did you offer that bitch?"

Carter swung around to face him, feeling the anger inside heat up.

"You did it, didn't you?" Michael asked.

"This is about more than money now," Carter answered. "We can't afford to have any enemies."

Michael's laugh was laced with his anger. "Forgive me, I was wrong. If she got you for that much, she's not the bitch. You are."

"Don't call me a bitch." Carter spoke just above a whisper, his hands clenched into fists.

Michael knew how much Carter hated being called that. It was the price you paid for pissing off the person who knew all your buttons. He leaned back against the table, folding his arms across his chest and widened his smile.

He had Carter's full attention as he slowly mouthed the word again. "Bitch."

Steven didn't need this pressure from Janet right now. "This is business, Janet. Why don't you just—"

Janet screamed as Carter slammed into Michael, pushing the table back about five feet. The china table setting went everywhere. Fists were flying. Michael kicked Carter away, hard enough to push him back into the vanity. Glass shattered and more china fell all over the place as Steven grabbed Janet out of the way.

"Stop it!" Janet screamed, but it was no use.

As soon as Michael was up, Carter came rushing back at him and slammed him against the wall. Michael aimed for Carter's chest, but Carter dipped and the swing slipped over his shoulder. A hard blow to the stomach had Michael doubling over, evading the painting that fell off the wall, just missing Carter.

Janet couldn't take it anymore. "Steven, please."

When she looked at her husband, Janet was disgusted at what she was seeing. Steven was just watching them. Not like he was enjoying it, but just letting it happen as if it was supposed to. It was some testosterone insanity she would never understand and wouldn't tolerate a second longer.

"Steven!" She grabbed his arm, jerking his attention to her. "Stop them, now!"

Steven watched as Michael hit Carter in his side. Carter groaned but didn't miss a step as he kicked Michael in the thigh, sending Michael to the floor.

"Enough!"

Both men stopped, looking at their father. Carter backed away from Michael, who was still on the floor.

"Are you both insane?" Janet asked. "I didn't raise you to act like animals. Look at this place, it's a mess."

"It's okay, Janet," Steven said. "I'll get Maya to take care of it."

"Is Maya going to take care of this family?" Janet came face-to-face with her husband, not understanding why he played these games with his sons; with her sons. "Because it's a mess too! That's not her responsibility is it, Steven? It's your family, so I suggest you figure out how to fix it now!"

He reached for her, but she pulled her hand away, storming out of the room. He hated upsetting her like this, but she never understood the dynamics of his relationship with his sons and theirs with each other. At least, not in the way he did.

"If you're done playing apes in the jungle," he said, "why don't you explain to me what you're both going to do about this offer?"

"I'm not doing anything," Carter said. "You want to change it, you do it. I'm out of here."

Steven stood in place, blocking Carter's way out of the dining room. He looked into the younger man's eyes, knowing that Carter wanted nothing more than to push him aside and leave, but he would never do it. As strong as Carter was and as angry as he felt, Steven knew he knew who his father was. He would stand there forever if he needed to teach him that lesson.

Carter wanted to strangle this man standing in front of him. This was another one of his games and although Carter had enough fight in him to last a while, he knew Steven wasn't his problem. It was Avery and the charges against him putting him on edge. So he stepped aside, like he always had and feared he probably always would and left the room.

Steven looked down at his remaining son who was laughing while wiping a trickle of blood from the side of his mouth. "Get off that floor, boy." Michael stood up, feeling Carter's hits hard. His father was staring at him like he wanted a piece of him, too. "What?"

"Why do you always do this?" Steven asked.

"Do what?"

"Goad him into a fight when you know he's gonna kick your ass. He always wins, so why do you do it?"

"Because one of these days," Michael said, straightening up, "I'm gonna win."

Michael saw a hint of pride in his father's slow-forming smile, knowing that was what he was expected to say. That smile meant the world to him, but as soon as he smiled back, Steven's face went flat.

"Well, that certainly wasn't today, was it?" Steven met his son's frown with a hard pat on his shoulder before turning and walking away. Janet had to understand, he knew what he was doing.

Besides, she wanted to decorate the room anyway.

"Don't move," Leigh whispered as her fingernails dug into Richard's back.

"What about now?" he asked after a while with a cocky grin on his face.

She sighed, her entire body rushing with liquid heat, before pushing him up. "Are you making fun of me?"

"I'm not. I would never make fun of multiple orgasms."

"Number ten on the list of one thousand reasons it's so much better to be a woman than to be a man."

He rolled over, lying beside her. "The rest of the equipment will be in tomorrow. We should all go out and celebrate."

Richard took her away from her worries, but reality was always waiting for her when she came back. "Richard, you know that I love you."

She felt his body stiffen in response to her words. This wasn't going to go well even though she hadn't done anything but rehearse what she would say to him since promising her mother this past Sunday.

"What is this about, Leigh?"

"I'm asking you a question," she said. "You know that I—"

"Just come out with it." He sat up.

"I can't keep my promise to you," she said. "About Leo."

"Dammit, Leigh." Richard got up from the bed and began putting his clothes back on. "You said you would end it with him."

"I know I did," she pleaded, "but you should have seen my mother on Sunday. She was—"

"You've known this since Sunday? How many times have we been together since then?"

"I didn't know how to tell you. This is so hard on everybody."

"Not too hard to have sex with me first, huh?" Leaning over his dresser, he used his arms to sweep everything off the top and let out a loud groan. "I can't believe I fell for that."

Leigh was horrified that he could think she would use sex to soften him, but she was more horrified by the fact that it might be true. "Nothing has changed about the way I feel about you. Remember what you told me last week?"

"Someone had just tried to kill your sister," he said. "You probably used that too, right? You knew I couldn't turn you away then."

"Stop it!"

Anger and resentment showed in his expression, his posture, his voice. "You let your mother guilt you into being her little puppet no matter who else pays for it."

"The clinic is going to open in a couple of weeks," she pointed out. "Just until then."

"Do you actually think there's a time limit on my pride?"

"You know what's going on with my family. I—"

Richard held up his hands to stop her. "I don't want to hear it, Leigh. No matter what you say or do, the fact is you're going to pick pleasing your mother before every-one and everything else; including yourself."

She could never explain to him how thin the line on her mother's sanity was. She could never explain to him how this need to please her mother had been driving her for her entire life.

"Just leave." He turned his back to her.

"Richard, please." Leigh rushed to him, grabbing at his arm, but he wouldn't turn around. "I promise you—"

He pulled away from her. "You can't make me any promises. I know you think what you're trying to do is right, but I can't be a part of it."

"But you are a part of it," she said. "You're a part of everything, because I love you and you love me."

"I'm taking a shower," he said, without looking at her. "I don't want you here when I get out."

Left alone, Leigh felt humiliated and rejected, standing in the middle of his bedroom naked in more ways than one. How could something so good, so well intentioned, turn into such a disaster?

Charlie didn't want to believe it when someone told him that Sean was working at his desk, but there he was. Sean was supposed to be on two weeks' unpaid suspension after taking a shot at Rudio, which was only the beginning of his problems. He hadn't taken well to Charlie's suggestion he take this time to reflect and put his priorities in order. He wasn't getting through to Sean. No one was and it was all because of that woman. A woman who slept with married congressmen.

He thought of the famous saying and found it almost biblical in its truth. It takes a woman twenty years to make a man of her son and another woman only twenty minutes to make a fool of him.

"What are you doing here, son?"

Sean didn't turn around. "Don't call me that."

"There's nobody around." Charlie wondered if there was more he needed to do. There was a line you had to draw as a parent when your children became adults. "You're not supposed to be here."

"I'm not working," Sean said. "Just doing some research. Can you please back off?"

Charlie grabbed him by the shoulder, swinging him around in the swivel chair. "You've gone too far with this woman."

"That's none of your business."

"You've made it everyone's business, Sean. You've made the detective squad look bad and you've jeopardized the case against Rudio."

"What case?" he asked. "Nothing is sticking. Davis isn't doing anything and Haley is stuck in God knows where."

"Why would you choose to get involved with . . . ?"

"Don't start with me about that wicked woman seducing me blindly." He wasn't the fool that everyone seemed to suddenly think he had become.

"That woman is no good. Look at what she's made you do already. Makes me doubt that attacking Rudio is the first time you've broken the rules for her. The fact that you're involved with her was the first."

Sean didn't care about the rules, values, and morals compromised in the quest for Haley. She had become some kind of an obsession for him over the last week. He was a young man, which meant he was basically always horny, but his desire to get his hands on that woman was taking it to a different level.

"If you don't get out of here right now, I'm going to report you and you'll get suspended for a lot longer than two weeks."

Sean looked up at his father, his eyes wide in disbelief. He could see that man meant it and he couldn't understand why he was turning on him. "You wouldn't do that."

"To help you get perspective," Charlie answered, "I'll do whatever I have to."

"Fine." Sean grabbed his keys, kicking his chair out of the way. He wasn't there to do research anyway and with the room as empty as it ever would be, it was time to do what he'd really come here for.

The detective's squad room was at shift change and most of them were at the lockers or downstairs. He had been keeping an eye on Davis for a few days now and he had to give it to him. Davis was a good detective when it came to protecting his information. He locked everything up even if he was just gone for a few minutes, with the exception of a bathroom trip.

Sean knew Rudio's file was the blue one, major case squad file. He did a scan of the room. No one was paying attention when he slid the file off the table. Sliding it in front of his own file, he stood against the wall speed reading. He caught the words that mattered right away. High Security . . . Penthouse . . . Century City. The name of the hotel wasn't listed, but Sean knew exactly where she was.

The Century City Villa. He had replaced the file and slipped out of the squad room in less than two minutes and not at one moment did he feel an ounce of guilt.

Carter was having one of those experiences when he felt like he was watching his life from outside his own body, trying to find perspective. Maybe it was the seven hundred dollar bottle of cognac he was finishing off, but he'd been feeling it all day. Looking over the balcony of his high-rise, he watched the sun set and wondered why his cab was taking so long. There was hardly any daylight now that November had crept up on him. He wondered how things might be now if he'd never walked into Essentials in September. He didn't have time to think about the past; he had a flight to catch and it was all about the future.

Carter could tell someone had turned on the light in his living room because it lit up the balcony, disturbing his peace. He took one final sip of the cognac, hearing footsteps behind him. He stepped off the balcony and headed toward the bar.

"What are you doing here?"

Laid out on the sofa, Michael grabbed the remote. "Since when do I need a reason to come by here?"

"I'm on my way out," Carter said. "You want a drink?"

He looked up at the cognac in Carter's hand. "How much you pay for that bottle?"

"Seven." Carter poured a glass for him, walking over to the sofa.

Michael sat up and Carter handed him the drink before sitting down.

Michael sniffed the glass; only the best. "I could get you that bottle for four hundred, you know that?"

"That's because it would be stolen," Carter replied. "You know that?"

Michael shook his head. "What is it, man? Why do you always worry about that shit? You're the consumer. It's not on you where it comes from."

They both looked at each other, smiling. That was all there ever was to it. They fought all the time, but in the end it never mattered. They hadn't talked since Carter had walked out of the house on Monday, and for both of them that hurt more than any blow from a fist.

"Thanks," Carter said. "I'll stick with my way."

"You're making a mistake, but that only figures. You're making a lot of mistakes lately, Carter."

"Dad must have sent you."

"Dad doesn't care about that Avery thing anymore."

That wasn't true, but Michael knew there was nothing they could do about the contract. Carter had handed

Avery the check Monday morning and she cashed it on Tuesday. They had the twenty shops and would be able to launch the line at the first of the year. Michael wasn't so sure about his promotion, but he was still hopeful. He worried about what Kimberly would do if it didn't happen.

"Then what are you talking about?" Carter asked.

"I'm talking about that." Michael pointed to the suitcase on the floor in the hallway.

"Avery is in Vegas." Carter looked at his watch again.

"You finally tracked her down?" Michael asked, not at all clear what Carter was doing. "Mom told me you were looking for her."

"I hired someone." Carter was ashamed of everything he'd done, but he knew Michael wouldn't tell anyone. "She's staying at the Bellagio."

"How do you know she's not with her sales boy?"

"She's not." Carter didn't know who she might be with but he had an idea what she was doing. She was looking for a sign and he was afraid she was looking in the wrong place.

"You're not supposed to leave L.A. You were arrested for attempted murder, remember?"

"Since when have you given a damn about rules?"

Michael placed his glass on the granite coffee table. "I'm worried about you, Carter."

Carter stood up, patting Michael on the head. "Don't worry. I know what I'm doing."

"That woman isn't right for you. You're making a mistake."

"That's funny you should say that," Carter replied, "because I remember about six years ago someone showed up on my doorstep to tell me he was marrying a woman he'd gotten pregnant on a one-night stand."

Michael leaned back, remembering that night clearly. Carter told him marrying Kimberly was a mistake and there was no way for him to know what he wanted that soon. It turned out to be the best decision he ever made in his life.

"That's not fair," Michael said.

"A model who used to be a teenaged runaway prostitute," Carter added.

"Hey!" Michael pointed angrily. "That's between me and you. Mom and Dad can't know about that."

"Have I ever said anything to anyone?" Carter asked. A promise to his brother was a promise for life.

Michael smiled with a nod and a shrug. "Don't expect me to like her."

The Century City Villa was the newest high-tech hotel for government officials, celebrities and anyone who had an ego large enough to believe someone wanted a piece of them. Cameras were everywhere and the security staff consisted of former FBI or CIA officials. When it opened, a few of the best cops on the LAPD joined the staff as well. The penthouse was the real deal and that's where Haley was staying. It was equipped with monitors, twenty-four-hour security guards with serious weapons, emergency buttons in every room, and its own elevator that only responded to a code that was changed every day. Even the resident wasn't given the code. For housekeeping, room service and all the other amenities, the penthouse had its own staff so there wouldn't be any mishaps with a stand-in or replacement. If the masseuse wasn't in that day, there would be no massage. The biggest selling point was the door that led to the roof of the tower with a helicopter pad.

So far, so good. The elevator opened up on the eighteenth floor and Sean stepped out coming face-to-face with two gun-toting security guards. He had a feeling his badge wasn't going to get him any further. "Take it easy, guys." He held his hands up, his badge flashing on the loop around his neck. "I'm a cop."

"That doesn't mean anything to me." This one was tall and skinny with dark circles around his eyes that made one think he hadn't slept for days. "No one gets up here."

"If I wasn't supposed to be up here," Sean said, guns still pointed at him, "then how would I know the code to the elevator?"

They had to think for a second. Sean had to use blackmail to get it and he didn't care to think about that. He hated turning on another cop, but he was desperate. He had been lucky to find one of them assigned to the building, sitting in the lobby in plain clothes. Jerry Laslow had a lot to be blackmailed over and Sean would have never chosen him for this detail. He wondered what other bad choices Davis was making.

"I know for a fact, you're not supposed to be here," the other guard said. "Detective Davis told us he's the only detective on the case."

"Things have changed a bit," Sean said. "I'm back on."

The first guard leaned into the second, whispering something in his ear. Both of their guns lowered.

"You really hit that scum?" the second guard asked.

Sean nodded.

The guard showed his LAPD badge. "Good job."

"Thanks." Sean looked at the door a few feet behind them.

"Still, you're not getting in."

The sound that came from inside the room was hard to describe. Something had fallen, crashed or broken and Haley screamed. Everyone reacted immediately, but Sean wasn't fast enough. The second guard pushed him back, pointing his gun at him.

"You can't go in there!"

"Something has happened to her!" Sean was tempted to keep going. He knew the guy wouldn't shoot him.

The first guard opened the door and before he could get a word out, a silver serving plate smashed against his head, knocking him to the ground as he yelled out in pain.

This was it! Haley jumped over the man and reached down for his gun. She was getting the hell out of this place even if she had to shoot somebody.

"Haley, what are you doing?"

When she looked up the surprise of seeing Sean was enough force to make her fall down, toppling over the injured guard.

"Get up," the second guard yelled at her. "Step away from that gun."

"It's okay." Sean rushed to Haley. "She's not going anywhere."

All thoughts of her attempted escape washed away as Sean helped Haley off the floor. Screaming like she won something, she jumped on him, wrapping her legs around his waist. For the last week she had been going insane. She had twenty-four-hour room service and a television with five hundred channels, but it was hell. Her cell phone had been taken away and she couldn't make outgoing calls. She missed her mother more than anyone, but she missed Sean more than anyone could have thought, and it was him she was thinking of all week when she planned her escape.

"How did you get here?" she asked.

"What did you think you were going to do, escape?"

"I can't take it here, Sean. I know it's good for me, but I can't stand it. I can't even talk on the phone."

"Well, that's got to be worse than murder."

"Don't tease me," she said. "Just get me out of here."

"He's going to need stitches." The second guard helped his partner up. Blood was dripping from his forehead.

Haley didn't feel a bit of guilt. He was there to face a

drug dealing killer, so a little nick on the head shouldn't mean anything.

"Send him down," Sean said. "You stay here and I'll stay with you."

"No way." He reached for his radio. "I'm calling down for approved backup."

Haley turned around with her back to Sean. Looking at the guard, she pouted her lips and widened her eyes in that helpless way stupid men loved to see. "Please, Len."

As soon as Sean closed the door behind them, Haley was all over him. He couldn't get his clothes off fast enough. They were going at each other like their lives depended on it, both feeling some kind of refreshing sanity. Haley wanted him so bad, she thought she would explode. One can only do so much for themselves she thought as she dragged him down to the floor with her. Sean was exactly what she needed; what she had needed for some time. For whatever reason, this guy did something for her and she needed him to do it now.

"Where's the bedroom?" Sean asked.

"Who gives a damn," she answered. "I'm right here, so what does anywhere else matter?"

She had a point. With one last bit of reason in him, Sean remembered that he hadn't locked the door behind him. Haley was right. It did make it a little more exciting.

Walking through Bellagio's casino, Carter was thinking of what to say to Avery. She was going to be angry that he was there in the first place, but he had to use this to his advantage. What he wanted from her was wrong, but this was Vegas and nothing really seemed wrong in this town. He'd spent countless weekends here losing a ton of money, drinking like a fish and doing things with women he wouldn't even tell Michael. After he could talk some sense into Avery, providing she hadn't lost all her money already, Carter was going to go to work on that wall she was building to hide the attraction he knew she felt for him.

The second he was beginning to think it might be too late in the evening, he saw her. She was sitting at the roulette table with a mound of chips in front of her and a drink in her hand. Carter was turned on by the sense of abandon that seemed to encircle her. In the way she moved, the way she flipped her hair back and laughed out loud after winning another spin. The way her legs rubbed against each other showing she was feeling the Vegas effect; turned on by everything. This city was crazy.

"Looks like you're on a roll."

Flipping her hair back, she turned, expecting anything but what she saw. She almost fell out of the chair and Carter grabbed her by the wrist to keep her steady. She squinted, unable to remember how many drinks she'd had. Was it possible that after so long of thinking about nothing but Carter, she was beginning to hallucinate?

She tried to speak and her mouth opened, but nothing came out. It was him all right. Standing there with that charming smile that told the world everything was going his way; that everything always went his way.

"Do you believe in coincidences?" he asked.

"After a few more drinks I might." She turned away, not wanting him to see the smile that begged to show itself. She should be angry thinking of whatever it was he used to find out where she was. "You Chases are very challenged when it comes to minding your own business."

"That's the good thing about being a Chase. Anything I want to know is my business."

"You're an asshole."

"It runs in my family. It's really not my fault."

She cracked a smile reluctantly. "You were right. I am on a roll, so if you don't mind."

"How much?" Carter wasn't sure whether or not he should be worried by her nonplused reaction to him showing up.

"Twelve grand." Avery placed her bets at the last minute. The game seemed to be getting faster or maybe she was just getting slower.

"Then maybe you should stop." He reached for her chips, but she slapped his hand away. "These things always turn around, Avery."

"I know what I'm doing." The dealer called out the number and slid her chips away. "See, you're jinxing me."

"Have you paid off all your debt yet?"

"Yes, Father." She couldn't think with him so close to her, but she didn't really want him to leave. "I am debt free with a little bit left over."

"To start a new business, remember? That's what you wanted and you're going to lose it all."

She grabbed one hundred dollars' worth of chips and reached for black twenty-seven, but Carter grabbed her by the wrist and pulled her arm back. She looked up at him and felt a rush of heat hit her at the angry look on his face. Even his impatience was attractive.

"Carter, please."

"No." Carter looked into her eyes. "What's this about, Avery? It's not like you."

"You don't know me," she said.

"Then tell me."

All bets were final and Avery put her chips back down. "If black twenty-seven hits, I'm gonna slap you."

"What makes you think I wouldn't like that?"

Avery sent him a wicked grin. "You've already used that one on me."

"Did I?" He shrugged. "I'm hoping the more I say it, the better my chances you'll actually do it."

"I'm not falling for your charm tonight. I'm here on a mission."

"To lose everything you have left?"

"It's my purpose," she answered. "I paid off all the debt from the shop, all my bills, everything, and I just sat there wondering what I should do next."

"Waiting for a sign from God." Carter wasn't that religious. He preferred to use his mind to figure things out than wait for a sign from above.

She wasn't sure if he was agreeing with her or making fun of her. She was a little drunk and everything around her was moving a little faster than her brain worked. The direction her life was taking was spinning her in circles and she needed to stop thinking so hard. Just feel and it would come to her. That was when Vegas came to her. No rhyme or reason, but she was going to follow it and so far it was working out.

"Yes," she said. "A sign from God."

"God told you to come to Las Vegas?" Carter asked. "I can't imagine it's one of his favorite cities."

"Twenty-first-century Sodom and Gomorrah!" Avery yelled.

Carter put his finger to his mouth. "You're being too loud."

"Is it possible to be 'too' anything in this city?" She lifted her index finger, gesturing for him to come closer. She wanted to smell his strong clean scent after a day full of cheap cologne and cigarette smoke. "That's what my father calls Vegas. Sodom and Gomorrah because . . ."

"I know the story," he answered. "Now, let's go before you turn to salt."

"Why are you here?" she asked.

"I guess it's my purpose, too."

"What?"

"You, Avery."

Her lips parted as his words sank in and anger and sadness came over her face, confusing him.

"I don't want your pity," she said. "I know I've become

pitiful, losing everything I've worked for, sacrificing my will to a man who doesn't give a—"

When his lips came down on hers, Avery almost fell off the chair. He grabbed her by the arms, pulling her closer, and she lit up like a stick of dynamite. Her hands slowly slid up his arms and behind his neck as the ache in her belly exploded.

"Does that feel like pity to you?" he asked, feeling his chest rise and fall from his heavy breathing. Just a taste.

Avery looked away. Who did she think she was, telling herself she could flirt with this man and not compromise her principles? She had already compromised everything else and there was no way she would get out of his grasp with any sense of honor about herself. She wanted him too much.

"Leave me alone." She swept her chips into her bucket, suddenly feeling so tired that she wasn't sure she could make it to her room.

"I can't do that, Avery." Carter wished he could go back to the days when women chased him. Avery changed all of that.

This exercise in humility was new for him. Even when he wanted a woman he shouldn't, he always got her sooner or later. More often sooner, but that wasn't going to happen here. Avery was fighting some demons inside of her and she had the spirit and will to win and that was more character than he was used to in any woman he'd ever wanted.

"Fine." She stood up, backing away from him. "Then I'll leave you alone."

"I don't think you can do that anymore than I can," he said.

He was right, but Avery wasn't going to give in to that now. She might have only a pinch of pride left, but she was going to stand on it. All she could do was hope Carter would become impatient and lose interest in her.

"If you follow, I'll call security on you and I don't think you want to get in trouble for stalking me while you're a suspect in my attempted murder."

Lot's wife looking back turned her into a pillar of salt, right? Avery kept on walking, fearing if she looked back at Carter, she would melt completely away. A certain calm came over her as she realized the anxiety she had been feeling all day was now satiated. All this time, she was waiting for something and she'd gotten it. He kissed her.

"What are you doing?" Haley rolled her naked body to the end of the bed where Sean was sitting.

"I'm getting dressed." Sean leaned down to kiss her.

"Only two rounds?" she asked. "I expected better out of a younger man. I mean, I've been with older men who can—"

"Haley!" He held up his hand to stop her. This woman didn't think for a second before she spoke. "I don't want to hear that."

"What's the problem?" Haley was definitely going to have to break him of his fragile ego.

"There isn't a problem." He pulled up his shorts. He wished she would put some clothes on. Looking at her made him want to stay.

Haley sat up in the bed, not bothering to cover herself. She got a kick out of how her incredible body made him nervous. He was good in bed, not the best, but something to work with. She would have to teach him a few things, but he had incredible potential. There was a bad boy underneath that holier than thou wrapping and she salivated at a chance to bring that bad boy to his knees.

"You know what I could really use right now?" she asked.

"I'm afraid to ask."

"Some weed." She rubbed her foot against his back. "You should have some, don't you?"

He looked at her like she was out of her mind.

"Cops always have the best stuff," she said. "That's what I hear, at least."

Hearing a door slam hard, Sean jumped up from the bed. Reaching for his gun from his holster on the chair, he turned back to Haley. "Get dressed."

Haley wrapped the covers around her, but was too scared to move.

Sean walked slowly toward the bedroom door, but it opened abruptly and he raised his gun only a few feet from Detective Davis's head.

"Put it down." Davis hadn't even blinked. He looked Sean up and down and then at Haley in the bed. "Isn't this nice?"

"What are you doing here?" Haley asked.

"I heard you tried to escape again." Davis helped himself to a chair just as Sean grabbed his jeans off the back.

In his late thirties, Davis had dark Irish features with black hair and piercing blue eyes. With an extra ten pounds all focused on his stomach, he didn't look like much of a genius but a man who was good at the one thing he did.

"He needed stitches."

Haley laid back. "I'm busy right now, so if you don't mind."

"I mind a lot," he said. "And so would your father. Both your fathers."

Sean zipped his pants up. "Davis, no one has to hear about this."

"How did you get up . . . ?"

Sean turned around to see what distracted Davis from finishing his own sentence and saw Haley getting out of the bed stark naked.

"Haley!" Sean positioned himself in Davis's line of sight. "What are you doing?"

"I'm getting dressed like you said." Going to the closet, she reached inside and pulled out a terry-cloth bathrobe.

"Don't worry, kid." Davis leaned back in the chair. "She's done it before."

"She's not doing it again." Sean glared at Haley, who stuck her tongue out at him as she returned to the bed.

"Detective," she said. "I'm hungry. Why don't you go down and order some dinner for me?"

"I think I'd rather call the captain and tell him about this little sex romp."

"Davis," Sean said. "This is complicated, okay?"

"I'll make you a deal," Haley said. Both men looked at Haley as if she were joking but she was dead serious. "I have something you could use."

"Haley, don't hold out," Sean ordered. "This is your life we're talking about."

"I was holding out for you," she said, "so I suggest you be more appreciative."

"Just tell me!" Davis yelled.

"Don't tell on us," she directed. "And then I'll tell you."

"Haley." Sean would never understand how this girl saw fit to play games with her own life. "What is it?"

"I remembered something else," she said. "I had a dream two nights ago and it came back to me. There was a woman on the boat. When the noise from the engine went off, she saw me first. She pointed to me and her mouth was moving like she was yelling to the other man. That's when they started pointing and then the gun."

"You can remember her, but not Rudio?" Davis asked.

Haley shrugged. "I can't tell you why, but I remember her because she had this horrible bleach blonde hair that went down to her butt."

Sean looked at Davis, who was waiting for more information. "I know who it is."

Davis eyed Sean. "You're not on this case, man."

"You let me help you and I'll tell you who it is," he said, taking a chapter from Haley.

"You're a cop, Sean. You'll tell me no matter what."

"Let's go." Sean turned to Haley. "Good job, Haley."

"Good job?" Was that all she was going to get? "What am I, a dog? Where are you going?"

"I'm going to pick her up."

"We're going to pick her up," Davis added.

"When will you be back?" she asked.

Sean looked back at Davis who rolled his eyes before leaving the room.

"I'll be back as soon as I can." He leaned down to kiss her.

"That better be soon," she said.

"It will." Without thinking, as he rushed out of the room, he quickly said, "I love you, Haley."

Had she heard him right? Haley shook her head, feeling a little sorry for him. He was a sweet guy, but he gave it up way too soon. He had a lot to learn. She knew he would fall for her, but he didn't know her well enough to know he should have kept it to himself. When a man told her he loved her, and they all did, Haley knew it was time to turn and run the other way. Love for men meant possession and ownership, trying to mold a woman who had most of what they wanted into being everything they ever dreamed of and she wasn't that type of woman. Either that or they would surrender their soul to her will and she would lose interest so fast it was like she never knew the guy.

Generally, she thought to herself, she would come up with a way to let them down nicely. If they didn't take the hint, she could make it ugly but that wasn't what Haley was thinking of right now. When she thought of Sean, her mind wasn't searching for excuses to run away. Maybe this time, at least for a little while, she might stick around and see what this brother was about.

CHAPTER 12

Carter took the last bite of his breakfast, keeping his eyes on his newspaper. He wasn't reading it, at least not anymore. For the last fifteen minutes, Avery had been standing on the edges of Café Bellagio staring at him. He could believe there was something spiritual in the fact that he sensed her before he saw her, but he wasn't in a romantic mood at the time.

After she left him in the casino last night, Carter decided to get drunk and lose some money. He didn't want to be a good boy, so he left the Bellagio and went to The Palms where he knew he could find a rowdy game and easy women. All night, he spent the big bucks and the women were all over him, but it didn't make a bit of difference. It wasn't like the first day he met Avery, and thoughts of her crept into his night with Lisette. Last night, he couldn't stop thinking of her and ended up going to bed drunk and alone. At least that he could remember.

He blamed Avery for every bit of it and under his breath told her she could stand there forever for all he cared. If he couldn't have her, he was going to be damned if he was going to let her keep him from enjoying other women. He wasn't interested in leaving Las Vegas without getting laid.

When she arrived at his table, he continued to look at his newspaper. He pretended like she wasn't even there, waiting until she said his name to look up at her.

"What took you so long?" he asked.

"What?" Avery felt the tightness in her chest begin to loosen.

"You've been standing over there like a fool, Avery."

"So you saw me?"

"Based on what I just said to you, isn't that a stupid question?" He stood up, tossing money on the table.

"This is the Carter I remember." Avery looked down at his plate; nothing but fruit. "Kind of a light breakfast for such an angry man."

"You'd rather I clog up my arteries with the shit all these other people are eating?"

Avery followed him out of the restaurant, strangely more comfortable with Dr. Jekyll than Mr. Hyde. "Carter, I know you hate me right now, but I want to apologize."

He stopped as she grabbed his arm. Looking at her, none of the anger he felt toward her could hold a candle to the look on her face. It all faded away and he felt himself relax.

"Come gamble with me." He wrapped his hand around hers, pulling her with him.

"I don't want to be your gambling buddy," she said. "I just want to apologize for being so rude to you last night. I know you were just trying to help me before I lost money and you probably saved me thousands of dollars."

"Sit down." He patted the seat next to him at the first blackjack table he found. "You make up for your attitude last night by bringing me good luck this morning."

"Can't I just say I'm sorry?"

"You don't have to do that." He gave the dealer three hundred-dollar bills. "You didn't upset me."

"I think I did." She would hate it if she was the only one who had walked away from that feeling turned around.

"I was a little mad." He accepted his cards, "but I washed it all away with a lot of scotch and a redheaded call girl." He looked at her, seeing her lower lip drop to the floor. "She was very nice. Very expensive, but a good listener. You know, cause I just like to talk."

"Please tell me you're kidding."

Carter played his hand, letting her wait. Then he turned to her with a schoolboy smile before she socked him in the arm hard enough to make him wince.

"That's not funny," she said, never meaning anything so much.

"Yes, it was."

"Vegas humor." She settled in. "What happens here, stays here, right?"

He knew what she meant and he wasn't about to leave that kiss behind. "We'll see, won't we?"

"It's the seduction of the city," she begged. "People do things they don't mean."

He could see pleading in her eyes, but he wasn't going to let her get away with that kiss. "Or things they've been wanting to do for a long time, but didn't have the nerve."

She made him want to feel like it had been all him taking advantage of her, but Carter knew the difference too well. He might have caught her off-guard, but her lips told him that she wanted that kiss.

Avery felt restless under his gaze, which she couldn't turn away from. She felt a sense of fear creep up on her, knowing that if he leaned in to kiss her she wouldn't be able to resist even though she swore to herself that she would.

"I have to go."

"I know you want to go," he said, "but you won't. Avery, I'm sorry but I'm not gonna be the gentleman and let you off easy."

The look on her face as she looked past him sent a chill through Carter. Her face went at least three shades lighter and her lower lip began to tremble. He turned around and in an instant Carter jumped off his stool and took off, pushing aside anyone in his way.

Craig saw him just in time, turning around to see who these people were yelling at for knocking them down. Carter saw the look of deathly fear on his face and it only made him run faster. When he leaped for him, Craig jumped away and tossed a bucket full of quarters at him. Carter felt someone try to hold him back while he was standing back up, but he pushed them away and ran after Craig.

Security was at the edge of the casino, but they were either too slow or didn't care because Carter yelled for them to stop Craig, but they just stared. Carter wasn't going to let him get away, so with one wide leap, he landed on top of the man and brought him to the floor. This was enough to interest the security guards and they started yelling threats to Carter, who was already pummeling Craig with his fists. It took two of them to pull him off.

"Get him!" Avery yelled, pointing to Craig. "He's wanted in L.A. for attempted murder!"

There were a few gasps in the crowd that was beginning to form around them. A security guard hesitated before going after Craig who seemed so harmless compared to Carter.

"Him!" She pointed at Craig again. "He tried to kill me. Check with the View Park Police Department."

Craig was mumbling something incoherent as the security guard pulled him up. He was bleeding from the lip and looked ten years older than the last time Avery had seen him. She couldn't stop staring at him. Seeing him in this unbelievable situation, Avery knew she wasn't crazy. There was a reason Vegas came to mind, and she had to believe there was a reason Carter had the mind to follow her.

"Eva Salazar." Davis repeated her name over and over again as he glanced at her rap sheet. "Did you see that play, *Evita*?"

Sean shook his head, losing his patience as they sat in Davis's car outside the town house of Eva Salazar. The house had to cost at least half a million and Eva was a music video dancer. Rudio was taking good care of her as he did all his women. Eager to bring her in, the only delay was the warrant for her arrest. They had to find a picture of her and bring it back to Haley to pick out among others. Fortunately, Eva had been arrested for prostitution a few years back and Haley picked her mug shot out right away. Now they were sitting outside her home for most of Saturday, but she was nowhere to be found.

"You didn't?" Davis asked. "I saw the movie with Madonna, but it was a play first. Everybody says she's not a good actress, but she was good in that one. I also liked her in that—"

"Please." Sean couldn't take his free association conversation a second longer.

"Hey, man, you should be happy you're even here."

Sean was grateful Davis hadn't told anyone about him and Haley. "I am, but I want something to come of this."

"For her?" he asked.

Sean looked at him. "To catch a murderer."

"You're not fooling anybody. This is all about that woman. If it had been anyone else, you would have handed this case over and went on about your business."

"It's not all about her." That wasn't true. Sean suspected Davis was smart enough to know anything involving Haley was all about her. She would see to it that it was.

"It's not a smart move," Davis said.

Sean didn't need anyone to tell him that. He was stepping onto a land mine with his eyes wide open. "It's out of my hands."

"That woman is going to rip you apart."

"Maybe so, but you have no idea what I've given up for her."

"Like what?"

My professionalism, ethics, and morals to name a few. Sean had been above reproach his entire career as a police officer and detective, but in a matter of a few months, he didn't even recognize himself and it was all because of a woman. What was more pitiful than that?

"It doesn't matter. All that matters is that I've earned the right to her and I'm going to have her."

Davis laughed. "Just remember that when you're reaching blindly to pick up the pieces of what she leaves behind when she's through with you."

They both sat up as Eva slid her black Mercedes convertible into the driveway. They briskly made their way to her while she was reaching into the backseat for a handful of shopping bags, completely oblivious to them. When she finally saw them, she didn't seem bothered at all. She was smacking her gum loud enough to be heard down the street. When Sean flashed his badge, she placed her hand on her hip and blew a bubble bigger than her head before it flattened all over her face.

"This is fine, Leo." Leigh stood at the entrance to her house, grateful that their lunch date with his parents was over.

She was completely creeped out by his behavior today and she wanted to get away from him. He'd surprised her with his parents and treated her altogether like she was his girlfriend. It ticked her off and even though he had been a perfect gentleman, Leigh felt a chill up her spine by the way he looked at her.

"I thought maybe I could come in?" he asked. "I don't have anywhere else to go today."

"I have to go to the clinic." There was that look again, like he knew her much better than he actually did.

"Leigh, I have to tell you that I haven't been this happy since . . ."

Leigh looked behind him, seeing the curtains in the foyer window shuffle. She saw finely manicured fingers reaching around before her mother's dark hair flirted at the edges.

"I love you."

Leigh's head jerked back, her eyes opening to the size of saucers. "What? What did you say?"

"I think I love you, Leigh."

Leigh didn't know how to respond. She felt awful, thinking of Leo's feelings the least in this whole ordeal, but couldn't think of anything she had done to make him go this far. "Leo, we hardly know each other."

"I want to change that."

"We haven't even kissed."

"I can do something about that, too."

Before she could respond, Leo pulled her to him and kissed her. Something in the way he held her arms, in the cruelty of his hard kiss made Leigh afraid to push away. She knew her mother was looking and didn't want to start a scene. Fortunately, it only lasted a few seconds before he let her go. Leigh looked behind him, seeing the curtains flutter. She turned back to Leo and the way he looked at her made her take a few steps back. This was all wrong.

The screeching sound of tires made her turn around just in time to see the back of Richard's Honda through the front gate speeding off. She started with a sprint, running as fast as she could to the street, but he was gone and Leigh knew she had just put a nail in the coffin.

"Who was that?" Leo asked, coming up behind her.

The man I love, she thought. "I thought it was a friend, but . . . Look Leo, I have to go. I'm sorry."

There was a hint of anger in his eyes as he flinched. "But Leigh, I just told you that I love you."

She could only think of Richard right now. "I can't do this right now. You have to go, Leo. I'll call you later."

She was already dialing Richard on her cell as she rushed into the house. Still, she felt Leo's eyes on her and made sure the front door was locked after she was inside.

Carter knocked on the open door to Avery's hotel room before entering. She was standing next to the police officer who finally came to arrest Craig and waved him over. The officer turned to him with a much less welcoming look than Avery.

"You've gotten yourself together, sir?" he asked.

"I already got the lecture from the other officer." Carter didn't feel as tough as he had before when it was revealed to him that Craig had a gun in his hotel room. "I just couldn't let him get away."

"You got lucky," the officer said. "Mr. Moon is on his way back to L.A."

Avery wrapped her arms around him and squeezed tight. She couldn't remember being this happy in a while. "They'll have to drop the charges against you."

"Charges?" The officer's brow rose.

Carter held Avery away. "There weren't actually ever any charges against me. I was arrested, but nothing . . . Never mind. Is that all?"

He nodded and was slow to say, "You two try to stay safe while you're in Sin City."

With the officers gone, Avery was finally able to really feel the effects of Craig. She wanted to scream loud enough to shatter the windows. There was suddenly a light at the end of the tunnel for her. The maddening turn was threatening to calm down. This had been enough drama to last her a lifetime.

Expecting him to be just as elated, Avery was confused at Carter's distant expression.

"Aren't you happy it's almost over?" she asked, sitting next to him on the edge of the bed. "Especially for you, right?"

The innocence in her eyes touched him. "There's a lot going on that you couldn't understand. It doesn't have anything to do with you, but too much has happened to really fix this."

"You talking about your reputation?"

"I've lost a couple of clients, but I'll get them back. It goes deeper than that."

"Your father?"

Carter paused, studying her. He had already told her too much about the tension between him and his father. No sense in hiding back now. "I've caused him a lot of pain."

"He's your daddy, Carter. He'll understand."

"Steven Chase is my father, Avery. He's not my daddy. Not in the way you think of when you say the word. And he doesn't understand anything about me."

Avery placed her hand on Carter's lap. "We can't have everything, you know. No one's parents are perfect. Maybe he doesn't understand you exactly, but he loves you and that's more important, don't you think?"

If love was all it took, Carter thought. Then they might actually be a happy family. An entire life of competition, unrealistic expectations and societal pressure had made his family much more complex than Avery could ever understand even though right now he desperately wanted her to.

He desperately wanted so much from this woman and when he leaned into her, smelling her perfect scent, looking into those angelic eyes, he had to have her.

She didn't resist for even a second when he kissed her. She gave in to all of it and was swept away from the start. She could feel his hunger and pain as his lips pressed harder and harder and Avery wanted him to let it go with her. She wanted to take his pain; feel it. Lying on the bed, Carter positioned himself on top of her, between her legs, unable to stop kissing her. Their hands were hungry and desperate to touch skin and they both made sounds that gave away any doubt in the other that this was what they wanted more than anything.

When the phone rang, it sounded like it was in another room through Avery's haze. She turned her head, seeing it right next to her bed, and groaned out loud while Carter's tongue traveled down her neck. She didn't want to answer it. All she wanted to do was be with this man who had the hardest, hottest body her hands had ever touched. She ignored the phone and turned her attention to getting Carter's shirt off.

Then her cell phone, sitting right next to the phone, went off and voices in the back of Avery's head started talking to her.

"No." Carter tried to pull her arm back as it reached out. "Let it go."

"I know it's my mother. I've . . . Just . . . a . . . second."

Carter sighed, lifting himself enough to let her roll away. Where women got their strength he would never know. He wouldn't have even noticed a fire if it started a few seconds ago.

"Hello? . . . Hi, Alex."

Carter looked up with a jolt and caught her eyes, which previously dancing were now tearing up with guilt and shame. When she turned her back to him, Carter felt a sense of defeat that he wasn't willing to get used to. Did he really want her or did he just want what he wanted?

No, he wanted her and when he closed the door to her room behind him, he knew only one thing mattered now. Alex had to go.

Seeing Janet sitting on their bed, reading peacefully, Steven wondered how she could be so calm at a moment like this. It was probably the Valium. He had taken her bottle from their bathroom, but knew she stashed more elsewhere because she never said anything to him about it.

"Kimberly said the boys are eating now." He joined her on the bed. "When they're done, they're heading out for the night and the boys are ours."

"That's fine." She rubbed his arm. "I want to know what's going to be done about Detective Jackson sneaking into Haley's hotel room."

Steven wasn't in the mood to hear any more of her ranting about that boy. He wasn't too happy about it either, but he couldn't deny he respected the young man's initiative.

"If he can get in," she said, "why can't that scum?"

"What's important is that he's making progress." He caressed her arm. "They have that woman under arrest and they're talking to her."

"What is she saying?"

"They can't tell us yet."

"Is he questioning her?"

Steven sighed, taking the book from Janet. "Janet, he's the best detective for this case. Everything went cold with Davis. I shouldn't have ever had him taken off."

"But you did."

"Everything is different now. Carter is going to be

cleared and I know this lead will turn out good for Haley. Sean assures me."

"You trust him?" she asked.

Steven nodded. "I'll admit I'm not too crazy about him with Haley."

"He can't handle her."

"That's obvious," Steven said, "but as long as she holds his interest, he'll work hard."

"He's still Charlie Jackson's son."

Steven sighed, feeling a rush of heat run through him. "Right now, I'm backing away, but trust me, I'm not finished with that man."

Janet leaned back against the pillows, feeling restless. "I just . . . Steven, I'm . . ."

"Things are getting better, Janet. That's all I'm saying."

Janet wasn't finished with Sean, but she knew when to move on. "When Carter gets back from Las Vegas, you need to be the first to hug him."

"He didn't even ask to talk to me when he called."

"Can you blame him?"

"I bailed his ass out of jail."

"Which he was in because of doing work for you that he shouldn't have been."

Steven handed the book back to her. "I'll call him."

"You will not call him."

"Okay," he said. "I'll go over there and talk to him. Then I'm going to ask him what he thinks he's doing running after that woman like a lovesick puppy."

When Avery arrived home from church, she was thinking of the sermon, remembering all the blessings she had to be grateful for, and realized that she hadn't thought of Alex. She wanted to blame him for all of this, but he wasn't responsible for her heart. She still wore the ring he gave her on her finger and when she found him sitting on her doorstep like a lost little boy she knew she still cared for him.

"How was church?" he asked, standing.

"Come inside." She remembered taking away her key during their last argument. It was childish in hindsight, but all she could think of to do.

Alex stood in the doorway. "First, you tell me what's going on. Are you sleeping with Carter?"

Avery held her breath for a while before answering, "No."

"Are you sure?" he asked. "Because I would expect you to slap me just for asking if you weren't."

"I've never hit you, Alex, and I never will. No matter how mad you make me."

"But you aren't mad, are you?" he asked.

"I don't want to be mad. I just came from church and Craig is going to jail. I've settled all my debts. Just be happy for me, Alex."

"What was he doing in Vegas with you?"

Avery sighed, unwilling to aid this conservation.

"Whatever his reason for being there," he said, his voice catching a bit, "he had to think he would get something out of that. I mean, don't you find that a little obsessive?"

"It was all for a reason," she stated. "It worked out."

"Avery." Alex took a deep breath to pace himself, looking down at the floor. "I don't want to lose you. I know I don't deserve you, but I . . . I do love you."

Avery couldn't remember the last time she heard him say the L word. The last time he stood before her so humbled. She felt sorry for him even though he was managing to once again make this all about himself.

"Then what's wrong with us?" she asked.

"We need a firm commitment," he said. "If we set a date, we could be committed to making this work. It'll be real for us."

It had always been real for her.

"Just promise me we can work this out." He reached for her.

She took his hand and let him pull her to him. She leaned up and when his lips came down to kiss her Avery felt nothing but guilt.

"I'll try, Alex. I promise I'll try."

"I swear to God, Michael." Carter loved his nephews, but they were like wild animals. They were running around his place like it was a backyard and his bachelor pad was not twin-proof. "If they break something, you're paying for it. Can you tell them to calm down?"

Michael shrugged. "I don't know what to tell you. It's those damn Rice Krispy Treats Maya gave them. I don't know how to handle them and Kimberly won't let me spank them."

"Won't let you?"

"You know her dad used to beat her up," he said. "That's why she ran away from home. She'd rather see me dead than lay one hand on them."

"I'm just saying—" Carter tried unsuccessfully to grab them as they ran by him screaming like they were on fire. "Why do you have them, anyway?"

"Kimberly is having dinner with your girlfriend." Michael delighted in the look on Carter's face. "I thought you'd like that."

"Avery isn't talking to me at all." Carter had been aching to call her since getting back from Las Vegas, but he couldn't. It was her game now. He knew she would reach out to him again, but she hadn't and he knew Alex was the reason why.

"Kimberly can get anything out of anyone." Michael knew that all too well.

"I need to get rid of Alex."

This was Michael's kind of game. "You wanna go get him?"

"Calm down, boy. I'm talking about the smart way."

"Sometimes it's smart to kick a guy's ass."

The object was to get Avery and she wasn't going to be impressed with violence. Carter had to find another way and he had to do it quick, while he still had the advantage of her slight in Vegas.

Daniel pushed Evan against the wall hard and Michael yelled at him.

"Don't worry," he said to Carter. "It's only a matter of time before they're knocked out."

"It's pinching my nerves," Carter said.

"You talk to Dad?"

"He talked to me. It's cool. He said what he could, but you know him with apologies."

"I can't stand this thing between you two," Michael said. "It's like you won't submit to his anger, so he directs it at me instead."

"I'm sorry, Michael."

"You could fix all of this. Just come work for him. You could be chief general counsel."

"You couldn't handle the competition."

"Very funny. Chase Beauty is going to be mine; you and I both know that. It would just make things so much easier if—"

"If I lived his dream for me."

Michael envied Carter for having the nerve to be the same person he would've been if he wasn't a Chase. Michael couldn't even imagine who he could be without his father or his last name. His father was God to him.

"Sorry," Carter said. "I've got my own dream and—"

The sound of glass crashing had both men dashing

down the hallway where Daniel and Evan stood staring at the vase, jumping out of the way of the water that trickled down the hallway's wooden floor.

"Are you hurt?" Michael asked.

They both shook their heads and said no at the same time.

"What happened?" Carter asked.

They looked at Carter, then at the broken glass and scattered flowers and then back to Carter before saying, "Nothing."

CHAPTER 13

Sean loved the sound Haley made when he slowly pulled out of her. It was like a satisfied whimper and it shot his ego to the roof. But he was only human and after three rounds, he rolled beside her sweaty and exhausted. Looking over at her, the smile on her face made him feel great, but the fact that she never tried to cuddle with him bothered Sean. Not that he wanted to; he hated cuddling after sex. He wanted to go to sleep or take a shower, but he always did it because that was what women wanted. Only Haley never wanted it and it made him wonder if he was as good as the noises she made told him. Haley didn't come across as the kind of woman to fake it to avoid hurt feelings. If he hadn't gotten her there, Sean was positive he would have heard about it.

"Sean?" Haley was curious why he always stared at her in silence after sex like he was waiting for something.

"Don't ask me if I have any weed."

"I'm being serious. It's about that woman. Eva whatever."

"She's not talking, but don't worry. She's still in jail and she'll break down."

"How long can you keep her?"

Sean didn't want to tell Haley that they wouldn't be

able to keep her much longer. They couldn't charge her with accessory to a murder they couldn't prove. "Don't worry."

"Maybe that works with your stupid girlfriends, but it doesn't cut it with me."

"She's scared, Haley. That's what we need."

"Is she scared of you or Rudio?"

She was smart. He shrugged and said, "Still Rudio right now."

"That's your mistake," Haley said. "You need to make her more scared of you."

Sean threatened Eva with prison and anything else he could think of, but she wasn't about to give up her meal ticket for more reasons than fear.

"Why don't you beat the crap out of her?" Haley asked.

"You don't mean that." Sean could tell from the look on her face she did. "We can't do that."

"If it's your manhood you're worried about, then get a female cop to do it."

"None of us can do it," he said.

"You mean none of you have the balls to do it." Haley would have liked a few moments with the woman.

Sean looked down at his watch. "Wow, is it emasculating time already?"

"Stop feeling sorry for yourself." Haley sat up in bed, wrapping the covers around her. "I'm the one he's trying to kill. You have to find out what matters most and take it away from her. What about her family?"

"She has a mother and a five-year-old boy," Sean replied. "I was planning on having them kidnapped this afternoon so I'm way ahead of you."

"What about her son? Use him to get to her."

"I've already told her she could have him taken away, but she doesn't even have him. Her mother takes care of him in Santa Barbara."

"Santa Barbara?" Haley thought for a second. "That's an expensive ass town. How is it that she's there?"

"I'm sure Rudio is bankrolling her, too."

"Take it all away, Sean."

"Haley."

"Take it all away and leave it up to her to get it back. She's not turning because her son is safe with her mom, but what if we make it so her mom can't take him, then he'll go into the system? Tell her that Rudio thinks she's talking and is going to get her son."

Sean sat up, not wanting to hear anymore. "Let me do my job, Haley. There are rules."

Haley leaned into him, running her hand up his bare chest. She looked into his eyes, knowing there really wasn't much work with him anymore. She'd had him quite some time ago.

"I love you, Sean." She hoped that was convincing. The look on his face made her believe it was. "I just want to be with you. Can't you break the rules for that? I need you."

If she only knew all he had done already. He didn't believe Haley loved him for a second, but it didn't matter. It felt too good to hear the words to let on that he wasn't buying them.

"I'll see what I can do." He grabbed her, pulling her to him for round four.

"Who is she?" Alicia asked, nudging Leigh aside at the window.

Leigh watched without a word as Richard stepped out of the baby blue BMW driven by an attractive, dark woman with long, flowing hair. He leaned in, saying something and she laughed, flipping her hair back before driving off.

"Have you seen her before?" Alicia asked.

Leigh ignored her, feeling her heart beat quickly as Richard made his way to the clinic. She hadn't been able to reach him since he sped off from her house despite several attempts at calling him, going by his apartment and even the hospital. He'd even been timing his visits to the clinic against her schedule, which was easy because of the demands Janet was making on her.

She wasn't giving up. Even if he never forgave her, Leigh had to explain to him what happened. The clinic was opening on December 1st and she couldn't let her stupid mistakes jeopardize its purpose.

"Hello, Richard."

After getting over a quick surprise, Richard mumbled her name and something else and kept on walking.

She followed him. "Who is that woman?"

Richard didn't look behind him. "None of your business."

"I'm sorry, but I disagree."

He swung around to face her. "Say one more thing and I'm out of here. I just came by to help put those lights up."

"You have to let me explain," she said.

"No more." His tone was flat despite the emotion in his eyes. "I don't want to hear it. You kissed him. That wasn't part of the promise to your mother, so don't try to make a fool out of me."

Leigh wanted to explain the fear that she felt when Leo kissed her. It was growing. Leo was calling her non-stop and she was doing all she could to avoid him. The tone in his voice seemed edgy even though he spoke articulately and politely. Her mother told her everything she knew about Leo and said it was all good, but Leigh was beginning to believe there was more her mother was keeping from her.

"I didn't kiss him. He kissed me, but I didn't push away and I should have. I know that's my fault but I don't have any feelings for him."

Richard was shaking his head wearily. "I found myself

sitting in my car in front of your house spying on you like some crazy stalker. When I saw you kiss him I wanted to get my tire iron and beat the life out of that man. I won't let you turn me into some obsessive monster because of some complex about your mother."

"I know what jealousy can do to a person, Richard. I just felt it when I saw you get out of that woman's car."

"Not quite an accurate comparison." He stared at her, seeming reluctant to give anymore, but finally sighed. "She's my neighbor and she's just giving me a ride because my car is in the shop."

Leigh wanted to hug him. "This is why I love you, Richard."

"Don't start that, Leigh. Words aren't going to make me give in this time."

"It's not my words," she said. "It's yours. Even after everything I've done to you, and it was all inexcusable no matter what reasons I gave, you were honest with me. Most men would have relished an opportunity to make me jealous just now. Just to play games and get back at me; to hurt me; but you didn't. That's why I love you."

His expression remained unchanged. "Are we finished, here?"

"I'm ending it with Leo and I'm going to come clean with my mother."

"Hmm, sounds familiar." He was sifting through a table full of tools. "I'm busy, Leigh."

"Things are different now. Carter was cleared and my mother is in a much better state because he's getting along with Daddy. She says there's progress in Haley's case, so—"

"I'm happy for you." He grabbed the hammer and sack of nails, brushing past her.

She followed him, trying to keep her emotions in place. If she cried like she wanted to, it would seem like a ploy. "We have to work together."

He turned around to face her with an impatient sigh. "I know that, but I can't do it if you're gonna keep this up."

"I just want to try to make things up to you." She reached out to him, placing her hand on his chest. This man had been open to her like no other man in her life and now he wouldn't even show her the most basic of feelings.

He backed away. "Actions speak louder than words, Leigh, and I don't want to hear another word from you."

Kimberly waved Avery over to her table at the country club. Today she got serious. Their first dinner, Kimberly made sure not to mention anything about Carter or the family in general and she sensed that Avery was more relaxed by the end of the conversation. She liked Avery and thought she might make a good friend, which was saying a lot from Kimberly who barely had any real friends. It was her honest opinion that women talked too much and she had too many secrets.

Kimberly also knew if Carter and Avery hooked up, which she knew they would, now was her chance to make Avery her ally before Janet got her claws into her.

"Sit down, honey." Kimberly gestured. "You look nervous. Trust me, Carter isn't hiding in the bushes or anything."

"I'm not nervous," she lied.

They paused to give the waiter their order and Avery had a feeling that today's lunch was going to be much different than their dinner last week.

"Any new news on Craig?" Kimberly remembered everything Michael told her. She was going to do even better than she promised. She lived to please her king. "He's still going to jail, right?"

"Yes, but he's bankrupt so I won't get any money back." Avery didn't want to talk about Craig at all.

"Carter more than made up for that with the offer," Kimberly said. "Michael said that Steven wanted to hit the roof when he found out what he gave you."

Avery thought about the tension between the two men and wished she wasn't any part of that.

"He hasn't been bothering you, has he?" Kimberly asked, waiting for Avery to speak. She simply shook her head and Kimberly knew she was trying to keep her cards close to her. "Is that okay with you?"

"Yes," she answered. "I don't want him to bother me." It was enough she was thinking about him every day. "Alex and I are committed to making this work. We've set a date."

Kimberly rolled her eyes. "You guys have had some problems, huh?"

"We're fine now. We've set a—"

"You already told me that." Kimberly paused while the waiter placed her oysters on the table. "You've been engaged for over a year, haven't you?"

Avery wished she had ordered something stiffer than lemonade. How did these people know so much about her? "We're getting married in June."

"Are you sure you want to do that?" Kimberly leaned in. "I mean, you guys are having all of these problems, not to mention Carter, and—"

"Every relationship has problems, Kimberly."

"Aint that the truth." Kimberly laughed. "But if it's like this now, what do you have to look forward to?"

"Can we talk about something else?" Avery slid an oyster down her throat and the horseradish made her eyes burn.

"Just tell me one more thing," Kimberly stated. "If it weren't for Alex, would you be with Carter?"

Avery sighed, knowing she should have known better. "Everything I tell you, you tell Michael and he tells Carter."

"That means yes, then."

"Kimberly, please."

"Actually, hon, my husband can't stand you. If you were interested in Carter, he would probably do everything to keep him from knowing."

Avery didn't know what to think of that. "Carter is a very compelling man, but I love Alex and that's all there is to it."

"That Chase thing." Kimberly smacked her lips. "Those men just have something. All of them just drag you to them. It's a curse, really."

"They seem to be dealing well with it."

"Not a curse for them," she said. "For the women who love them. Don't get me wrong, I know Michael loves me. He would never hurt me, but you have no idea how many women make a career out of trying to snag him away."

"That must be hard on you." Avery was certain she was hearing more than she should.

"What are you gonna do?" Kimberly asked. "I mean, men are men and I think hell, he's gonna cheat on me one of these days."

"How can you say that?" Avery didn't understand why so many women, especially black women, accepted cheating as if there was no other choice. People will treat you how you let them.

"They all do it." Kimberly was laying it on thick and lying her butt off. If she ever caught Michael cheating she would cut his head off. Both of his heads.

"They don't and if you expect it, you're only asking for it to happen to you."

"So you're trying to tell me that if Alex cheated on you, you would give up all the work you've put into him?"

"Yes, I would!" She was indignant. "Even if I found

some way to forgive him, I would never trust him again and if you don't have trust, what's the point? I mean, if we can't trust each other, what is it all for?"

Kimberly shrugged, downing the last of her martini. This woman was way too open and trusting. Kimberly would have figured she'd learned her lesson after everything that had happened, but you could never tell with some people.

"Just be ready," she warned.

"Ready for what?"

"Marrying into black royalty ain't all it's cut out to be."

Avery wouldn't justify that statement with a response. She was marrying Alex Conner and that was all there was to it.

Sean was taken back by the look on Davis's face. He knew what it was: disgust. Davis had been sitting there listening to him threaten Eva with things he knew they would never do, could never do. Sean studied the law carefully. He knew he wasn't breaking any rules even though he was bending them beyond recognition and repair. Davis wasn't enjoying the show, but Sean ignored him, turning back to Eva whose crocodile tears had no effect on him. He reminded himself who this woman was, what she knew was going on and felt justified in hiding it. She was no victim. Haley was the victim and he was willing to break Eva down to save her.

"Your mother is going to jail, Eva." He looked down at her menacingly. "She's going to jail and your boy is going into the system."

"You're lying! You didn't find no drugs at her house. My mother would never, ever—"

"We found it," he said. "Pills and cocaine, Eva. I don't know how it got there, but it was there and it's her house."

"You planted it!" Eva pointed her finger at his face. "You set her up."

"Good chance with that," Sean said. "The mother of an ex-prostitute now video ho who happens to also be a drug dealer's girlfriend having drugs at her house. It's not a stretch. Two View Park detectives with spotless records planting drugs in an old lady's house in Santa Barbara? That might be a bit to prove."

"You have to let me out of here," she pleaded. "I have to get my son."

"He's with the state!" Sean slammed his fist on the table. "You won't get him back. As soon as you're convicted of accessory to murder, you'll never see him again."

"You can't do this!"

"What you can't do is get away with murder. Someone is going down and you're the only one that can be ID'd."

"He'll kill me!"

"Either way, you're on his hit list."

"Not if I don't tell."

Sean swallowed a bit, an acid taste filling his mouth. "But you did, Eva. That's what the word is, at least. You're talking and we're going to let you go free. No charges. He won't believe you just walked out for nothing."

"Just tell us," Davis advised. "Let's get this over with and we'll help you."

"How?"

Davis explained the witness protection program to her, sending Sean a few dirty looks when he promised to drop charges that didn't exist against her mother and get her son out of state custody, where he wasn't. Sean wasn't concerned with his opinion. Davis hadn't been able to do anything on his own and he didn't give a damn about Haley.

Eva's face fell into her hands as she agreed to tell them

everything through choked sobs. Sean slid a pad and pen across the table to her, letting her rip out a litany of swear words in Spanish at him. He deserved it. After he left the interrogation room, he leaned against the wall and took a deep breath. Nausea swept over him and he couldn't make eye contact with Davis even though he knew the man was staring him down.

"You can't go back from this," Davis said. "You gave up something today, man."

"I caught a killer!"

"Hopefully that will keep you warm at night." With that, Davis turned and walked away.

He wouldn't understand, so Sean didn't bother to tell him. Haley was going to keep him warm at night and that was going to be enough to make him forget anything else.

When he walked into his father's home office, Carter recognized a lower level of anxiety than usual. Steven was making an effort with him, which meant he only yelled at him half as much as usual. He wasn't going to rock the boat, thinking of what Avery told him. His father loved him and that would have to be enough.

"Think fast!"

Carter leaned to the left, letting the football Michael threw fly past and hit a bookshelf, knocking down a pile of magazines. "Very smooth, kid. Where is he?"

Michael circled around in his father's chair. "Had to go back to the castle room for something."

The castle room was their name for their parents' bedroom. The room was massive, taking up a quarter of the entire second floor.

"What about what I told you?" Michael asked. He had relayed everything Kimberly told him from her lunch and Carter merely thanked him and hung up.

Carter sat in his usual chair. "I'm not going to sit around and wait for him to cheat on her. And I know what you're thinking and the answer is no."

"You can set him up." Michael didn't even like Avery, but salivated at the chance to bring this guy down for his brother. "I'll take care of it."

"Michael, don't do anything." Carter could just imagine him hiring a call girl and having it all blow up in his face.

"It's all in the woman you choose," Michael said. "Some trick isn't gonna make it work. A man who has a woman like Avery isn't going to be interested in anyone for hire; at least not anyone who looks like they're for hire. It has to be someone you can trust and you pay her well."

"I wouldn't trust anyone who would do something like this." It was childish for him to even engage in the conversation.

"I left something out." Michael wanted to see his face when he relayed the good news. "They set a wedding date. June."

Carter sneered at his brother's sly grin. "It'll never happen. Trust me, I'll have her by then."

"Why are you willing to wait? That's a weakness, man. Dad says—"

"Don't give me one of Dad's psychotic business philosophies. She as much as told Kimberly she wanted me. I know what I'm doing."

"What about Lisette?" Michael was all surprises today and Carter didn't have a response. "Didn't know I knew about her, did you?"

"There's nothing to know."

"She needs a hundred grand."

"I already turned her down and she told me she found another sponsor."

"That fell through."

No wonder she was leaving so many messages for him these past few weeks. "Since when are you her close confidant?"

"Not that I relish being second choice, but since she really doesn't matter, I—"

"Please do not tell me she propositioned you, too."

Michael nodded. "Can you believe it? The amazing thing is she was staking me out and trapped me in the garage of the damn health club. That just tells you she's perfect."

"She can stake him out," Carter said. "Still, she wouldn't do it."

"She was willing to do it with me." Michael didn't really care to remember the moment. There was something inherently wicked about Lisette McDaniel that did appeal to him, but he hadn't considered it for a second.

"Not gonna happen."

"You offer her two hundred and she'll do it. I'll put in fifty for the hell of it."

"Shut up." Carter wanted him to stop talking about it because the more he did, the more it became an option and he didn't want to think of himself like that. "I can't do something like that."

"You're feeling a little hesitant, I understand. You've been through a lot, but that's all the more reason."

"Reason for what? To hurt someone I care about so I can take advantage of their pain?"

"You won't be hurting her," Michael said. "Alex will and you'll be her savior. You can't look me in the eye and tell me that you've come this far just to wait. That's the same as losing."

"Chases never lose."

Carter swung around as Steven walked by him. Michael jumped out of his seat, stepping a few feet away.

"Have you been listening?" Carter asked.

"I've got better things to do with my time than listen in

on you two." Steven exchanged glances between the boys. Michael had that look on his face; like a wolf salivating at the smell of rabbit. He loved that look. "Carter, what have you come so far to lose?"

"Nothing." Carter's expression threatened his brother if he spoke a word.

"You're up to something," Steven said. "Right now, I'd advise you to take it easy. You don't need any more trouble."

"I agree," Carter said.

"Then again," Steven added. "I'd rather get in trouble and win than play it safe and lose."

"My thoughts exactly," Michael said.

"Now"—Steven leaned back in his chair—"let's talk business. We need to hire someone to manage our salon chain. I have some candidates."

Carter watched as Michael accepted the folders from Steven and usually would have taken this time to protest the purpose for him even being here, but his mind was a million miles away right now.

Haley stuffed her mouth with strawberries dipped in white chocolate, blasting rap music on the stereo. Sean should have been there by now. If there was anything she didn't tolerate it was a man making her wait. There were too many other men out there who would show up on time to put up with that.

She turned the radio up a little more, knowing it drove the morning security guards crazy. Haley knew she was evil, but ticking other people off was just something to pass the time. Real revenge, well, that was something to look forward to. She had been thinking of ways to get back at Carly. Jail would be too simple for her. She needed to suffer and Haley was going to make sure she did.

Then there was Rudio and all the things Haley wanted to happen to him. When Sean told her they arrested almost everyone in his crew but couldn't find him anywhere, she should have been frightened, but not Haley. She had enough hate for the man who she was certain if he ever showed up she could kill him just by will alone. She would never be satisfied with him going to jail; he had to die and Haley didn't understand why he wasn't dead already. If it had been Leigh whose life he tried to snuff out, Haley was sure her father would have Rudio six feet under in no time. His precious little Leigh would be worth that, but Haley would be fine locked in a hotel room away from everyone and everything.

She blamed her father for everything and always had. If it hadn't been for Steven's coldness toward her, maybe she would have never gone after a man like Jack Flay. The only time she ever got her father's attention was when she upset him and barely even then. He hadn't even been there when she was born. He'd been traveling in New York with a wife nine months pregnant in L.A. Knowing she could give birth any day, he still hopped on a plane and went for the cash. He'd been there for every birth but hers and Haley would never let him forget it.

There were so many times when she wished she wasn't his. She imagined some day her mother dropping the bomb and finding out her real father was someone who gave a damn. Only as she went to the bathroom and looked in the wide mirror, Haley saw her father's face everywhere and she knew that was just a dream. Her mother would never cheat on him. After all, he was good to Janet. He was good to everyone but his little waste of time and money, Haley.

Why are you so angry, her mother always asked her, but she didn't understand. No one understood. Haley wasn't angry at anyone, she just didn't give a damn and for a woman that was unacceptable. Because she was a woman she was supposed to be emotional, nurturing, sacrificing and accommodating. That was why women always got the short end of the stick and stayed ten steps behind men.

Most men were worthless. Haley didn't need any more years under her belt to know that. All they cared about was sex and money and had the nerve to be offended when a woman proclaimed they felt the same way. They were good for what they could do for you, because in the end they would only disappoint you. Not all men of course, but Haley wasn't willing to allow herself to fall in love with any man until she found one with balls bigger than hers.

She was pretty confident Sean wasn't that man, but there was something about him that made her want to stick around and see. The sex was getting much better; so good now that she didn't remember the first time anymore. He saved her life and seemed to care more about helping her than anyone else except for her mother. He worshipped her, which wasn't unique, but he wasn't a taker, which was good because she was. She could trust him even though he would be a fool to trust her. He was all she had right now and that scared her.

She heard noises outside her bedroom and she knew it was him.

"Haley?"

She heard his keys drop to the floor and the snap as he undid his shoulder holster. By the time he reached the bathroom door, Haley felt her entire body tingling. Sean was a really good man and that might be boring, but when it came to what really mattered, he got the job done.

"Didn't you hear me calling you?" he asked, coming up behind her.

He wrapped his arms around her waist watching as she looked at herself in the mirror. Her eyes slowly closed and he was already hard. His hands slid down her hips, dipping under her satin nightgown. Slowly they slid up and she wasn't wearing any panties.

She leaned forward, grabbing the edges of the sink as he spread her legs apart. She arched her back as he lifted the nightgown, waiting not so patiently as he unzipped his pants. Men loved it from behind. It made them feel powerful. A lot of women pretended otherwise, but Haley knew they loved it just as much.

"Come on, baby." She lowered her head, ready.

He didn't make her wait any longer.

When Avery saw Carter through her peephole, her heart jumped. She hadn't seen him since Vegas and even though she told herself she didn't want to, she knew the truth. Every day, she waited for him to call or come by, but he hadn't. She hoped he would stay away just long enough for her to get out of Los Angeles. Then time could just work through everything.

She opened the door a bit, leaning against the post.

"I need to talk to you."

"I wish you would stay away."

"I already told you that's not gonna happen and I don't think you really want it to."

She flung the door open. "Who do you think you are, telling me what I want?"

"Why do you need me to stay away from you?" he asked.

"Because I know what you're intentions are, and—"

"Bullshit, Avery. It's because you don't think you're strong enough to stay away from me."

"Good-bye, Carter." She reached for the knob, but Carter pushed the door open wider and invited himself inside. He turned back to her. "You can close the door now."

She slammed the door shut.

"I've stayed away from you since Vegas," he said. "I've given you time to work things out with Alex."

Avery couldn't believe this man's arrogance. "So, one kiss from you and I'm throwing away the last three years of my life? I don't think so."

"So what do you plan to do? You can't avoid me, Avery. We gravitate toward each other."

"In your huge, huge head we do. Carter, it was one moment of weakness and—"

"More than one."

"However many times there were." She hated the smug look on his face. "It was all a reaction to what was going on in other areas of my life and that's all over. Craig is going to jail, my debt is paid off and I have enough money to start a new business. Alex and I are—"

"Spare me."

"You came over here, Carter. As much as you like to listen just to the sound of your own voice, you had to know I was going to say something."

"I didn't come over here to watch you struggle to make your affection for that man seem genuine." He helped himself to her living room sofa, looking around. "I came to make you an offer. What's with the boxes?"

"We've already done our business." She cleared her throat, not relishing telling Carter the truth. It might give him time to change her mind.

"The boxes, Avery." He had a bad feeling about this.

"Alex and I are mov—"

"Do you think that's going to help things?" he asked, feeling too pensive to even let her finish. "Moving in with him isn't going to solve your problems."

"Stop it!" Her hands clenched in fists; when she reached him he leaned away. It was good he thought she would hit him because she wanted to. "Since when have you been an expert on relationships? You go from woman to woman, Carter. Everyone knows about you."

Carter held his chin up, his eyes setting on hers. Her fire turned him on and Michael's words chipped away at him. "I came here for business, Avery."

"You came here to piss me off," she said. "You want to punish me for not falling under your spell. Your ego is bruised, Carter. You'll get over it."

No need to get over something that wasn't finished. "I came here to offer you a job." She sat down across from him and he appreciated being able to shut her up for once. "It's with Chase Beauty. My father is looking for someone to run the salon chain. You have the experience and you have a business degree. You have an understanding of what's important to the clients and my father needs that to balance his hunger for the bottom line."

"Your father wants me to work for him?" Avery couldn't believe that. She couldn't believe she actually liked the sound of it either.

"He doesn't know yet, but bear with me."

"He hates me," Avery said. "You know that."

"Well, you hate me, so that'll make you two best friends."

"That's not funny, Carter." She did hate him for making her feel compassion for him. "You don't understand. Alex and I are—"

"The salary is one hundred grand, with bonus and a car because you'll have to be traveling to the salons a lot."

"Don't tell me any more." *Please don't.*

"I know what you're going through," he said. "I felt the same way when I came back home. I was supposed to go work for my father. It was what I was groomed for. All the years and money was meant for one thing, like you and the shops. When the time came I wanted something else. So I compromised."

"What do you mean?"

"I followed my dream of opening up my own law firm and I made Chase Beauty my first client. That way I could have a little bit of the old dream with the new one. You can keep the dream you had with Essentials, but in a new venture."

She couldn't think of words to say for a moment, she was too busy trying to convince herself this didn't sound perfect. "Carter, I—"

"I'm barely there, Avery. You won't have to see me."

"It's not you, Carter." It was him. Everything seemed to be about him and that was the point. "It's me. I'm leaving L.A."

He blinked before he could catch himself. "You're running away from me?"

"I'm not," she answered. "Alex is getting transferred to the Phoenix office."

She turned away from him, unable to handle the blank stare on his face.

"This is convenient." Carter knew he was never going to let that happen.

"It's not a coincidence." She ordered the magazines on the coffee table, trying to keep her hands from shaking. "We're making a fresh start."

"Your family is here, Avery. That has to mean everything to a person like you."

Whatever he meant by that, he was right. The thought of being away from her family, especially her mother, was killing Avery, but she'd made a promise to Alex and if this was what it took, this was what it took.

"I need you to leave, Carter."

"We all need a lot of things." He reached into his jacket pocket and pulled out his business card. He plopped it on the table even though she knew exactly how to reach him. "Call me when you come to your senses."

Carter was driving with the top down even though it was chilly outside. He needed the air. He was selling his soul to the devil and it wasn't settling well with him. Neither was the idea of going out by letting a man like Alex beat him. The man wasn't even worth a thought, let alone his resentment. As he headed for the expressway to downtown, he hoped Lisette was still staying at The Westin.

"He's here to see me." Leigh nodded to Jay, the only bodyguard left at the house who generally stayed either inside or outside the front door.

This was why she had asked Leo to come to her house and she had no intention of letting him get out of Jay's sight. She had broken up with guys before, but she had a feeling that Leo wasn't going to be happy. He hadn't done anything to make her think that way. It was just the way he looked at her the last time they were together. That look was why she refused to be alone with him ever again.

Leigh rushed to the car as a confused Leo stepped out. "Shouldn't I just come in?"

She opened the passenger-side door. "Let's talk here. There are a lot of people in there."

Back in the car, the eager look on his face made Leigh feel like she was the worst person on earth. She swallowed hard and apologized a few times before he asked her just to come out with it. When she told him she couldn't see him anymore, she expected him to get angry but he didn't get anything and that worried her more. He went expressionless, as if he were barely awake. If it weren't for his eyes boring into her, Leigh wouldn't even believe he had heard her.

"Why?" he asked in the same voice he would greet a stranger.

"I'm just not feeling this," she said. "I think you're moving so fast . . ."

"I can slow down." A little crack in his voice slipped through.

"It's not you." She felt bad for even suggesting that he

was the reason this wasn't working. "You're great, Leo, but I'm just not interested in seeing you as anything more than a friend."

Leigh bit her lower lip, waiting for something as he turned away and faced the front of the car. She glanced to her right to make sure Jay was still there. When she turned back, Leo had closed his eyes and his breathing was picking up. When he started slamming his head against the steering wheel, Leigh's reaction was to reach out for him, but he wouldn't stop.

"Leo! Please, stop it. Leo!" She looked back at Jay, who wasn't paying the least bit of attention to them.

"You little bitch!" When he turned to her, the words spat out of his mouth, his eyes turned to slits and blood trickled from his left eyebrow.

Leigh gasped, but wasn't about to argue with him. She reached for the door handle, but just as she put her hand on it, she heard the click of the locks.

"Unlock the door, Leo." The way he stared at her made Leigh shake all over. He looked like a completely different person. "Unlock it now!"

"It's Richard, isn't it?" he asked.

Leigh froze. "Who?"

"Don't play games with me. It's Richard, right?"

"How do you know him?"

"Through you." His smile was a straight line, not showing any teeth. "I've seen you with him; at his apartment. You never even gave me a chance."

Leigh couldn't take any more. She turned to the window and began pounding on it, screaming for Jay to come to the door.

"You women," Leo said as if she wasn't in a panic. "You call us dogs, but you treat us like dirt with a smile and an apology. You think that's enough?"

Finally Jay noticed her and after leaning to the side, he rushed to the car.

Just before he reached them, Leigh heard the locks click and didn't hesitate. Jay caught her falling out of the car.

"What's going on?" he asked.

Leigh jumped out of the way as Leo did a quick circle around her and Jay and sped out of the driveway.

"Do you want me to go after him?" Jay asked.

"No!" She grabbed him since he was already heading for his car. "Don't. It's okay."

"Was he locking you in there?"

"We were just arguing," she explained. "I was being dramatic. I'm sorry."

Jay didn't seem to be buying it. "You looked like you were scared to death."

"It's okay," she said, trying to pull herself together.

It wasn't okay, but Leigh wasn't going to do anything. This was her fault and she'd paid the price. It was over and that was all that mattered. As she ran into the house, she decided to keep this to herself.

CHAPTER 14

Carter ignored the women who rubbed against him as he walked through the strip club. Even though The Playground was Los Angeles's highest end strip club, he couldn't get past the amount of female customers in the place. Times were changing. The women here were as hot as any he had ever seen, but all the money in the world couldn't make this place more than a strip club and it just didn't do it for him.

He saw Michael sitting at a table in the front, leaning back, enjoying the show, and sat down next to him.

"What took you so long?" Michael asked.

"Why did you want to meet here?" Carter leaned away from a woman trying to get his attention.

"'Cause this is where I was gonna be." Michael smiled at a woman who caressed his chin walking by. "Get a drink, man."

"Hell, no."

Michael looked at his brother, sighing. "What's the matter with you, man? This is the nicest strip club in L.A. You're single. You should be up in this bitch on the regular."

"Yeah, I'm single. What would Kimberly say if she knew you were here?"

Michael laughed, pointing behind him. "She's over at the bar getting another drink."

Carter swung around and there she was, standing at the bar laughing with the bartender and looking better than any woman around her. All Carter could think was, *damn*.

"Did you do it?" Michael asked.

"You could have asked me that on the phone."

"I wanted to see your face when you answered me." Michael didn't think he looked too good right now, but that was okay. "Did you do it or not?"

Carter nodded, looking away, and Michael shook his head. "What's wrong?"

"I guess I can't believe I actually dated someone who would do something like this."

"You're someone who would do something like this." Michael socked him in the arm. "Come on, man. All that matters is that she's doing it and I wouldn't call what you did with her dating."

"Well." Carter was looking down at his hands trying to clear the cloud in his head. "It's done."

"You should be happy that it went that easy; that quick." Michael slammed his glass on the table. "What's the matter with you? You're going to get what you want."

"You wouldn't understand. Unlike you, human beings actually experience guilt, regret, and maybe some shame when they do something they know is wrong." Carter tasted bile in this throat when Lisette agreed to set Alex up after he raised the payment to two-fifty. She wasn't at all surprised, which made him believe that Michael had already spoken to her, but he didn't ask. He just wanted to get it over with.

"You're damn right I wouldn't understand." These were the times Michael felt like he was the older brother. "Feelings that don't help you get what you want aren't worth having."

"Is that another one of Dad's philosophies?" Carter asked, feeling his father all over that deranged sentiment.

"You feel bad now"—Michael shared his attention between Carter and the woman on stage—"but it won't last. When Avery falls into your bed, things will change. You'll feel like a God because you'll know that you can really have everything you want. You've proved it to yourself and it'll get easier the next time."

"I'm not doing this shit again."

"You say that now, bro." Michael leaned toward him. "But just wait until it works. Trust me, you'll do it as many times as you have to."

"Which one of you is Michael?" A blonde with long legs and a chest that made her look like she was going to fall forward any second stood between them. She was dressed in a leather zebra striped bikini ready to bust apart. She directed her attention to Carter until he shook his head, pointing to his brother.

"What can I do for you?" Michael asked, leaning forward.

She positioned herself between his legs, wrapping her arms around his neck. "Your wife wants to watch me dance for you."

Michael leaned back, looking toward the bar. Kimberly waved him over before slowly sliding her hands over her hips. He stood up, glancing down at Carter who had a look of disbelief on his face.

"Anything you want," Michael said before letting the woman take his hand and lead him toward the private rooms.

Carter shook his head, laughing to himself. He didn't want everything like Michael did. He just wanted Avery and even though he knew he was going to get her, this feeling haunted him. He was no angel. He had done things that were wrong and immoral. He had been greedy and selfish most of the time. He had been cruel and spiteful, but this seemed different. He was manipulating other people's lives, their hearts, to suit his own need. He had crossed a line he never believed he would. There was no going back now.

"I have a surprise for you." Haley opened her bathrobe the second Sean entered the room, revealing a skimpy Brazilian bikini.

"I have something for you, too." He tossed his holster on the chair and grabbed her in his arms, kissing her. "We think we know where Rudio is."

"Where?"

"Florida. We've been keeping surveillance on his mother for the past couple of days and she's been acting suspicious, changing her regular schedule. We think he's there or he's on his way."

Haley grabbed Sean by his collar and pulled him to her. "You have to kill him, Sean. No one else will do it. They won't understand. They'll just arrest him."

"I don't want to go through this again." He pushed away from her, feeling his frustration mount. "I'm not going to kill him, Haley. Not unless I have to. Jesus, haven't I broken enough rules for you?"

"I want him dead, Sean."

Sean walked past her to the room service table showing the remains of a lobster lunch. "What's my surprise?"

She came up behind him and wrapped her arms around his waist. She reached down and rubbed him back and forth. "I got something good for you."

He reached behind him, grabbing her by her hair and pulling her in front of him. He pulled her head back and leaned in to trail his tongue from just above her breast to her chin before planting his lips on hers. A ripping pain hit him as she bit his tongue and he backed away.

"Dammit, Haley!"

"I needed to calm you down," she said. "You're getting too hot too soon."

"Well that's not a problem anymore." He tasted blood.

"My surprise is downstairs." She grabbed his hand. "Let's go, Daddy."

He pulled her back. "You're not leaving this room."

"Have you ever had sex in a Jacuzzi?"

"Yes, I have." Even though he hadn't. The most exciting place he'd been was the backseat of a car and that didn't go too well.

I don't believe you," she said. "It's exciting."

"Haley, if you tell me about the many times you've had sex in the pool, I'm leaving."

"Don't worry, little girl." She closed her bathrobe, walking toward the door. "I've gotten the head of security to close the private pool after the lunch rush just for me. I can bring one of the guards down and you have your gun, so let's move."

"It's not a good idea."

Her expression became completely serious. It was too far into this relationship for him to still say no to her. "Sean, I went through a lot of trouble to get this done, so I don't think you want to disappoint me."

"I don't mind disappointing you," he answered. "Getting you killed on the other hand . . ."

"By who? Rudio is in Florida and all his guys are in jail. Who's gonna come here, get past security downstairs, find their way to the private pool area, get past the guard I'm bringing with me, and get past you?"

"How long ago did you set this up?" he asked.

"I'm done explaining to you, Sean. Let's go." She opened the door knowing that if she looked back he wouldn't come.

"Come on, Danny." She nodded to the security guard and heard the door close behind her. She turned back to see Sean rushing to catch up with her. They were all so damn easy.

Sean pushed Haley's hands away from his crotch for the third time. She was acting like Danny wasn't in the elevator with them. There wasn't much point to it; everyone knew why he came there. Still, with Haley biting on his neck practically climbing his body, he was grateful when the elevator opened up and they could get out.

Danny blocked them, looking down the hallway. He waved to someone. "There's a security guard down at that end."

"Another one?" Sean asked.

"Come on out." Danny stepped aside for them.

Sean looked down the hallway. He saw the profile of the security guard, but he was too far to get his face. He was short and had a stomach that made him look like he was in his third trimester. "I thought you only had Danny?"

"I said one guard." Haley started the other way, toward the pool. "Maybe he thought he was supposed to provide it. Come on, Sean."

"You can stay here," Sean ordered Danny as they reached the door to the pool. He looked at the guy's grin. "Turned that way."

"I get it." He laughed. "Don't worry. I'm not into looking."

Every guy was into looking, but that wasn't on Sean's mind. "Just keep an eye out."

When they got to the pool area, it was enclosed and dimly lit. Haley wasn't the romantic type, but it suited her fine. She tossed her bathrobe away and stepped into the Jacuzzi, turning it on. She looked up at Sean who was searching the walls. "What in the hell are you doing?"

"I'm looking for the lights." Finally seeing them, he flipped the switch and the room lit up. "Better."

Haley watched him grab towels and bring them to a chair and began to slowly undress. She took off her bikini top and threw it at him. "I'd like to do this today if you don't mind."

Sean held his gun in his hand, looking around. He thought to place it on top of the towels, but something wasn't right. He looked around, seeing Danny standing at the doorway. Yeah, he was looking. He nodded an apology before turning around.

Sean grabbed a towel and wrapped it around his gun. He wanted it as close to him as possible. He was feeling something eerie and with a half naked Haley a few feet from him, he shouldn't have been feeling anything but her.

He placed the gun under the towel at the edge of the tub and got in. He took Haley by the waist as she reached up and placed her bikini bottom on his head. He jerked it away, leading her against the edge.

"What are you doing?" she asked.

"Just stay over here," he said. "This is dangerous, you know."

"That's the whole point, Papi." She licked her lips, but leaned away as he came in for a kiss.

He grabbed her arms. "I don't like games."

"Are you sure?" she asked, laying her hands on his chest. "Because I think you like them a lot and I have a good one for you. It's called, how long can you hold your breath under water?"

She was wicked and he cursed that he wouldn't have her any other way. Sean took a deep breath and submerged himself under water. He was good for a couple of minutes at a time.

When she felt his touch inside of her, a sensation ran through Haley making her arch her back. She wanted to let go, but she knew that meant a lot of noise and Sean would get upset with a guard just outside the door.

She turned to see Danny, and as she expected, he was looking right at her. She had caught him and his face went red. She smiled, twirling her fingers to gesture for him to turn around and he did. Then he jerked and Haley blinked.

He leaned over and then leaned back against the glass. Slowly, his body lowered and it wasn't until she saw the trail of blood on the glass above him that she realized what was happening.

Haley opened her mouth, but nothing came out. The door burst open and the other security guard stepped onto the deck. He tossed his cap aside, taking a black wig with it.

Rudio smiled at Haley, showing all his gold teeth, and raised his gun. Haley let out a bloodcurdling scream and miles away, Janet, who was standing in the middle of her kitchen, felt a sharp pain run through her. She dropped the glass of water in her hand and it shattered everywhere.

Carter looked up from his computer when Michael came into his office with a dangerous grin on his face. Whenever Michael had that look, he was interested in starting something.

"Whatever it is," Carter said, "the answer is no. I've got work to do."

"It's Friday, man. You should take off early. Patricia is obviously gone and you're worthless without her. Let's go check out a movie or something."

He walked to the window, noticing a shiny new gold telescope. "What's this?"

"A present from a client." Carter turned his computer off. "What about the family?"

"Kimberly has the boys in this little toddler fashion show thing." He leaned into the telescope, focusing it on the building across the street. "You know how she is when anyone mentions modeling."

"Why don't you let her do any modeling?"

"She's got enough being my wife and raising our kids." The truth was he was scared if Kimberly got a taste of how much money she could make as a model she wouldn't be satisfied being anyone's wife. "Have you found any naked women or people having sex with this thing?"

"That's not what it's for. Don't you ever take a rest?"

"No rest for the wicked." He lowered his brows, staring at his brother. "And you're no different from me, so give it up."

Carter laughed. "Try the top floor on that building with the red brick sides. You'll find something good there."

"Carter!"

They both turned to Alex Conner who stormed into the office. He looked from Carter to Michael and seemed disappointed Michael was there.

"Mr. Conner." Carter leaned back in his chair, clasping his hands behind his head. "This is a nice surprise."

"I know what you're up to," Alex exclaimed.

"I don't think we've met," Michael said. "I'm—"

"Fuck you!"

Michael laughed a little too hard for Carter's sake. It was that laugh that warned only those who knew him that he was about to start something.

"What did you think you could do by offering her that job?" Alex asked. "You think you could get her to stay?"

Carter knew Avery wouldn't tell him anything. "You found my card."

"She told me what you were doing there, but I know it's about more than that."

"You're smarter than you look." Carter let go of any attempt at politeness.

"So you admit you're trying to take my woman away from me."

Carter placed his hands flat on the desk, tilting his head slightly. "Now, Alex, let's be honest. If Avery was still your woman, you wouldn't be here."

His hands clenched into fists, Alex started for the desk. Carter shot up from his chair and Michael took a couple steps forward and Alex backed away. He looked at both of the men and was clearly intimidated. His hands loosened and he focused just on Carter.

"This isn't over," he said.

Carter checked his adrenaline, having shot up at the prospect of beating the crap out of this man. He relished the opportunity even though he knew it would work against him in the long run. "You're wrong. This was over some time ago. Now get the hell out of my office, bitch."

Alex swallowed hard, pressing his lips together. His eyes were like daggers at Carter, who stood calmly with his eager, smiling brother just behind him. When he turned and walked out, Carter sat back down looking up at Michael.

"I didn't need you," he said. "I can take that guy by myself."

"I know." Michael went back to the telescope. "I just couldn't help myself. This is a great move, Carter."

"I know." Carter rested his chin on his folded hands. "He's feeling real emasculated right now."

"His manhood has been threatened." Michael focused on the red brick building. "He's ripe for the next woman who comes along."

Carter picked up the phone. He'd had enough of this game. Lisette needed to get this done.

Sean's head shot up, his eyes stinging when he opened them. He looked at Haley who was shaking all over, digging her nails into his shoulder. When he turned, he saw the security guard standing with a gun and realized then . . . Rudio. He looked at the towel covering his gun behind Haley, but knew he wouldn't have time to reach for it before Rudio got at least two shots off.

"Don't stop for me." Rudio moved the gun between the two of them as if he wasn't sure who he wanted to kill first. "If I gotta go out, that's how I'd want to do it."

Haley saw the sickening grin on his face and she felt the hatred inside of her begin to take over her fear. She whispered, "Where's your gun?"

"Not now," Sean whispered back, slowly pushing Haley aside so he could get in front of her.

"Don't." Rudio took a few steps closer. "It'll be easier on you if you accept right now that there aren't going to be any heroics this time. No close misses, no sorry security guards or scared bitches who can't follow through."

"She can't hurt you," Sean said. "She never saw you."

"You think this is still about her?" Rudio laughed.

Sean made a conscious choice not to look at the towel. If Rudio caught on, Haley would be dead. "I told you I would get you and I did it, not Haley."

"You're so smart, huh? So how did I get here, then?" He paused like he was expecting Sean to help him along. "I followed you. You couldn't stay away from that little whore. You were so lit up, you didn't even notice me. It only took me a day to get a uniform. And you know the best thing? I'm inside for less than ten minutes before another security guard reminds me to tell everyone the eighth floor pool is off-limits. That's how smart you are."

He kept his eyes on Rudio. "You know this is about you and—"

"Don't try to reason with me! I've got nothing to lose so you got no room for negotiation."

"Then why don't you just do it, you bitch!" Haley yelled out.

Sean slid in front of her, certain they were both going to get shot, but Rudio just laughed.

"Till the end, huh?" he asked. "That's fine. I want you to get your sweet ass out of that little pool. We're gonna talk."

"Kiss my ass," Haley spat.

"Why don't you just talk to me?" Sean asked. He could jump out of the Jacuzzi and conceal reaching for the gun behind his legs. "I'll get out."

"Don't worry," Rudio said. "I'm gonna kill you in a second, but I want you both to listen while I tell her why she's gonna die. I want to give her a few seconds to hate her father."

"What did you do to my dad?" Haley asked.

"This is about what he did to me. I was gonna leave you alone because you're a stupid spoiled brat who hadn't seen anything, but your father wouldn't stop. He tried to take away my club and close down my restaurant, and don't think I don't know he was trying to get me killed. That shooting didn't work out, but I know it was him. Now get out of that damn pool. I want to watch you bleed to death so I can tell your daddy your last thoughts were that all of this was his fault."

Haley couldn't believe what she was hearing. Why would he lie now? Her father had tried to help her.

"I'm not getting out!" she yelled, wishing Sean would do something quick.

"Okay." Sean turned to Haley. "Haley, get out."

She gasped, hitting Sean on the arm. "No, he'll kill me."

"I won't let that happen," he said. "I know what I'm doing. Get out."

She shook her head, not moving an inch. "I'm naked."

"Since when did that matter to you?" He smiled, but she didn't smile back. "I know you're naked, and I know no man can avoid being distracted by that body of yours. Just get out."

Rudio was yelling something, but Haley wasn't paying attention. She took a deep breath, looking into Sean's eyes. They promised her he would not let her die and any thought that she might washed away. He had bigger balls than she did and that made her love him.

"That's what I'm talking about." Rudio was laughing boyishly as Haley slowly started to get out.

She didn't want him looking at Sean, so as she walked to him, she made eye contact with him. He licked his lips as he slowly looked her up and down. He tilted his head, rubbing his chin with his free hand. "Damn, woman, you are fine."

Haley hadn't heard the shot, but she screamed when she saw the bullet go through his forehead and his limp body drop. She rushed to Sean who was backing out of the Jacuzzi with his gun still trained on Rudio, but he held his hand out to her.

"Get out of here," he said.

She didn't want to leave. She wanted him to hold her. "He's dead, Sean. It's okay. It's over."

Standing over Rudio's body, Sean kicked his gun away. There was barely any blood and that grin on his face at the sight of Haley's naked body was still there.

"Sean?" At first she thought he was leaving and she rushed after him, but he was only checking on Danny. "He's dead, too. Forget him."

"Stop it." Her indifference to a man who had died protecting her grated on Sean, but he knew she wasn't thinking straight right now. "Get dressed."

Haley was confused by his coldness. She held her hand out to him as he walked past her, but he ignored her. She loved him and needed him and all he could do was stand over Rudio's dead body looking like he regretted killing the man who was certainly going to kill them.

Sean looked up at Haley who stood there staring like she was waiting for something he didn't have the mind to give her right now. She started to move toward him, looking down at Rudio. He was jolted when she spat on him even though he wanted to understand. He was disgusted by everything and wanted to get this over with.

"You're still naked," he told her.

She looked up at him feeling insulted by the disgusted tone of his voice before saying, "So are you."

Janet was losing her patience with Steven and she resorted to yelling over the phone, a completely classless thing to do. "Steven, I'm telling you something is wrong with Haley!"

"Janet, please. Get a hold of yourself."

"You have to understand me," she pleaded. "She's my baby and I can feel her. Do something now or I'm going over there."

"Don't do that, Janet. I'll call Sean and get back to you, okay?"

"Right away, Steven."

Janet hung up, slamming the phone down on the foyer console table. She put her hand to her aching stomach; the pain hadn't gone away. Something was terribly wrong and she wasn't going to rest until she talked to every one of her children.

Hearing voices yelling on the other side of the door only made her worry more. Opening the door, she was surprised to see Jay struggling with a young man trying desperately to get inside. At first she feared he had something to do with Rudio, but he was dressed in a doctor's coat and was yelling for Leigh to come to the door.

"What do you want?" she asked.

"I need to talk to Leigh!" Richard pushed away from Jay.

"Something's wrong with this guy," Jay said. "He practically drove his car up the steps."

"Who are you?" she asked.

"I'm Richard. I'm her boyfriend. Please, Mrs. Chase."

His voice was straining, his eyes desperate. "You have to let me talk to her. Something is really wrong."

The way she was feeling right now, Janet wasn't willing to take the chance he was lying. "She's upstairs, but tell me what you mean."

Richard pushed Jay away, storming into the house. "Where's her room?"

"You tell me what's going on and I'll take you to her."

"I was talking to her on the phone." Richard spoke through quick breaths. "She called me, crying. She said she needed me and she was afraid. Then she hung up."

When they burst into Leigh's room screaming her name, they found her sitting on the bed, hugging her knees to her chest with tears rolling down her face. Janet rushed to her, wrapping her arms around her and it only made her cry harder.

"I'm so sorry," she kept repeating. "I'm so sorry."

"What happened?" Janet asked. "What are you afraid of?"

Leigh couldn't hold back anymore. "It's Leo. He's crazy, Mom."

"What are you talking about?" Janet asked.

"I . . . I . . ."

"Calm down, first." Janet began to run her hand gently over her hair to soothe her. "Tell me what he did."

Leigh took a deep breath, looking at the floor because she was too embarrassed to look anyone in the face. "I broke things off with him because I love Richard and I want to be with him."

"Did you tell him that?" Richard asked.

She shook her head. "No, but he knew. He's been following me and he knows all about you, Richard. He started to bang his head against the steering wheel."

"Did he hurt you?" Janet asked.

"I thought he was going to, so I tried to get out but he locked the door." Leigh looked up just in time to see

Richard's hand clench into a fist. This was what she wanted to avoid. "Don't be mad. He didn't touch me. He was just so upset, but he let me out after I yelled for Jay."

"Then what?" Richard asked, his voice almost growling.

"He just drove off, so I thought it was over." She looked up at her mother. "I didn't want anyone to be upset because things were going so well with Carter and Haley's case."

"You have to tell me these things." Janet wondered how she could have been so wrong about Leo. "Has he bothered you since?"

She nodded. "He just called me on my cell phone. I picked up because it was from the hospital."

"My hospital?" Richard asked.

She nodded. "He must have called me from there knowing I would think it was you and pick up. He said I was going to be sorry for doing this to him and I hung up."

Richard picked up the phone. "We need to call the police now!"

"No," Leigh pleaded. "Don't do that. Everything was just calming down."

"She's right," Janet said. "I'll call my husband first. He'll know what to do."

Leigh looked up at her mother, not comfortable with the calm look on her face. "Mom, please don't tell Dad to do anything. It will pass, I'm sure."

Janet smiled at her. "It's okay, honey. Your father and I will fix everything."

"What can you do without the police?" Richard asked.

Janet just looked at him and the expression on his face seemed to show he understood. "We can do whatever needs to be done. Give me the phone."

* * *

Haley was waking up, but Janet wished she wouldn't. She enjoyed looking down at her baby sleeping peacefully in her own bed. Because she was the youngest, more than any of the other children, Janet still saw a baby when she looked at her. She saw the wide, curious eyes and the curly hair that went all over the place. She saw that stubborn mouth and those fat kissable cheeks. Wiping a tear from her own cheek she said another prayer, thanking God for protecting Haley and bringing her home. She wouldn't thank God that Rudio was dead, but she was grateful he was.

Haley opened her eyes, thinking at first she was still in that hotel room, but when she saw her mother staring down at her, the present rushed back to her and she beamed, stretching her arms wide.

"Morning." Janet leaned down to kiss her cheek.

"What are you doing?" Haley asked.

"Watching you." She sat down on the edge of the bed. "It's eleven, sweetie."

"Where's Sean?"

Janet's smile faded. Haley had never asked for a man so much. She hadn't let him leave her alone since Rudio's death Friday night. "He's at work, dear. It's Monday."

Haley sat up. "He said he would come by this morning. What did Maya make for breakfast?"

"Stop being so spoiled." Janet offered Haley's bathrobe to her, but she didn't take it. "Go on downstairs and make your own breakfast. It's time to get back in the saddle."

"You make me breakfast," Haley said. "Please."

"Please? When was the last time I heard that word from you?" Janet stood up. "Sorry, dear, but I'm having lunch with your father."

"Is he here?"

"He's at work."

"Mom, you know what he did for me? He tried to . . ."

Janet put her finger to her mouth to silence her. "I know, but we won't talk about that."

She nodded. "Why are you leaving?"

"I don't want you worrying about anything. Now get up."

Haley frowned, kicking her covers away. "Leigh, right? Everything is about Leigh."

"Don't be so selfish."

"I'm not being selfish. After what I've been through, all anyone can talk about is Leigh and her stupid boyfriend calling her on the phone." Haley got out of bed, grabbing the bathrobe from her mother and tossing it to the floor. "Doesn't anyone care about what happened to me?"

"You know we do." Janet sighed, looking at her watch. There wasn't enough of her to go around today. "You're just upset. Now—"

"Sean!"

Janet watched Haley's entire demeanor change as she rushed to hug Sean, who was standing in the doorway. When Haley told her that she was in love with Sean, Janet took it with a grain of salt. It was Haley after all, but now she wasn't so sure.

Sean leaned away from Haley's kisses, conscious of Janet's stare. "Hello, Mrs. Chase."

"You can call me Janet," she offered.

"I told you," Haley stated, dragging him to the bed. "He doesn't think you like him, Mom."

"Don't be silly," Janet said. "I wouldn't have any justification for not liking him. Sean made sure of that when he saved your life."

Sean felt a chill from the plastic smile Janet gave him before excusing herself. It was okay, he knew she was just angry. She was angry because he could do no wrong now and she wasn't going to be able to keep him away from Haley ever.

"Are you feeling better?" Haley took hold of his chin, turning his face to her.

"I'm not sick, Haley. I told you that. I'm sorry for the way I acted Friday, but it's not easy killing someone."

"You don't think I can understand that, but I can." Haley leaned in to kiss him gently on the forehead, still not believing she could feel this way about someone and not be scared. "I love you, Sean. I know you didn't want it to end like that even though I did."

"I'm fine now."

"I'm glad you're feeling better." She wrapped her legs around him. "Now, you could make me feel better."

He moved away from her, taking everything he had to resist her. "I can only stay a few minutes. I've got to get back to work. I'm on a new case. It's—"

"I gotta get out of here, Sean." Haley was up, heading for her vanity. "I'm not talking about for the day. I mean I can't live here anymore. Now that Leigh's back, everything is about her again and I just get a bad vibe here."

"Where do you want to go?" he asked, wishing she was out of this house, too. He couldn't imagine doing anything with her in her parents' house. It made him feel too juvenile.

She laughed. "Silly, I'm gonna move in with you."

He swallowed hard, expected to feel panic, but he didn't. He felt anything but. "Sounds like a plan, but my place is very small."

"I don't doubt it." Haley was trying hard to ignore how much Sean's tax bracket bothered her, but she was working on that. She was going to get him a job at Chase Beauty and he had to get a college degree. She couldn't date a high school graduate. "We'll get a place of our own somewhere downtown. I've always wanted to live where Carter lives. That's the hot building."

"Those places are expensive, Haley."

"Carter's condo only cost about three million dollars. That size would be fine for us."

"Excuse me?" Sean hoped she was joking. "I don't think so."

Haley ignored his gesturing, choosing to brush her hellish hair instead. "I have to get my hair done and a pedicure and manicure. Since I'm at it, I better just get a massage. My eyebrows need—"

"Haley, are you listening to me? We can't afford a condo." Sean couldn't describe Haley's expression, but it was as if he were speaking a foreign language.

"Don't worry, Sean. Daddy will buy it for us."

"No, he won't."

Haley wasn't interested in hearing this. "Yes, he will. If he's willing to kill someone for me, he won't object to a stupid condo."

Sean stood behind Haley, placing his hands on her shoulders, massaging them gently. "You know I won't take money from your father."

"I'll take it from him," she said. "You don't have to be a part of it."

"If I'm living there, then I'm living off of him and I can't do that."

"Then what do you expect me to do?"

"We'll get a place we can both afford." There was that look again, but he was sure he was speaking English.

"What do you mean, like pay rent? Please, Sean. Next thing you'll be telling me to get a job."

Janet waited while Steven dismissed the two men in his office and she smiled kindly to them both as they walked by. There had always been an understanding between them; when Janet came to the office she would not be made to wait for even one second. In return, she rarely came by unless she knew Steven would be free, which was never.

Steven closed the door behind the men, pecking his wife on the cheek. "You're early."

"Just a few," she said. "I wanted to talk to you while we're still alone."

"Who are we having lunch with?"

"David and Elisa Fox." She helped herself to a seat on the sofa while he returned to his desk. "She's new on the museum board, so I'm trying to make her feel comfortable."

Steven leaned back in his chair, knowing that when Janet used this extremely proper tone of voice she meant to ask him something he didn't want to tell her.

"I spoke with Giovanna this morning," she continued. "She told me Leo has been missing for a few days now."

Steven's expression didn't change. "I'm aware of that."

"Steven, I know you spoke with him after I called you about Leigh, and—"

"Janet, I've taken care of it."

Janet found it so difficult to reach him when he turned to stone. "I know, but . . . Steven."

"I'm not going to talk to you about this." He stood up. "Let's go to lunch."

"I know what you did with Rudio," she said. "It didn't work, but I know you tried to—"

"Janet." Steven gave her an admonishing stare.

"I'm just worried about Leigh."

"Leo is fine," Steven said. "He'll show up soon. What did you say to Giovanna?"

Janet knew she would never hear another word about this. Steven promised to never betray her, but he had secrets and he made it very clear to her there were things she didn't want to know.

"I told her I was able to find out that Leo had been arrested for abuse a couple of times, but her husband had it wiped away. Also, he was kicked out of three prep schools from junior high through high school for violence. She had nothing to say to me."

Steven walked over to Janet, joining her on the sofa. He wrapped his arms around her, wanting to take away what he knew was the guilt she was feeling. He was afraid it would only lead to her taking more pills. "It wasn't your fault. Giovanna deceived you. You shared that with her?"

"I think I was very clear," Janet said. Giovanna's position in Los Angeles society was over before it even got started.

Avery dumped another stack of books in the closest box. She was exhausted having packed all day, but seemed to be getting nowhere. She had so much stuff she knew she should throw away but it was proving harder than she expected. Everything she had, even the junk, held some memory of family, friends, and better times. The idea of being in Phoenix without these things was too much for her.

It was only a few states over, but seemed like a million miles to Avery. Carter had been right. She wasn't the type of girl to be away from her family. She knew she was on her way to making her own family, but it didn't sooth her worries. Avery wasn't sure she could make it without her mother close by.

Things weren't getting better like she hoped setting a date would make them, and she only had the courage to share that with her mother. After Alex found Carter's business card, he accused her of having an affair with him. She had to tell him the truth about the job offer, but Alex had been cold to her since. He could be a fool, but he wasn't an idiot. He knew as well as anyone that Carter hadn't needed to come over to offer her the job. He came over to see Avery and Avery hadn't sent him away. Alex had every right to be upset.

Avery got up, walking to the telephone with every intention of calling him at work just to talk to him. She needed to reach out to him and reassure him, but the second the phone was in her hands, she couldn't think of a thing to say. How could she reassure him of something she wasn't sure she believed in anymore herself? It would take some time, but they had to be able to work it out. She put the phone down, deciding instead to go through her mail. Anything was a welcomed distraction from the reality of leaving Los Angeles. She slit open a wide manila envelope with no return address and out slipped a piece of paper written on stationery from The Westin Los Angeles.

Avery,

You don't know me, but I've been in love with Alex for some time. I didn't know about you until a week ago, which is why I'm writing. When I heard Alex was moving to Phoenix, I wanted to go with him. That was when he told me about you. The truth is, I feel relieved to be rid of him. This is not an act of revenge, but a warning. I didn't think you would believe me so I hid a video camera in the room we meet in at The Westin. Don't worry. I've destroyed the video, but I've left you a couple of still photos for proof. Do with them what you will.

A stunned Avery lifted the envelope an inch more and out slipped two pictures.

CHAPTER 15

"I can't imagine your mother will be too happy with this." Richard stepped into the elevator of his building behind Leigh.

"She's fine." Leigh didn't know how her mother would react to her staying overnight at Richard's apartment, but she needed to be with him. She felt safer with him than anyone else.

They hadn't talked much about Leo in the past few days, but Richard told her he was beginning to wonder if it was the right idea not to call the police. Leigh didn't want to drag Richard any farther into it, but she couldn't hold back her concerns about what her father had done. A few people, including Leo's mother, had contacted her asking about him. He hadn't shown up at his job either. Richard pretended not to care, but she could tell he was worried. She didn't understand how her father operated, and when it came to this type of thing, she didn't want to understand.

Leigh thought of the look on her mother's face after she got off the phone with her father about Leo. Her mother was scared. She refused to tell Leigh what he'd said. Now Leo was missing and if her father had hurt him or worse, it could come back to hurt him and it would all be her fault. Richard was insistent that it was Janet who was to blame, but Leigh didn't want to hear it.

"You don't have to walk me to my car." She stepped off the elevator. "It's really cold outside."

Richard laughed. "I'm from Chicago, remember? This is spring for me. Usually by Thanksgiving we're knee deep in snow."

Leigh shivered at the thought. "Speaking of Thanksgiving, you'll come, right?"

"Of course I will." At the door to the building, he wrapped his arms around her. "I don't think your mother is crazy about me, but I'll brave it."

"She likes you," Leigh said. "It was her idea to invite you. With Leo, the fund-raiser and the clinic, I forgot all about it."

"No more Leo," Richard said. "I won't ever let you do anything you don't want to just to please someone else; even your mother."

"You'll keep me honest." Leigh nudged him with her elbow.

"The best path to heartache is trying to please everyone but . . ."

Following Richard's stunned gaze, Leigh's heart jumped into her throat.

It was hard to tell from far away, but all of her car windows had been smashed or cracked. There were large dents on the driver's side of the car and the hood. People were gathering around and Leigh began to feel closed in by them. She looked around, expecting to see Leo. He could be anywhere and now, not only was he mad at her, but he had revenge on his mind for whatever her father had done.

"That's it," Richard said. "I'm calling the police."

Leigh grabbed him before he could get away. "You can't, Richard. If my father has done something, he could—"

"Your father can take care of himself," Richard said. "I'm going to take care of you."

Janet was flawless at making the deliberate seem anything but. Which is why, as he descended the stairs in the Chase mansion, Sean would never believe she had been waiting there for him.

"I didn't even know you were here." She stood at the foot with an innocent smile.

"We went to lunch," he said.

"Did Haley tell you she and I had a spa day yesterday?"

Sean nodded, trying to figure out what this woman was up to.

"She told me about your plans," Janet said. "Your plans to live together."

"I was meaning to talk to Mr. Chase about that."

"She's already told him, but that's not the issue."

"Is there an issue, Mrs. Chase?"

"Janet, please." She headed for the foyer, knowing he was following. "The issue is the life my daughter is accustomed to."

Sean knew this would come eventually. "I don't have a lot of money, but I love her and I know how to take care of the woman I love."

Janet believed every word he said, but that didn't matter. "Except when that woman is Haley. You can't take care of her. Look around this house, Sean. Haley has had this all her life. She doesn't appreciate it as a blessing."

"I wouldn't blame her for that." Sean didn't bother mentioning who he would blame.

"If you think it's because we spoiled her, you're wrong. Haley was raised the same way all of my children were. She is the person she is because it's who she's meant to be. She was this way from the day she was born."

"I think this experience has changed her somewhat." *Think* being the operative word for Sean.

"Trust me, it hasn't. Add to that, a father who feels guilty for never being home so he gives her everything she wants. You're a proud man, Sean. I know you won't be able to deal with that."

"You don't know me as well as you think you do," he said. "I'll deal with what I have to in order to make Haley happy."

"I believe you." Janet felt a sort of pity for him. "You're a good man. It took me a while to understand that, but I do now. You love Haley because you have no choice. You couldn't do anything but love her."

Sean didn't want to respond to that, because he knew the shoe was about to drop. In retrospect, he didn't see how this could have come out any other way.

"The problem is," she continued, "you're already thinking of what she needs to change about herself." Janet waited for her words to sink in and appreciated that Sean tried to hide their effect as much as possible. "You don't have to hide it. Haley is . . . let's just call her one of a kind."

"You underestimate her." Sean was feeling increasingly uncomfortable.

"On the contrary," Janet said. "I've never underestimated my child, but you have. You want Haley to be nurturing, caring, and supportive. You believe with time and love she can be that person, but she can't. The problem I have is that because she believes she loves you, she—"

"Believes she loves me?" Sean wasn't able to hide his anger now. "Are you suggesting that she doesn't?"

"She could. I mean, there's a first time for everything. I personally believe she thinks you're her hero and as soon as this whole situation wears down, it will fade."

"I need to get going." Sean headed for the door. "It was nice talking to—"

"Wait." Janet approached him, holding the door. "I'm not trying to hurt you, Sean. Let's say she really does love you. The problem is, because of that she'll try to change. She'll try to be something she's not and it won't work because it just . . . it just can't."

Sean pressed his lips together to keep from cursing this woman out. "Good-bye, Janet."

Janet grabbed him by the arm, turning him to her. "This is the point you have to understand. Because it won't work, you won't be happy and my daughter will begin to feel like she's not good enough."

Sean let her pull him closer to her, her eyes compelling his to stay locked.

"That," she said, "is something I will never, ever let any of my children feel."

Without a word, Sean jerked his arm out of her grasp and turned away from her. Heading for his car he tried everything to calm his temper, but it was no good. No matter how early he got up in the morning, he was never going to be one step ahead of Janet. That was because she knew Haley better than he ever could and every word she'd said was right.

After staring into his refrigerator for ten minutes, Carter grabbed a bottle of beer. He wasn't hungry for the various takeout leftovers. He wasn't hungry for anything right now. He was anxious and uptight about what he had done to Avery and what he was supposed to do next. He needed to prep for that meeting, but his mind was scattered since yesterday, when Lisette called him and told him Avery had gotten the pictures.

Carter wanted to reach out to Avery, but he couldn't let on that he knew anything about this because Alex was already accusing him. When Carter arrived at work earlier that day, he was met with an angry, threatening message from Alex. He knew he had to play this right and that wasn't going to happen if he held onto any of the guilt that had been following him all week.

In the living room, he grabbed the remote and flicked away at the channels on his sixty-inch flat screen television. He settled on a Lakers game, but just as he sat down on the sofa, the doorbell rang.

He leaned against the door. "Who is it?"

"Carter?" The voice came like a whimpering child.

When he opened the door, Carter felt air escape him at the sight of her. Avery's eyes were bloodshot and she looked like she hadn't slept for days. It hit him that this was entirely his fault, but his survival mechanisms kicked in and he looked at her as if he couldn't be more surprised.

"What are you doing here?" he asked, trying not to reach out to hold her.

"Can I come in?" Avery felt cold all over. Her legs hurt from walking for two hours. "I need to talk to you."

"What's the matter?" he asked, stepping aside.

"You trying to tell me you don't know?"

Carter kept his game face. "I'm sorry, Avery. I just didn't think it was any of my business."

"Whatever." Avery tossed her purse on the floor as she sauntered unsteadily over to the living room sofa. "What are we watching tonight?"

Carter stood above her. "How much have you had to drink?"

"I lost count." Avery reached for the remote, but Carter grabbed it out of her hand. "I don't think you want to piss me off, Carter. I'm inclined to cut off the balls of every man I see at this point."

"Did he really do it?" Carter asked, sitting next to her.

Avery looked at him, wondering if he was playing with her. She couldn't tell and right now, she didn't care. "What do you think?"

"All I know is I come to work this morning and he's leaving me threatening messages. Saying he knows I'm the one who did it."

"Oh, no." Avery laughed. "Don't worry about that. He's the one who did it, but he did mention that it was your fault. Then he mentioned it was mine."

"Yours?"

"I'd rather not go over it." She lay back on the sofa, hugging a pillow to her chest.

It was the best acting job Avery had ever seen. First he denied it, blaming Carter for putting thoughts in her head. When she showed him the pictures, he blamed Carter again and suggested that it might have even been her mother since she never liked Alex. When Avery threatened to leave, he finally admitted to sleeping with the woman but promised it was a one-night stand and continued to claim victim to being set up. He denied an affair, a relationship of any kind. Avery was at her sanity's end when he came out with the kicker.

Maybe he did cheat, but it wasn't his fault. It was Avery's fault for being so cold to him and playing him against Carter. That was when she pretty much wrecked his entire place, breaking everything she could find, knocking over his prize television and throwing as many of his sales awards out the window of this twelfth floor apartment before he pushed her away.

"So you don't believe I had anything to do with it?" Carter asked.

"I would," she said, "but for a couple of things. First, I have pictures so I know he did it. Second, he admitted to it. Third, I know you would never do something like that."

Carter swallowed hard. "You do?"

She tried to smile, but it wasn't in her. "Maybe a few months ago, I would have thought you'd do it, but not anymore. It's not you."

"You think you know me. so well?" Carter heard the voices in his head telling him to shut the hell up, but he couldn't.

"I think I do." Avery tossed the pillow aside, sliding next to him. "You try to act like this cold, slick player like when I first met you, but you're not. You've shown me that you care and you went above and beyond with the payment for Essentials, and—"

"Stop, Avery." Carter didn't want to hear anymore. "I did all of that for my own interest."

"I'm not buying it." She placed her hand gently on his chest, looking into his eyes.

"Why did you come here?" Carter backed away from her a bit.

"I don't know," she answered, feeling desire creep through her, making her skin tingle all over. "I've been in a haze these past few days. Drinking and walking for hours. Why, don't you want me here?"

"You're drunk." He stood up, heading for his phone. "I'll call you a cab."

"I couldn't stay away from you." She was finally able to find a smile as he turned back to her. "So maybe it was my fault."

Carter hated himself. "You don't think that, Avery. You're angry, hurt, and drunk. Alex never deserved you."

"And you did?" Avery stood up, approaching him. She looked into his eyes searching for some give but he was so guarded right now. "That's what you thought all along, right?"

"I don't deserve you either." He'd never said anything so true.

She grabbed the bottom of his sweatshirt, pulling him to her and sliding her hands up his bare chest. She felt his hard, flat stomach contract and it made her feel powerful. He grabbed her hands stopping them halfway.

"You don't think you deserve me?" she asked. "But you can have me, Carter. You knew all along that you could. I knew all along that you could and I fought you because I thought I had something with Alex."

Carter moved her hands away, stepping back. His mind was losing the battle with his body. He felt like an ass already, so why not just be a man and take what was offered to him?

Avery laughed at his useless attempt to resist her. He didn't understand. She didn't care about anything anymore. She had been such a fool to feel guilty and to think she could fix everything and for what? She kept her eyes on him, biting her lower lip as she savored the anticipation of finally getting what she had been denying herself for too long.

When Avery's hands went to the edges of her blouse, Carter knew what was coming and when she flipped it over her head, the voices lowered to a whisper. He was listening to something else now.

"Avery, I know you feel bad, but I'm not going to . . ."

She reached behind her back, unsnapping the clasp of her bra. "Take advantage of me?"

When her bra fell to the floor, revealing her full breasts, Carter could only shake his head. This wasn't going to go as he planned. His hands went to her waist by instinct. Her skin was so damn soft, Carter couldn't resist pressing her flesh with his fingers. When he did, she closed her eyes and slid her hands up his arms.

"I've wanted you," she confessed, "since that night at the restaurant. Do you remember?"

"The red dress." It was emblazoned on his mind the way her fingers traced the edges of the wineglass.

"The way you looked at me." Avery wrapped her fingers gently around his neck as his hands slid down the small of her back and reached into her pants. "You made me feel naked and I hated you because I liked it."

Carter leaned down and kissed her passionately on the lips, his entire body hitting a lava flow. Yes, he heard a whisper telling him, this is what made it all worth it. He knew he would have to pay the devil in some way for what he'd done, but he couldn't think about that now.

Their clothes were off in a second, and he was consumed by her naked body, her silky skin, and the erotic sounds she made when he put his mouth on her. He made love to her trying to be gentle and slow despite his body wanting to be urgent and forceful.

Forgetting about Alex and everything else, Avery escaped in the pleasure of letting this man take her in a much rougher way the second time. She felt lost in the best sex she had ever had and began to remember what feeling good meant and the power of a man's strong arms around her. When he rubbed her thighs and she opened her legs for him a third time, she was firm in her belief that this was what was meant to happen, so she would be grateful.

"This is it." Sean stepped aside, letting Haley enter his apartment for the first time.

He could tell from the look on her face it was all that she expected; unfortunately. He was twisted inside wondering what he should do. It had almost become painful being with her these past few days as Janet's words rang in his ears constantly. Since then, Haley had done nothing to reassure him that her mother was wrong, but he couldn't ignore the fact that he loved her.

Haley looked around, not too interested in seeing any more than what was right in front of her. None of this was making it into their condo. "When are we going out to dinner?"

"You said you had something to show me."

She gave him a sideways smile, reaching into the pocket of her two thousand dollar leather jacket. "You're going to love me for this."

He wanted to say he already loved her, but it couldn't come out. Not that it wasn't true. He just wasn't sure why it was true and he wasn't at all sure it even mattered. Not in the long run at least.

Haley handed him the piece of paper and waited eagerly. "It's just the cover page. The actual lease is about five thousand pages."

Sean saw the stationery on top. Reagan Properties. As he read on, he couldn't even think of what to say. The condo was set at five hundred thousand dollars. He looked up at Haley with his mouth open and his temper flaring.

"How could you do this?" He crumpled up the piece of paper and threw it across the room. "I told you not to do this."

"You never told me anything and even if you had, I don't take orders from you." Haley retrieved the paper. "Look at what you've done. This is our official copy."

"Undo it now," he ordered. "Let's go to wherever we need to go now and undo this."

"It's done. My father took care of it today and I would expect some appreciation."

He threw his hands in the air. "I told you I can't afford this! You need to understand something if this relationship is going to work."

"Excuse me?" Haley's hands went to her hips.

"You have to take me seriously, Haley. I'm not kidding when I tell you that your lifestyle is going to change with me."

"Who do you think you are?" she asked. He needed to understand that her lifestyle was going to be whatever she wanted it to be. "I'm moving out of a mansion, remember? With a maid and a pool. If that's not change, I don't know what is."

She was right. Even what was out of the question for him was a huge step down for her. "I just can't afford it and I'm not letting your dad pay my mortgage."

"You can afford it, Sean." She went to him, wrapping her arms around him. She was forgiving him for his out-burst and he better appreciate that. "That's the rest of my surprise."

"I don't think I want to hear any more."

"Daddy is gonna give you the chief of security job at Chase Beauty."

Sean backed away from her, wishing he'd heard her wrong. How many times had he wished that since he met this woman? "You've gone too far now."

"He has to get rid of the current chief of security," she said, "but it pays six figures and with Daddy paying my half of the mortgage, you can afford the other half."

Sean began pacing the floor, shaking his head. He began to laugh even though he found this anything but funny. He was enraged when he turned to her. "Who do you think you fell in love with, Haley?"

Haley pressed her lips together hoping to prevent say-ing what she wanted to. She hated when people asked her stupid questions trying to make her say what they wanted to say themselves. She just had to remember that she loved him and hope that was enough, because patience was never her strong point.

"I'm a detective," Sean said. "It's in my blood and it's always going to be. I can tell you with my hand to God that I will never, ever be anything else."

"There's no money in that," Haley stated. "I'm just trying to help you. You can't get by in life making sixty grand."

It was forty-five actually, but that wasn't the point. "I've been doing it just fine so far."

"Well, things are different now. You're with me and if you're going to be with me, it's not fine." She couldn't believe he was so against bettering himself. She was going to be the best thing that ever happened to him and it was like he was fighting it.

Sean sighed, lowering his head. His mind was pulling a blank when he searched for something to fix this. "It's going to have to be, Haley. If you're going to be with me, it's going to have to be."

Haley huffed, wishing she could slap him back to reality. She loved him but the world would end before she revolved her life around anyone but herself. "Do you have any idea of what I've done to accommodate this archaic need you have to define your manhood through denying me?"

"I can't believe what you just said." If he could even understand it.

"I thought of everything you've said to me. I wanted the same condo Carter has, but I knew that was too expensive, so I asked Daddy to get the smallest one they had instead."

Was she joking with him? Sean couldn't be sure. She certainly looked serious, but the words out of her mouth seemed more like a comedy sketch.

"Then to appease you further," she continued, "even though Daddy wanted to buy the place, I told him to only pay the down payment because I knew you wanted to pay your own mortgage."

Sean heard Janet's words swirling around him and everything Haley was saying made perfect, painful sense.

"Not to mention," she went on, "this job. He wanted to give you just any job on his security force, but I told him you were too good for that. That he had to give you the top job because I knew you wouldn't be happy unless the challenge was great. I was only thinking of you."

"I believe you," he said, "but it's not enough."

She meant every word she said and it cut through his gut to realize that these sacrifices were more than Haley had ever done for anyone in her entire life and they didn't even come close to what he needed from her. She was trying to make him happy and getting nowhere. She would try harder and that angry, tortured look on her face right now would turn inward. Sean wished he was a better man and could tell her the truth, but he couldn't. He did love her and he hoped there was some way that would fade with time. Everything did, didn't it?

As his expression saddened, Haley felt a heavy pull in her stomach. "Before you tell me why what I'm giving up for you isn't enough, you tell me what you're giving up for me."

He was giving her up.

For her and for himself, because as much as he wanted her, Sean knew the man he was and before he met her he had been proud of that man. Most importantly, he wanted that man back and he knew that could only happen if he accepted the man he wasn't. He wasn't a man who found a way to fit the drama into his life that was destined to be a constant. He wasn't a man who could be selfish enough to keep a woman around just because he wanted her even though he knew it would only cause her pain. He wasn't a man who was prepared to deal with a mother who would fight him every step of the way and never give up because her purpose was stronger than his.

"Haley." He reached out, taking her hand in his. Looking into her eyes, the only thing Sean was sure of was that he was going to love her for a long, long time. "We need to talk."

Standing outside the clinic, looking up at the flashing sign, Richard wrapped his arm around Leigh and she loved the idea that what felt good could outweigh what felt bad once again. It had been the other way for long enough.

"One more week," she said. "Are we ready?"

"We're more than ready."

"I'm afraid." She wrapped her arms around him and buried her head into his chest. "I don't want anything to go wrong."

"It won't." He rubbed her back reassuringly.

"As long as Leo is still out there anything can happen. He knows the first of December is the grand opening. After my car, I think—"

"The police are going to find him, Leigh. Even if they don't by then, we'll have a ton of security here. It'll be okay. Let's go."

She was too exhausted to argue and she wanted to believe him anyway. "Will you come home with me?"

"I'm not staying at your house," Richard said. "Stop asking."

"Just until they catch him," she pleaded.

Richard was typing in the alarm codes. "I'm not afraid of him."

"It'll just be easier." She helped him push the heavy steel door closed. "Thursday is Thanksgiving dinner at my house, which you're coming to anyways and Saturday is the fund-raiser, which is at my house as well. It'll just be—"

Leigh was startled when Richard grabbed her arm and his finger came to her mouth. She looked at him for an answer, but he just shook his head and looked around.

"I thought I heard something," he said.

Leigh looked around in the darkness. Most of the streetlights on this block were knocked out, something she was still battling City Hall to fix. "Let's hurry, then."

They rushed down the walkway toward the car, parked right in front, but a shadow loomed in front of them and Leo stepped out from behind a thick bush where the only light working was shining on him. He had a black left eye and a reddish-purple bruise that covered his entire right cheek. His lower lip was cut right up the middle.

Leigh screamed just as Richard pushed her behind him. He stared Leo down, but there was a look on Leo's face that made it seem like this wasn't happening.

"It's okay," Richard whispered to her. "Look, man, I know this whole thing has been a big mess for you, but we're both men here. You're taking this too far."

Leo smiled at him like they were old buddies. "You're right. We're both men, but we both know I'm the better man and the better man always wins."

Leigh slowly reached her hand into her purse, searching around for her cell phone. "The police are already looking for you, Leo. Don't make this worse."

"How could it get any worse?" he asked. "I have an arrest warrant out on me. I got kidnapped and beat up by some thugs who threatened to kill me for two days before leaving me for dead. I've been fired from my job and my parents wouldn't let me in their house. My own mother told me she didn't have a son anymore because I've harmed her reputation."

"That isn't Leigh's fault," Richard said. "She was trying to do what was right and she's sorry you got hurt."

"She can speak for herself, can't she?" Leo looked behind Richard. "Can't you, Leigh? Can't you tell me why you destroyed my life after I came here to start over?"

Leigh's finger slid across the back of her cell phone and she carefully wrapped her hand around it.

"There are cameras all over here," Richard said. "They scan this whole walkway. Any movement is recorded, so if you think you're going to get away with anything, you're wrong."

"I don't expect to get away with anything." He reached under his jacket, pulling out a gun. "I never did."

Before she could react, Leigh's entire body was tossed

to the ground. She fell flat on her stomach and screamed when she heard the gunshot. Then another shot. She swung around just as Richard slumped to the ground. Barely able to breathe, she crawled to his motionless body and held his face in her trembling hands.

"Leigh?"

She looked up at Leo. The gun in his hand brought her back to reality. She felt almost numb to the fact that she was going to die because she just didn't believe it. How could this happen?

"Leo." She was barely audible. "Please."

"Don't worry, Leigh." He lowered the gun. "I was gonna kill you, but then I thought that would just make you the victim. Everyone would feel sorry for you even though this is all your fault!"

She looked down, pressing her hand hard over the spot where Richard was bleeding most. She reached for Richard's limp hand, placing it against the other wound. He was still breathing, she could feel him and she worried that Leo would try to finish him off.

Leo took a few steps closer. "I'm gonna let you live, Leigh. Live knowing this could have all been avoided if you'd given me a chance. He's dead because of you; and so am I."

Leo put his gun to his temple and the doctor inside of Leigh screamed out no as she jumped up and reached out to him; but the gun went off and he fell to the ground like a rag doll. Leigh wanted to be shocked, but she was a doctor and that wasn't allowed. She went back to Richard, pressing on his larger wound with one hand as she scrambled to find her phone with the other.

"Leigh?" he whispered.

"Don't talk, Richard." She dialed 911, trying to hold back the tears that wanted to come at the gurgling sound he was making. Blood was trickling out of his mouth now.

"It's going to be okay. I have to go back inside to get what you need. I'll be right back."

Carter pulled up to the Jackson's modest Baldwin Hills home just as Avery stepped onto the porch. He was going to act casual for her benefit, but the truth was he was happy as hell. After their night together, Avery asked for some time to think about things and it worried him because he hadn't intended to sleep with her that night. He only hoped that she hadn't seen it as medicine for an angry woman to be taken only once. When she called him that morning, Carter knew there wasn't anything to worry about. She wanted to take it slow, but wanted to see what would happen. He was going to let her take as long as she needed to figure out she belonged to him.

"Right on time." Avery slid into the car. "I like that."

"I'm just being good because it's the beginning. After a while, I'll be fifteen, twenty minutes late on average."

"You do realize it's November?" She lifted her hands to the air, gesturing at the lack of car top. "It's freezing outside."

"I'm not ready to give in to the season." He started the car. "Unless you're too weak for a little breeze."

"Gun it."

As he sped off, she settled into the seat, feeling much more comfortable than she expected to. Instead of nervous and uncertain, she was excited and hopeful. The pain of Alex's betrayal was still with her and she knew it would be in some form for the rest of her life. She had loved him, but the finality that was forced on their relationship made her so relieved she was ashamed to share it with anyone. She felt selfish indulging in a man as incredible as Carter, but after all she'd been through, Avery wanted to be selfish for a while.

"Did you mention me?" he asked.

"No." She reached across, placing her hand on his thigh. "Don't take it personally. The whole truth about Alex is more than enough for them to take right now. I just want to keep my dad from killing him before he gets to Phoenix."

The whole truth about Alex. That was something Carter was going to have to keep for himself. Living with lies wasn't as impossible as people thought. He was living with other lies, holding onto secrets he would keep till his grave. Better men have done worse for less.

"I want to show you something." He slowed down, turning onto the familiar street. He slid up to the curb and parked.

Avery looked around seeing nothing in particular. When she turned to Carter, the look on his face made her nervous. "What? What's going on?"

"Remember when you came to my house for dinner?"

"Are you seriously asking me that?"

Carter laughed. "Of course you do, but what do you remember the most?"

"That's easy." She leaned into him. "When you told me about going to school and living in . . ."

He was happy, because she got it quicker than he expected and the only explanation for that was that she had listened and she cared.

"Which one?" she asked.

He pointed to her left and when she saw it, the house that Carter grew up in, a smile warmed her face. It was the biggest house on the block, lily white with black shutters and a hunter green door that curved into a half circle at the top. It looked like something off a painting and she felt incredibly touched that he would share it with her.

"What about that job, Avery?" Carter asked.

She turned back to him with a shrug of her shoulders. "It sounds good, but I don't—"

"You're afraid," he said, "and you should be. Working

for my father is no picnic, but I know you can do it. You know you can do it. Don't let fear make your decisions for you."

"It's a white space for me," she admitted. "It would be safer if I just—"

"Avery, my father gave me some advice once. He said life is for the living. If you don't want to live it, then get the hell out of the way."

This wasn't helping her any. "I didn't think he wanted you to start your own law firm."

"Actually I was seven when he told me that." He smiled when her eyes opened wide. "On my grandmother's grave, I'm not lying. This is the man you'd be working with."

She laughed, feeling closer to him than it made sense to feel. She couldn't trust her emotions right now because of all she had been through, but Avery was confident she was going to fall in love with this man.

As soon as the elevator opened up, Janet and Steven lurched out and headed straight for the hospital desk. Michael and Kimberly were right behind with Haley taking a little time picking up the rear.

"Leigh Chase," Steven said. "Where is she?"

The woman behind the counter looked down at her computer, shaking her head. "I don't have that name."

"She's up here!" Janet gripped the edges of the desk, leaning forward. "She's in surgery."

The woman shrugged, punching various keys on the computer. "There's no one by that name—"

"Listen to me!" Steven slammed his fist on the desk. "You find someone who knows where she is now or I'm going into every one of these rooms to find out for myself."

"You can't do that." She backed down when Steven gave her the look of death. "I'll see who I can find."

"Where are you going?" Steven reached for Janet who was already heading down the hall. "Wait here, Janet."

Janet could hardly breathe, trying to free herself from Steven's grasp. "I can't wait. Where is she? Sean said that—"

"She's up here." He wrapped his arm around her, turning to Michael. "Have you reached Carter?"

Michael reached for his cell phone. "I'll try again."

Steven placed his forehead against Janet's and whispered words of assurance to her. She was losing it and he wasn't far behind.

The evening had been ending innocent enough. With the exception of Haley raising hell over Sean dumping her throughout dinner, the boys had been put to sleep and everyone was relaxing for the evening. Steven had gone off to do some work, leaving Janet to deal with Haley when Maya rushed into his office. The look on her face cut his annoyance short as he grabbed the phone.

It was Sean calling to tell him that something had happened to Leigh. There was a shooting outside the clinic, Leo was dead, and she was on her way to L.A. General. Sean only knew what he heard over the police wire. She was being taken straight to surgery. Steven felt a sense of dread come over him as he couldn't believe what he was hearing. What had he caused to happen?

"Mr. and Mrs. Chase?" Sean cautiously approached them, not wanting to interrupt the intimate moment.

"Where is she?" Janet reached for him, taking his hand in hers. "You know?"

Sean glanced behind her, noticing the look of pure hatred and disgust on Haley's face at the sight of him. He almost regretted that he had heard about Leigh's situation, because this was the last thing he wanted. He had to call Steven even though he knew the entire family probably hated him now. His breakup with Haley had been one of the ugliest scenes he had ever experienced, and that was saying a lot for a homicide detective.

"She's in six-forty," he said, after Haley turned her back to him and walked away.

"Where is that?" Steven followed Sean's eyes to Haley, not missing the scratch marks along the right side of his face that he had no doubt was his daughter's work.

"It's down the hall." Sean held onto Janet who tried to pass him. "You don't understand."

"What?"

"She's okay," Sean said. "She wasn't shot."

"Oh, my God!" Janet fell back into Steven's arms. "Thank you, Lord."

"What happened?" Steven felt like he wanted to cry at the news. "Why is she in there?"

"Leo shot Richard and then himself." Sean understood their confusion. "I don't know why he didn't shoot her. I'm not sure. She hasn't talked to anyone yet. She's in there with Richard. They're letting her stay because she's a doctor."

"Is he going to be okay?" Janet asked.

"I don't know," Sean said. "There was a lot of blood."

Janet turned to Steven, burying her head in his chest. Leigh was all right. Her baby wasn't going to die. She was relieved but still in pain just from the thought of it. "I want to see her, Steven."

"I'll make that happen." Steven turned back to Michael. "She's okay. Tell Haley."

Michael nodded, looking back at his little sister who was sitting on a bench down the hallway. "Carter isn't answering his cell. I think he's with Avery."

"Excuse me?" Sean asked, but Michael barely acknowledged him.

"What's that about?" Kimberly asked her husband.

Michael looked at her, unsure of what to say. "He's with her now."

"How did that happen so quickly?" she asked, remembering Avery's vow of lifelong commitment to Alex less than two weeks ago.

"Not now, Kimberly." He pecked her on the cheek and headed for Haley. He wasn't going to be able to tell Kimberly the truth. This was something he promised Carter he would hold onto.

Sean absorbed the look Michael gave him when he approached him and Haley. He knew Michael would rather punch him, but the situation put a lot in perspective. What was a breakup compared to murder? To Michael it was probably nothing, but Sean could see his brotherly instinct and knew under better circumstances this might have been taken outside.

"Get the hell away from me." Haley couldn't believe he had the nerve to approach her, looking at her as if he gave a damn. She could barely control the hatred inside of her at the sight of him.

Sean didn't know what to say. He still loved her so much and he hated himself right now for hurting her the way he had. She went ballistic when he told her it wasn't going to work. She didn't believe him at first and from out of nowhere he came up with a reason that she seemed to buy. His attraction to her was due to the excitement of the situation they were in. The danger and the savior syndrome had gotten the best of him and now that it was over, he just didn't want to go forward. Now that it was over, all he could think of was how he wasn't willing to make the changes necessary to make something unworkable work.

After attacking him so aggressively he had to physically push her away, Haley went through a litany of threats as she tore up his apartment. He wanted to try to calm her down, but she tossed a lit candle on his sofa and he was too busy trying to put out the fire to notice she had left. He drank himself to sleep that night, wondering how he could have thrown away a woman who made him feel the way Haley did. There was no explaining it, but it was done and he had to live with it. That would only be possible if he could stay away from her, but that wasn't working so far.

"She doesn't want to talk to you," Michael said.

"I just wanted to see if you were okay." He reached for her, but she slapped his hand away.

"You'd love it if I wasn't, wouldn't you?" She wasn't going to give him the pleasure of knowing she'd cried herself to sleep that night.

There wasn't going to be any more crying. She made the stupid mistake of falling in love and learned her lesson the hard way. As far as this bastard standing in front of her, his lesson was just beginning.

Sean looked at Michael, his eyes pleading for a moment. Michael just stared at him. He wasn't going anywhere. "This isn't about us. It's about Leigh."

"She's fine," Haley said. "So fuck off!"

"She's not fine," he said. "She's going to need—"

"Haley doesn't need you to tell her what her sister needs." Michael didn't give too much of a damn about Haley's ongoing sexcapades, but he had never known any guy to dump her and that alone was enough to interest him.

"Michael." Haley stood up. "I want to be alone with Sean for a second."

"Fine." Michael headed back for his family.

The only reason she didn't try to kill Sean now was because being where they were, someone would probably be able to save him.

"I wish you hadn't left like that," Sean asserted.

"Did you expect me to stay and cry?"

"No, I . . . I'm just sorry. I really am."

"You have no idea how sorry you're going to be." She relished the look of surprise on his face. "That's right,

Sean. You made a bigger mistake than you think. No one dumps me."

"I didn't dump you, Haley. I—"

"I gave you more than I ever gave any man," she said. "Men much better than you and you tossed it away. Did you think you could just walk away from that?"

"You're upset. You don't really mean what you're saying."

"I'm not upset anymore, Sean." She leaned back with a calm look on her face. "I'm focused. I'm focused on one thing and one thing only. I'm going to make you pay for using me. I'm going to make you pay in a way that you didn't imagine even a bitch like me could think of."

Sean sighed, feeling the pain shoot through him from the look on her face. He didn't want to think she really meant what she was saying, preferring to believe it was a broken heart that would heal. Only this was Haley and she didn't bother to lie because she didn't give a damn what you thought of the truth.

"I'm glad your sister's okay." He turned and walked away, determined to get back to work and somehow get back to the man he used to be.

Oh, yeah, and he planned to watch his back.

Haley wasn't sure how she was going to do it, but she intended to devote everything she had to hurting Sean in a way he wouldn't recover from. She had her father's money and sheer will, which the detective had greatly underestimated. Somehow she was going to take away from him the one thing he thought meant more than she did; his promising career in law enforcement.

"Janet." Steven grabbed his wife, who was leaning into him, and turned her around just as Leigh made her way to them.

Janet gasped, feeling weak in the knees. Leigh, her angel with the softest heart, was covered in blood and had a demolished look on her face. She went to her, but Leigh held her hands up to keep her away.

"Are you okay?" Janet was confused by the anger she felt emanating from Leigh.

"Richard's dead." Hearing herself say the words brought the pain rushing back and Leigh's legs gave way.

Steven grabbed her just in time to keep her from falling to the floor. His heart ripped into pieces at the sight of her like this. What kind of father was he if he couldn't keep his daughter from such pain?

"Baby." Janet tried to wrap her arms around Leigh, but was shocked when she was pushed away.

Finding strength in her anger, Leigh stood up straight. "This is your fault!"

Janet gasped. "No, Leigh. I didn't know—"

"All of this happened because of you." Her words spat out like venom. "Because you held the Foundation above me like a string to control my choices. Because you can only give when it's on your terms. You always have to be happy and it's always up to me to make that happen because you convince me you can't count on anyone else."

"Leigh." Steven reached for her. "You don't know what you're saying."

"Are you happy, Mom?" She threw her hands in the air. "Look at me. I'm covered in the blood of the man who I betrayed for you. The man who is dead because I dragged him into my sick addiction to pleasing you!"

"Please," Janet whimpered through tears. "I'm so sorry."

"No more," Leigh said. "I'm not gonna let this happen anymore because you don't exist to me anymore. I don't ever want to look at you again."

Janet gasped, her hand flying to her chest as she

watched Leigh walk away from her. She turned to Steven, unable to speak.

"It's okay," he said. "I'll get her. It'll be okay."

As Steven rushed after Leigh, Kimberly watched from a distance.

Janet stumbled to the desk and held onto it for dear life. The look of total destruction turned the seemingly perfect woman into a pile of nothing. A sense of calm came over Kimberly as she watched Janet fumble through her purse for that little pill she hoped would make it all go away.

At that moment something came to Kimberly. What she had always wished for; what she had always wanted since meeting that witch became so clear to her.

It was wrong to have wanted to get out of that house; to get away from Janet. As she looked at the annihilation of this seemingly untouchable woman it became clear how utterly touchable she was. Instead of getting out of that house, Kimberly knew what she really wanted was to get Janet out and she couldn't think of a better time to get that ball rolling.

"Are you okay?" Michael gently caressed his wife's cheek, unable to decipher the look in her eyes.

"I'm fine," she answered. "I'm perfect. Go to your mother. She needs you."

The following is a teaser from
the second installment of
Angela Winters' exciting View Park trilogy.

ENJOY!

Six months later

Kimberly's hard work pays off as she brings a long-lost secret that Janet would do anything to hide back to View Park. It threatens to put a woman already on the brink due to prescription drugs and strained family relationships over the edge and destroy her marriage.

Just as their life together has them heading for the altar, tensions rise between Avery and Carter as she tries to deal with what it means to be a part of America's black royal family and Carter tries to deal with the woman who threatens to tell Avery how Carter won her heart if he doesn't give her more money.

Back from a wild binge in Europe, Haley returns to View Park only to get caught up with a nightclub owner who drags her into his illegal lifestyle and dark, sexual world. When Taylor Jackson gets involved, Sean has to save her, which means dealing with Haley who still wants to see him pay for hurting her.

To keep updated and learn more about the Chase and Jackson families, visit the View Park Web site at www.viewparkonline.com

Don't miss Angela Winter's
A PRICE TO PAY
Available in trade paperback in June, 2009
wherever books are sold!

1

Thirty-one-year-old Carter Chase was standing impatiently in the foyer of his family's famous and often photographed home, the fifteen-thousand-square-foot Chase Mansion in View Park, a suburb of Los Angeles. He was impatient for a couple of reasons. First, his parents, Steven and Janet, were late. Church let out at eleven and it was twelve-thirty. They had promised to be home by noon at the latest. Second, he was always impatient to see his baby girl, Connor, especially considering he only had another eight hours with her before her mother would come pick her up from his house.

Connor Chase, the newest addition to America's wealthiest and most famous black family, was born six months ago and Carter's life was changed forever. Only a few months earlier, he'd been knocked in the face with the reality that her mother, Avery Jackson, the woman Carter loved and had wanted to marry, was married to another man, and pregnant.

He was only temporarily jealous of the other man, college professor Anthony Harper, because he had little right to be. Carter understood that he drove Avery away trying to control her and keep secrets from her. He was wrong and deserved to have his heart broken, which she did when she left L.A. to live in secrecy with relatives outside Miami. But he'd never stopped believing he would get her back. And as much as it hurt that she had been with another man, he wouldn't pass judgment on her. He'd been sleeping with any woman he could get his hands on in the six months after Avery left California, just to stop thinking about her for a few moments.

But the pregnancy was another thing. He was certain that Connor was his from the moment he saw Avery's belly, but Anthony had convinced Avery to lie and say the baby was his. He'd conspired with a local doctor who owed him a big favor to create medical records to support the lie. The idea that Avery, the woman he loved with all his heart, was having another man's baby had floored Carter.

Being a Chase, a member of America's black royal family, Carter had always gotten everything he wanted. He'd had a charmed life, always able to win any contest and influence or buy his way out of whatever he needed to. He was an heir to an empire, Ivy League educated and in charge of his own successful law firm; not to mention having that whole tall, dark, and handsome thing in his favor. He was six feet tall with chocolate brown skin and hazel eyes. His smile and style added to making him one of the most eligible bachelors on the market, with his pick of the best women. Which was why everyone was surprised when he hung it all up for a middle-class girl next door, Avery Jackson.

But they just didn't know. He hadn't expected to fall in love with her at all, but Avery quickly became everything in the world to him. She was perfect in every way that mattered. She grounded him, made him feel like a king regardless of his last name or his wealth. Carter felt a connection to Avery that he hadn't believed could exist between a man and a woman. But he'd made mistakes to get her away from her first fiancé, Alex, and even more mistakes to keep her. Unlike the other women he'd dated,

Avery didn't care about the money, the glossy high life or the power. She didn't care about all the things that came with being a Chase, so for the first time in his life a woman didn't put up with his crap, and she had left it all behind.

Like with any other obstacle, as soon as Avery returned Carter was determined to win her back, regardless of her marital and parental status. And he'd almost done it. He'd gotten her to the point where she admitted she wanted him—loved him—but there was one problem. Avery actually believed in fidelity and the sanctity of marriage. She wouldn't cheat on Anthony and she wouldn't leave him even after the truth of Connor's paternity came out.

But he was a Chase, so there was always a plan B. It would take a lot of patience, but he would get Avery back. And although he had been angry with her when she finally told him that Connor was his, moments after giving birth, it only made him more determined to get her back. Now it was about more than the woman he loved; he had a family.

So while it hurt to see Avery with her husband, Carter knew it was only a matter of time before he'd have her back. Meanwhile, he took every moment he could to spend with his daughter, whom he loved to no end.

That is, he took every moment that he could get Connor away from her doting grandmother, Janet Chase.

"They're coming." Maya, the caretaker of Chase Mansion, stood at the archway between the foyer and the great room.

She looked tired, although Carter never really saw her do anything but cook. She always hired contractors to do heavy work, but he knew his mother loved Maya, who had been taking care of the Chase clan for almost fifteen years.

"I can hear the car, Maya. Thanks."

"Are you sure I can't get you somethin'?" Although she'd been in the country for more than twenty years, Maya's Caribbean accent was still very strong. "You know how she likes to stall when she has the baby."

"Not this time," Carter said. "I have to get going. I'm meeting Julia for lunch."

"How nice."

Carter noted that Maya rolled her eyes like she did whenever the name of Julia Hall, Carter's current girlfriend, was mentioned. Maya had loved Avery because Avery was kind and warm to her, while Julia maintained a clear class distinction in the very few times she even acknowledged Maya was there.

Carter smiled at the sound of his baby's voice. Before the front door even opened, he could hear her laughter and cooing.

Janet Chase, a woman of the best breeding, class, and social mastery, had always placed her family first. She was the image maker of the Chase name, and tough as nails when it came to her family. She was also a sucker for a grandchild, and her only granddaughter simply brought her to her knees. She hated giving her up, but as soon as she walked into the house, she could see from the look on her oldest son's face, that she wasn't going to get away with her stall tactics today.

"Don't start," Janet said as she handed the baby bag to Maya. "We tried to leave, but they wouldn't let us. Ask your father."

"Who is they?" Carter asked, delighting at the squeal Connor gave as soon as she saw him and reached out for her daddy. She was so stinkin' cute.

"Everyone at church." Janet reluctantly handed Connor over. "I tell you, she looks more and more like Leigh every day. She looks ridiculously cute in her new dress."

Janet spent an obscene amount of money on dresses for Connor. There were two other Chase grandchildren, twins by second son, Michael, but Connor was a girl and that took Janet's indulgence to a whole other level.

"You're not letting people, strangers, hold her, Mom." Carter gave Connor a big, fat kiss on her lips.

"Of course not." Janet smoothed out her cobalt blue, Diane Von Furstenberg cashmere wrap dress. She was a very beautiful woman, who still turned heads in her fifties because she looked at least ten years younger than she was, and she had an air of unattainability about her that men loved.

She turned to Maya. "Can you please serve lunch in the Florida room in about an hour?"

Maya nodded, handing the baby bag to Carter before leaving.

"Hello, son." Steven Chase closed the front door behind him, greeting his son briefly before reaching down for his vibrating smartphone.

Carter would have replied if he thought his father was paying any attention, but he knew he wasn't. Steven Chase was head of a billion-dollar empire, Chase Beauty, and that empire came first. There was no ignoring him once he walked into a room. From even his youngest days, Steven had a presence that sucked up all the attention in the room. This included his own children, his sons especially.

Carter and his father had been at odds as long as Carter could remember, with brief periods of peace. Right now was a period of peace where they got along, but that still didn't guarantee he'd get any attention from his father.

"You're making me late for lunch with Julia," Carter said to his mother.

"Why didn't you tell me you were having lunch with her?" Janet asked. "I can keep Connor while you both . . ."

"No thanks," Carter said. "You'll see Connor again soon. We have to . . ."

"You know," Janet interrupted, "this wouldn't be an inconvenience if you actually came to church."

Carter gave his mother an annoyed glance. "You know that's not going to happen, Mom."

"You should open your eyes, son." Janet leaned forward to kiss Connor on her tiny, brown nose. "That God you've decided not to believe in gave you this blessing."

"Science and genetics gave me this blessing," Carter replied. In choosing to govern his beliefs by logic and rationality, he had made the decision while a Harvard undergrad to believe in evolution over creationism, and his mother had given him a hard time about it ever since. Avery gave him hell for it.

"Carter." Steven hung up his cell, getting his son's attention. His salt-and-pepper temples added a distinguished looked to his dark, masculine figure. "Come in the office. I need to talk business with you."

"I can't," Carter said.

Chase Beauty was the largest client of Chase Law, the small firm that Carter had decided to start instead of joining his father's company. This, in addition to his sense of entitlement and assumption of power and control over everything, made Steven expect Carter to jump at the snap of his finger.

"I have to meet Julia for . . ."

"Now," Steven said definitively. He was already walking down the hallway toward his office.

Janet joyously reached her arms out. "I'll hold her while . . ."

"Nice try," Carter said as he headed down the hallway with his baby in his arms.

"Close the door," Steven ordered without looking up from his desk.

"Dad, this has to be quick."

Steven looked up, ready to remind his stubborn son

that a one-hundred-thousand-dollar-a-month retainer meant he could take as much time as he wanted, but thought better of it. They were getting along, as much as Steven and Carter could ever get along. These periods of relative peace between them never lasted long, so Steven let it go. "Did you read that Luxury Life report I sent you?"

"I read all the reports weeks . . ."

"No, this is a new one I had my marketing department put together. I sent it to your office Wednesday."

Carter shook his head. "I haven't gotten around to it."

"Dammit, Carter!" Steven leaned back in the detailed leather chair of his finely furnished home office, one of seventeen rooms in the house. "That's the only thing I asked you to do for me this week."

Carter pretended to bite Connor's tiny fingers as she put them over his mouth. She laughed as if it was the funniest thing ever. "You know I have that big antitrust case right now, and two new clients."

Steven sighed. "As your father, I'm glad your firm is growing. As your client, I don't give a damn. Read the report by Monday."

That was a lie, Carter thought. He wasn't glad as a father either. Although he had interned in the Chase Beauty legal department during Harvard Law, Carter's decision to go out on his own instead of join the company, as expected, had always been a sore point between him and his father. A sore point was putting it lightly.

"I'll get to it tonight, after I drop Connor at Avery's . . ."

"Carter, I know you're happy you have a baby and all that, but you can't let it interfere with your work."

"Maybe I can do like you did, Dad." Carter's voice was laced with extreme sarcasm. "Just ignore my kid altogether. I'm sure she'll understand like we all did."

Steven sneered, wondering if Carter thought he was too old to get knocked upside the head. No, he hadn't been the best father, but he was building an empire and they had Janet. He still loved them all more than his own life.

"You've never appreciated the sacrifices I've made for this family," Steven said, "but you seem fine with benefiting from them. Read it. I need to make a decision now."

Carter wanted to ask why his father wanted to expand Chase Beauty, which had already added real estate and a chain of beauty salons to its hair-and-makeup product line, to include publishing, but he wouldn't. He didn't have the time for the answer.

"Look, Dad, I was supposed to meet Julia at Beso five minutes ago. I'll read it later."

"She can wait if you tell her to," Steven said. "She'll do whatever you want."

Carter frowned. "What the hell does that mean?"

"You know what it means," Steven answered. "Julia wants to be Mrs. Carter Chase. She'll put up with anything if she thinks it will get her closer to that goal. I'll call her if you don't have the balls."

"You know that's not going to happen." Carter's tone reflected his confusion. "Why would you even say that? You know that . . ."

"I know six months ago you said that Julia was just a temporary amusement until you could get Avery back. She was part of your plan to make Avery believe you were over her so she wouldn't be so cautious around you."

"She still is," Carter said. "But it's not as if I don't like her. You don't expect me to be celibate until I get Avery back?"

"Julia is in love with you. She's told your mother several times."

Carter believed Julia was more in love with the idea of being with a Chase than anything genuine. "I can't do anything about that. I'm going to marry Avery. That's it."

"Tell that to your mother," Steven said. "She's already picking out invitations."

"Mom doesn't need to know anything about this," Carter said with a warning tone. "Dad, you promised not to tell her."

"I haven't said anything," Steven said. "Now just read the report."

Carter got pissed off when his father acted as if he didn't understand the master plan, which was two-fold. Part one was to make Avery believe that he had truly gotten over her, had no intention of interfering with her marriage, and only wanted to deal with her in terms of being good parents to Connor. It was working. Carter even believed that Avery was a little jealous of his relationship with Julia at times. Because of their chemistry, Avery had previously refused to be alone with him. That was changing. Once her guard was down, she wouldn't be so reluctant to spend time alone with him. That was all it would take.

Part two was much more complicated. Carter had to create a situation in which Avery would be willing to leave Anthony and not hate herself for cheating on him. This had begun by completely emasculating Anthony at every opportunity possible without it seeming obvious to anyone but Anthony. When placed against Carter, very few men could measure up.

Steven smirked. "You remember, kid, it was my idea for you to crowd her husband out slowly, before I knew she lied to you about Connor not being yours. I'd prefer you be done with her. Julia is more suited to our circles anyway."

"You're starting to sound like Mom," Carter said. He placed Connor in the other arm. She was getting heavy.

Twenty-six-year-old Julia Hall came from a prominent Dallas family of doctors. She had made a departure and gone into corporate finance, but this positioned her perfectly for a financial analyst position at Chase Beauty. Janet had intended for her to distract Michael from Kimberly, but Julia had wanted Carter from the start. She was a bona fide, black blue blood like his mother: those who had money, power and social standing dating back to the 1800s.

No one else belonged in these circles. New money, acquired in only a generation, didn't count. What was worse was money from entertainment or sports. They always wanted in, and people like his mother and Julia always wanted to keep them out.

"That wasn't your background," Carter reminded his father.

"This isn't about me." Steven was well aware that his middle-class background would never have gotten him where he was now if he hadn't married a woman like Janet. "This is about you wanting a woman that has rejected you countless times and . . ."

"You're exaggerating," Carter said. "Avery admitted that she wants me, but all that Bible blah, blah and . . ."

"Marital fidelity isn't Bible blah, blah, Carter. It means something to a lot of people."

"Well, nothing means anything to me except Avery and Connor. So, fuck her marriage and that teacher."

"You better watch it," Steven warned him. "If your animosity shows, it will force Avery to side with her husband.

"Don't worry about me." Supporting Connor had been the perfect excuse to make Anthony look inadequate. "I've taken every opportunity, and his growing frustration has only worked in my favor. I've undermined him without Avery catching on. She seems more and more annoyed with him every day. I've got her keeping secrets from him, thinking she's doing what's best for his pride. But it's only making him more jealous and possessive and when those secrets come out, he'll explode."

"Pitiful." Steven couldn't help but appreciate Carter's tenacity. He got what he wanted and that was what he had instilled in all his children from the beginning. The best education, training, and guidance had created four exceptional people. Well, at least three. Haley was something else entirely.

Carter felt no pity for Anthony. He was the one who convinced Avery to keep Connor away from him and guilted her into feeling obligated to him because he had been there for her when she ended her engagement to Carter. Avery was loyal and wanted to do what was right. Anthony was counting on that and Carter would crush him for it.

Steven chose not to press it any further. If there was one subject he couldn't change Carter's mind about, it was Avery. "Call me tonight after you've read it."

"It might be late," Carter said, grabbing the baby bag and turning to leave.

"I don't care," Steven answered. "And son . . ."

Carter turned back to his father, trying to move away from Connor's tiny hands that were blocking his eyes.

"Be careful with Julia. Women like her have one thing in mind: getting a ring on their finger. If she catches on that she's just a means to an end, you'll have trouble."

"She won't catch on." Carter really did like Julia. He just didn't love her. "I got it under control."

And Carter truly believed he did. In the last six months, he'd been as meticulous in his social life as he was in his professional life. Avery was just an inch away from him. He could taste her.

"Which one is it?" thirty-year-old Michael Chase asked his seven-year-old son, Daniel, who was twisting and turning on his lap.

Daniel pointed to the computer, but didn't say anything. He was getting bored and Michael knew he should probably let up. It was good enough that, at seven, both Daniel and his twin brother, Evan, were acing educational software games aimed for eight-to-twelve-year-olds. But they were Chases, and doing better than expected was the least that was expected.

He'd had this conversation with his sons many times. Fate had them born into a family that lived under a microscope. The Chase family, in all their power, money, success and philanthropy, had become more than just a rich family. Their reign over the upper crust of black society, and powerful role in white society, made them unlike any other family of their kind, and the expectations would only rise with every generation. Carter was the Harvard lawyer. Michael was the Columbia finance whiz. Leigh was the Duke doctor and Haley . . . Haley was the spoiled socialite. Every rich family had to have one.

As the third generation of this dynasty, Evan and Daniel, now joined by Connor, would be expected to be at the top of their private schools, get into the Ivy Leagues, and project the appearance of perfection in career success, family, and commitment to the community. It was a lot of pressure, but it came with advantages too numerous to even mention, including a hefty trust fund.

"You're a Chase, Daniel. We don't give up. If you pick the right one, you'll get a card and can move to the next level."

Daniel sighed, lowering his head back to where it rested against his dad's chest.

"Jellyfish!" yelled Evan as he jumped around on the other side of Michael's desk.

"You can't even see it." Daniel sat up, seeming energized by the challenge of his brother.

"I already finished it." Evan jumped on the black

leather settee nestled in the middle of Michael's home office, one of ten rooms in the six-thousand-square-foot, Tuscan-inspired house nestled in the ultra-lux Hollywood Hills.

"I told you about yelling the answers," Michael warned the son that was becoming more and more like him every day.

Daniel and Evan were fraternal, but looked almost identical. Both were a smooth, chocolate brown like their mother with dark, fierce eyes like their father. Daniel was reserved and thoughtful like his Uncle Carter. Evan was always on and eager, like Michael. Michael only hoped they would grow up best friends as he and Carter had. They certainly fought as much.

"They're all jellyfish, stupid." Daniel leaned forward. "It's a Bubbler Jellyfish."

Michael smiled. "You mean Blubber, right?"

"That's what I said."

"It isn't," Evan said without even looking up.

"Michael!"

They all looked up as twenty-nine-year-old Kimberly Chase stormed into the office. Despite wearing a T-shirt and jeans, no makeup, and her long hair in a loose ponytail, what always struck one first about Kimberly was that she was distractingly beautiful. Both men and women stared at her everywhere she went. The society papers gave her the title of "most attractive Chase."

"Mommy!" Evan jumped off the settee toward his mother. "I finished first. Daniel still takes forever."

"Did not!" Daniel yelled out in his defense.

"Go play," Kimberly ordered curtly. She was trying her best to hold her temper until the boys were out of the way.

Both boys looked at their father, which only made Kimberly angrier. Michael had always been the disciplinarian in the family, but in less than six months she had ceased to have enough authority over her own children to be listened to alone.

"We're learning," Michael said. "Play time will come later."

"Okay," Kimberly said, holding up a cell phone. "I just want to know who Shana is."

Michael reached for his pocket and felt that his cell was still there. He lifted Daniel off his lap. "Okay, you boys can go play."

Without hesitation, they ran out of the office. There was no glance toward their mother. Michael was all the authority they seemed to need anywhere. He was turning her own children against her and Kimberly wanted to kill him for it.

"Why is this bitch calling me?" Kimberly closed the door behind her.

"I don't know what you're . . ."

"Aren't you tired of that?" Kimberly asked.

"Tired of what?"

"Pretending like you don't know that I know you fuck anything that moves!" She tossed the phone at him.

Michael ducked to avoid the flying iPhone. When he looked back up, his dark eyes were intense. "I don't have to explain myself to you."

And he hadn't. Ever since Kimberly had done something that could destroy everything the Chase family had worked to create. That was six months ago. Since then, Michael never answered to Kimberly for anything, including his affairs.

"Besides," Michael said, "you don't fuck me, so why do you care who does?"

Kimberly was disgusted. "Don't flatter yourself, asshole. I don't care, but what I do care about is when one of those skanks calls me on my cell phone. How did this Shana bitch get my number?"

Michael wanted to know the answer to that too. "I'll handle it. Is there something else?"

Kimberly thought about the question. Yes, there was. He could give her a divorce and let her take her children as far away from him and his crazy family as possible. That's what she wanted, but Kimberly knew she wasn't going to get it. Michael wasn't going to give her a divorce unless she agreed to ask for nothing. And he would never let her take the kids. He told her she would never even see them again. She tried to leave with the boys six months ago, but he'd found her and gave her no choice but to come back to L.A. She couldn't be separated from her kids.

It used to break her heart that her husband had turned so cold to her. She used to worship Michael. He was her knight in shining armor. From an abusive, poor childhood to being a teenaged street hooker, meeting someone like Michael Chase just wasn't supposed to happen to someone like her. But then again, there was that beauty. She was modeling in New York when she had caught his attention the way she did every man that crossed her path. She was attracted immediately. He looked like a young Sidney Poitier, but it wasn't his good looks that got to her. It was his presence. There was a power about Michael that anyone would recognize. She'd had no idea who he was until after their one-night stand.

Her entire life, all the men Kimberly had known had treated her like a doormat. Michael was the first man who loved her and needed her. It didn't matter that she would never be accepted by his mother and they would have to lie to everyone about her past. Although she wasn't willing to get another abortion, she hadn't asked him to marry her when she found out she was pregnant. He asked her. And for almost seven years, he loved her and gave her the world.

Things began to change more than a year ago when
Kimberly schemed to get rid of Janet Chase, the woman
who made her life hell by reminding her she wasn't good
enough for the Chase name. By dredging up a skeleton
from Janet's past—an affair with another man after her engagement to Steven, which resulted in an abortion—she
set off a chain of events that led to Janet's overdose on prescription pills and alcohol, while almost exposing the
family for what it was: truly dysfunctional.

As with every other scandal, and there were too many
Chase scandals to count, Steven and Janet's money and
influence kept it a secret from the world. But Michael,
who lived for his father's approval even more than his
wife's love, hadn't been the same since. She had gone behind his back and almost destroyed his parents' marriage
and his family's image.

But he still loved her and he did not leave her. He
worked hard to forgive her, and even though the rest of
the family had turned cold to her, Michael stayed. But his
relationship with his father had taken a serious blow and
Michael made it clear to Kimberly that she couldn't tip
the boat again. He'd lose everything.

So when her old pimp, David Harris, came to California to blackmail her, Kimberly tried to handle it without
telling Michael anything. But it wasn't money David
wanted. He wanted revenge against Michael, who'd had
him framed and put in a Mexican jail to keep Michael's
parents, or anyone else, from finding out about his connection to Kimberly. David promised Kimberly he'd leave
if she slept with him. She thought it was over when she
complied, but it was only beginning.

Kimberly found out that David had taped their sexual encounter and was planning to post it on the Internet for the
world to see. They struggled for the tape and David ended
up dead. When she realized that someone else, hiding in
the closet, had witnessed the accident and stolen the tape,

Kimberly had no choice but to tell Michael, who had no choice but to tell his father and explain everything.

Kimberly's life had been miserable ever since. While he was eager to help her hide David's murder, when Michael found out she'd slept with David, he lost it. That, on top of the fact that his father now blamed him for almost destroying the entire family, was the end of their marriage. Michael made sport of humiliating her, isolating her from the rest of the world. He controlled every aspect of her life. She couldn't take a step outside the house or spend a penny without his knowing of it. He demeaned and degrading her when it suited him and still had the nerve to want sex.

Sex, she refused, but everything else she put up with. She didn't have much of a choice. Steven and Janet backed Michael's threat that she would never get the children. Kimberly wasn't just afraid for her own life. She was afraid of never seeing her boys, the only good things in her life.

"Yes," Kimberly finally answered. "I'm going out to eat with Avery."

"No you're not." Michael pressed the Exit button to release the CD-ROM.

"The boys want to see Connor."

He rolled his eyes. "Can you do anything but lie?"

"Can you be anything but a hypocrite? Your whole life is a lie."

Michael shot up from the desk and smiled when it caused Kimberly to jump. "I have you to blame for that."

It was Kimberly's turn to smile. "Which I take pleasure in every day."

Michael slowly came around the desk, enraged by the sight of her. Not because he hated her, but because he couldn't hate her enough to get rid of her. "The boys will see Connor at her birthday party next week."

"I'm going." Kimberly turned to leave, but Michael

was at her side in a second, pulling her away from the door.

"I said no." Michael glared menacingly. "You walk out that door and you don't come back. Do you understand?"

"Is that so?"

"You heard me, bitch!"

"Yeah, I heard you now and when you said it last week and the week before."

Michael let her jerk her arm free. "Don't push your luck."

"If I had any luck," Kimberly said, "you'd drop dead!"

When she opened the door to his office, Michael slammed it back. He leaned against her from behind, pressing her body against the door. He could hear her let out a gasp and it turned him on. Touching her always turned him on and he hated her for still having that power over him.

"Baby." He nestled his head into her neck, rubbing against her. "You have as long a leash as I want you to."

Kimberly's elbow jutted back and hit him in the chest. "Unless you want me to throw up on you, you'll get off me!"

He leaned away, looking down at his watch. "Be back by five. I'm going out tonight."

Kimberly was shocked by what she saw when she opened the door. Her babies were standing there with sullen looks on their faces.

She had to come up with some way out of this. She had to get away from Michael and take her babies with her. It was the only way to save them.